Ourselves
and
Immortality

Logan Sage Adams

For permission requests, contact Logan Sage Adams at LoganSageAdams@gmail.com.

Editing by Mild Mannered Editors

Cover by Aliz Reka @rain1940commissions

Published by Logan Sage Adams

Dedication

For every person who has ever felt broken, othered, or too strange for this world—

You're perfect exactly as you are.

Content Warnings

This novel includes the following sensitive topics that may trigger reactions for some readers: period-typical homophobia; references to off-page deaths of family members (including the passing of a child and deaths of parents); period-typical neuro-ableism (including mild internalized neuro-ableism, though it is not explicitly named as such because of the time period) and period-typical ableism (experienced by one MC in the past as a result of his stutter); past homelessness (experienced by one MC as a child); references to one MC having lived in an orphanage for a short length of time; references to past sexual coercion (not by one of the MCs, but his ex-lover); references to infidelity (not by one of the MCs, but his ex-lover); scenes involving funerals and embalming; on-page lying and thievery; and explicit sexual content involving consenting adults.

Author's Note

*O*urselves and Immortality includes a mixture of Victorian funeral customs (e.g., funerals taking place in people's homes, the creation of mourning jewelry, the practice of hanging ribbons or wreaths or scarves outside the home, etc.) and more modern ones (e.g., embalming, funeral services being held in churches, etc.), which will, I hope, reflect the transitionary nature of this time period in history. During the late 1800s and early 1900s, funerals were changing, moving away from being a more public event, when social etiquette placed an emphasis on public mourning in Victorian times, to an increasingly private one. Something else that changed in the 1800s was the prevalence of embalming, which became a more respectable trade as a result of both the Civil War, when deceased soldiers started to be embalmed before being shipped home to then be buried by their loved ones, and Abraham Lincoln's traveling funeral, which exposed even more people to the idea of postmortem preservation. Toward the end of the 1800s, mortuary schools began to open around the United States, and so, more people began seeking these services. While I used many sources for my research, much of the information for the late 19th century and early 20th century funeral practices included in this novel came from *Clarke's Textbook on Embalming* by John Henry Clarke, which contains a section on funeral etiquette. All of this is to say that some of the particulars included in John and Calvin's story may not have been widespread across the entirety of the United States. Additionally, John and Calvin's funeral services would have likely only been accessible by folks in the middle or upper class. Keep this in mind when reading. If this kind of historical information is of interest to you, I encourage you to subscribe to my newsletter, in which I periodically include fun nuggets of information on these topics for my readers.

One other thing I wanted to note is that John, the shy mortician in *Ourselves and Immortality*, is neurodivergent-coded with a persistent stammer. I tried to write what I hope is an overall optimistic, but still accurate portrayal of someone like him who was alive in the late 1800s and early 1900s. However, I acknowledge that every neurodivergent person has a unique lived experience; this is as true today as it would have been back then. Still, I hope that folks will read his story through a historical lens and celebrate his happily ever after.

Prologue
John

John Hall was working the coarse sandpaper over the edges of the newly made coffin lid when the sound of shoes shuffling on the footpath nearby caused his concentration to waver. With a shake of his head, he returned his focus to his work. Tomorrow was to be the funeral for one of the most beloved women in town—Ida Miller, who had once owned Media, Pennsylvania's best flower shop. Even though John considered every request for a casket or coffin to be an honor, this one felt especially important. Because Ida had been one of those rare people who celebrated people's eccentricities rather than finding fault with them. She had been kind to John throughout the years, no matter how others had occasionally perceived him. Grateful for the warmth she had often shown him, John was intent on making sure that her coffin turned out exactly as she had requested before she had passed.

When the barn door opened, a perfectly timed breeze brought with it the heavy scent of manure from nearby farms. Even though the scent tickled John's nostrils strongly enough to cause him to wrinkle his nose, he remained mostly unperturbed by it, and continued rubbing the sandpaper along the wood.

While John stayed focused on finishing up the coffin lid, smoothing out one of the stubbornly rough edges, his brother, Michael, came up behind him.

"I haven't seen one like that in a while," Michael remarked.

In response to Michael's observation, John simply let out a hum. True, no one else had requested one of these old-style coffins—a hexagonal shape with individual handles on its sides rather than a continuous bar—in a very long time. Probably not since their father had first started teaching John how to make coffins.

Sharp pain began to prickle in John's chest as one of his favorite memories of his late father sprung to his mind, the scene playing in his head like the fast-flipping images of a mangled kineograph whose images were either missing or marred because of the passage of time.

John heaved a sigh as the memory faded from his thoughts. He missed his father. Even though Samuel Hall had been one of Media's most visited physicians, he had eventually become the borough's main undertaker as well, mostly because he'd had a talent for carpentry (something he had learned from *his* father), but also because he had been a trusted pillar of their little community. His father hadn't exactly *enjoyed* making caskets, but he had never once complained, and when John had eventually shown an interest in learning the skill, he had taught John everything he knew without hesitation, possibly so that the two of them could have something to bond over.

After John's father had passed, John had taken up the mantle of casket-maker for their small town, though his reputation in Media wasn't such a positive one. Probably because he rarely ever talked to anyone other than Michael (well, besides to find out what kind of casket he should make for an upcoming funeral).

Resting a hand on the wood, Michael said, "Nice work. Are you *certain*, though, that *this* is the type of casket her family wants for her?"

At once, John's stomach soured, the critical tone in his brother's voice making him feel small.

"It's what Ida w-w-wanted," John managed in response, squeezing his eyes shut as he stumbled over the last word.

Michael clicked his tongue once. "Strange."

But it wasn't strange, really. Ida wanted her coffin to match her late husband's.

Instead of correcting Michael, John set the sandpaper aside and took hold of the edges of the lid. Grunting, he hoisted it up over his head, and Michael backed up a few steps.

"John, I need to talk to you about something," Michael said as John bent over to place the lid on its base.

Straightening up, John rubbed his sweaty palms back and forth a few times on the fabric of his work pants before turning to face his brother. From Michael's expression—the fixed look in his eyes and the way he was chewing the inside of his cheek—John knew that it must be important. Probably something Michael was nervous about, which was rare.

Michael shifted his stance, and John tilted his head inquisitively.

"Uncle Frances wants me to work with him," Michael said.

John's eyes widened. While that bit of news shouldn't have been surprising, John still hadn't expected it because, though Michael was certainly intelligent enough to help their uncle run his carpet factory, the building was located in Philadelphia. Which meant that if Michael were to work with their uncle, he would have to move. Michael had friends in Media. Many of them. So the prospect of working with their uncle must have been quite enticing if he was willing to leave his current life behind.

"Oh, that's . . . that's w-w-wonderful," John said, pushing through yet *another* invisible verbal blockage, one that he worried made him sound hesitant or even critical of Michael's choice, even though he wasn't. In fact, John felt confident that Michael would enjoy working in the city. Sharp and personable, Michael was the sort of man who ought to be somewhere like Philadelphia. Somewhere that would permit him to really make his mark on the world. Of course John was happy for his brother. But . . . why had Michael seemed so nervous to tell him?

"And I want you to come with me," Michael tacked on.

Ah, that was why.

Dipping his head, John shoved his hands in his pockets. Unease clawed up his throat.

"I-I'm not interested in the f-factory. Too many people."

"Don't worry, I know you're not interested in factory work," Michael said. "But I think I found something else for you."

Arching a curious eyebrow, John peered up through his lashes to meet Michael's eyes. He could hardly imagine what kind of work he'd enjoy in a city like Philadelphia.

"Did you hear that they opened a, uhm, a mortuary school?" Michael asked, and John's other eyebrow rose to meet its twin. "The Eckels College of Mortuary Science. I thought that since . . . well, since you seem to like helping with the funeral preparations, and since I know that you'd prefer to find some way to make money that would involve you working mostly by yourself as well, you could make a business out of this. Uncle Frances told me that organizing funerals has become a real profession now. Something respectable. And the way things currently work out here—family members preparing and laying out the body, people burying their relatives in the churchyard—will be a thing of the past soon, especially in the cities. I mean, there's no room in those churchyards anymore, and everyone has started to come around to the, uh, the concept of preservation."

"Embalming?"

"Right," Michael said. "It seems that there's a need for more people who know how it works. So, I thought you would like to learn. Eckels College only opened a few years ago. They're eager to find students."

John furrowed his brow. While opening up a funeral business was, on the surface, a nice enough idea, the prospect of working with other people was . . . not exactly inspiring. How would he even manage to make the sorts of connections necessary to start and cultivate a new business? How would he ensure that his clients were satisfied with the services he could provide? Despite the fact that John knew everyone in his hometown, he *still* had trouble talking with them. He wasn't sure how he'd ever run a business of his own in a city like Philadelphia. After all, it would entail communicating with strangers fairly regularly. Where would the funerals even be held? Would he have to visit people's homes?

John swallowed past the tightness in his throat and said, "Where would I work?"

"I'm not sure, exactly," Michael said with a shrug. "I think you'd probably prepare the bodies in people's homes, and perhaps bring the casket there as well. If you're the one making it, that is, though I heard that in the cities, there are shops where people can purchase them now. So, then, while working in the Philadelphia funeral business would still be *somewhat* similar to how things work out here in Media, it would be something new."

John frowned as he considered the suggestion. Perhaps he *could* stomach it. Almost everyone nearby requested his help whenever someone passed. In addition to crafting the casket, he had also taken on other funeral responsibilities, like preparing the gravesite and transporting the body to the churchyard. Still, John never thought of it as his *profession*—he only ever wanted to be paid for the materials—but as a way to help the community. Could he really turn it into a legitimate business?

"I can't leave without you," Michael said. "I need to sell the house so that I can find one in the city. I'd rather not rent."

"Perhaps, instead, I could . . ." John paused while his brain worked frantically to come up with some acceptable alternative. "I could find my own p-p-place out here. Someplace smaller. Someplace cheap."

"Doubtful. Furniture-making would barely even bring in enough money for necessities. Besides, it's not your . . . *passion* to be making tables and chairs and other household furnishings," Michael said.

John couldn't miss the way Michael had wrinkled his nose the moment he had uttered the word "passion." While not surprising, seeing Michael's expression still made John feel as though his insides were twisting together. Or maybe becoming flattened, like they were being put through a clothing wringer.

Shame trickled up the back of John's neck. He couldn't control his preoccupation (or, as Michael sometimes liked to call it, his "fixation") with burials and cemeteries and everything that came with them any more than he could control his stutter. He had struggled with his words ever since he could remember, and his fascination with funerals had also started very soon after his earliest memories. It wasn't as though John had *chosen* for his brain to become stuck on the subject of mortality. It was simply who he was.

And since it was who he was, Michael was probably right. What other type of work could John ever tolerate? Or, perhaps, enjoy?

John's eyes fell to the floorboards. "Alright, I'll c-consider it."

"Do you think you could tell me by the end of the week? I'd like to take Uncle Frances up on his offer soon. And we'll have to sell the house here first."

Unwilling to even try to meet his brother's eyes, John mumbled a soft "of course," his stomach churning from unease. Dread was making his palms sweat even worse than working on the coffin had. Instinctively, John wiped his hands on his pants as he watched his brother's black leather shoes vanish from view.

After Michael was gone, John walked over to his workbench and sat. He ran a hand through his brown, pomade-coated locks, letting out a long breath as he replayed the conversation in his mind, and then his eyes fell upon the newly made coffin near the entrance of the repurposed barn. Soon, Ida would be reunited with her husband here on earth. Well, as reunited as they ever could be. Perhaps they were together now in heaven.

John lifted his chin to see the wooden beams running from one end of the barn to the other. And then, he looked beyond them to the ceiling. Sunlight streamed in through the spaces between the slats. Before John could catch himself, he began wondering what it might be like to see beyond them to the sky. And beyond the sky too. All the way beyond the world itself and the stars and the planets and the expanses of the universe.

And he wondered what it would be like to finally be with Lucy again.

Chapter One
Calvin

April 1902

Loitering on Market Street near city hall, Calvin Wright was starting to panic. He took a long inhale to try to calm himself, breathing in the scent of that morning's rainfall, but still, his heart continued to race. After only weeks of being unemployed, Calvin was running out of both time and money, and if he couldn't manage to cough up the cash for his one-room rental in the boarding-house soon, he'd wind up back on the streets. Working at the textile mill hadn't panned out. It had been too noisy, too busy, too . . . too nausea-inducing. Each time he'd operated one of the machines, it had brought up painful childhood memories. Memories he wished he could forget. Besides, working fourteen or more hours each shift, completely exhausting himself, for eleven or twelve bucks a week? What a cheat *that* was. He couldn't—*wouldn't*—continue subjecting himself to it.

Despite the fact that only a few months prior, Calvin had promised himself he would try to lead an honest life, he had yet to stomach even one of the menial factory positions he'd tried, which, unfortunately, were the only positions within reach for someone like him—an unmarried man with no family connections and no formal schooling beyond the handful of years he'd completed in one of New York's common schools.

Because Calvin still hadn't found work that suited him, he was starting to feel like living a life without crime would forever be unreachable. Which was fine. Or, well, it had to be fine. Besides, he had only made the promise to himself that he'd change his ways when he had experienced a particularly rough night—one that had entailed barely escaping a thrashing for having cheated in a game of faro. Calvin hadn't been thinking straight then. Not while he'd been running for his life. But, really, the men with whom Calvin had been playing had simply overreacted. He could see that now. All it had taken for Calvin to win that round had been a well-placed comment, something that had pulled everyone else's eyes away from the cards for a moment, followed by a sleight of hand to move his bet to the next card on the layout. Nothing worth ending someone's life over, even if he *had* "won" a fair sum of money. He'd have won even more had he not been caught trying to pull the same stunt a second time.

But why should it have been *his* problem that people, on the whole, could be so easily fooled? Moves like the ones he'd pulled shouldn't even have been considered cheating. It was more like . . . like Calvin had simply been collecting a tax. One that was sorely needed, too. Levied against those who liked to think they were entitled to muddle through life so completely absent-minded that they opened themselves up to being tricked by a man with a charming smile.

Of course, none of the other players would have seen it that way, even if Calvin had possessed the wherewithal to come up with that perfectly reasonable explanation for his cheating the moment he'd been found out. And so, Calvin had run, and while he had been sprinting through the streets of Philadelphia, he'd promised himself that if he managed not to receive a physical beating from those petty card-playing bums, he would find real work. Real, honest work.

But, sadly, though perhaps unsurprisingly, real, honest work had been really and honestly terrible.

Calvin sighed. If he couldn't stomach returning to the factory that had been employing him, then he'd have to figure out some other way to make money.

But how? He could set up a three-card monte table. Somewhere busy, somewhere he'd blend in, somewhere with room for him to run if he needed to. Chestnut Street, maybe? Or one of the immigrant neighborhoods?

Blowing out a breath, Calvin spun in a little circle. He wasn't *exactly* familiar with Philadelphia yet. Not like he had been with New York. Why, he and David had practically been running that city. Alright, maybe *that* was a slight exaggeration, but still, the two of them had been raking in cash left and right. Between the card tables (where they'd won by cheating most of the time) and fooling unsuspecting rich folks with either three-card monte or their wallet-drop maneuver, he and David had easily come up with enough money to pay for their one-bedroom (yes, one-*bedroom;* two rooms total) rental without having to work. Hornswoggling people never felt like *work*. It was fun. And the two of them had only ever targeted people who they'd thought had it coming—other petty criminals and wealthy snobs who had way too much money.

But, of course, now David was with Ed. Calvin curled his lip as an image of Ed flashed in his mind. Ed, who had once been nothing more than the slightly surly tenant who lived at the end of the hall. Ed, who had a hideous mustache and wouldn't know a nice suit if it kicked him in the rear. Ed, who, *despite* the hideous mustache, was really very handsome, which was really very . . .

Calvin let out a small scream of frustration. He had to stop thinking about David. It was for the best that he and David weren't together anymore, anyway. It was better not to rely on other people for things like shelter or food or love. Loving other people only ever meant heartbreak. Making a home only ever meant losing it. Life's pleasures were best enjoyed alone.

It was time for Calvin to figure out how to make some money. Fast. While nervously cracking his knuckles, Calvin searched the streets for a target. He'd better come up with something subtle. Something sly. Something that wouldn't catch too much attention. Without huge crowds of people, Calvin wouldn't be able to slip away so easily if things went sideways.

Not more than a minute later, Calvin caught sight of his pretty little privileged target half a block over—Katherine McGough. Katherine was the daughter of Patrick McGough, the ugly bugger who owned the shoddy mill where Calvin had been working up until a few weeks prior. Patrick McGough—what a bastard he was, paying his workers a measly couple of bucks in exchange for hours and hours of hard labor. It was a wonder that so many people could stand to work there. Give folks a couple of breaks and a bit of sunlight and they'd conveniently overlook the fact that their boss was cheating them, paying them a pittance compared to what he pulled in sitting on his rear end eating doughnuts. Patrick McGough was such a horrible man, too. Mean for the sake of it.

Calvin continued watching Katherine for another few seconds. Her red curls were spilling out beneath her hat, unable to be tamed even with the tens of pins she probably had in her hair.

Wringing his hands together, Calvin racked his brain, trying to come up with a way to force Patrick McGough to pay for his current month's rent. Maybe next month's, too. Or, even better, a whole year's worth. Wildly whipping his head around to try to spot something, *anything*, he could use, Calvin's eyes found the city's statue of beloved William Penn perched atop the new city hall, and a wolfish smile stretched across his face. Perfect.

Calvin hurried over to a man nearby, one who looked like he must have had a lot of money, too, judging by the cane he was carrying. Calvin eyed the cane's elaborate silver head with contempt. And ... *maybe* a little envy.

What made the man the perfect unsuspecting accomplice, though, was not the fancy walking stick he was clutching with his left hand, but the thing he was holding in his right: a brand-new brown leather notebook. Strange thing to be carrying, maybe, but perhaps the man owned more than one business nearby, which, therefore, necessitated having more than one office and required the man to move between them. He certainly seemed wealthy enough for that to have been the case.

"Excuse me, sir!" Calvin called out. "Mind if I borrow your notebook for a moment?"

Slowing his walk, the man eyed Calvin with suspicion, not yet willing to either stop or speak with him.

"*Please,*" Calvin implored, his lightly touch causing the man to stop. "Do you see that beautiful woman over there? With the blue hat?" Calvin asked, pointing over at Katherine McGough, who was now talking with her companion—a brown-haired woman whom Calvin had seen once or twice, probably either friend or a relative—as they traveled farther from city hall. "I bumped into her and her friend there, thinking that I'd recognized her from church, and so, we started talking, and it so happens that her father owns some sort of clothing factory. Now, it turns out that I hadn't been correct about having recognized her, but wow, what a stroke of luck it was to talk to her! See, I need to find work, and she very kindly offered up the name and street address of her father's factory for me, but I know I'll never remember it for long. Ever since I fell off that horse last year in Kensington, I've struggled with remembering things for very long. If I could just write it—"

"Yes, yes," the man said, interrupting him and holding out the notebook. "That's fine."

"Oh, thank you *so much*," Calvin said, trying for an earnest smile.

Not that Calvin had a pen, but that wasn't important. He wouldn't need one.

Tucking the notebook in the crook of his arm, Calvin rushed over to Katherine, pushing past the handful of people on the Market Street sidewalk on the way.

"Thank heavens!" he said as he approached. "Katherine Mc-Gough! Will your father be here soon, then?"

"Uhm, I . . ." Katherine looked over at her companion, who merely shrugged. "I'm sorry, who are you?"

"Apologies, ma'am. I thought you'd recognize me from—"

"Oh! Aren't you one of the laborers in my father's mill?"

Calvin faked a hearty laugh. Damn. He hadn't planned on her recognizing him. "*Laborer?!* No, ma'am, though I have visited your father's mill over on Broad several times. My name is James Johnson. I'm in the business of building restoration. Now, your father said that he'd meet me here today to talk about the statue of William Penn. You know, the one perched on top of the new city hall building. We're replacing it."

"Replacing it?"

"Yes, well, when I sent my men up there to clean it, they noticed that it had a small crack. Like the Liberty Bell, see? So, we're replacing it. And your father, the savvy businessman that he is, wanted to purchase the original. Should be worth a bundle in a few years. If I had his kind of money, I'd purchase it myself." Calvin pretended to search around. "Where is he? We were supposed to meet here to talk specifics. I have what will be the proof of sale tucked away in my notebook here. Once your father pays, he can sign it, and then we'll have the statue sent to your home."

"Oh." Katherine's brows knitted together as she lifted her chin so that she could look up at Billy Penn. When she shifted her attention back to Calvin, she had an apologetic look in her eyes. "He must have lost track of time."

Calvin blew out a frustrated-sounding breath. "Well, that's a shame. Do you see that man over there?" he asked, pointing to the man from whom he had borrowed the notebook. "He's next in line to purchase it. If your father isn't here . . ." Calvin shook his head, feigning upset, but then snapped his fingers. "Actually, I could hold his spot if I secure some cash." Did women carry cash? Calvin wasn't sure. He ought to suggest something else. Just in case. "Or, uhm, some . . . jewelry, perhaps?" He'd better try to explain that one. "You know, something to show good faith in his future purchase. And then I could come by his business tomorrow instead. We only wanted to meet here today because I'll be sending my crew up in a little while to take the statue down. Do you happen to have—"

Katherine cut him off. "What about my necklace?"

Calvin's eyes flitted to Katherine's necklace—a thick, white rope chain from which hung a beautiful pendant, one with a sapphire in the center—and he wet his lips as he considered how much money he'd make from it. Once he sold it, he'd not only have enough for rent but perhaps a bet or two at the racetrack as well.

"Yes," Calvin said, keeping his voice as level as possible, though his heart began thudding excitedly in his chest. "I think that would work."

Katherine reached behind her head to unclasp the necklace. While she worked to unfasten the chain, Calvin began tip-tapping the notebook with the pads of his fingers, a small swell of nervousness mixing with the excitement he'd been feeling. Hopefully she wouldn't rethink her offer while she was fiddling with the clasp. Calvin continued strumming his fingers, praying that she'd think that he was becoming impatient, which, then, should keep her from taking time to reconsider handing her necklace over to a total stranger.

"Sorry," Katherine said. "Sometimes it—"

"I can help," her friend or relative or whoever she was offered, circling behind her.

"How rude of me," Katherine said. "Mr. Johnson, this is my friend, Mrs. Ruth Meyer."

"Nice to meet you," Calvin said with a polite nod, though inwardly, he was begging her to hurry up before either of the women could come to their senses.

After a brief moment of Mrs. Meyer fussing with the chain, the clasp came unhooked and the necklace fell free into Katherine's waiting hands. Without hesitation, Katherine held it out for Calvin to take. Calvin's chest swelled with excitement as the pendant and chain coiled together in the palm of his hand. Quickly, Calvin shoved the necklace into one of the inner pockets of his suit jacket.

"Thank you, Ms. McGough," he said.

"Oh, it's Mrs. Hall now," she said. "Recently married."

"Ah." Calvin cringed internally. If that was the case, he was more or less stealing from whoever her husband was, rather than her terrible father. Oh well. It wasn't as though he could back out now. "Apologies, Mrs. Hall." He touched his palms together and widened his smile. "I hope your marriage is a long and happy one. Now, I should probably return to Mr. White over there"—Calvin nodded toward the man with the expensive cane—"to tell him that he lost out on the purchase. Poor fellow."

All that was left was to return the man's notebook. Or . . . maybe not? Calvin kind of wanted to keep it now. Should he keep it? Calvin took the notebook in his hands and ran his fingers over the soft leather. God, it was a nice notebook, wasn't it?

"Shouldn't I sign something?" Katherine wondered. "Or perhaps you could provide me with a receipt?"

Well, Katherine had essentially made Calvin's choice for him, then. He couldn't very well refuse her a receipt and then calmly walk over to return the notebook to Fancy-Cane Man.

"Uhm . . ."

Calvin looked back and forth between Katherine and her friend.

And then, he took off running.

While Calvin was sprinting past the man from whom he'd stolen the notebook, he heard Katherine cry out, "Help! I think that man stole my necklace!" And he only barely fought the urge to call back "You fucking handed it to me!"

Calvin bolted toward city hall. Drawing near, he made a left on Broad and kept running for several more blocks. Once his body began protesting the exercise, his lungs burning and brow starting to perspire, he slowed to a walk, knowing he'd be able to slip inside his building soon. By the time either Katherine or Fancy-Cane Man notified a policeman, Calvin would be relaxing on his ratty old sofa. Calvin continued to catch his breath for the last block of his trip home. He let the sounds of the city—the clamor of occasional conversations of passersby, coupled with the faint clip-clop of horses transporting folks from place to place—wash over him, calming his still-racing heart, though the elation he felt from having completed his first successful con in Philadelphia was still simmering beneath his skin.

Soon, Calvin reached home. Or, well, the building in which he was renting a room, which had never really felt like *home*. After entering through the front, Calvin started up the stairs, hoping he wouldn't run into one of the other tenants on the way to the third floor. He was one of four men renting from Gladys Donaldson, a widow who had turned her modest home into a boarding house. Since her home itself had been modest before the modifications, the rooms she rented out were, in a word, mediocre. Not only were they tiny, but the paper-thin walls between them meant that Calvin barely had any privacy. It was maddening. If only he could somehow make enough money to rent a house of his own.

Once Calvin reached his rented room, he fell onto his tattered beige sofa and stretched. His feet hung over the edge. How unfortunate that there wasn't space in here for a proper bed. Not with Calvin's bookcase, which he had filled to the brim in less than six months, and his tiny kitchen table. Still, even though the space was small, it was a step up from the rental he'd had with David in New York, which had not only been small (two rooms, both of them tiny; the main one fitting only their bed, a table, and a bookcase) but unsafe too, the whole place more or less crumbling around them, plaster falling off of the walls in chunks.

Lolling his head to the side, Calvin scanned the spines of the books, most of which had been "borrowed" or flat-out stolen, before his gaze settled on his father's pocket watch resting on the middle shelf. When Calvin closed his eyes, he felt a pinch in his chest, and his thoughts returned to the last time he'd seen his father wear it.

Sitting with his father in the stands of Polo Grounds, Calvin was constantly shifting positions to try to see past the tall men in front of him, though their towering, black opera-style top hats were nearly making it impossible. Whenever the mid-October breeze blew past, Calvin hugged his arms to his chest, the cold pulling his focus from the players on the field. As soon as Calvin heard the crack of the bat hitting the ball in the eighth inning, his father hooked one of his arms around Calvin's shoulders, shaking him several times.

"Did you see that?" his father exclaimed, happiness practically radiating off of him.

"Not really," Calvin nearly blurted out, but instead, he only smiled back, not wanting to ruin the moment.

Calvin's father loved baseball. Before marrying Calvin's mother, his father had been a player for a small baseball club in Brooklyn. Of course, once he'd met the love of his life, he had started to focus his efforts on his work as a carpenter, soon saving enough money to become his own boss (and hiring a few less-experienced carpenters to work for him). Still, William Wright's fondness for the sport had never faded. And it was obvious to Calvin, even at only twelve years old, that his father wanted his son to love it too.

One of the men seated in the row behind them tapped Calvin's father on the shoulder.

"Do you have the time?" he asked.

When Calvin's father pulled out his pocket watch—a beautiful brass piece with a clamshell-style lid, a thin layer of silver circling the perimeter, and a little anchor on the watch's face where the numbers were—Calvin found himself staring, the conversation between his father and the man behind them and the noise of the ballpark fading to a hum while he remained transfixed on the timepiece. Calvin didn't really understand why, but staring at the watch made him consider his future—what sort of man he might someday become—and he found himself hoping that he would make his father proud.

Moments later, his father's snort of amusement brought him back to the present.

"Nice watch, isn't it?"

Calvin nodded.

"Well . . ." His father unfastened the chain from the button of his vest. He held the watch out for Calvin. *"Maybe you can keep it safe for me for a little while."*

When the weight of the watch and chain settled onto Calvin's palm, his breath caught in his throat. Somehow, it felt to Calvin like there had been a shift in his person that very moment—a change from boy to man.

Even back then, Calvin had been struck with the feeling that his life was about to change.

If only he'd known it would be for the worse.

Melancholy pressed heavily on Calvin's heart. Along with the sorrow came a sense of shame, the feeling starting as an uncomfortable heat at the base of his neck and eventually creeping upward to color his cheeks. His father would never be proud of the man he had become.

Calvin stood and retrieved the watch from its shelf in the bookcase. After plopping back onto one of the couch cushions, he breathed a sigh and began to turn the watch over in his hands, the cool metal sending a shiver up his spine as the pads of his fingers traced the patterns on the watch's face.

Dangling the watch from its chain, Calvin followed the pendant as it swung. Back and forth, back and forth.

And so, too, did Calvin's emotions swing, from sorrow to shame.

Back and forth, back and forth.

Chapter Two
John

Howard Price was on John Hall's portable cooling board. Towels had been placed to encircle the table, catching the water from the melting ice packed beneath it. Gripping his scalpel in his right hand, John's thoughts began to wander from the present moment, and soon, he found himself worrying over the upcoming funeral, which was to take place within a week. Worry settled in John's stomach, making it churn. After taking a breath, John tried to will the thoughts away, reminding himself that even though he had practically ruined the last four funerals he had been hired to organize, he had come up with a plan this time, one that was *sure* to help him be more personable.

Before the service, he would fill a flask with whiskey and then tuck it inside the front breast pocket of his suit. Prior to the start of the funeral, he would force himself to have some, telling himself to think of the pungent brown liquid as medication, rather than the recreational substance most people considered it to be. And the whiskey would then work its magic. After all, Michael had never not seemed relaxed once he'd had a few sips of the stuff, and so, it stood to reason that imbibing a bit of whiskey would help John be more relaxed as well. With the help of the miracle beverage, John would transform into the calm, collected, *personable* person he was supposed to be for these things.

Despite clinging to the hope that his plan would be successful, John couldn't shake his unease, and his mind continued to pummel him with worrisome thoughts over the fact that his funeral business was floundering. While it wasn't true that his entire business hinged on the success of Howard Price's funeral, it certainly felt that way, and John couldn't seem to stop fretting. Would he remember everything he needed to remember for the funeral? Would he be friendly enough? Professional enough? Would he make some kind of error? Heaving a sigh, John returned his focus to the embalming.

With his free hand, John lifted Howard Price's right arm so that he could locate the brachial artery. After finding the little cord, he made an incision—two inches long near the bend of the elbow—and then, with an aneurysm needle, he raised the artery and veins to separate them. Every task that followed, John completed with ease, the repetition of movements that were becoming second nature to him soothing some of his lingering worries over the funeral. Once the arterial and venous tubes were in place, John began working the manual pump, each squeeze of his hand pushing more embalming fluid into the circulatory system and, in turn, pushing out the blood.

Minutes passed. Soon, John couldn't keep a small, bemused smile from tugging at the corners of his lips while he watched the blood exit the end of the tubing. How funny it was that most people would be bothered by such a thing. Blood never bothered John in the least. Michael had been right—embalming seemed to be the perfect profession for him. Perhaps it really was John's calling.

Unlike the rest of funeral planning. When John pictured the flood of Philadelphians who would come to Howard and Marjorie Price's brick home on Fourth Street for the viewing and then to the church for the service, his small smile fell away, and nervousness began to twist inside him again.

Someone burst into the sitting room, the *whoosh* of the swinging door startling John out of his thoughts. Whirling to face the threshold from where the noise had come, John lost his balance, and his foot kicked the large four-quart embalming jar, causing it to topple. Blood spilled onto the tile floor.

"Oh, for heaven's sake, John!" exclaimed Michael, rushing over. Quickly, John scrambled to right the jar and replace the tube in its opening. By the time he stood back up, Michael was already rummaging through his black bag for some linen.

"I'm not even sure if there's enough here," Michael lamented, pulling out a couple of squares of cloth. "I'll have to pester Marjorie now. I know *you* won't be able to."

Immediately, John crumpled in on himself, slumping forward while lowering his head. The moment he and his brother locked eyes, however, Michael's fury seemed to fall away, his face softening and tension leaving his shoulders.

"Sorry," they said to each other at the same time.

Michael rubbed his forehead. "No, really, *I'm* sorry."

John wanted to explain himself—to tell Michael that he was nervous about the funeral service—but the words stuck in his throat. Michael tossed him the cloths. He caught most of the pieces, though one square landed in the little puddle of blood, and then, before John could even thank Michael for his help, his brother turned to leave. John bent down to soak up as much of his mistake as he could.

Not much time passed before Michael came back with a ratty old towel that John could use to clean up the rest of the mess. Luckily, Michael informed him, Marjorie Price hadn't been too upset to find out that her late husband's blood had been sent splashing across the floor. After John cleaned everything up, he set to work on finishing the preparation of the body, and then he and Michael shifted it over into the casket, which was waiting in the next room.

"I won't be able to be your assistant forever, you know," Michael said. "Uncle Frances wants me to start taking on more responsibility at the factory. I think he wants me to take over for him. Every week I see him, he looks thinner and thinner and, well . . ."

"I know," John said softly.

Gently, Michael rested a hand on his brother's shoulder and squeezed. Smiling half-heartedly, John reached up and patted it.

Michael said, "So, I was thinking, maybe it would be best if *you* receive the guests for the viewing and the funeral both. I'll stay back and watch. It *is* your business, after all."

After a moment, John managed a nod, nervousness churning in his stomach once again. It wasn't as though he harbored some kind of hatred for people. Not individually. But John hated crowds. And he hated *emotional* crowds even more. Because he had no clue how to handle them. John's only saving grace was that he wasn't expected to (nor was he really *supposed* to) offer many words of sympathy to his clients. Still, he knew that they would probably appreciate it if he managed to look stoic rather than mildly repulsed throughout the service. Weeks prior, Michael had said that whenever their clients requested for John to be present for either a viewing or a funeral service, John spent the entirety of it looking as though he was harboring a deep hatred for the person in the casket.

When John was finished with the embalming and all the preparations he'd needed to do that day at the Prices' home, he and Michael rode home in the hearse, with John holding the horse's reins and Michael sitting beside him. Because of the nature of John's funeral business, Michael had purchased a corner home in the city, one with enough property in the back for a small horse stable separate from the house itself, rather than one that was connected, like a mew. He'd have been fine with a mew, though. It was the fact that John wasn't forced to constantly borrow a horse from one of the city's livery stables that made everything easier. John would have found coordinating that *incredibly* stressful. And Agathe was a sweet horse. John liked tending to her. He liked talking to her, too (much to Michael's chagrin).

Inside, Michael's wife, Katherine, was playing cards with a few of her friends in Michael's office. While passing by, John caught Katherine's eye and managed a tight smile before hurrying toward the basement, which had become his favorite room in the house. No one bothered him while he worked there. Since John's clients typically purchased their caskets elsewhere, John had taken up some other hobbies, like teaching himself how to create little funeral trinkets, such as mourning pendants, which could be used for pins or necklaces. Not that such things were still in fashion, but it kept John busy. Busy enough not to have to interact with the many people who visited their home. Both Katherine and Michael had become very popular. On the few occasions when John had accompanied them to church, he had witnessed firsthand how well-liked both of them were. Which was lovely to see. But . . . stressful.

Ever since Michael and Katherine married, Katherine had kept busy by entertaining in their home, typically by hosting luncheons for friends or suppers for folks whom Michael knew from work (other business owners and their wives). Probably Michael and Katherine would have children eventually, which might be nice, not because John relished the thought of tiny feet padding through the halls, but because Katherine might not want to host people so often once she was busy being a mother.

Although, perhaps it wouldn't matter whether or when Michael and Katherine expanded their family. Because the moment John felt more comfortable running Hall Funeral Services by himself, Michael and Katherine would move, probably to someplace closer to the factory, which was something they both wanted. Still, John couldn't be sure that he'd *ever* be comfortable running the whole business by himself.

When John neared the end of the hall, he looked back over his shoulder, catching Michael's eye. Michael simply nodded before returning his focus to Katherine and her friends, whom Michael had been conversing with while standing in the entryway of his study. Thankfully, Michael never chastised John for not being more social with their friends. Michael knew that John was neither eager to befriend members of Philadelphia's social elite nor interested in courting Katherine's unmarried friends. John's reluctance to marry wasn't solely because he couldn't fathom fumbling through the whole courting process, but because he wasn't romantically interested in women. Only in men. Michael would have probably been more upset over that fact had John not been too shy to even *think* about trying to find someone else like him. Muddling through some sort of secret relationship? John couldn't even imagine it. He wasn't the type.

Sometimes he found himself wishing that he was, though.

Determined to make a positive impression when people showed up for the viewing, John was rechecking his reflection in a nearby ornate circular mirror that was hanging in the front room of Howard and Marjorie Price's home. It was of the utmost importance that he look professional. Friendly, too. Studying his reflection, John worked through his mental checklist. Unfurrow the brow. Relax the forehead. Strive to look impersonal yet personable—not smiling but not *not* smiling, perhaps?—while still seeming a *touch* sympathetic. Once John felt moderately confident that he had his facial expression right, he reached up to fix his hair, brushing away a few strands that had fallen over his forehead.

Leaving Michael behind in the front room, John went through the kitchen to reach the small study in the back of the house where he'd last seen Marjorie. He lifted his hand to knock, but paused and then reached into his pocket to retrieve the flask of whiskey instead. *Medicine*, he told himself. *It's purely for medicinal purposes.* John took a small sip, and the moment the bitter liquid sloshed over his tongue, he recoiled, scrunching up his face. How on earth could people enjoy the taste of whiskey? After returning his flask back to his pocket, John lightly rapped his knuckles on the wood. He thought he heard Marjorie say "come in" from the other side, but he couldn't be sure. Nervous that he may have misheard, John simply stayed in the hallway, wondering whether he should try again.

He was still working up the courage to either knock a second time or call out to Marjorie to verbally confirm that he could come inside when Marjorie came out instead.

"Hello, Mr. Hall. Have you hung the scarf so that people know they can come pay their respects?" she asked, her eyes red and raw.

He nodded once.

"Would you like to come sit with me? I have coffee."

"No, thank you, Marjorie. I'll stay in the sitting room with m-m-my brother."

He turned to leave, but she touched his forearm, stopping him.

"May I see Howard now?"

"Of course," John said.

He led her back to the front room where Michael was waiting, and as soon as Marjorie started toward the casket, John slipped back into the kitchen. The sound of a faint sniffle reached his ears as the swinging door swiveled shut behind him. After blowing out a long breath, John took out his flask so that he could force himself to have a few more sips of whiskey before the funeral. Bringing the flask to his lips, John screwed his eyes shut, his body tensing as the unpleasant-tasting beverage found his taste buds again. It was horrible. Really horrible. Definitely not worth the potential relief he might feel from continuing to torture himself with it. Frowning, John replaced the cap. When the sound of one of Marjorie's choked sobs broke through the walls, John winced. Mind elsewhere, he placed the flask in his outer breast pocket, rather than returning it to his inner pocket where he had been keeping it before. Then, he made himself head back out to the front room.

Not long after, guests began pouring in. One and then four and then twelve. Water had to be fetched. People had to be welcomed. Everything moved much too fast. Before John could even orient himself, Marjorie was tapping on his shoulder, wondering where to put the harpsichord player, whom she had hired to play first in her home and then the following morning at the church as well. Then, while John was trying to remember some of the other tasks he'd have to complete throughout the service tomorrow, more and more people started to come into the house, and it felt as though every one of them had set their sights on bumping into him on their way to see the body. Soon, the room was so packed that John could scarcely breathe, and every time John heard someone whisper something, he found himself becoming worried that people were making nasty comments about him, probably lamenting the state of the room, saying the service wasn't organized well enough, or (maybe even more likely) remarking to each other that John's speech cadence was strange and oh, what a shame that was. John cringed as memories from childhood flickered through his mind.

One from when he was seven or eight.

"Why are you so strange, John?" Michael remarked, coming up behind John in the churchyard cemetery. "Stop spending so much time out here. Everyone thinks there's something wrong with you."

Another from when he was eleven.

"Is that Lucy's rag doll?" Michael sneered, turning up his nose the moment he came into the bedroom and saw John stroking the doll's yellow hair. "Why do you still have that?"

One more from when he was thirteen.

"Casket-making?!" Michael scoffed, meeting John outside the barn. "Of course you'd want to help Father with that. And you'll probably enjoy it too."

And the worst one, the one that he thought of most frequently, the one that brought him the most shame, from when he was only six.

Michael slammed his palms on the table, interrupting John's latest Lucy-related commentary, the sound causing both John and his parents to flinch.

John had been telling everyone that Lucy wouldn't have liked the carrots they were having for supper because she would have found them to be too crunchy. Apparently, he shouldn't have been.

"Can't you see that no one else wants to talk about her anymore?!" Michael roared, his eyes wide with fury.

Michael's voice continued to echo in John's ears, only now the words were no longer playing in Michael's high-pitched soprano of their shared childhood but in the tenor he spoke with today. John's memories often unfolded like this, making him feel as though Michael was still saying these things to him, even though neither of them had brought up Lucy to the other for a *very* long time.

Each iteration of Michael's cruel words boomed like the harsh, powerful notes of a church's pipe organ. John's palms began to sweat, and he started wringing his hands as shame flared to life on his cheeks.

Michael had been right back then. John *had been* strange. He still was.

Shortly before six, when Marjorie was ready to stop receiving guests, John forced himself to bury his lingering feelings of self-reproach so that he could carry on with the rest of his responsibilities, the most immediate one being to close the coffin and let everyone know that it was time to leave. It was the last of his duties for the day. Then, tomorrow, the other men he'd recruited would help him move the casket outside to the hearse so that it could be transported to the church and then to the cemetery.

When John pushed himself to stand, he pushed the last of Michael's still-echoing words out of his head, too, and then walked toward the casket, his mind foggy from multiple hours of reliving some of the most shame-filled moments of his childhood. A moment later, John reached the front of the room, and he wiped his sweaty palms on the front of his pants so that he could close the casket. Just before he touched the lid, someone's hand came to settle on his shoulder. He flinched and turned.

Thankfully, it was only Michael.

"I'll take it from here," Michael said. "I can sense when you've had enough."

John replied, "No, I'll be f-fine. I *am* f-f-fine."

"You're not," Michael said flatly, reaching up for the lid.

John's hand shot out to stop him. "Stop. I have it."

"No."

"Yes."

Michael tried to wrestle his hand away, but John tightened his hold, which only made Michael pull harder. And then . . .

John tripped forward, his sudden stumble sending the flask that had been in his outer breast pocket to the floor. It struck the hardwood with a clatter.

Someone—possibly the elderly woman seated closest to them in a nearby rocking chair—gasped.

"Jesus Christ, John," Michael muttered with a sigh. "Were you—"

Heat rushed to John's face. Blood began whooshing past his eardrums, the sound so loud he couldn't even hear the rest of Michael's sentence, though he knew what Michael had probably said. Humiliated, John scooped up the flask and then bolted outside. He knew he shouldn't leave his brother to handle the rest. But . . .

Embarrassment set the rest of his body ablaze. He couldn't stay. Not now. Ashamed of his constant ineptitude, John tucked the flask inside his suit pocket and started for home on foot. He never once stopped to look back.

Why couldn't he seem to make this whole "mortician" thing work?

Later, while John was sitting in front of the fireplace reading a book, someone came into the house, and whoever it was must have been in a hurry because they flung open the door with enough *oomph* to cause it to crash into the wall.

"Michael!" Katherine called out as she traversed the hall. "Michael!"

Listening to the click-clack of her heels on the floorboards, John's muscles tensed. He liked Katherine well enough, but she was . . .

"Michael!" she shouted.

Loud.

Katherine entered the room with a big sigh.

"John, have you seen Michael?"

Keeping his eyes fixed on the page, though he was no longer reading the words, John replied, "He's finishing up with the P-P-Price viewing."

"Without you?"

Before John could respond, they both heard the door to the back of the house open and close. Michael strode into the room not more than a moment later, smoothing out his suit, his movements looking intentionally more pronounced than usual, possibly to communicate to John how much he'd had to endure as a result of John fleeing early.

Or maybe that was all in John's head.

At least John was saved from the embarrassment of having to tell Katherine that he'd run off, leaving Michael to finish the Price funeral on his own.

"Someone stole my necklace!" Katherine cried out the moment she saw her husband.

Curious, John shut his book and looked up, though shame was preventing him from meeting Michael's eyes.

"Off of your neck?" Michael asked, shaking his head in bewilderment.

"Well, not exactly . . ." Katherine twisted the ring on her index finger one way and then the other. "He said he wanted to sell Father the statue of William Penn."

"Wait. Billy Penn? From the new city hall?"

"I know how it sounds, but he was very convincing," she huffed. "He told me that it was cracked."

"Like the Liberty Bell?" Michael asked, now laughing.

"Yes! See, it happened before, so why shouldn't I have believed him? He told me that my father was supposed to meet him there to . . . to pay for it and to sign the proof of sale or—"

Michael continued to laugh. He looked over at John, seemingly expecting John to be laughing too. John forced a smile and a chuckle, though he couldn't help but feel sorry for Katherine. It never felt nice to be tricked.

"It isn't funny!" she exclaimed.

"Well, what would you like me to do, love?" Michael asked. "Report it to the police?"

"Yes! And maybe . . . maybe we can find him. I *knew* I had recognized him, but then he . . . well, he spun his tall tale and confused me. I swear I've seen him working at my father's mill."

"Do you think that the police will throw him behind bars based on hearsay?"

"Not hearsay! Why, I'm sure they'll find my necklace if they look."

"Criminals work fast," Michael said with a shrug. "He might be selling it as we speak."

Katherine sucked in a breath. "No! I *loved* that necklace!"

"If you loved it, why—"

"It was *William Penn*, Michael!"

"Ah, so you love William Penn more than me?" Michael asked playfully. "That was the first necklace I ever bought for you, you know."

"Yes, I know! I feel terrible!"

Michael's expression softened. "We'll try to retrieve it, Katherine."

Michael wrapped her up in an embrace. For a moment, John couldn't help but stare. Envy stirred inside him, making his stomach harden. What would it be like to be that close with someone?

But then, the feeling of envy faded as soon as Katherine sniffled and Michael began stroking her hair. It was probably for the best that John hadn't found someone with whom he'd like to spend his life. He couldn't fathom having to comfort someone else, to help the person he loved make sense of bad things that happened, even to lovely people. He would be completely inept at that sort of thing.

"We'll talk to your father, see if he remembers someone who fits the description of your necklace thief," Michael said. "Hopefully we'll be able to find him. If he's sold it by then, maybe I can see to it that he pays us something."

"Thank you," Katherine said, her voice slightly muffled by the fabric of Michael's shirt.

Michael placed his hands on her shoulders and urged her back a bit so that he could see her face. "Mind if I talk to John for a little while? Alone? I'll meet you upstairs."

Katherine sniffed and shook her head. "No, not at all."

She walked off, wiping her face with her fingertips on the way, her retreating footsteps mimicking the fast-rising beats of John's heart. John's eyes fell to the floor, and once the sound of Katherine's heels had become soft enough to provide John with a reassurance that Katherine was no longer within earshot, he began to explain himself.

"I only had a couple of sips to try to calm myself. I promise I wasn't s-s-s . . . I wasn't s-*slopped*."

Michael let out a sigh. "Well, that's somewhat of a relief." He knelt to catch John's eye. "But I'm worried about you. I want Katherine and I to have our own place soon. I'd like to be closer to work. And I want to take on more responsibility there. I won't be able to keep taking over for you, but . . ." He sighed again. "John, I'm worried you'll start losing clients. No one will ever recommend Hall Funeral Services to their friends or relatives if you keep—"

"I know," John said softly. "I should have stayed back in Media."

"Come on, I couldn't have left you there. We both know that. I mean, would you have even talked to anyone else in town? It seems like Katherine and I are the only people you talk to in this entire city. Other than your clients, whom you only speak with when I force you to. And even with Katherine, I'm fairly certain that you only *barely* tolerate her because she's my wife."

"No, I-I like Katherine. Just, she's—"

"Life is about *connections*, John."

"I know." John's eyes wandered to his hands. He began twisting them in his lap, one way and then the other. "But it's . . . it's hard for me. Always has been."

"Only because you barely ever try."

"I can't seem to connect with people. Even wh-wh-*when* I try."

Michael's hand came to rest on John's knee. "We need to find someone else to work with you. Someone who can handle the things that you . . . can't."

John stopped twisting his hands, pausing to let Michael's words settle in. His brother was right, wasn't he?

"Alright," he forced out. "I'll try to write something up. Something we can have printed in the n-n-newspaper."

"Perfect." Michael clapped his hands together and stood. "Now, I need to try to find the fellow who stole Katherine's necklace." He clicked his tongue once. "Good God, I can't believe she let herself be tricked like that. Not that I'm upset with her. It's sweet how trusting she can be. I mean, she tries to see the best in people. How could I not love that?"

Love. Once again, a flicker of envy flared to life in John's chest, tugging on his heart for the briefest moment before being snuffed out by the harsh reality of his own situation. He'd never find someone to love.

"But this . . . this is inconvenient," Michael continued. "I mean, she really liked that necklace. I think." Michael let out a puff of air. "William Penn—my God!"

Michael chuckled, and John pretended to laugh, too.

Then Michael turned and walked out, leaving John alone. John reopened his book but soon found that he wasn't able to focus on the words. Instead, he kept thinking about those little blips of envy he'd been experiencing over what Michael had with Katherine. Back in Media, John had never been very concerned with finding romantic companionship, but it seemed like living in the city, being constantly surrounded by people, by *couples*, especially while he was organizing funerals, was changing something in him, making him want to find someone with whom he could experience real closeness. Someone who would love him for who he was. Someone who would tolerate his shortcomings, of which there were many.

But, realistically, John knew he would just have to try to be content with his continued solitude.

Chapter Three
Calvin

Calvin was relaxing on the sofa reading one of his favorite books when a series of knocks startled him out of the story. He looked up from the page, furrowing one of his brows. Strange. Earlier that morning, Calvin had paid Mrs. Donaldson the rent, thanks to the fact that he had managed to sell the stolen necklace the previous evening. He hadn't made any real friends in the city yet. And he was barely even cordial with the other tenants who lived in the boarding house. Who could be knocking? Perhaps the fellow across the hall? Some time back, Calvin had borrowed the man's coat, and he had yet to return it. Truthfully, Calvin had been holding on to the hope that the man would forget he had even borrowed it. It was a nice coat. Calvin wanted to keep it.

After stretching out his legs, Calvin stood and made his way to the door to see who had knocked. His mind was busy coming up with excuses to explain why he needed the coat for a while longer, even though it was the middle of springtime, and when he finally opened the door, a burst of fear slammed into him with such force, it nearly knocked him back a step. Standing there, in the hallway of the boarding house, was the redheaded woman whose necklace Calvin had stolen. Katherine . . . Holloway or something. Katherine No-Longer-McGough. Quickly, Calvin moved to slam the door shut, but the man who was with her—probably her husband—caught the wood, and Calvin's stomach nearly fell out of his ass.

"Where is it?" the man asked.

"Um . . . where's what?" Calvin replied.

Damned Mrs. Donaldson. It seemed that she would let just about anyone into her home.

"Is this not him?" the man asked, turning to Katherine.

"It *is* him!" she said before pointing a finger in Calvin's face. "*You* stole my necklace."

"I seem to remember you handing it to me," Calvin said smugly.

"We'd like it back," the man said. "I can't believe you'd prey on a sweet young woman like this. Katherine's father said you weren't even fired from the shoddy mill, either. Just up and left before the end of one of your shifts. Which means that the stealing wasn't even some sort of revenge for having lost your paycheck. Just malice."

"Not *malice*," Calvin said, which was kind of a lie, but oh, well. "I needed money for rent. But I couldn't keep working in the mill. I mean, look, I nearly lost one of my fingers!" He held up his index finger to reveal a scar that was *at least* seven years old, though hopefully neither Katherine nor the man who was probably her husband would be able to tell that from its appearance. "I'm not coordinated enough to work those machines."

"So, you con people out of money instead of finding other work?" the man asked, leveling a look.

"No! Or . . . sometimes." Calvin sucked on his bottom lip, trying to work out how to win their favor. Making people feel sorry for him had worked in the past. He could try that. "I've been on my own since I was little." Was twelve little? Maybe not. But Calvin needed their sympathy. "See, I'm an orphan. It's not like I'm proud of stealing." Alright, maybe *that* was a little bit of a lie. Beneath his shame, Calvin was a *tiny* bit proud of his skills. "But I need to eat. How else am I supposed to keep myself from starving and ending up on the streets? I'm not suited to factory work, but there's nothing else for me out there." Over the years, Calvin had learned that it was best to pepper in the truth with one's lies. "I can't keep working in textile mills, but I have no other skills, either. I never meant any harm. Besides, it was only a necklace."

"It was my *favorite* necklace," Katherine said. "It was important to me."

Calvin fought back the urge to say that she had handed it over fairly easily for something that was supposedly so important to her. Instead, he lowered his eyes to the floor and said, "I'm very sorry."

"Can we have it back, then?" the man asked.

"I . . . uhm . . . I sold it," Calvin said, softening his tone in order to try to sound sheepish. He bit his lip for extra effect. "I'm so sorry."

"Who purchased it?" Katherine said. "Perhaps we can buy it back."

Calvin scrunched up his nose. "Can I be honest? I sold it to a random person I encountered outside the . . . uhm . . . the racetrack." No need to let either Katherine or her husband know that he had ventured over there with the intention of placing a few bets, right? "I went there to . . . to see the horses. Just . . . wanted to watch the race." What a sorry lie that was. Although, Calvin *did* like horses. "So, see, the buyer wasn't someone I know personally. I mean, I'd played cards with him a couple of times in the past, I think. But I have no clue where he lives."

"We'll take the money instead, then," the man said with a tired sigh.

Calvin cringed. "I spent most of it. On food and rent."

Well, those things as well as a couple of losing bets and a new book.

The man let out a huff and said, "I suppose that leaves me no choice. I'll have to turn you in."

Fear struck Calvin in the chest once more, and his heart skipped a beat.

"With what evidence?" Calvin spluttered, his head snapping up to meet the man's eyes. "No one else heard our conversation. And I won't confess to the police. It'll be your word against mine."

"Lucky for me, I happen to be friends with the chief of police," the man said in a pompous tone. "Katherine's father is friends with the mayor too."

Calvin narrowed his eyes to study the man's face. Was the braggart merely exaggerating? Lying outright? Calvin couldn't tell. Damn. He *really* couldn't let himself be thrown in prison for stealing a stupid necklace, especially not for stealing one that had only yielded enough money for a month's rent, some food, and one measly book.

"I'll pay you back," Calvin said.

"How?" the man scoffed. "You have no income. You said so yourself! Unless . . . maybe Katherine could convince her father to let you come back to work."

Calvin threw his head back and groaned. Not the Goddamned mill!

"No. *Please*, no," Calvin implored.

Desperate for a solution, Calvin began scrutinizing the man's appearance. His clothes seemed nice enough. Did he own a business? Soon, Calvin's eyes found the man's cuff links. His *very nice* cuff links. Gold, most likely. With . . . were those *real* emeralds? Calvin's eyes widened, his suspicions more or less having been confirmed. Clearly, this man was no laborer, but a business owner of some sort. Calvin could work for him. Maybe. Not that the man struck Calvin as a pleasant person to be employed by. But if Calvin could keep himself out of prison by working for him, he'd consider it. Especially if the man owned a business *other* than a textile mill.

"Maybe . . . I could work for you instead?"

"Well, sure, if you wouldn't mind working in a carpet factory," the man replied, his voice thick with sarcasm.

Calvin frowned. Damn.

Katherine tapped on her husband's shoulder.

"I think I might have a suggestion," she said to both of them before narrowing her eyes at Calvin. "But I'd like to speak with my husband privately first."

Donning a fake smile, Calvin said, "Not a problem. Shall I . . ."

He tried to step out into the hall, wondering if he could simply run off and return for some of his things later, but the man placed a hand on Calvin's chest, stopping him.

"Wait here," he commanded before shoving Calvin back into his room.

With one swift pull, the man shut the door in Calvin's face. Frustrated by both the man's pushiness and his own ineptitude, Calvin let out a huff.

And then he put his ear to the wood to listen.

"What if he worked with John?" Katherine suggested.

"I can't subject John to someone like that," the man replied.

"What do you mean?"

"He's a criminal!"

"Well, who else could stomach John's kind of work? And John really needs to find someone who can help him run his business. Especially if we move soon." There was a pause. "I want our own place. I like living with John, but some more privacy would be lovely, wouldn't it? And you've been saying that you'd prefer to live closer to work. Besides, we could finally hire a maid—someone to help me with cooking and cleaning and washing clothes. I mean, the only reason

*why we haven't found someone is that John feels uncomfortable with
it, even though we would pay the woman well."*

"*I know, love. I want to move too. I nearly have enough money
saved to purchase our own place outright now. But . . . God, Katherine, could I really propose that this man work with my brother?"*

"*Well, you're tired of working with John yourself, aren't you?"*

"*I . . . am,"* the man admitted, though he sounded reluctant to say
it. "*Still, John could wind up hurt working with someone like that.
He's clearly a thief. What if he steals something?"*

"*John can still handle the money. Wouldn't they only be together
a few hours a week?"*

"*I . . . suppose."*

Calvin pursed his lips. What kind of work was this?

Katherine continued on. "*And, oh, Michael, the poor man's story!
He was orphaned!"*

So, the man's name was Michael. And Katherine was kind
enough to still think Calvin was worth helping. He hadn't expected that. Now he couldn't help but feel a tiny bit bad for stealing
her necklace.

"*Oh, who knows if what he said was true,"* Michael remarked.

"*It sounded true to me."*

"*Katherine."* Michael sighed. "*You're too trusting."*

"*I feel sad for him. At least offer him the chance to pay us back.
His employment could be . . . temporary. Sort of like . . . well, sort of
like practice for John. And you know that John's not used to working
with people. If he makes this man uncomfortable, well, then it won't
matter so much since he's . . . well, he's no one."*

Calvin held in a scoff. Well, that was a little harsh, wasn't it?
No one! Calvin wasn't *no one*! Or . . . well, maybe he *was* no one,
but it was cruel of Katherine to say such a thing out loud. Wealthy
people. What self-serving snobs.

Before Calvin could press his ear back to the wood, Michael pushed the door open. Calvin righted himself quickly, doing his best to look innocent as ever.

"So, what's the suggestion?" Calvin asked.

Michael said, "We think you might like working for my brother."

Calvin crooked an eyebrow. "It's not factory work, right?"

"Right."

"What kind of work is it, then?"

Michael and Katherine exchanged a look, both of their faces pinching with what looked to be unease, which, in turn, made Calvin uneasy too. His stomach churned nervously.

"Let me talk to my brother first. About the salary," Michael said.

"Is the work that bad?" Calvin tried to tease, huffing a shaky laugh.

"Not *bad*, exactly, but, well . . ." Michael paused, his brow furrowed.

"It's *unique*," Katherine said, and she clasped her hands together. "Would you like to come by tomorrow?"

"Uhm, sure."

What on earth was he setting himself up for?

"Do you have a piece of paper? I can write down our address," she said.

Calvin held up a finger before stepping back into his room. He retrieved the notebook he'd stolen and then located a pen.

After Katherine wrote their address and they settled on a time for their meeting, Michael pointed a finger in Calvin's face and said, "And if you run off—"

"I won't," Calvin cut in, the false promise leaving his mouth before he even had a chance to think on it. But then, as Calvin took the pen back from Katherine, he realized that maybe it *was* true. After all, he wasn't keen on taking his chances with the law. If Michael was telling the truth about his and Katherine's supposed "friends," it could certainly complicate Calvin's life for a while, whether or not he ended up being thrown in prison. He hated to think of having to start his life over in yet *another* city. After leaving New York, it had taken a long time and a lot of creative "borrowing" for Calvin to build up his new collection of books. So, maybe what he'd said *was* true. Maybe he *wouldn't* run. "I won't," he reiterated, this time with more sincerity. "I promise."

"See?" Katherine said, smiling up at her husband, who merely rolled his eyes.

Michael held out his hand for Calvin to shake.

"Until tomorrow, Mr. . . . ."

"Wright," Calvin said. "And you're Mr. . . . Holloway?"

"Hall," Michael corrected.

Calvin nodded. "Right, Hall. Michael Hall."

Michael tilted his head. "How'd you know my name was Michael?" His eyes widened. "Were you . . . oh my God, were you *listening to us* earlier?!"

Flashing a simpering smile, Calvin retracted his hand.

"It's not like I was *trying* to listen."

Katherine snorted, and Michael immediately shot her an irritated glare.

"I have a feeling I'll regret this," he said. "See you tomorrow, Mr. Wright."

"Tomorrow," Calvin confirmed.

When they left, Calvin let out a long breath.

Well, he had successfully kept himself out of prison. Barely.

Whatever this position was that Michael and Katherine had in mind for him, Calvin hoped it wouldn't be too strenuous. It would be nice to have a steady source of income. For a little while, anyway.

As Calvin crossed the threshold into the front room of Michael and Katherine Hall's home, his heart started to hammer, and within a few paces, his brow began to perspire as well, nervousness percolating inside of him with such ferocity that he thought he might retch. God, this was stressful. Because no matter what the employment entailed, Calvin couldn't exactly say no to the offer. Not without fear of being thrown in prison.

Attempting to focus on something other than his troubled emotional state, Calvin surveyed Michael and Katherine's home as he followed them through it. Calvin had already figured out that Michael and Katherine were wealthy, but the sheer size of their home still surprised him. Beyond the large street-facing front room, which had a few chairs as well as an impressively sized bookcase, they moved into a long hallway. Traversing it, they passed by what was either a little library or an office and then by a sitting room, both on the right. They then passed a kitchen to the left (there was a room beyond the kitchen, too, probably where the Hall family took their meals; Calvin could see the edge of a table in there), as well as a set of stairs to the second floor. At the end of the hall, there was a little vestibule with a solid wood door at the back, maybe leading to a basement.

They all stopped in front of the door. Michael knocked on it and called out, "John?"

Stairs creaked on the other side of the wood, and then, the man who must have been John answered. And the moment Calvin locked eyes with him, his heart stuttered and he sucked in a breath. Because—*oh, God*—John was very, very handsome.

"John, this is Mr. Calvin Wright, the man I told you about," Michael said. "And Calvin, this is my brother, John Hall."

It took Calvin an extra second to register Michael's words. It was as though his mind had stalled the second that he and John had made eye contact, the beautiful man's presence causing Calvin's thoughts to twist and tangle like snarled yarn. Hoping to free the threads, Calvin shook his head. Never before had he encountered a man who could make him feel as though his mind was as useless as an old throstle frame spinning machine.

"Hello!" Calvin spluttered, his brain still trying to catch up with the present, and then, before Calvin could think better of it, he blurted out, "Whatever it is you need me for, I'm ready," in a playful tone of voice that was *way* too flirtatious.

Oh, God, what was wrong with him?

In response to Calvin's strange behavior, John shot Michael a look of confusion, his mouth twisting up on one side while he raised one of his eyebrows. Michael simply sighed.

"Doesn't he know—" John started to say.

"Not yet," Michael cut in, holding up one of his hands as though to stop John from finishing his sentence. He turned to Calvin. "First, the salary. You'll be paid by the job, which could be as low as three dollars . . ." He paused, and Calvin caught himself curling his lip. It sounded as though, salary-wise, it would be similar to working in a mill, which, in truth, wasn't very appealing. "Or as high as seventy-five."

Calvin nearly choked on his own spittle. "*Seventy-five?!*"

"That isn't t-t-t-typical," John clarified, squeezing his eyes shut while he stumbled over the *t*'s. "M-more likely, you'd receive twenty."

John's cheeks reddened to the loveliest shade of crimson, and Calvin's heart pitter-pattered a little from the sight. Goodness, the man was handsome. Was John's stammering making him feel embarrassed? Calvin couldn't see why. Despite the fact that Calvin was familiar with society's strong views on the condition, he himself had never thought of it in a negative way. Not that Calvin had talked to very many people who stuttered, but still. Everyone had their . . . eccentricities.

Was *this* why Katherine had implied that Calvin might not like working with John? Because of a simple speech irregularity? It couldn't be.

"What's the work entail?" Calvin asked.

Even though Calvin had hoped that John would be the one to respond, Michael cut in instead.

"John needs someone who can talk to people. Organize events."

"Easy," Calvin said, though he still couldn't understand why everyone was talking *around* exactly what this business of John's was, rather than being forthcoming with information. "What kind of events? Weddings? Parties? Government events?"

"Funerals," John said, lowering his eyes. "I'm a m-m-mortician. I suppose that's what I'm supposed to call myself now. Undertaker had been the term before. Until recently."

"*Undertaker?*" Calvin balked. Jesus, no wonder everyone was worried that Calvin wouldn't want the job. "So, you mean you handle the . . . uhm . . ."

"Embalming," Michael said, finishing for him. "Yes, but *you'll* mostly be handling the living. And you'll make a pretty penny from it too." He looked over at John, whose cheeks were still rosy, his eyes fixed on the floor. "Much more than I had originally suggested, but John thought it would be best if you were compensated *fairly*." Michael rolled his eyes. "Almost as much as John, in fact, which, honestly, seems completely absurd. I mean, John went to school for his work, while you . . . well, you stole from me."

Calvin tried a charming smile. "Well, with this kind of salary, I could repay what I owe you fairly easily."

"Yes, I suppose there's that," Michael said, his voice slightly weary. "So, you'll take the position?"

Calvin bit his lip. Truthfully, he wasn't sure. He'd make a nice salary. He wouldn't be laboring in some overcrowded factory. Nor would he be stealing or otherwise putting himself at risk of prison time. But to be organizing funerals every week? How sad. And strange. Too strange, maybe.

While Calvin was thinking it over, he and John locked eyes for the briefest moment before John immediately looked away. John then raked a hand through his hair, causing some of it to stick up this way and that. Calvin's cheeks began to warm. John really was handsome.

Handsome *and* intriguing. Calvin couldn't help but feel a little fascinated by him. What kind of man would choose *this* for a profession?

Before Calvin could respond and indicate that he might, in fact, be interested, John said, very shyly, "Don't feel bad if you don't want to w-w-work with me. I know that this isn't the type of thing most people would enjoy."

"Oh, it's not that I'm *not* interested, but . . ."

"I-I could offer you m-more money, perhaps, or—"

Michael scoffed. "*More money?!*"

"Or somewhere to live," John said before taking a pause and clearing his throat. "We have an extra room."

"Extra room?!" Michael threw up his hands. "John, I *told you*, this would be a *temporary* thing. Someone to work with for a *little while* so that you might eventually become comfortable—"

"Yes, I-I know, but you said that the building he lives in is . . . well, I won't repeat the word, but it wasn't a n-n-nice one."

Calvin might have been offended had that not been true. He had to respect John's willingness to be tactfully honest.

John continued, "And it w-w-would be easier for me if Calvin lived here. Otherwise, I would have to travel to his home whenever we had a c-client." He shrugged. "Unless you think we ought to pay for a . . . a telephone?"

Michael heaved a sigh. "No, not while I'm saving up to move while *simultaneously* trying to purchase a larger factory space." He muttered something to himself, something Calvin couldn't make out, though he was certain he heard a bit of profanity in there, and then Michael reached up to massage his forehead. "John, I need to speak with you. *Alone.*"

Without hesitation, John turned and went back into the basement. Michael followed. Calvin and Katherine continued to stand in the hall, listening to their retreating footsteps, the basement stairs creaking while the brothers descended. Calvin stuck his hands in his pockets and rocked back on his heels.

After a moment, Katherine said, "I think you should take it."

Instead of responding, Calvin continued to rock back and forth a couple of times as he thought it over. *Should* he take it? He wasn't sure. Despite the fact that he could certainly benefit from free housing, he wasn't thrilled with the prospect of living with other people. Or even just one other person. He was starting to like living by himself. It was nice to make his own choices regarding the living space. Not that there was much space. But still. David had been so particular about everything. Calvin couldn't have hung a couple of stolen curtains without the man criticizing the look of them.

Besides the fact that Calvin was enjoying the freedom of having his own place, he couldn't help but be worried that if he lived *here*, he'd become too entangled with these people. Attached, even. Maybe not to Michael since he seemed like a bit of a bastard, but maybe to John. Because Calvin was finding himself thinking some . . . interesting thoughts about the man. Interesting and . . . forbidden. How could he not think these sorts of things, though? Filthy things. John had such a nice face. He had a soothing voice, too, even with the stammering. And the stammering itself . . . Calvin might just be feeling a smidge enchanted by it.

Calvin stopped rocking and blew out a breath. God, what a nightmare it would be if he took the position only to then continue having this terrible fascination with his employer.

"I know it would be the *logical* choice to take it. Decent money. Housing." Calvin scratched the side of his head. "But I'm not sure if I should."

"Why not?"

Well, Calvin couldn't exactly tell her the real reasons, but maybe he could hint that his hesitation was partially because of John. Without revealing that it was because he was becoming *a little bit* enamored with him, of course.

Calvin said, "Well, what's John like? Would you work with him?"

"Would *I*?"

Calvin snorted. "Well, not *you*, specifically, obviously, though I think it's kind of silly that women are expected to stop working once they're married." He threw Katherine what he hoped she'd see as a platonic, but friendly, wink. "I'm sure you'd make a fine embalmer."

Katherine laughed softly, and Calvin smiled in return.

"John's a sweet man," she said, "but he struggles a bit with people."

"Are you referring to the fact that he seems to fumble over his words?" Calvin asked.

"No, not that. Not *only* that. But . . ." She frowned. "He's very reserved. Poor man. He had a hard childhood. It wasn't like most people's. He had a hard time making friends. Michael's childhood wasn't easy either, I suppose, but he seemed to handle certain things better."

"Oh." Calvin nodded thoughtfully. "Well, my childhood wasn't like most people's either. Or, well, there were plenty of other children in the orphanage so maybe it wasn't so uncommon."

Katherine's brow creased with what Calvin knew was pity. Almost everyone made the same face and said the same things whenever he brought up either his parents or the orphanage. Everyone said the same things, and yet . . . no one ever seemed interested in hearing Calvin say much more on the subject. Even David hadn't wanted to learn more than the bare minimum about either Calvin's early childhood or the loss of his parents.

"I'm sorry," she said, predictably.

Calvin pressed his lips together into a thin line, shrugging as though it was nothing.

But the fact that he'd once lost everything felt so far from "nothing."

Seconds passed. Calvin was ready to move on to a new topic when Katherine said, "How, uhm, how old were you when you . . . ended up there?"

Calvin blinked twice. He could hardly believe that she wanted to know more. It seemed like she . . . like she cared. But why would she? After all, Calvin was a nobody. He was a nobody who had stolen from her. Katherine had said so herself. Why was she asking him this?

Cautiously, Calvin said, "Uhm, twelve. Not *so* young, maybe, but . . ." Shame flared to life on Calvin's face as he recalled his time in the orphanage. God, he'd been so lonely. Lonely and . . . heart-broken. Life had felt so hopeless back then. And many times since. Pushing past the shame, Calvin tried to respond with honesty. "But I think that was worse in some ways. Not being young. No one wanted to take in a twelve-year-old. Not even my relatives, few that I had."

"Gosh, that's . . . that's horrible."

Deep sadness was etched on Katherine's face as she fixed a lock of her hair that had fallen across her forehead, tucking it back into the mess of red curls piled up high on top of her head. Calvin felt a little pang of regret over having stolen her necklace. It was only right that he should try to pay her back for it.

Calvin opened his mouth to tell Katherine that he'd work with John, but Katherine started talking first.

"I *really* think you should take the position, Mr. Wright."

Calvin's lips curled into a small smile. "Calvin is fine."

Katherine smiled back. "Well, then, Calvin, I think you should take it. Based on what you've said, I can imagine that you've spent years hoping for a better life for yourself. Better than life working in factories. I know my father doesn't pay well. Probably many men who run these factories try to pay as little as possible."

Calvin's mouth fell agape. He was shocked—pleasantly shocked—by her candor.

Katherine chuckled. "I'm not supposed to say that, but it's true. And John won't only pay you fairly, but he'll treat you kindly as well. I'm not sure if he'll manage to find someone else to work with him otherwise. Plenty of people will try for the position once they see it in the paper, I'm sure, but would they stay? And *if* they stayed, would they be kind? I'm not hopeful."

"Why would *I* stay?" Calvin asked.

Katherine shrugged. "Because you have nowhere else to go."

"How do you know I'll be kind?"

"Just . . . a feeling I have."

Calvin pursed his lips. He narrowed his eyes, studying her.

"I'm surprised by your honesty," he said.

"Gullible, but honest," she said. "I suppose that's me."

Maybe. But Calvin thought there was probably a better way to say it. Twisting the truth was helpful even when, or perhaps *especially* when, it was about yourself. Katherine wasn't only *those* things. She was caring, too.

"Kindhearted," Calvin said. "I think that suits you better."

Katherine smiled warmly. "I like that. Thank you."

Michael and John came back upstairs a moment later, stopping just inside the vestibule.

"So," Calvin began, "if I take the position, will I have housing too?"

"Yes," Michael said through a strained smile. "If you would like to live here, that would be fine with us. Somehow."

Even though Calvin could sense that it was very much *not* fine, he thought he might as well show enthusiasm, "Great!" He exclaimed before holding out a hand toward John. "I'd love to work for you, then, Mr. Hall."

John hesitated. "Really?" he said, taking Calvin's hand.

Calvin's heart leapt the moment he touched the man's slightly calloused skin. What was wrong with him?

Michael clapped Calvin on the shoulder.

"When would you like to start?" he asked, squeezing hard enough to make Calvin release John's hand.

Calvin wriggled out of Michael's grasp. "Whenever you'd like. I can move in soon. Actually, Mrs. Donaldson might return some of my money if I move out within the week. It's only the start of the month."

"Alright, well, I'll let you and John talk, then," Michael said. "Katherine and I should be leaving for the theatre now. We're meeting some friends there soon."

With that, Michael and Katherine retreated into the hall. Calvin shifted his weight from one foot to the other as he waited for them to gather their things and ready themselves to leave.

And then, Calvin and John were alone.

"So . . ."

Calvin trailed off while John shuffled his feet, his shoes making a soft scuffling noise on the floorboards. Portions of John's hair were still sticking up every which way, and Calvin could barely bury the urge to fix them. He shoved his hands into his pockets to make sure he wouldn't be tempted.

After a minute of painful silence, Calvin said the first thing that popped into his head. "What were you doing in the basement? Were you working on something?"

As soon as Calvin said the last word, a sharp pang of unease hit him in the stomach. Good Lord, were there bodies in there? Why had he asked that?

"I can show you," John offered.

Calvin faked a hearty chuckle. "It's not a *person*, is it?"

Please let it not be a person.

"No," John said with a small, bemused-looking smile. "Don't w-w-worry."

After turning on his heel, John started down the basement steps, and Calvin followed. He clutched tight to the railing so as to prevent potentially tripping on the steep set of stairs. Or from fainting. Even though John had said that he hadn't been *working on* a person, couldn't there still be a body somewhere? He wasn't sure how these things worked.

Halfway down, John looked back over his shoulder and asked, "Aren't funerals . . . common? Are you really that squeamish?"

Calvin tried to keep his voice level. "Well, first, embalming isn't *that* common, is it? Or, it hadn't been back when I was young. Which is probably why I'm not really comfortable with these sorts of things. I haven't been to a funeral since . . . well, since my parents passed. I've successfully stayed away from them ever since."

Calvin expected John to say something sympathetic like Katherine had, but John only let out a short hum, and then continued to the basement in silence. Calvin's heart clenched from . . . from what, exactly? Disappointment? It wasn't as though he *needed* to hear what would probably have been fairly empty-sounding words of sympathy, but he had *expected* to hear them. He hadn't expected such true kindness from Katherine, but he expected *something* from his future employer. Confessing to losing his parents only to be met with silence was . . . upsetting. It left Calvin with a strange sinking feeling in the pit of his stomach. Grief woven together with nausea. Was *this* why Michael and Katherine had insinuated that most people might not like working with someone like John? Because he was cold? Callous?

When Calvin reached the bottom step, he paused to take in the space. It was set up like a workshop, one that reminded him of his father's. Seeing the pieces of wood and the tools scattered about—saws and hammers and scrapers—was like a swift punch to the stomach. Calvin winced, and tears sprang to his eyes as he inhaled the scents of pine and oak and whatever other kinds of wood were down here. God, he missed his parents. He missed them so much. It was as though Katherine's earlier kindness—the fact that she seemed to truly care to learn what Calvin's life had been like—had broken something in him. Ripped through his veil of fake apathy as easily as shears slicing through linen.

Standing on the bottom step, pathetically struggling not to burst out crying, Calvin nearly turned to leave, but then John started talking, and the softness of the man's voice somehow soothed some of Calvin's lingering sorrow.

"I'm m-making something for a client I had last week," John said, taking what looked like a small silver pendant off of the work-table and holding it out for Calvin to see. Calvin blinked back his tears and came closer, his sadness waning more with every step, and oh, how thankful he was for the way that John had pulled his mind out of the past and back to the present.

"Just a pin," John said.

Calvin inspected the pendant through still-slightly-bleary eyes. In the center of the sparkling silver border, there was a pattern made with what looked to be . . . oh, *God*, woven hair?

Instantaneously, the topsy-turvy feeling in Calvin's stomach returned, though this time Calvin wasn't thinking of his parents, but of whoever would receive that trinket. And whoever's hair that had been, too. He took a shaky step backward. Even though most people might not have batted an eye to see the pin, Calvin was not most people. Death was a part of life, sure, but it wasn't part of *Calvin's* life. Not anymore. How would he ever manage to be this man's assistant?

Apparently oblivious to Calvin's unease, John continued on. "I know these haven't been popular for a wh-wh-while, but I still thought I would offer."

After clearing his throat, Calvin managed to eke out, "Why would someone want something like that?"

"Closure," John answered with a small shrug of his shoulder. "At least, that's what I learned from Eckels."

Still contending with waves of unease—the ripples of which were so intense that his skin was starting to itch—Calvin tried to find something else to focus on, hoping that maybe talking about something other than *human hair keepsakes* would make him feel better for having stupidly agreed to being a mortician's assistant.

Glancing around the room, Calvin noticed what looked to be a half-finished casket in the corner, and his stomach folded in on itself. In a flash, he was transported into the past, standing in front of his parents' closed caskets in the church, and he had to fight the urge to retch.

"Does he know?" he heard Aunt Mildred say in a hushed voice from a few feet away.

"About the orphanage?" Uncle Thomas whispered back. "Not yet, no."

Grief started to bubble its way to the surface, but Calvin tried to swallow it, which only served to make his stomach even more upset. Queasy, Calvin took one more step backward, knocking into a stool. He grabbed it so it wouldn't fall, and as he righted it, his eyes flitted over to the stairs. Once again, he wondered if he should leave. But then he remembered Katherine's kindness, and guilt slammed into him. He had to pay her back. Didn't he?

Calvin closed his eyes. He could bury this feeling of remorse. He had succeeded in burying it so many times before. Clearly, Katherine had plenty of money. She probably had other necklaces, ones that were *at least* as nice as the one that Calvin had stolen. He couldn't stay here. Couldn't work with a mortician. Couldn't be surrounded by sorrow and loss when he'd never even moved on from his own. Couldn't—

"Mr. Wright, I want to be honest with you," John said. "I only offered to make this p-pin because I n-n-needed to rectify something." Calvin opened his eyes. John's eyes were fixed on the pin he cradled his hands. "See, I-I ruined the funeral. I took the b-b-b-body to the wrong church. So, then, I was late. Embarrassingly late." He blew out what sounded like a nervous breath, turning the trinket in his hands, and a moment later, he huffed a short, uneasy laugh. "I'm not very good with people. Which is why I need to find someone who can handle that part of the business.

When I'm nervous, I flounder. I take c-c-caskets to the wrong church or knock over embalming fluids or lose my . . . my words. Even more than now, I mean." He looked up and met Calvin's eyes. "I need someone to work with me. I need . . . help."

Watching John's nervous fingers tinker with the pendant—his hands trembling slightly while he turned it this way and that—Calvin felt a rush of warm sympathy bloom to life in his chest. The feeling melted away the trepidation he'd had over taking the position, banishing the *couldn'ts* completely like the summer sun evaporating the morning dew. Now, the prospect of a fair salary and nice housing weren't the only things making Calvin want to stay. Neither was the promise of repaying Katherine. Instead, it was John. Seeing John standing there, his cheeks pink from shame, looking both pained and lost, Calvin found himself wanting nothing more than to help him.

Coming closer, Calvin said, "Well, I *am* fairly personable. At least, I'm personable enough to trick people into things like trusting me with their money or buying bottles of tonic water for their health—which, let me be clear, probably had the opposite effect. And I need *some* kind of income. I can't keep working in factories or textile mills. I'm not suited to it. I shouldn't keep stealing either. I'd prefer to stay out of prison. And out of one of those," Calvin said in what he hoped John would hear as a playful tone as he pointed over to the half-finished casket. John smiled back. "And you can call me Calvin, by the way."

"Alright." John nodded once. "Calvin."

"May I call you John?" Calvin asked. John nodded once more. "Well, John, I would be happy to help you. It'll take me a little while to stomach some of it, but I think I would come to love working with you."

"Thank you," John said with a small, hopeful-looking smile. "Really. I-I . . ." He let out a long breath. "Thank you."

Calvin's heart fluttered as he and John smiled at each other. Seconds passed before John finally looked away, running a hand through his hair and mussing it up even more in the process. Calvin's breath caught. Jesus Christ, John was stunning, especially with his hair sticking up every which way like that. It reminded Calvin of how David had sometimes looked while they were being intimate. But John was . . . well, John was *much* more handsome than David.

Calvin began chewing on his bottom lip. Oh, hell.

After clearing his throat, John said, "W-w-would you like to move in soon, then? It would benefit both of us if you could move in within the next few weeks. I never know when someone might come knocking in n-need of my services."

"I would love to," Calvin said. God, was he in trouble. He would be sharing a home with one of the most handsome and intriguing men he'd ever met in his whole life. "Um, I can start moving my things tomorrow. Do you have a carriage I can borrow? I noticed a stable in the back."

"In a way," John said. "It's a . . . hearse. If that wouldn't be too strange."

It was a hearse. Because why wouldn't it be?

Calvin huffed a laugh, unease clawing up his throat.

"Just as long as it's empty," Calvin tried to tease.

With a sort of hum-chuckle, John responded, "Yes, it w-w-will be."

Calvin's heart fluttered a bit. He really liked John's laugh.

"Perfect," he said. "I can come by to borrow it."

After a slightly awkward parting, one where John stumbled over a thank you while Calvin tried to insist that he should be the one thanking John for taking a chance on a criminal (though John was not aware of the number or extent of Calvin's past crimes),

Calvin left for home, opting to walk rather than try to catch one of the trolleys.

On the way, he said a little prayer that the position would work out. Even if it was temporary. Because the more Calvin ruminated on it, the more he realized that he *wanted* to plan funerals. He liked the notion of using his charms to *help* someone, rather than hurt them.

And not only *someone*, but John Hall. Impossibly handsome, strangely endearing (and endearingly strange) John Hall.

Imagining John's shy smile and kind eyes, Calvin felt that same surge of warmth bloom in his chest.

Dear God.

Calvin would have to keep these maybe-romantic, very-much-sexual feelings from continuing to blossom, not only because lusting over one's employer seemed like a terrible idea but also because, in all likelihood, John fancied women, not men, and so, nothing could ever happen between the two of them, regardless of how charming Calvin ever tried to be. Not that Calvin should be trying to charm the handsome mortician in the first place. Of course not. Truthfully, he shouldn't even be entertaining the idea of courtship. After what had happened with David, Calvin ought to be focused on keeping his heart safe.

When Calvin reached the corner of Market and Third, he paused to let a carriage pass by. While waiting, he closed his eyes and envisioned putting these burgeoning feelings for John into a little box. And then locking that box. And then kicking it off of a bridge.

Calvin had seen plenty of handsome men before. He had spoken with many of them over the years. And they had been easily forgotten. Ergo, it wouldn't be hard for Calvin to stop fawning over John Hall.

Hopefully.

Chapter Four
John

Seated in the box of the hearse carriage next to Calvin, John held tight to the reins, his stomach in knots as they traveled together to the boarding house on Walnut Street where Calvin had been staying. Even though Calvin would have likely preferred to simply borrow the hearse, John hadn't felt right letting him. It wasn't because he thought that Calvin might steal it (though that had been Michael's primary concern; John had received an earful from him over it while they'd had supper the previous evening), but because he was worried that Calvin might not take to Agathe. Or, more likely, that Agathe wouldn't take to Calvin. Agathe was a well-trained horse, but she very clearly preferred John holding the reins. She tolerated Michael fine here and there, but still, John felt a responsibility toward her. Besides, he wanted Calvin's move to proceed without complications, especially any complications related to a slightly stubborn horse. It was a miracle that Calvin wanted to work with him in the first place, and John didn't want anything to make Calvin change his mind.

When they turned onto Walnut, Calvin looked over at John with a cheery smile, and the knots in John's stomach tightened as he forced himself to look elsewhere. He fixed his gaze on Agathe's mane and prayed that Calvin wouldn't try to start a conversation.

Because every chat they had was one more chance for John to make Calvin regret his choice to work for Hall Funeral Services.

Despite the fact that Calvin had been perfectly kind to him, John couldn't help but worry that he was a hair's breadth away from scaring Calvin off, probably by saying something off-putting. He had come close to it yesterday when he had shown Calvin the mourning pin. John cringed internally as Calvin's mortified expression popped into his mind. God, Calvin had looked as though he'd been on the verge of throwing up. John had been forced to use every bit of courage he possessed to confess the reason *why* he was in need of help, practically *begging* Calvin not to reject the position outright. Calvin could still back out. Especially before the move. John needed to be careful.

Calvin pointed to one of the brick row homes ahead. "That's the one."

John nodded and then searched for a nearby hitching post for Agathe. After scanning the street for about half a block, he spotted one near the corner of the next cross street and steered over toward it.

"I hope you're ready to carry crates of books half a block," Calvin said, hopping out once Agathe came to a stop. "I wouldn't mind if you stopped right out front of my building instead. You could wait outside with your horse."

Walking the reins over to the cast-iron hitching post, John's eyes flickered over to Calvin, and he tried what he hoped would be a friendly enough smile. "I'll be f-fine. I'm happy to help."

John breathed a sigh of relief that Calvin didn't seem ready to back out of their agreement as he tied the reins to the post.

Calvin shrugged his shoulders in an overly exaggerated manner, lifting them up almost to his ears. "Suit yourself."

Once Agathe was secure, John and Calvin started back toward the boarding house. John kept back a couple of steps, letting

Calvin lead the way. After they reached the right building, John stayed on the sidewalk while Calvin headed up the two steps to let them in. He was struck with the sudden worry that he'd have to talk to whomever Calvin had been renting the room from. Or that he might be forced to speak with one of the other tenants.

After fiddling with the lock, Calvin looked back over his shoulder and said, "Mrs. Donaldson shouldn't be home. In case you're worried that you'll have to meet her. On Tuesdays, she meets up with her sister to play bridge. I'm not close with the others here, so I can't imagine they'd bother us either."

John's eyes widened, his eyebrows lifting in tandem. How had Calvin known? It was as though the man had read his mind.

"Well?" Calvin said, motioning for John to follow him inside. "Come on."

Blowing out a breath, John started up the steps. Even though he was itching to ask Calvin about his apparent telepathy, he kept his mouth clamped shut as he followed Calvin through the house. It was probably too familiar of an inquiry. He and Calvin barely knew each other.

Calvin's room was located on the third floor. So far, John hadn't noticed anything wrong with the building itself, not like Michael had implied. Even though the home was a modest size, it was well kept with fresh floral wallpaper lining the walls and woven wool carpets covering much of the hardwood. John felt a little foolish for suggesting that Calvin move in with him. Clearly it was only for his own benefit, not Calvin's. Calvin would be losing his privacy. Walnut Street was a convenient location, too. Only a short walk from various shops and markets.

But then, Calvin pushed open the door to his room, and those thoughts immediately fell out of John's head. John's face set to a frown as he crossed the threshold. While Calvin walked over to a stack of wooden crates in the corner, John leaned his weight on the doorframe, pausing to take in the space. Not that there was much to take in. It wasn't even large enough to fit a bed. Where had Calvin slept? On the sofa? God, it probably wasn't even long enough for him. Had Calvin spent his nights with his feet hanging over the edge? Didn't that hurt? Over time, sleeping in such a position might even cause problems with circulation.

Calvin bent to pick up a crate, but stopped. He looked up at John, who was still stuck in the same spot, sorrow and confusion preventing him from coming any farther into the room. Calvin huffed a light laugh and straightened.

"Do you want a tour?" he said, clapping his hands together. And though there was levity in Calvin's tone, there was something else there, too. Bitterness, maybe. John forced himself to take another step into the room as Calvin faked a laugh. "I warned you that it wasn't much."

He had. John's eyes found their way back to the sofa. Calvin strode over and fell back onto the cushions.

Reclining, Calvin said, "It's a little small for me, but . . ." He rolled onto his side and curled into a half-ball. "I slept like this so it wasn't too bad." He sat up and smacked the cushion with his hand a couple of times. "Better than a park bench. I know from experience."

Calvin's words struck John in the chest. In only a matter of what seemed like milliseconds, they burrowed into him, sticking into his heart like straight pins. He winced from the pain. Calvin tilted his head to the side as though waiting for John to reply. But John stayed silent. How was one supposed to respond to something like that? John couldn't even begin to know.

Ba-dum, ba-dum, ba-dum. Calvin began strumming his fingers on one of the cushions, clearly still waiting for John to say something. John lowered his head, shame coiling in his stomach as his

heart continued to bleed for Calvin. He wasn't reacting right, was
he?

Before John could even try to say something, Calvin sighed and
stood.

"Let's take some books to the hearse, shall we?"

John swallowed thickly. "Alright," he managed.

Over the next twenty minutes or so, John and Calvin carried
crates out to the hearse. On one trip, Calvin brought two sacks
of clothing, but otherwise, the only thing they took were stacks
of books. Throughout the move, Calvin said relatively little, only
making a couple of comments here and there as they relocated his
belongings.

Shame sat heavy in John's stomach. Calvin must have been
thinking to himself that John was strange. That there was something wrong with him. If John couldn't change Calvin's mind, it
seemed quite unlikely that Calvin would want to work with him
for very long. What if Michael moved out and then Calvin left
before John could even find someone else to work with? Before he
became even a *little* comfortable running the business by himself?
Goodness, what if Calvin left even *before* finding other, steady
work himself? John could foresee Calvin coming to the conclusion
that he was too peculiar to live with. Or work with. How horrible that would be. Poor Calvin obviously needed the money. He
needed the work. And John was happy that he had helped him by
offering him the position as his business counterpart.

By the time they were nearly finished moving Calvin's things,
with only two crates remaining in the much-too-small room, John
knew he had to at least attempt to make conversation.

"Wh-wh-wh-where'd you find the crates?" he tried as they
walked back into Calvin's room.

Calvin stopped and placed his hands on his hips.

"Oh. Uhm . . . I took them from one of the markets. I think they'd been keeping produce in them?"

John hummed. Calvin had "taken" them. Did Calvin mean to imply that he had stolen them? Or that the market hadn't needed them anymore?

"Don't worry," Calvin said with a wave of his wrist. "I'll bring them back."

So, the former.

"Right," John said.

Together, they picked up the last two crates. While heading back to the hearse, John noticed that Calvin looked wistful, his eyes fixed on the books in the crate he was holding. John craned his head to see which book Calvin might have been looking at with such fondness. It was *Dracula* by Bram Stoker. John hadn't read that one yet himself. He wondered how many of these Calvin had read. Did he read often? It seemed so. Unless he was only keeping these for sentimental reasons. Perhaps some had belonged to his parents or something.

"Do you . . . like to read?" John asked as they neared the hearse.

"No. I hate books," Calvin replied flatly before looking over at John with a cheeky smile and a raised eyebrow. "Yes, obviously I like to read."

John's cheeks warmed. Calvin chuckled.

"Do *you* like to read?" he asked, opening the cabin of the hearse.

Embarrassment was still pressing on John's vocal cords, preventing him from replying. Had Calvin meant to hurt his feelings?

"John, I was only teasing you," Calvin said. "You know, trying to be funny?" He set the crate next to the others. "I thought you'd laugh."

Squeezing his eyes shut, John shook his head. "Right. Sorry."

He placed his crate next to Calvin's.

"Let me make sure we haven't left anything behind," Calvin said. "Be back in a minute."

Calvin hurried back toward the house, while John leaned against the hearse's cabin and nervously moved a hand through his hair. He had to figure out how to connect with Calvin somehow. But try as he might, he couldn't think of anything.

When Calvin returned, he stopped very suddenly a few feet from John, and his face lit up with what looked to be . . . some kind of tenderness. It was the same sort of expression he'd had when he'd been looking at his books.

Grinning, Calvin said, "Thank you for helping me move."

John only shrugged. Calvin would be helping him keep his business. Moving a few crates of books seemed like the least he could do.

While John untied the reins from the hitching post, Calvin climbed up into the box seat. Soon, the two of them were off, traveling back to John's home in Frankford.

After a couple of blocks, Calvin bumped John's knee with his own.

"Do you like to read too? You never said."

John's stomach churned from nervousness. He hoped he wouldn't reply incorrectly this time. Maybe he could try to be funny. Calvin would probably like that.

"No," John replied as seriously as he possibly could, though he was barely fighting back a smile that was threatening to burst forth. He watched as Calvin's face swiftly fell, and then he couldn't hold back anymore. With a soft laugh, John smiled and said, "N-n-no, Calvin, I love to read."

Calvin let out a puff of air and rolled his eyes.

"You had me for a moment there," he said before bumping John's knee once more. "See, I think the two of us will get along just fine."

John's chest swelled with both hope and happiness.
He really hoped so.

Chapter Five
Calvin

After Calvin set his final crate of books onto the floor of his new bedroom, he straightened his posture, rested his hands on his hips, and smiled proudly. Despite having been thrown out onto the streets like trash mere months before, Calvin had somehow managed to find not only real, honest work with a real, honest-to-God incredible salary but a real home, too, one where he'd have space for both his books *and* a bed. No more low-hanging wall sink that was supposed to be used as a urinal in the nighttime, either. He'd be welcome to use the main bathroom whenever he pleased. How unbelievable it was that he had found such perfect employment. All thanks to a con, too.

Calvin was still standing there marveling at his new bedroom when John came up beside him, his head low, wringing his hands together as though he might somehow light a fire with them. Calvin wasn't sure what had John so nervous, but he knew he needed to fix it. Was John worried that he would run off?

"I'm excited to work with you," Calvin said, which wasn't exactly the truth, but it was far from the biggest lie that Calvin had ever told. He *did* want to work with John. He'd just prefer for them not to be working on corpses. "I'm really happy that you asked me to live here with you, too."

John's lips curled into a small smile. "I had to."

Calvin wasn't sure if John meant that he had to offer the room because it was more convenient for him if Calvin lived there or if John meant that he had to offer because Michael had insulted the condition of the boarding house. Perhaps it wasn't important what he meant. Calvin was here now. Thankfully.

John shifted his stance and said, "Should we return to Mrs. Donaldson's for your b-b-bookcase or . . . ?"

"Oh, I'm not keeping that. It wasn't the nicest piece of furniture, was it? Loose shelves. Scratches on the wood. I found it on a street corner when I first moved here."

"Where'd you live before?"

"New York," Calvin said. "Grew up there."

Nodding, John hummed. Calvin wondered if he'd bring up the sofa next. Probably. It would be the logical thing, wouldn't it?

"Obviously, I'm not returning for the sofa, either," Calvin said. "It was an old, ratty thing. Mrs. Donaldson can offer both pieces to the next tenant."

John looked stunned for a moment, probably because Calvin kept successfully predicting what John wanted to ask about. It was a skill that Calvin had picked up years back. Anticipating the needs of others. When it came to trickery, this skill had served Calvin well.

After seeming to recover from his mild shock, John said, "Do you need a . . . a bookcase, then? I have a small spare. In the basement."

Calvin's eyes widened. "If you're really offering."

John nodded, and Calvin's heart fluttered. God, that was kind of him.

Just as he was about to thank John, someone knocked on the door, startling both of them. Calvin turned to see Katherine standing in the hallway.

"I brewed some tea for you two," she said. "It's in the study. I thought you both might want to relax once you were finished moving what looks like a library's worth of reading material."

Warmth swirled in Calvin's chest. Katherine was only being polite, but still, it was . . . nice. Really nice. Calvin couldn't remember the last time someone had brewed him tea.

"I'd sure like some," he said before turning to John. "What do you think, John? Shall we take a break to have some tea? Maybe you can tell me a bit more about the funerals. Teach me what's involved. Before. During. After." Calvin shrugged. "Everything."

After all, Calvin needed to learn. And perhaps John would feel a little more comfortable once they'd engaged in some more conversation, especially if the topic was one that John was clearly interested in.

"I-I'd like that, yes."

Calvin swept his hand through the air, gesturing toward the hallway.

"Lead the way."

John and Calvin followed Katherine to the first floor, where she then left for the kitchen while John and Calvin went into the study. Waiting for them on a wooden tea cart was a porcelain teapot—white with a ring of blue flowers—and matching teacups on saucers. It was a beautiful set, and it reminded Calvin of one that his parents used to have.

Calvin bent low to have a closer look.

"Gorgeous pattern," Calvin said, picking up one of the empty cups.

Calvin turned the cup over in his hands, letting his fingers brush over the pretty blue flowers. He considered bringing up the subject of his parents, but hesitated. He wasn't sure how John would react.

When Calvin had mentioned some of the bleaker parts of his childhood to Katherine yesterday, it had felt so strangely nice to tell her a little bit about his experiences. Today, Calvin found that he was still chasing that feeling. Craving it, really. Because, God, it had been magical. Acceptance and sympathy and care all rolled into one. But Calvin hadn't forgotten that each time he'd brought up his woes to John, either current or past, he had soon regretted it.

Calvin fought the urge to sigh. On the surface, John was nothing like David, and yet . . . and yet John's silence was probably his way of saying that he had no interest in listening to Calvin moan about his life. Had no interest in hearing Calvin recant the ways in which life had been unfair to him. David had never been interested in talking about such things. Even though David had been an orphan himself, he hadn't wanted to spend time wallowing over the things he had lost.

Calvin's unspoken sorrows pressed heavy on his heart as he set the cup back on the saucer. Better to leave these unpleasant things in the past. Especially if Calvin wanted to hold on to his position at Hall Funeral Services.

While Calvin was lost in thought, John came up next to him and poured himself a cup of tea. Then, he poured one for Calvin, too. Afterward, they each took their cups over toward the fireplace and sat next to each other on two brown leather chairs. Two *really* comfortable brown leather chairs. God, this was nice.

Calvin blew on his tea and took a sip. John followed suit.

"Alright, tell me what my tasks will be for the funerals." Calvin crossed one leg over the other. "I want to learn everything." He thought for a moment. "Well, maybe not everything. I want to learn everything *except* for embalming."

John let out a low chuckle that made Calvin's stomach flutter. Damn, he really liked that laugh.

Over the next half hour, John talked. And it was *wonderful*. Despite the occasional trouble John had with his speech, Calvin found himself captivated by everything John said. He loved the man's voice. It was melodic, in a way. Soft and soothing. Almost musical. What was even more wonderful than listening to John's enchanting voice, though, was watching John become more confident and comfortable as he talked. By the end of the lesson, John seemed to be much more relaxed. His stammer persisted, but it seemed less frequent, though maybe it was only John's own reaction to it that had changed. He seemed to be less troubled by it as time went on. Calvin's entire body hummed with excitement. Working with John would be nothing short of sublime.

Eventually, Katherine called John and Calvin into the kitchen for supper. Nausea roiled in Calvin's stomach as the intermittent happy flutters he'd been experiencing were replaced with an overwhelming sense of unease. He'd have to eat supper with Michael. *Oh, God.*

Following John to the kitchen, Calvin let out a breath and concentrated on keeping his face neutral. He couldn't let Michael see how intimidated he was. Besides, at least Katherine would be there. Right?

Sure enough, Katherine was in the kitchen transferring pieces of baked chicken onto a large, circular metal serving platter. When she looked over her shoulder, Calvin caught her eye. Katherine offered a friendly smile and pointed through to the connected room.

"Michael's waiting for you two."

Grimacing, Calvin's eyes flitted over to the threshold. Of course Michael was already waiting, probably grumbling that they were taking too long so he'd have something else to blame Calvin for.

Despite Calvin's inner turmoil, John didn't seem bothered in the least, and he gave a curt nod to Katherine before turning and heading to the dining room. Calvin followed begrudgingly. Michael was sitting at one end of the long table, scribbling in a notebook, his brow furrowed in concentration. When Calvin stretched up onto his tippy-toes to try to see what Michael was writing, Michael must have sensed it, because he swiftly covered the text with his palm before lifting his eyes and shooting Calvin a slightly threatening look.

"Writing a novel?" Calvin said, trying for a joke, but his voice came out what had to be a whole octave higher than its normal range.

"Budgeting." Michael's curt tone made Calvin's stomach roil some more. Michael placed his pen on the table and slammed the notebook shut. Then he gestured to the empty chair on the other side of the table, raised both his eyebrows, and said, "Don't you want to sit?"

Calvin eyed the free chair with suspicion. Part of him wondered whether Michael may have placed a tack on it.

"Of course," he said, circling around to make his way over to the chair.

Calvin sat. Thankfully, without injury. John was already seated across from him, placing a white linen napkin on his lap. Calvin copied him. It had been a while since he'd had such a formal mealtime experience.

"How was the move?" Michael said.

Calvin opened his mouth to reply, but closed it again when he realized Michael had been speaking to John.

"Fine. Not too strenuous," John said. "It m-m-mostly consisted of carrying crates of books."

"Books." Michael pursed his lips and nodded a couple of times, looking thoughtful. Or perhaps pretending to. Turning toward Calvin, he tilted his head. "Didn't you say that you barely had enough money to eat? Where'd you find the cash to purchase so many books?"

Calvin's face caught fire. *"Didn't,"* he nearly said, but caught himself. He'd stolen almost every book he owned, and Michael seemed to know it. Michael must have wanted Calvin to say it, to provide John with a reason to rescind his offer of employment, to provide *himself* a reason to call his friends in law enforcement.

So, Calvin stayed quiet.

Michael clicked his tongue once and said, "I see." He pressed the tips of his fingers together, forming a steeple with his hands, and turned back to John. "By the way, I had someone come over earlier and install locks on our bedrooms. I think you ought to start keeping your money in the safe as well."

Calvin clenched his teeth. John's eyes found Calvin's, and the brief moment of eye contact made Calvin's cheeks burn even hotter, shame coiling in his stomach. Letting his eyes fall to the table, Calvin muttered a few choice words to himself. He wondered if John could tell how infuriating and humiliating this was for him. God, Calvin had only stolen the *one* necklace from Katherine! He had promised to pay Michael back for it, too. Calvin could only imagine how Michael would react if he ever found out the extent of Calvin's other crimes. He'd have never let Calvin work for his brother. All Calvin wanted was a chance—one measly opportunity to learn a new skill, to make some *real* money (and *not* by working in a factory, either), and to use his charms for good. All while helping an enchanting man like John.

But Michael wanted Calvin to pay for stealing that necklace. Not only with his money. But with his dignity, too.

Calvin continued to stare at his empty plate. How badly he wanted to say something back to Michael, to spew some biting retort. But he couldn't. Because now Calvin's entire livelihood hinged on his ability to hold his tongue.

John hummed. "So then where should Calvin k-k-keep his money? Should we purchase him a safe of his own?"

"Calvin can keep it wherever he pleases," Michael said with a smug smile. "Perhaps he can tuck it away with his socks."

Bastard.

While Calvin was busy silently seething, his eyes burning a hole in the porcelain, Katherine came in with the platter of chicken. She set it in the middle of the table next to a pan of roasted vegetables.

"Time to eat," she said.

Glancing up through his lashes, Calvin caught her eye. Katherine offered Calvin a warm smile, one that made Calvin's heart sink. Because no matter how much he liked either Katherine or John, and no matter how much they liked him in return, Michael would never let Calvin forget one simple thing: He wasn't welcome here.

He recalled what Michael had said to John the previous morning.

"I told you, this would be a temporary thing. Someone to work with for a little while . . ."

Calvin's face set to a scowl. *Temporary.* He had nearly forgotten himself. None of this was meant to be permanent. Didn't matter how much he ended up liking it here. Sure, the room he had here was better than the one he'd had in the boarding house, but it wasn't and was never meant to be a *home.* Calvin was only supposed to work here until either he paid Michael back or John no longer needed him. Whichever came first, most likely.

Gripping the edge of the table, Calvin pushed himself to stand.

"I'm not feeling very well," he said. "I think I'll skip the food for now. Organize my books."

John's brows pinched as the two of them locked eyes.

"Do you n-need help?" he asked. "I could bring the bookcase."

"No, thank you. I'll be fine," Calvin said. "I'll pile them into neat little stacks."

And with that, Calvin left the room. Every step, he felt more and more foolish for having let himself become excited over this peculiar setup. *Temporary.* Calvin repeated the word to himself as he moved through the house. When he reached the study, he paused to look in. Seeing the teapot still resting on the cart, its contents no doubt now cold and bitter, Calvin heaved a sigh.

He turned to head upstairs but stopped as something shiny caught his eye. Sitting there, on one of the small end tables, were Michael's cuff links, the emeralds shimmering in the low yellow light of the sun pouring through the window.

Michael's. Cuff links.

"I can't subject John to someone like that."

Calvin's hatred for Michael began to burn.

"He's a criminal!"

It burned even hotter than his shame. Calvin's entire body caught fire, flames flaring from the rush of upset.

If Michael thought he was a criminal, well, then, he'd be a criminal.

Heart pounding, shame and frustration and fury roaring in his ears, Calvin strode over to the end table and snatched up the small buttons. At least when his *temporary employment* came to an end, Calvin would have something he could sell to help him start over. He knew exactly where he'd keep them, too.

He'd tuck them away with his socks.

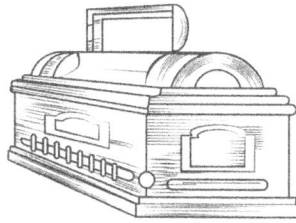

Chapter Six
John

John was sitting on his bed trying to read, as he had been for at least a half hour or so, but couldn't seem to focus on the words. Instead, he kept ruminating on how unpleasant things had been between Michael and Calvin for the last few days since Calvin had moved in. Back when John had first extended the offer for Calvin to take the spare bedroom, he hadn't realized how upset Michael would be to have Calvin staying in the house. Logistically, it was better this way. Besides, Calvin's old room had been too small for him and his things. It hadn't been the nicest room either. John could have sworn he'd seen a miniature toilet hanging from the wall right next to the bookcase. No, John couldn't have left him there, especially now that John had spent some time with him.

Despite the fact that Calvin had stolen Katherine's necklace, he had otherwise proven to be a pleasant person. He wasn't too loud. He wasn't mean. He had a sense of humor. One that John liked, too.

Still, Michael was *not* happy that John had convinced him to let Calvin live in the extra bedroom. Not only was Michael not happy, but he wasn't *hiding* the fact that he was unhappy, either. It was wearing on Calvin a little. John could tell.

John heaved a sigh. Hopefully, Calvin would prove himself in time, and then, once Michael realized that Calvin wasn't a threat, he would lighten up. Probably.

After John returned his focus to the page in front of him for the umpteenth time, Calvin knocked. John knew it was Calvin because neither Michael nor Katherine was home. Before John could tell Calvin that he was welcome, Calvin strolled in.

Snapping his book shut, John looked up at Calvin, brows pinching in exasperation. Why couldn't Calvin wait for John's reply before entering? Ever since the night he'd moved in, Calvin had been barging into John's room seemingly whenever he pleased. Every time John had tried to point this out to Calvin, his frustrating shyness had strangled the words in his throat. Oh, how he *loathed* that he hadn't managed to push past this lingering nervousness and speak clearly. Or, well, as clearly as he could with his persistent stammer. But John couldn't reprimand Calvin. He hated the thought of saying something that might make Calvin feel unwelcome. Michael was making Calvin feel unwelcome enough. Still, John wished he could gather the courage to *ask* Calvin *nicely* to *please* not enter his room before John invited him in.

He did feel quite lucky to have Calvin working with him, though, regardless. It was fortunate that he'd found someone with such confidence and charm. And even if Calvin didn't have any manners, he was a kind man, especially for a criminal.

Dear God, what a sentence *that* was.

"What?" Calvin said, probably noticing John's either sour or weary expression.

"Nothing," John said, forcing himself to soften his face.

"Right. Well, I think I've come up with the perfect slogan," Calvin said before swiftly shoving a piece of paper at John.

Rearing back slightly, John reached up to take it. He read the text.

Good Mourning!

His eyes widened at the absurdity of it. Did Calvin *really* think this was a good idea as a slogan for funeral services? Unable to fake enthusiasm for such a travesty, John let out a scoff instead, one he hoped wouldn't sound too harsh. He held out the paper, trying to return it to Calvin, but Calvin wouldn't take it.

"No? Why not?" Calvin asked, incredulous. "We need something that'll catch people's eyes while they're scanning the page. Don't you know how many other businesses will be in the paper?"

"M-many," John said. "But they won't be offering funeral services."

Calvin stroked his chin as though he had a beard. It made John smile a bit.

"We have to figure out *something* to put in there," Calvin said. "I mean, you've already paid for the spot."

"Yes, to find someone to w-w-work with me."

John would have been fine letting the paper keep the money for nothing.

"I know. And now you have me," Calvin said. "And you're supposed to *trust* me. I'm the personable one, remember?"

John closed his eyes and pinched the bridge of his nose. Calvin was confident, yes, but maybe *too* confident. Regardless of what Calvin thought, making light of someone's loss with a slogan like *Good Mourning!* was *not* the way to find more clients. It couldn't be.

Calvin said, "Look, I know what you're thinking, and I have to say, humor *is* a perfectly fine way to pull in new clients."

Groaning, John covered his face with his hands, letting the paper fall onto his lap. When would Calvin stop reading his thoughts? How on earth was it even possible?

Instead of letting his mind linger on Calvin's obvious telepathy, John began racking his brain for a slogan. Something better than

Good mourning! Something funny, too. Because if the two of them *had* to try to be humorous, John hoped that they could be cleverer than *that*.

After a minute or so, John thought of one. He held out his hand, silently requesting a pen. Somehow, Calvin knew exactly what John needed and retrieved one for him. Balancing the piece of paper on his knee, John wrote: *Rest assured, we'll help your loved ones rest.*

Calvin scrunched up his nose the moment he saw it.

"We're not running an *inn!*" he said.

John's cheeks burned. *Of course* Calvin wouldn't like it.

"Is it *absolutely necessary* that we try to make people laugh?" John asked, his voice tired and his face still tingling from embarrassment over his suggestion.

"No, I suppose not," Calvin sighed, taking back the paper and pen.

Rather than leave, Calvin hoisted himself up onto John's desk and sat. Right on top of it. Even though there was an empty chair. How could Calvin make himself at home so easily? John couldn't help but wish that he himself possessed that same ability.

Several minutes of silence followed. Calvin simply sat there twiddling his thumbs. John watched Calvin's fingers move. Normally, John liked the silence. Silence was cozy. Comforting. It provided his brain with much-needed time to rest. But not this. John couldn't enjoy this sort of silence. Because he *knew* that he should have been trying to make conversation with Calvin. Over the time John had spent observing Michael with friends and clients, John had learned that most people expected conversation. And John needed to be the one to provide it. Especially because they were in *his* room. Which meant that John was Calvin's host.

If only John could think of something to say.

One more minute passed.

"Are you . . . settled in?" John finally asked.

Calvin shrugged. "I think so."

Back to silence. Well, that had not been very successful.

John frowned. Hopefully he could learn how to truly connect with his business partner soon. Yes, *partner*. Despite the fact that Calvin was only supposed to be John's assistant, he was starting to think of Calvin as his partner instead, mostly because making Calvin an equal would mean that John could stick to what he liked best—embalming and making the caskets—and not feel horrible that Calvin would be taking on all of the other funeral-related tasks without being fairly compensated for them.

John hadn't managed to tell Calvin any of this yet. He hadn't managed to tell Michael, either. He might *not* tell Michael, though the thought of keeping something so important from his brother was making his stomach churn from unease. At the very least, John would have to tell Calvin. Soon. And Calvin would be pleased, wouldn't he? He could have half the money from their work this way, rather than the one-third that John and Michael had previously settled on. Still, there was a chance that Calvin wouldn't like the potential permanence of a true business partnership. Michael had presented the position to Calvin as a temporary one. It wasn't like Calvin had *set out* to co-own a funeral service.

After a few more moments of silence while John thought on this, he realized that he should try one more time to make conversation.

"Do you feel ready for your first service later?" he asked.

Crossing one leg over the other, Calvin said, "I think so. It shouldn't be that hard, right? Greet the mourners. Collect the payment."

"Right." Under his breath, John muttered, "It *shouldn't* be that hard, should it?"

Luckily, Calvin had the sense not to respond to that.

Calvin spent the next five minutes lingering in John's room before returning to his own. Even though John found some of his nervousness waning once Calvin left, there was part of him that somehow missed Calvin's presence, like there was a little hole in John's chest, one that made it feel heavier, not lighter, as though a *hole*—which was supposed to be a *lack* of something—could cause such a thing. Ignoring the empty heaviness in his chest, John picked up his book and tried to read. Only a couple more hours were left before the funeral. He and Calvin would be spending time together soon enough.

Unfortunately, those hours passed slowly. John barely managed to read his book. When it was finally time to leave and Calvin knocked, John let out a small sigh of relief. Thank God he wouldn't have to continue to torture himself with the book anymore.

John and Calvin took the hearse to the funeral, empty casket in tow. Since the funeral was to take place only one neighborhood over, it wasn't a long ride. After only ten minutes, they reached the home of Richard and Sarah Brown, Hall Funeral Services' newest clients. The funeral was to be for Sarah's father, Horace. It was the perfect first funeral for Calvin to run. Since Horace hadn't exactly been young when he'd passed, hopefully Calvin would find it easier to stomach the service. Horace had lived a full life. And John was prepared to remind Calvin of that fact if he needed to.

After John found a spot for the hearse—thankfully, there was a hitching post only a few houses away since this was a fairly populated area in the city—the two men walked together to the Browns' residence. Once they reached the stoop, John removed his hat and knocked, some of his worry tempered knowing that he had Calvin there with him. But then, while they waited, John looked over at Calvin only to see *him* still wearing *his* hat. Didn't Calvin know that he needed to take it off? John kept staring, hoping to catch Calvin's eye so that he could silently remind him to remove it. But Calvin kept his eyes straight ahead. Desperate, John nudged Calvin with his elbow.

Scoffing, Calvin rubbed the spot where John had prodded and then let out a very exaggerated, unnecessarily loud, "Ow! Jesus!"

Before John could explain himself, Mr. Brown opened the door.

"Mr. Hall. Mr. Wright. Thank you for coming," he said. "Come in."

Mr. Brown turned to head back into the house, motioning for John and Calvin to follow. As Calvin stepped across the threshold, John reached out and swatted Calvin's shoulder with the back of his hand.

"What is *wrong* with you?" Calvin whispered, turning back to shoot John a confused-yet-furious look.

With a roll of his eyes, John tapped himself twice on top of his head with his index finger.

"Oh, right."

Quickly, Calvin removed his hat.

Both men then followed Mr. Brown through the house toward the kitchen. The body was waiting there on John's cooling board, having been embalmed the previous morning. More often than not, John would come to embalm the body as soon as the family in need contacted him, and then he would set to work on the casket right after he finished the embalming. Sometimes, though, like in the case of Marjorie Price's husband, he might make the casket before the person passed. That, however, usually only happened when that someone was either very ill or very old and the family knew that the person's passing was imminent.

John hoped that him having prepared the body early, by himself, would make Calvin's first funeral experience easier, too. Most people would find the embalming process hard to watch, and

Calvin was likely to be no exception. Additionally, rather than having the body viewable for one or two entire days prior to the service, Mr. and Mrs. Brown were having a small viewing and service here at their home before then having a larger one later at a church. Since many clients asked John to stay for the length of the viewing, this particular setup would mean fewer hours spent with the body, which might be easier on Calvin, too.

Once they were in the kitchen, Calvin froze, his eyes fixed on Horace's recently embalmed body on the board. Sympathy bloomed in John's chest, heavy and uncomfortable. Should he say something to Calvin to make him feel better? Even in front of Mr. Brown? John wasn't sure.

Seconds passed with Calvin only staring wordlessly at the body, not yet having moved a muscle, while John stood nearby, shifting his weight from one foot to the other and praying that Calvin would come to his senses so he could confirm the specifics for the upcoming service.

"So . . ." Mr. Brown looked at John expectantly.

Oh, God, this was supposed to be Calvin's role! John cleared his throat, hoping to pull Calvin back to reality. But Calvin stayed frozen. Unease twisted in John's stomach. He tried once more.

Blinking several times in rapid succession, Calvin shook his head.

"Sorry." Calvin turned toward Mr. Brown, twirling his hat in his hands. He thumbed over his shoulder back toward the main room, where there was an expansive window. "We'll bring the casket in through that window, then?"

Mr. Brown replied, "Yes, we were hoping to have a small viewing here for immediate family, and then—"

"Take Horace to the church for the service. Afterward, we'll travel together to the cemetery in East Falls, yes?" Calvin said, finishing for him.

John cringed, making a mental note that Calvin could stand to work on his manners.

"Um, yes, that's right," Mr. Brown said, his expression hardening a little.

John reached up to rub the back of his neck, secondhand embarrassment making his cheeks burn, but his tongue was leaden in his mouth, preventing him from trying to rectify the situation.

"Well, we'll start on setting everything up now," Calvin said. He rubbed his chin. "We shouldn't need help hoisting the *empty* casket up into the window, but we'll need help moving Horace back out once the service is over. We'll have a few more men to help us lift it back out later, yes? Because, I mean, it'll be much too heavy for the two of us"—Calvin whipped his finger back and forth between himself and John—"once the body is in there."

Mr. Brown shut his eyes. He started rubbing his forehead, seemingly frustrated or offended by Calvin's lack of tact. John's face burned hotter.

"Oh, Calvin, what in heaven's sake is wrong with you?" he wished he could say.

After a moment, Mr. Brown said, "Yes, we'll, uhm, we'll have Sarah's brothers here to help carry the casket to the hearse. I've asked them to be pallbearers, so they know what's involved with regards to the transportation."

Mr. Brown then excused himself from the room, and John took Calvin by the sleeve and pulled him closer, his forceful tug causing Calvin to stumble.

"Calvin, p-p-*please* try to be more respectful," John implored in a hushed voice.

Calvin's mouth twisted up in confusion. "What do you mean?"

John sighed. "Don't forget that these people are hurting. Just . . . try to be k-kinder when you're speaking about the logistics of m-m-moving the body."

"Who are you to criticize?" Calvin sneered. "I thought you wanted me to handle these things because *you* couldn't."

John's muscles tensed, his face burning hotter as his second-hand embarrassment swiftly transformed into shame. Swallowing thickly, John tried to push past it. Calvin may have had a point, but he still needed to improve his manners.

"I-I know what I'm *supposed* to say. Most of the time." John ran a hand over his face. "But I can't ever make it . . . come out right."

Instinctively, John shrunk in on himself, pulling his shoulders in as though he could make himself smaller. Because that truth . . . it certainly made him *feel* small sometimes.

Calvin clasped John's shoulder and squeezed.

"Sorry, yeah, I'll try harder," Calvin said, unmistakable tenderness in his voice.

John lifted his eyes to meet Calvin's, and Calvin's lips curled into a smile that looked both warm and sincere, like maybe Calvin could actually sense the intensity of John's struggles. John smiled back.

When Mr. Brown came back, Calvin removed his hand, and then began reviewing the rest of the logistics with him while John stepped back. Sure enough, Calvin's tone was softer. Gentler. Mr. Brown seemed pleased.

As the two of them talked, John moved to a nearby chair and sat, letting out a breath as relief washed over him. It would work out. Calvin seemed to be understanding his role now, and he was proving to be the perfect business partner that John had hoped he would be.

Fortunately, the service went well. Better, in fact, than every funeral John had ever organized so far, even the ones he'd run with Michael. Once in a while, Calvin said something that was a little too curt or blunt or forward. But, overall, Calvin was . . . charming.

After the burial, John and Calvin started back home toward the Frankford section of Philadelphia. They were planning on returning to Richard and Sarah Brown's home the following morning to pick up the cooling table as well as the funeral chairs, which meant that they were finished with work for now. Thankfully. Despite the fact that the funeral had been a success, business-wise, it had still been tiring. It would be nice to relax back at home.

For the first few minutes of their trip home, John and Calvin stayed quiet, listening to the clip-clop of Agathe's hooves on the pavement and cobblestone, and then Calvin bumped John's knee with his own.

"Should we celebrate?" he asked.

Arching an eyebrow, John said, "Celebrate?"

"Why not? It was a successful first funeral for me, I think. Other than those first few minutes there. We ought to stop at a tavern."

John cringed internally, the memory of his mishap with the flask flashing in his mind. He shut his eyes as his insides twisted together from unease.

"Oh, the prospect of spending some more time with me can't be *that* bad, can it?" Calvin said through a laugh. "Come on, it'll be my treat."

But John couldn't shake the shame that had suddenly been unearthed over his blunder with the flask of whiskey. "I'm not the sort of p-p-person who likes crowds."

"Wow, that's surprising," Calvin said, his voice thick with sarcasm. Chuckling, he bumped John's knee once more, and the contact made John's stomach tumble in a strange way. He really wasn't used to this much familiarity. "I promise it'll be fun. We'll leave if you aren't enjoying yourself within . . . let's say ten minutes."

John turned Calvin's suggestion over in his head.

"Five," he said. He could probably stand five minutes.

"Cheer up. It'll be my treat, remember?"

After a pause, John relented.

"Alright," he said. "Just tell me where to go."

It took a while for them to reach the place that Calvin had chosen. Even though they had passed a few taverns by the time they reached Fairmount, Calvin had insisted that they venture farther into the city toward Rittenhouse Square. By the time they found a spot for the hearse carriage, John was eager for them to relax in a tavern together, though he wasn't sure if whiskey or beer or whatever else he might have would help with that or if it would only make him think of his mishap at the Price viewing. Furthermore, while John was happy to spend time with Calvin, the thought of being in a crowded tavern was unsettling. Hopefully this whole ordeal wouldn't be too painful. Perhaps Calvin would somehow make it fun.

After parking the hearse, John and Calvin walked Agathe over to a small nearby stable. He would have tied her to a hitching post, but not only was John unfamiliar with this part of the city (and so, he wasn't sure whether there were hitching posts nearby), he also wasn't certain how long they would be in the tavern, and he wanted Agathe to be comfortable.

When they were sure Agathe was settled, they walked the two blocks to the tavern, and John started becoming more and more nervous the closer they got, his stomach twisting and turning with every step. He had to focus on keeping his chin up, head held high, though his instinct was to instead tuck his head in toward his shoulders and pull his homburg over his face instead. What if he made a fool of himself somehow? What if he said something that made Calvin think he was strange? Although . . . Calvin probably thought that already, what with John's chosen profession. Still, John liked that Calvin had suggested they spend more time together. He just hoped he wouldn't ruin it.

John's heart was still thudding violently as they stepped inside, but the moment John took in his surroundings, he breathed a sigh of relief. Seven Stars Tavern wasn't crowded or loud or rowdy. It was a tiny place. Quiet, without many other patrons. In the single room on the first floor, there was only a wooden bench nestled in the far corner and a long bar counter. Some of John's icy tension melted away. Perhaps it wouldn't be so bad trying a cocktail or two.

After John followed Calvin to the bar, Calvin ordered for both of them. Because of course he did; he was *Calvin*. Ever-confident, Calvin hadn't had trouble knowing either what to order or what he should say. He had ordered their two cocktails with ease.

While they waited for the bartender to prepare their beverages, Calvin threw John a wink, and John's stomach flip-flopped in that same maddening way as when Calvin had bumped his knee in the box seat of the carriage on the way over. He wasn't quite sure what was wrong with him, but he prayed that his stomach would settle soon.

A minute or so later, the bartender set two cocktails on the bar in front of them. John eyed the creamy yellow liquid, bending low to inspect it.

"Thanks much," Calvin said to the bartender. He removed his hat and placed it on the counter. "We're certainly in need of something to lift our spirits. Just came from the East Falls cemetery." He sighed very dramatically. "Funeral."

Clicking his tongue, the bartender frowned. "Ah, sorry about that."

"Gosh, it's hard to . . . to say goodbye," Calvin said, shaking his head sadly, his voice cracking the tiniest bit.

John's mouth fell agape. Calvin wasn't trying to trick the bartender, was he?

"I know what you mean," the bartender said, clearly eating up every word of Calvin's performance. "I feel like I've been to a lot of those myself lately. Doesn't matter how many people I lose, it's never easy." He tapped the counter twice with his index finger. "On the house today. Whatever you need."

"Wow, thank you. I can't tell you how much we appreciate it," Calvin said, peppering in that silly fake voice crack once more and hiding what John knew had to be a faint smile behind his raised hand. "Don't we, John?"

God, Calvin. Why?

John bit his tongue. Literally. Unwilling to outright lie to the poor bartender, John threw the man a tight-lipped smile and a nod instead.

When the bartender then turned to serve someone else, Calvin smacked John's bicep with the back of his hand.

"You're welcome," Calvin said playfully, picking up his cocktail. He winked. "For the cocktail *and* the location. I knew it'd be pretty calm in here. It's one of the few taverns I know in the city so far."

"Yes, it is rather nice," John said. "But . . ."

"But what?"

John's eyes fell to his tumbler. He'd have rather paid for the cocktail himself. Unfortunately, John couldn't bring himself to tell Calvin that.

"Nothing."

After picking up his glass, John shook his hand, swirling the liquid, and then brought it to his nose to sniff. What kind of cocktail was it?

Anticipating John's inquiry, Calvin said, "It's a whiskey fizz."

John pursed his lips. Whiskey fizz. He had never heard of it. After one more sniff, John took a slow sip, and as the liquid slid over his tongue, he was pleased to find that the cocktail was *much* more enjoyable than the straight whiskey had been. He supposed it ought to be, what with the sugar and soda that the bartender had obviously mixed in. Something else too. Lemon?

"Lemon, sugar, soda, and whiskey," Calvin said. "Pretty simple, really."

Letting out a small huff—half amusement, half incredulity—John turned to face him.

"How is it that . . . that you always seem to know wh-wh-what I want to say?" he asked.

Calvin smirked. "Just a little trick that I picked up. Anticipating what people want or need or what kinds of concerns they have." Calvin took a swig of his cocktail, a mischievous twinkle in his eye. "It's been helpful for sure."

John hummed. By now, it was clear that Calvin had stolen much more than Katherine's necklace over the years. John took a couple more sips of his cocktail, thinking about this. How *much* had Calvin stolen? He'd been orphaned, hadn't he? At one point, Calvin had made a remark about sleeping on park benches. Probably he'd been forced to steal in order to survive. John's eyes found the yellowish liquid in his tumbler. Obviously, Calvin had taken to stealing other things too. But no matter what Calvin would likely say if prodded, a whiskey fizz was *not* a necessity.

John took another sip and let out a low moan, relishing the slightly smoky yet sweet taste as the liquid sloshed over his tongue. God, that was tasty.

Over the next couple of minutes, John took many more sips of his cocktail. He had nearly finished it when Calvin leaned in close, startling him.

Calvin whispered, "I might be wrong, but I take it that you're not someone who enjoys cocktails very often, are you?"

"Not often, no," John said even though he should have probably said "not ever." He finished off the rest of his cocktail. "Is it obvious?"

"Just a hunch." Calvin flicked John's empty glass. "Be careful with these."

"I'm f-f-f-f—" John cleared his throat to try once more, a small twinge of embarrassment over his verbal blunder bringing with it a pinching feeling in the pit of his stomach. Oh, how he hated that he still struggled with his words like this. And to become so tongue-tied in front of a personable person like Calvin. It was humiliating! He restarted his sentence, set on pushing past the blockage in his throat. "I'm f-fine," he forced out.

Calvin just nodded thoughtfully, seeming unperturbed by John's verbal struggles. Embarrassment over his stammer still lingered, however, and John raised his empty tumbler and caught the bartender's eye. John shook it once, silently ordering another. Somehow, Calvin wasn't even halfway finished with his. But John needed another cocktail. He needed *something* to focus on. Something other than how he had fumbled over such a simple word.

Calvin bumped his elbow. "Don't be embarrassed," he said, his tone gentle.

Once again, Calvin had read John's mind. But it only made that tiny pinch of embarrassment worsen. John's muscles shook slightly as he strained them, his face becoming hot from shame.

Oh, how John wished he could be confident like Calvin. Even *half* as confident. But John could never manage that, not with his eccentricities. Growing up in Media, most residents hadn't been the kindest to John with regards to his speech problem, especially other children. Even here in Philadelphia, not much had changed. People still looked at him oddly. He still felt like he didn't fit in.

Calvin then leaned in closer, and John mentally braced himself for what he thought would be some kind of ridicule.

But instead, Calvin said, "You know, before we met, it had been a long time since I'd spoken to anyone who had a stammer."

He paused to take a slow sip of his whiskey fizz. "I find it . . . fascinating. Not in a bad way. Just . . . it's intriguing."

John lowered his eyes to the countertop. He'd rather be ordinary than "fascinating." Especially if ordinary would spare him from ridicule.

When John looked back up, he and Calvin locked eyes. Calvin's small smile broadened, and John's stomach twinged excitedly. Alright, well, maybe he liked the thought of *Calvin* finding him fascinating for some reason. Who would have thought that someone like Calvin—someone who seemed so worldly—would be intrigued by such something as a peculiar pattern of speech.

Calvin said, "I promise you, John, I'm not fazed by it. Not *negatively*, I mean. If, for some reason, you think that this particular eccentricity of yours impacts the way I see you, you're wrong. Don't try to hold back when we're chatting. Not if it's because you're worried about your speech. Because I like talking to you. Actually, it's becoming one of my favorite things."

Calvin's lovely words settled in John's mind, soothing him like a cool, wet cloth pressed to the forehead to temper a fever. Hot embarrassment transformed into the most exquisite warmth, one that was both comforting and heartening.

Calvin enjoyed talking with him? God, how . . . how wonderful.

In a soft voice, John replied, "Thank you, Calvin."

Still smiling a crooked, boyish smile, Calvin winked once in response.

John's stomach fluttered. *Again.*

Both men stayed silent for a few moments while they waited for John's second cocktail to be made. Fears over his speech somewhat abated, John shut his eyes, letting himself enjoy the tavern's surprising tranquility, the low murmur of conversation like a pleasant hum in his ears.

Once John was served his next whiskey fizz, the two men started chatting, first about the books they both liked to read and then about some of the other things they enjoyed. John told Calvin how he had become interested in carpentry from his father, who had taught him how to make caskets. He couldn't quite make himself bring up Lucy, though she wasn't far from his mind. Calvin neglected to say much about his past, other than to tell John that his father had been a carpenter, too, as a profession, not a hobby. But Calvin had never learned. Throwing back the last bit of his cocktail, John wondered if Calvin would ever want to learn woodworking. He'd love to teach him. He'd teach Calvin embalming someday, too, if he was ever interested. All John wanted, in that moment, was for them to keep spending time together.

Watching his leftover ice float this way and that, from one side of the otherwise empty tumbler to the other, John smiled to himself. He had a friend.

Hoping to finish the last *tiny* bit of watery cocktail left in the glass, John picked up the tumbler, but suddenly, the condensate was *way* too slippery. Cursing to himself, John fumbled, nearly letting the tumbler fall.

He looked up to see Calvin smiling, his lips twisted up into a wolfish grin. John's cheeks warmed, and Calvin chuckled.

"I warned you," Calvin said.

John pursed his lips. Warned him? About what? About . . . carpentry? Or maybe the cocktails? Raising an eyebrow, John waited for Calvin to elaborate, but he only snickered. Infuriating. John wished he knew what Calvin was hinting at, sly little thing that he was. John studied Calvin's face. Sly and . . . and handsome. Attractive. Wildly so. John hadn't really let himself see it before, but Calvin was a handsome man, wasn't he? He had the softest looking light-brown hair with eyes that were a near perfect match in color. Strong cheekbones, too, but not so strong as to remove the boyish charm he had about him. And Calvin's ears . . . the little lobes were connected to his head, which was so . . . so peculiar. But in a pleasant way. John couldn't recall ever meeting someone with ears like Calvin's before. Probably he had, only he had never noticed.

Without meaning to, John found himself smiling impishly, his eyes transfixed on one of Calvin's ears.

"What are you so happy about?" Calvin asked.

"N-nothing," John said, still unable to tear his eyes away. "You 'ave interesting ears."

Immediately, Calvin began touching both of his ears, opening and closing his fingers repeatedly as he moved them from top to bottom.

"Why? What makes them interesting?"

Lost in a blissful haze, John reached up to touch one of them. He pinched the silly lobe between his index finger and thumb.

"They're funny," John said with a little hum.

With a playful scoff, Calvin took hold of John's hand and lowered it.

"Well, now we know your limits," he said.

"Limits?"

"One whiskey fizz is the *most* you can tolerate. I bet you're not even feeling the second one yet, but here you are, massaging a stranger's ears."

"Stranger?" John said, leaning more of his weight on the bar counter. "Calvin, you're not a stranger. You're m-m-my business partner."

Calvin rolled his eyes. "I'm your *assistant*."

"No, no," John insisted. "P-p-p-*partner*."

Crooking an eyebrow, Calvin said, "Really?"

"Really," John replied firmly. "We'll split everything in half. I'll take the embalming and the casket-making—"

"And the creation of off-putting hair trinkets," Calvin teased.

Chuckling, John lowered his eyes, heat coloring his cheeks. He really *had* come close to fouling everything up by showing those to Calvin, hadn't he?

"Yes, the . . . the mourning jewelry as well." John took a pause to try to push away his embarrassment. "Meanwhile, you can take care of organizing the service and everything having to do with t-t-talking to anyone."

"Are you sure?" Calvin said. "Because it seems like you talk plenty once you've had a couple of cocktails."

Groaning, John closed his eyes, feeling completely and utterly mortified by that statement. Because Calvin was right. Even with his mouth feeling strange and his tongue feeling leaden, John had been sputtering nonsense, like pointing out how funny Calvin's ears were. God, he hoped that he could remedy this somehow. Or at least avoid embarrassing himself further.

John was busy regretting the number of cocktails he'd imbibed when Calvin said, "Well, if I'm really your partner, we ought to change the name of our business. We'll have to rethink our slogan for the paper, too. What if we try something like, 'Wright and Hall: The right funeral is just down the hall.'"

John sputtered a laugh. "*No,*" he said emphatically.

"Why not?"

John continued to laugh. Calvin was so ridiculous sometimes.

"Are you trying to be f-f-funny? Because that makes *no* sense."

Hoping to be funny too, John shut one of his eyes, trying for a wink, though he wasn't sure he managed to make it look nearly as smooth as Calvin always did (probably because he had never, in his whole life, winked at someone before). And then said, "Calvin Wright: He's . . ." John paused to try to compose himself, praying that he could force the next words to come out right or else the tease might not be very effective. "He's always wrong."

Calvin reared back, making a sound that was something like a combination of a scoff and a chortle. And then John burst out laughing from his own stupid remark. Despite knowing how ridiculous this was—both the play on words and the fact that he was losing his mind over his own humor—he couldn't stop, and soon, his entire body was shaking from happiness.

Calvin clasped his shoulder. "Alright, yeah, we need to head home before you start making a fool of yourself here." Even in his haze of bubbly laughter, John knew that was sensible, though he was too preoccupied with trying to recover from his outburst to respond. Calvin threw on his hat and began leading John toward the exit. "*I* think you're funny, but I have a feeling you'll wake up tomorrow morning with some interesting feelings about this whole experience. Regret, most likely. If we stay here, I can't even imagine what else might fly out of that typically-tight-lipped mouth of yours. I may have only known you for a little while, John Hall, but I can tell that you're the sort of person who prides himself on being reserved."

"I'm not *reserved*," John blurted out, stumbling a bit as he tried to keep up with Calvin. "I'm shy."

"What's the difference?"

"One is p-purposeful."

"Uh-huh. Right."

When John stumbled once more, Calvin hooked arms with him. John's heart slammed into his ribcage. Never before had he been so physically close to someone who was not an immediate member of his family.

John's heart was still somersaulting as they neared the hearse.

"Oh no," John lamented, tripping over a bit of uneven pavement. "I-I can't hold the reins like this. Poor Agathe. I could hurt her."

"Is that your horse's name?" Calvin asked, and John nodded. "*I'll* hold them. Don't worry, I've handled carriages before. I know how to steer. I won't make her lead us anywhere scary."

"Scary?"

"Scary. Dangerous. Whatever. I won't steer us off a cliff. How's that?"

John huffed a laugh. Calvin was never not entertaining.

Once they were only a few steps from the hearse, John pulled away from Calvin. However, he soon realized that trying to walk on his own was a bit of a mistake. His legs wobbled beneath him as he walked in a slight zigzag. When they came to some more unevenness in the sidewalk—one slab that was higher than the other—John's toe caught the edge, and he nearly toppled. Fortunately, Calvin caught him, placing one hand on John's back while clutching his sleeve.

"Almost there," Calvin said. "You're even worse than I thought."

"I'm fffine," John lied, knowing very well that he was not, in fact, fine.

Calvin helped John into the box seat, and then John waited there while Calvin fetched Agathe from the stable. Before John knew it, Calvin was back and had hitched the horse up to the carriage. After climbing up next to him, Calvin patted John's knee in what looked to be mock-sympathy. Each *tap* sent a little blip of excitement surging through John's veins. God, what was wrong with him?

Seated next to Calvin in the box seat of the carriage, John fought to stay upright as they made their way through the city. Every second, he was becoming more and more unsteady, swaying back and forth as they clip-clopped through the streets. Having never been intoxicated before, John wasn't used to his mind being so muddled. Or his body feeling so tingly.

When they went over a bump, John's hand shot out to clutch the front edge of the seat so that he could keep himself from falling.

"Are you worried that we'll ride off a bridge or something?" Calvin teased, looking pointedly at John's hands. John followed Calvin's gaze and noticed his knuckles were turning white. "I only had *one* beverage, and I am *a lot* more experienced with keeping my wits about me than you seem to be."

"No, I'm . . . I'm worried I'll fall over," John said. "Somehow, I seem to be feeling worse with every passing m-m-minute."

"Did you really not know you'd feel this way?"

"Not really, no." John bowed his head. He'd have covered his face with his hands if he could have convinced himself to pry them off of the seat.

"Let's try something," Calvin said, scooted closer. He linked his nearest arm with John's. "How's this? Do you feel safer this way?"

Safer, yes. Only, now John's heart was threatening to fly out of his chest.

"Yes, that's . . . yes," he managed to say.

For the remainder of the ride home, John hugged tight to Calvin's arm. Luckily, Calvin seemed not to mind, though he probably *would* have minded had he known how John was feeling about the closeness.

When John caught a whiff of Calvin's scent—earthy, maybe, but sweet, too—he let out some silly involuntary sound, one that was like a sigh and a whimper melded together, and he immediately chastised himself inside the confines of his head. How could he be so unprofessional? Not only that, either. Unprofessional *and* unconventional. Which was putting it kindly.

Most likely, Calvin was interested in women. Just like practically every other man John had ever met. John cringed internally. He'd better rid himself of these warm, fluttery feelings. Quickly.

Because soon, Calvin would try to find someone he wanted to marry, perhaps print a few of those calling cards or whatever they were called. John vaguely remembered Michael fretting over such things when he had first been trying to court Katherine. Since John hadn't ever wanted a wife, he hadn't really been paying attention back then, but now he sort of wished he had been. At least he'd know what to expect when Calvin would inevitably find a woman to court in the near future.

Imagining Calvin trying to woo some pretty woman—maybe one of Katherine's friends—was making John's stomach hurt. Without even meaning to, he found himself clutching tighter to Calvin. Calvin reached over and patted John's hand. His touch set John's body ablaze.

"Almost home," Calvin said. "No more free cocktails for you, though."

"Sorry," John mumbled.

When John then tried to hide his face by shrinking in his seat and lowering his head, his new position had the unfortunate consequence of making it seem as though he was trying to cuddle Calvin instead.

How nice that would be.

"Do you feel sick?" Calvin asked.

"Somewhat," John said because he was making himself sick with these thoughts of snuggling up with his business partner.

"Once we're home, I'll make you some tea."

One more forceful breeze blew past, causing Calvin's scent to catch in John's nose again. He closed his eyes and tried not to like it.

But of course he liked it. He liked it a lot.

Over the next fifteen minutes, John tried not to think about how much he liked the way Calvin smelled. Or how handsome Calvin was. Or how fun. Or how clever, too. While the two men rode through Philadelphia, John tried not to think about any of those things.

He was not at all successful.

Chapter Seven
Calvin

While Calvin was busy fixing his tie in the mirror, readying himself for the upcoming viewing, John passed by the bathroom. His heavy footsteps sent Calvin's heart aflutter. Ever since he and John had spent time together in that tavern, Calvin hadn't been able to stop obsessing over the way it had felt to cuddle up with John in the carriage on their ride home. Even though John had only huddled close because he had been scared of falling out onto the street, their temporary snuggles had unearthed a powerful longing in Calvin's heart. And . . . elsewhere. Every night for the last week, Calvin had been letting himself think of John in a sexual way while pleasuring himself in bed. Which would have been bad enough on its own, but worse, Calvin was thinking of John in a romantic way too. Every morning, he'd wake up imagining what it would feel like to be held by the enchanting mortician. Every evening, he'd close his eyes and wonder what John's lips would feel like on his own.

Oh, God, he was falling for John, wasn't he?

Calvin sighed. *Temporary. Temporary. Temporary.* Damn, how many times would he need to repeat that word to himself before it stuck? He couldn't let these misplaced romantic feelings continue to blossom. He had to bury them. Otherwise, he'd end up heartbroken. God, he'd probably end up heartbroken as it was. He'd soon lose his home. Sure, John had called Calvin his partner. But he had been intoxicated. Being called someone's business partner willy-nilly wasn't some sort of ironclad contract. *Surely* he was still a temporary employee. Especially if Michael had a say in the matter.

John flew past the bathroom entrance once more, and Calvin's heart leapt, his breath catching in his throat.

Damn.

Calvin stuck his head through the doorway into the hall so he could see what the fuss was about.

"I'm looking for my hat," John said, still pacing, peeking into one room and then the next. "I need my homburg, but I can only find my f-f-flat cap. I-I-I can't wear that one to the viewing. It isn't even black."

John only ever talked this much, verging on rambling, when he was nervous. Or, well, when he was intoxicated, too. Calvin's expression softened, warm sympathy flickering to life in his chest. Fondness then pulled at his heart. He couldn't have tempered it even if he'd tried.

He stepped out of the bathroom and walked toward John.

"Does it really matter?" Calvin asked. "You'll be removing your hat before you even step foot inside their home."

"I *know*, but—"

"Just wear your flat cap. Or, hell, leave that too. No one will notice."

"But—"

"John," Calvin said, his tone soft but stern. "We have to leave soon."

"Right," John said, letting out a breath. "You're right."

John's eyes were still filled with worry, and the sight pulled at Calvin's heart some more. He could hardly stand it.

Calvin tried a half smile. "What if I take us there while you sit in the hearse? No one will even know that you were missing your hat."

Exhaling a second nervous breath, John ran a hand through his hair, mussing it up, which then had Calvin's whole entire body buzzing with the urge to reach out and fix it. Despite the fact that his employment was very likely still intended to be temporary, Calvin found himself wanting to take care of this beautiful, wonderful man. John was such an interesting person. Shy. Uncertain. Befuddled by everyday life. John was beautiful and fascinating and definitely, obviously in need of Calvin's help.

And Calvin wanted to provide it.

"Oh, John, you're falling to pieces," Calvin said. "It's only a hat."

Calvin reached up to smooth down John's brown locks, and the moment his fingers touched the strands, he froze and his heart slammed into his ribcage. Oh no. God, they were *business partners*, not lovers. Calvin's muscles tensed, and he braced himself for John to scold him for being so familiar.

But John only said, "Oh, is my hair a mess?"

Calvin swallowed thickly. "Um, yes. Do you mind if I fix it?"

"No, Calvin, of course not," John said. "I think I w-w-w—" He paused to collect himself, squeezing his eyes shut. Probably he would start the sentence over. Calvin had come to expect this from time to time. "I think I would lose my entire head without you."

Calvin's stomach tumbled. How splendid it was to be needed. Because as long as he was needed, he wouldn't lose everything he had found—his shelter, his salary, his new life. John.

"We're lucky I'm here, then," Calvin said, moving his fingers through John's slightly waxy locks, heart still fluttering madly. After a moment more, Calvin removed his hand. "Try not to touch it too much now."

John smiled shyly. "Nervous habit."

"I know," Calvin said. He retrieved a handkerchief from his pocket to wipe the pomade off of his fingers, wishing that he could somehow wipe away his intense fondness for his shy business partner too. "Let's head over."

After they arrived at the home of Frank and Angelina Baker, Calvin purposefully flung his hat inside the hearse carriage so John wouldn't be insecure that he was the only one not holding one. When they reached the steps, Mr. Baker welcomed them before either of them even had a chance to knock. He must have been waiting for them. Once John and Calvin were inside, Calvin let John check on the body while he talked to Mr. Baker some more.

The viewing was for a man named Harold, Angelina's brother, who had been, Calvin came to learn, a so-called "confirmed bachelor." Harold had been living with the Bakers for several years. Since Harold hadn't been with someone, romantically, when he'd passed, all of the funeral planning had fallen to Mrs. Baker.

After Calvin was finished talking to Mr. Baker, he took a seat in a small chair in the back room. He knew he should probably confirm that everything was set in the front sitting room instead, where Harold's body was waiting, lying in a casket the Bakers had purchased elsewhere. But Calvin was still too uncomfortable to spend too much time with corpses to make himself move. He still preferred to spend as little time close to caskets as possible.

Not two minutes later, John bolted into the room.

"Calvin, we forgot the scarf!" he said, his eyes wide with fear.

"Scarf?" Calvin asked with a tilt of his head. It took him a moment to realize what the hell John was referring to. "Oh, the thing we're supposed to hang outside?"

"Yes, right, exactly."

Calvin shrugged. "So what? Will anyone care?"

John's mouth hung open with shock. Even though John had no emotional connection to these funeral customs himself, he was insistent that Hall and Wright Funeral Services follow every one of them he'd been taught at Eckels. And so, Calvin knew what John was thinking: How could Calvin *ever* even *think* to insinuate that people who were mourning the loss of someone they loved might be too busy to notice that there wasn't a silly scarf hanging outside? Calvin pursed his lips to keep himself from chortling. John could be so rigid sometimes.

"I think I saw a white one in the hearse," Calvin said, pushing himself to stand. "I'll fetch it."

"White?!" John scoffed. "Harold was f-f-fifty-six. White scarves are for—"

"Children," Calvin finished for him, becoming frustrated. "*I* know that, and *you* know that, but will everyone else—"

"Of course they'll know!"

"Alright, calm down," Calvin said, resting a hand on John's shoulder. "I will find one for us. What if I check with Mr. Baker?"

Somehow, that comment made John look even more horrified.

"No! Please, I . . ." John pulled his shoulders in, lowering his head. "I-I'm too embarrassed that we forgot it. I'm on my way to becoming the . . . the worst mortician in Philadelphia."

"It was a simple mistake."

Ears noticeably reddening, John squeezed his eyes shut. "No, it wasn't. Earlier, I lost my hat, and n-n-now, I've lost the black scarf. Why can't I . . ." He trailed off and ran a shaky hand through his hair.

Affection unfurled in Calvin's chest like a spring flower, its softness transforming Calvin's irritation into tenderness instead.

"I will fix it," Calvin said, reaching up to straighten John's hair again, flattening the strands that were sticking up. Even when John's hair was back to normal, Calvin kept touching it for a few more seconds, telling himself he was only trying to comfort his very frazzled business partner. It had nothing to do with Calvin relishing the chance to be closer to John. Nothing at all. "That's why you hired me, right?"

"Not to fix my mistakes, no."

"Well, I thought we said that you would handle the embalming and the creation of unsettling trinkets and the casket-making, while I would handle everything else. Didn't we?" John nodded. "I think this falls into the category of 'everything else,' right? Same with your hat, really. So, John, I take full responsibility for both of these mistakes." Slowly, Calvin let his hand fall to John's cheek and then to boldly cup John's chin, his stomach leaping into his throat the moment he felt the prickle of stubble on his fingertips. He lifted John's chin, encouraging John to look at him. "And I will fix this one. I promise."

Calvin's pulse roared in his ears as he and John looked into each other's eyes for what felt like forever, the fondness that Calvin felt toward his peculiar-yet-endearing business partner suddenly so great, so *heavy*, he began finding it hard to breathe.

Inhaling a shallow, shaky breath, Calvin wondered whether John might feel something toward him, too.

Finally, John smiled a little and said, "Thank you."

Calvin let his hand fall and then clapped both of them together. Rubbing his palms back and forth, he racked his brain to come up with a way to procure a black scarf. Perhaps they could simply borrow one from a neighbor. Practically everyone had one.

"What if I check elsewhere?" he said. "Maybe one of the neighbors has one that we can borrow."

"But what if the neighbors say something to the Bakers? Then they'll know that we borrowed one. They'll know that I hadn't been p-p-prepared. Calvin, I'm worried that I'm making a . . . a reputation for not being able to m-make it through a funeral without ruining it somehow."

"It's a silly custom," Calvin tried, though he knew he'd never manage to make John see it that way.

"It isn't. It's how people know that our clients are open to receiving people for the viewing."

"Alright, so, even *if* it's important, borrowing a scarf from a neighbor to follow this *very* important custom is . . . horrible for some reason?"

"Well, maybe the—the Bakers won't ever want to hire us in the future."

"Because of a scarf," Calvin said, his tone flat. He heaved an overly exaggerated sigh, frustration taking hold again. "Oh, for heaven's sake," he muttered. "What about we find one here then? And we borrow it without either Mr. or Mrs. Baker knowing? We'll return it once they want to end the viewing. *Still* without them knowing, of course."

John shook his head. "How? I checked the c-c-closet in the front room before. No scarves."

"They're probably upstairs, then. Everyone has scarves. More importantly, everyone has a *black* scarf. Every man in Philadelphia, anyway."

"I'm not sure if that's—"

Calvin held up a hand, cutting him off. "Mr. Baker has one. I'm sure of it." He began strumming his fingers against his thigh while he thought some more. "Have you offered to make them some of that creepy mourning jewelry yet?"

"No, why would I have? Neither of them would be interested."

Calvin smirked. "I bet I could persuade them."

"Why . . ." John raised an eyebrow. "Why would you want to?"

"Well, maybe they'll invite me upstairs so that we can choose something for you to work on. Once I'm in the bedroom, I can find a scarf."

John rocked back and forth on his heels a few times. "Seems unlikely to work, Calvin."

"Trust me," Calvin said, clapping him on the bicep. "I can be very convincing." Truthfully, Calvin wasn't really sure if this half-formed plan *would* work. But confidence was *always* the first and most important element of a successful con. Hence, the name, probably. "Stay here," he said. "Actually, no, come with me."

"Wh-what if I ruin—"

"You won't."

Starting toward the front of the house, Calvin motioned over his shoulder for John to follow. When they reached the room where the service would be held, Calvin called up the stairs for Mr. Baker.

A moment later, Mr. Baker started down the stairs. "Is everything set, gentlemen?"

"Almost, Mr. Baker," Calvin said. "But we still need the necklace."

"Necklace?" Mr. Baker asked, pausing at the bottom of the staircase.

"Or brooch or whatever you'd prefer. John here will be making the mourning jewelry."

Mr. Baker narrowed his eyes. "Mourning jewelry? Aren't those—"

"Becoming popular again? Yes, very. Even for siblings. *Especially* for siblings like Harold. You know, men and women without spouses or children. Which makes sense. It's sad to think that once poor Harold is laid to rest, you won't have much to remember him by otherwise."

"We hired a photographer. He came yesterday."

"Photography?!" Calvin asked through a little fake laugh. "Well, sure, photographs are nice, but with mourning jewelry, your wife can have a piece of her brother—"

"Twin brother," Mr. Baker corrected.

Nearby, John sucked in a loud breath before proceeding to lose himself to a coughing fit. Calvin winced. What the hell was happening? Was John trying to ruin Calvin's practically perfect scheme that had maybe a twenty percent chance of working?

"Is he . . . ?" Mr. Baker started to ask.

"He'll be fine," Calvin said with a dismissive wave of his hand. "Anyway, Mrs. Baker can carry a piece of her twin brother with her for the rest of her life. Isn't that sweet? Especially since, if I remember correctly, you said that she has no other living family."

"How much will it cost?"

"Oh, uhm, two . . . or . . ." Calvin looked at John who slyly pointed up to the ceiling. "Three?" John tilted his head from side to side, considering the number, before nodding once. "Yes, three dollars."

"*Three?* Wow."

"Yes, well, it's very intricate and—"

John chimed in, his voice low, his face reddening as he talked. "And I-I may have to be a little more c-creative with this one since Harold's hair is so short."

Mr. Baker rubbed his chin and sighed. "Alright, I think we can manage it. Do we really not have to purchase a new piece? Seems strange."

"Oh, no. It's customary for us to use something you already have."

Calvin had no idea if this was true, of course, but he had made it *sound* true, which was the important thing.

"Well, then I'll run upstairs to see if Angelina can choose something."

"I'd be happy to ask her myself," Calvin said with what he hoped was an innocent enough smile.

But from the face John was making—his teeth visible as he cringed hard—Calvin could tell that he had made some sort of error. Probably it was some kind of a social misstep to offer to spend time with Mr. Baker's wife in their bedroom by himself.

"No, I'll take care of it, thanks," Mr. Baker said slowly, his tone a bit suspicious.

Damn.

Once Mr. Baker was out of view, Calvin turned to John. His lips were pressed together into a thin line. His expression seemed to be saying *"oh, yes, this is working perfectly,"* in the most sarcastic tone imaginable, which sent a little burst of frustration through Calvin's veins. His face turned hot, even though John hadn't really said those words. *"I'm not finished!"* Calvin wanted to shout back.

Moments later, the Bakers came downstairs together. Mrs. Baker was carrying a brooch.

"Thank you so much for the offer," she said, handing the brooch over to Calvin. "You know, my mother had a necklace with my late sister's hair. I had nearly forgotten that you could have something like this made. Perhaps you can replace the face of the brooch with a hair weave?"

"Definitely," Calvin said, turning the brooch over in his hand a few times.

Panic started percolating in his stomach. How would he ever make this work? Mrs. Baker had chosen the piece so quickly. Just as Calvin was losing hope, Mr. Baker excused himself to find his checkbook and left for his study. With Frank temporarily out of the way, slipping upstairs *might* be easier.

Calvin said, "Mrs. Baker, would you mind helping John with the . . . uhm . . . the . . ."

Dammit. With what?

"Cookies," John spluttered. "We still have to put out the . . . the f-f-funeral cookies."

"Oh . . ." Furrowing her brow, Mrs. Baker shook her head in confusion. "Had we talked about that? I'm sorry if we had and I'd forgotten. I'm not sure where my mind has been this past week."

"It's customary," Calvin said.

"Sometimes," John clarified before clearing his throat. "Not everyone serves refreshments, but . . . but . . ."

"But we thought *you'd* like to," Calvin said. "Do you have something else that would work in lieu of cookies?"

"I haven't baked anything special, but I think I still have some leftover shortbread in the kitchen."

"Perfect," Calvin said. "John can help you set some pieces out."

Mrs. Baker left for the kitchen with John trailing behind. Briefly, John looked back over his shoulder, catching Calvin's eye before Calvin hurried up the stairs. He raced through the hall on his tiptoes, heading for the bedroom with the open door. Thankfully, it seemed to be the main one, at least by the looks of it. Hastily, Calvin threw open the closet, only barely managing to catch the door before the handle smacked into the wall, and then searched for a scarf. Just as he thought, Mr. Baker had several black ones sitting on the top shelf, neatly folded. Hah! He swiped one and bolted back downstairs, praying he wouldn't be caught.

Once he reached the front room, he let out a long breath. No one had come back yet. What luck!

Swiftly, Calvin stepped outside. He wrapped the scarf around the knob and hurried back in. Not two seconds later, Frank returned with a check.

"Just hanging the scarf," Calvin said with a nervous, out-of-breath laugh.

"Good, good," Mr. Baker said, his eyes still on the check as he approached. He handed it to Calvin. "Here's the payment for everything including the, uhm, brooch."

"Wonderful, thanks," Calvin said, folding it and shoving it in his back pocket. "Tomorrow, we're heading to the Church of the Holy Trinity for the service itself, right?"

"Right."

"Perfect," he said as John and Mrs. Baker came back with the shortbread.

Calvin caught John's eye and winked, hoping it would silently communicate that he had taken care of everything. Sure enough, John seemed to have understood. He visibly relaxed a bit, his shoulders lowering, probably releasing some of the tension he'd been holding. And then, silly John, he ran a hand through his hair again, making a complete mess of it. Calvin had to purse his lips to contain his smile as his whole body warmed from the sight.

"Perfect," he repeated to himself.

Because John really was perfect, wasn't he?

Hours later, once Harold's viewing was behind them, Calvin and John were riding home together, sitting next to each other in the box seat of the hearse while Calvin held Agathe's reins. As soon as they were out of view of the brick row home, John started to laugh. It began as one of those low hum-chuckles that Calvin loved, but soon intensified to a roaring belly laugh. Which then made Calvin laugh, too. He wasn't sure what had John so tickled, but it was nice to hear his laughter, regardless. John had what was probably the most beautiful laugh that Calvin had ever heard.

"What are we laughing for?" Calvin asked.

"I can't believe you p-pulled it off," John said.

Calvin knew that John was referring to the scarf.

"Ah, it was easy," Calvin said, puffing out his chest a bit.

"Really, Calvin, that was too much," John said. "It was wrong of me to have even asked that of you."

"It wasn't."

"Why'd you . . ." John's smile faltered. His eyes fell to his hands, which then started twisting in his lap. "Calvin, you could have refused. Michael w-w-would have told me that . . . that I was being ridiculous, and then he'd have asked Mr. Baker for the scarf himself. But you m-m-made this whole, intricate plan. Why?"

"It's fun to trick people," Calvin said with a half-hearted shrug, though that obviously wasn't the real reason. Or, not the *full* one.

Calvin had concocted that whole, silly, elaborate scheme because he was falling in love with John. He couldn't even pretend otherwise anymore.

Temporary.

Calvin's heart clenched. He shut his eyes for a moment to block out the small rush of pain.

John said, "I've never liked being tricked. Or the thought of . . . of tricking people. But I suppose no one was hurt in this case." He shifted in his seat. "I've been m-m-meaning to ask this, but . . ."

Shifting the reins to one hand, Calvin reached over and covered John's still-twisting hands with his free one, steadying him.

"Whatever it is, I won't be offended."

John's face softened, the worry lines that had been creasing his forehead slowly vanishing. "Alright." He nodded, and Calvin took his hand away. He tried not to focus on the way his skin tingled from remnants of John's warmth. "Before you came to work with me . . . you tricked people often, didn't you?"

Shame settled heavy in Calvin's stomach.

"Yes."

He wouldn't lie to John.

"Are you a . . . a . . . wh-wh-what's the term? Con man?"

Calvin swallowed hard. "Yes."

Furrowing his brow, John pursed his lips, seeming to think this over. Calvin's stomach continued to roil. Would John kick him out?

"I thought you might be," John finally said.

Calvin waited for more. He waited for John to chastise him, to scold him, to call him a thief. But John only stared straight ahead. Still thinking, perhaps, but . . . maybe not mad?

"I won't ever steal from you," Calvin said earnestly. "I promise."

John smiled and said, "I trust you."

"Am I . . . still your business partner, then?"

"Of course." John's brows pinched together. "Why wouldn't you be?"

Calvin nearly laughed. Why wouldn't he be? Because he was a criminal!

Unless . . . maybe . . . maybe he wouldn't have to be one anymore.

"Permanently?" Calvin asked, hopeful.

"Hmm?" John looked confused.

"Well, when we first met, you'd said . . . or *Michael* had said that my employment with you was . . . temporary. Is it . . . not temporary?"

"Do you want it to be?"

"No, I . . . I like working with you, John," Calvin said emphatically. "And I'd love to *keep* working with you. For as long as possible."

Without even the smallest pause, John said, "I'd like that."

Calvin's stomach fluttered, and that lingering, heavy shame vanished, leaving behind a wonderful, comforting lightness, one so unlike anything Calvin had ever felt before.

Calvin smiled. John smiled in return.

"I like working with you too, Calvin."

Chapter Eight
Calvin

After Calvin finished washing up in the bathroom, he went looking for John. First, he checked John's bedroom, but it was empty. Next, he checked the stable, but John wasn't there either. Earlier, when John and Calvin had first come home from the viewing, Michael had pulled John into his office to talk to him privately. Calvin had ventured upstairs to read, but had then lost track of time. It seemed that John was probably still with Michael, then.

Calvin scrunched up his nose, the mere thought of Michael sending a wave of worry, followed by an even larger wave of irritation, flowing through him and making his heart race. Even though only hours before, John had essentially confirmed that Calvin's position with Hall Funeral Services (or, Hall and Wright Funeral Services) was permanent, Calvin still couldn't shake the worry that Michael would try to throw him out on his rear end if he ever could.

Determined not to keep thinking about Michael, Calvin tried to find something to busy himself with. He wandered through the house, looking for Katherine, but then remembered that she was visiting her terrible father. Passing by Michael's study, Calvin heard Michael's muffled voice through the walls and scowled. He made his way into the kitchen, thinking he'd nibble on something, but he couldn't find anything that he wanted.

When Calvin stepped back out into the hall, his eyes found the entrance to the basement. He could still remember the scent of freshly shaved wood, and he recalled the momentary magic—heart-wrenching though it had been—of being transported back into the past to his father's workshop. Calvin hadn't managed to sit with those emotions for very long. He'd been surprised by them. Scared, even. Terrified of their power. But ever since he'd visited the basement with John, those feelings—heartbreak over having lost the only two people who had ever truly loved him and the wistful sort of sorrow he'd felt for wishing that he could turn back time—had been percolating inside him. He wasn't so terrified of them anymore. Instead, Calvin wondered if maybe he could stomach their full intensity now.

Slowly, Calvin walked toward the basement, his heart thudding fast, practically slamming into his ribcage with each beat, like the picker on a power loom knocking the shuttle. Inhaling a long breath, Calvin reached for the handle. When he opened the door, the smell of pine filled his nostrils with his next breath, memories of his father's work-worn hands kicking him in the teeth. But Calvin took the hit and stepped forward onto the first stair. And then the next. And the next. Soon enough, he was back down in the basement. Childhood memories still whirling through his head, Calvin paused to take in his surroundings.

Minutes passed. The pain subsided. Calvin walked over to John's workbench and sat. On the tabletop, there was a chisel. After a pause, Calvin picked it up. What a shame it was that he had never learned his father's trade.

Behind him, the stairs began to creak. Calvin turned toward the sound.

"Calvin?" John said, making his way into the basement. Once John reached the last step, the two of them locked eyes, and John tilted his head slightly. "Why are you here?"

"I was bored," Calvin said. "I thought I'd explore a bit."

"Not much to see," John said. "I'll probably stop making c-c-caskets soon. It's hard to constantly have to find enough lumber and to bring the w-w-wood here. You know how frustrating it can be to bring the caskets upstairs too."

Calvin turned the chisel over in his hands. "Will you miss it?"

"I will," John confirmed, walking over to meet him. He knelt and tapped the chisel. "Do you know how to use one? I seem to remember—"

"No," Calvin confirmed, some sorrow in his voice. "Never learned."

"I could teach you."

"I thought you said that you wouldn't be making caskets anymore."

"We could m-m-make other things." John pointed over to a casket lid resting up against the wall. "And I still have one more to f-f-f-... to finish."

"Alright," Calvin said, a flicker of warmth igniting in his chest. "Yeah."

John pushed himself to stand and fetched the lid. Calvin scooted his chair backward as John balanced the lid on the tabletop.

"All that's left is to refine the trim," John said. "We won't need a ... a bench chisel for it." Gently, John plucked the tool out of Calvin's hands. "We'll need a p-paring one."

While John found a second chisel, one with a longer handle and a finer tip, Calvin stood and moved his chair out of the way. Hooking his hands behind his back, Calvin watched John strip away bits of wood. He found himself smiling as he recalled his father embellishing an entryway table for his shop. With the memory came a pinprick of pain, but, sure enough, it wasn't as harsh as it had been before. After a few minutes, John turned to Calvin and silently offered him the tool. Calvin reached for it, but hesitated, his hand hovering over the handle. He looked over at John, who nodded once, encouraging him without even saying a word. Calvin took it.

He knew what John wanted him to try. John had left this side of the lid unfinished, the last third or so remaining. Pressing the blade to the wood, Calvin took a breath and pushed, shaving some of it away. He paused to wait for John's commentary. But John stayed quiet. Calvin moved to try once more, only for John's hands to settle on top of both of his. And this time, when they pushed together, Calvin could feel a change, the weight of John's hands silently instructing him to press harder. John's hands stayed on top of his for a few moments longer. All the while, Calvin's heart continued to stammer.

And he wondered whether there was something between them. Something more than a business partnership. Something wonderful.

Desperate to know whether he was simply imagining things—seeing a connection, perhaps even a *romantic* connection, where there was none—Calvin shifted his hand, lifting up his thumb. Shaking slightly, Calvin stretched it, hooking his thumb to rest it on top of John's. He braced himself for John to reject him, to pull his hands away in horror. And then Calvin would have to pretend that he'd only been trying to improve his hold on the chisel. He'd lie. He'd lie like he had lied so many times in his life. He'd lie to ensure that John wouldn't end their business partnership.

But John huffed a tiny, barely-there laugh instead.

Calvin's face caught fire, and the flames spread through him, setting his body ablaze with hope as he replayed the sound in his head.

Carefully, Calvin resumed shaping the wood, John's large, lovely hands lingering on top of his, the sound of John's soft chuckle echoing in his very soul.

Sometime later, mid-stroke, John moved his hands away and took a step back to let Calvin finish the task by himself. Calvin missed his touch instantly. Scraping the blade over the wood, Calvin's heart burned with the hope for something he was so very terrified to hope for: companionship.

Calvin only worked for a little while more by himself. Once Calvin completed what remained of that first edge, John took over, finishing the rest of the lid himself while Calvin watched.

Beneath the still-present longing for love, Calvin felt something else too. He felt gratitude. Watching John work seemed to be bridging the chasm between Calvin's lost childhood and the present. Here, in the basement of his new home, Calvin felt more connected to his father than he had in years.

John finally set the chisel back on the workbench. Sweeping his hands back and forth on his pant legs to wipe off the wood shavings, he turned toward Calvin, his eyes fixed on the floor in front of him.

More gratitude swelled in Calvin's chest as he watched the flecks of wood fall.

"Thank you," Calvin repeated. "Truly."

John lifted his head to meet Calvin's eyes.

"Anytime."

All of a sudden, that wonderful fullness in Calvin's chest waned as long-buried memories of his father's workshop flashed in his mind. He could remember sitting on his mother's lap, watching his father work on something, and though the something was blurry, Calvin could *feel* the care that his father had put into every stroke of the chisel. Calvin winced. Grief overtook him, pulling him beneath the surface, and tears welled in his eyes. He missed his parents. He missed them both so much.

Choking back a sob, Calvin shut his eyes, trying to stop himself from crying.

"God, John, being here . . ." He inhaled a trembling breath. "It makes me realize how much I miss my parents." He exhaled slowly. "Dammit, I'm sorry."

Calvin spent the next few minutes trying to collect himself. Keeping his eyes closed, he took long, slow breaths, hoping to rein in his emotions. All the while, he waited for John to say something. He waited for John to comfort him. Yearned for John to try to help ease the pain. Because John cared for him. Didn't he?

But John stayed quiet.

Calvin opened his eyes and looked at John pleadingly, silently and pathetically begging for comfort. He so badly hoped to find sympathy. But John's face was expressionless, his brown eyes empty of care. It was reminiscent of the hardened stares David would give him whenever Calvin had tried to bring up his family. David, who had never truly cared for him. David, who had cast him aside. David, who had broken his heart. God, David had only ever thought of Calvin as someone he could use. Sexually. Financially. David had only been with him out of convenience.

David had never loved him.

And John would never love him, either.

"I like working with you too, Calvin."

John liked *working* with him. Nothing more. John may have told Calvin that his employment could be permanent. But it couldn't be, could it?

Because Calvin couldn't let himself spend the rest of forever pining for someone who very clearly had no interest in being close with him. Judging from John's repeated responses to Calvin's silent pleas for comfort, John wasn't interested in intimacy, not even of the platonic kind.

Calvin swallowed, fighting the tightness in his throat.

"I . . ." He sniffled and shook his head, forcing his sadness to the wayside. "I think I'll read for a while in my room." He kept his voice steady and even, removing every trace of emotion from it as best he could. "Thanks for the lesson."

Without waiting for John's reply, Calvin turned and hurried toward the stairs, thanking the Lord that he still had financial insurance in Michael's cuff links he'd hidden in one of his socks. When Calvin's foot touched the first step, he scolded himself for being so vulnerable, for tricking himself into thinking that John cared for him, and for letting himself want what would never be his. Every step that Calvin took, he repeated the same thing over and over in his head.

Temporary. Temporary. Temporary.

Chapter Nine
John

Days later, John and Calvin were traveling out to Media to provide their embalming services for a family John had known since childhood. Mr. and Mrs. Hutchens had specifically requested that John be the one to embalm their son and their daughter-in-law, both of whom had only been in their late twenties when they'd passed. Apparently, they had contracted some sort of illness, one that had unfortunately taken them both, and had left behind a ten-year-old boy.

Try as he might, John couldn't remember either of the people he would be embalming. He remembered Mr. Theodore Hutchens, though, who had run one of the local meat markets. Despite the fact that John hadn't spoken to the man since moving to Philadelphia, Mr. Hutchens had still wanted to hire him, perhaps out of loyalty to the Hall family (most likely, out of loyalty to John's late father, specifically), though there probably weren't many morticians outside of the city for them to hire otherwise. Back when John had first enrolled at Eckels, the program had been fairly new, and so, the likelihood of there being a mortician in Media itself was slim. Perhaps in a few years' time. Regardless of the reason why the Hutchens family had requested him, John was happy to help, especially since he hadn't needed to make the caskets himself.

When John and Calvin neared the western city limits, John's palms started to sweat, his stomach tightening from nervousness. He still hadn't told Calvin the specifics of the embalming they would be helping with. All Calvin knew was that they wouldn't be staying for the service (John had been surprised that Calvin still wanted to come, though he'd never refuse Calvin's company). Now, John couldn't help but worry that Calvin might become upset once he learned that the folks whom John would be embalming had left behind a child. God, Calvin had nearly fallen to pieces in the basement earlier that week when John had been teaching him a bit of carpentry. John cringed internally as the image of Calvin's sorrowful face floated into his mind, shame coloring his cheeks over how he had reacted.

Or, well, how he *hadn't* reacted.

John simply hadn't known *how* to react to Calvin's tears. Truthfully, he *still* wasn't sure what the correct response would have been. Should he have tried to comfort Calvin somehow? If so, how? John hadn't received much comfort himself as a boy. Not even when Lucy had passed away. What would he even have said to Calvin? How *could* he have said something comforting, something impactful, when he himself often struggled to make the right words come at all?

Grimacing, John tried to force the thoughts from his head by telling himself that the unpleasantness of that experience was behind both of them now. Hopefully Calvin wouldn't be too upset by the embalming. John could (and probably should) encourage Calvin not to watch him work, which might help prevent a recurrence of the basement catastrophe. But, in the event that Calvin *still* became upset . . .

John shifted uncomfortably in his seat. Well, if Calvin became upset, then John would have no choice but to try to comfort him. Somehow.

When the hearse carriage reached the corner of State and Monroe Streets, John's stomach tightened. Goodness, they only had a few minutes before they would ride up to Mr. and Mrs. Hutchens's home. He had to tell Calvin everything before they arrived. Slowing their hearse carriage, John turned north on Monroe and then pulled back on the reins ever so slightly, urging Agathe to slow her pace even more.

John cleared his throat.

"Calvin . . ." He paused to wet his lips, but his entire mouth had suddenly become parched, which made him feel as though he was instead rubbing sandpaper over a piece of wood. "I know I should have m-m-mentioned this earlier, but . . . the . . . the person we're embalming . . . it . . . well, it isn't *one* person. It's two. And they . . . well, they left behind a . . . a little boy."

Bracing himself for upset, John shut his eyes. He couldn't stand to look at Calvin yet, to see the inevitable sadness or shock or horror on Calvin's face. Oh, God, why had he taken this embalming job? What a fool he had been.

Moments passed. John listened for sniffles or sobs or whimpers, but the only thing he could hear was the clip-clop of Agathe's hooves on the pavement. Cautiously, John peeked one eye open. He found Calvin staring off ahead.

"Are you upset?"

"No," Calvin said, his voice strangely devoid of emotion. "Just thinking."

"Oh." John opened his other eye. "About the . . . embalming? Because I won't n-n-need you to be present for it, if that's what's bothering you."

"No, not that. I can sit with you while you work. Actually, I'll probably prefer that to, uhm, to being alone. But . . ." Calvin blew out a breath. "I was thinking about how tragic it is when these things happen."

"Yes," John confirmed, preparing to speak slowly as though he was navigating a minefield. "It is tragic. But the boy . . . he has other family who will be taking him in."

Calvin let out a short, bitter laugh. "Small mercies."

"Yes. Small m-m-mercies."

Both men went silent. And for the last small stretch of the ride, John's heart continued to bleed for his business partner and friend.

When they arrived at Mr. and Mrs. Hutchens's home—two stories (three, if the small attic could be counted), sage colored, with a well-kept, white wrap-around porch and nicely placed brown and yellow shingles surrounding the third-story window—John steered Agathe toward the stable in the back of the house. Once they were stopped, he unhitched Agathe from the hearse while Calvin began unloading their embalming equipment—John's black bag of tools, a few empty jars meant to hold body fluids, and several full containers of embalming solution. After Agathe was secure inside the stable with Mr. and Mrs. Hutchens's horse, he helped Calvin carry everything to the porch.

Mr. Hutchens opened the front door as they approached.

"John," he said. "I'm so touched that you came."

"Of course, Mr. Hutchens," John said, carting his bag up the porch stairs. "I couldn't believe the news. Wh-wh-when your brother, Walter, came to the city to tell me . . ." He shook his head, unable to find the words.

"I know," Mr. Hutchens said, his voice softer, face turning sullen. "You can call me Theodore, by the way. We've known each other for ages."

"Thank you, Theodore," John said as Calvin came up beside him, brown luggage bag in tow. "Sorry, this is Calvin Wright, my business p-partner."

Calvin and Theodore both bowed their heads.

"So, when can we start?" Calvin asked. "Are the, uh, the bodies inside?"

God, Calvin was still so blunt sometimes. Mostly when he was uneasy. Despite his lingering feelings of sympathy, John had the urge to thump Calvin upside the head. Lucky for both of them, Theodore seemed not to be bothered by what Calvin had said.

"Lewis and Rose are in the kitchen," Theodore replied. "We borrowed two cooling boards from neighbors nearby."

Well, thank God for that. Lewis and Rose had died . . . probably over forty hours ago. Without the cooling boards and Walter's immediate trip into the city . . . John shuddered. He'd rather not imagine the state of the bodies.

"Perfect, thanks," Calvin said, picking up two of the empty containers. "We'll start right away, then."

With a solemn nod, Theodore turned to head back into the house. John sighed, his heart hurting for his old family friend. He wished Theodore and his wife wouldn't have to endure what had to be such a heavy grief.

Over the next half hour, John and Calvin transferred everything into the kitchen and John laid out his tools, preparing to begin the embalming process. Before he could start, Theodore came by, but stayed back, hovering in the entryway.

"We only have the one spare bedroom," he said. "I'm not sure if my brother had mentioned that, but I hope it won't be a problem. It'll probably be nightfall before you're finished."

Shoving his hands in his pockets, John swiveled to face Calvin, hoping to gauge his business partner's reaction to this bit of news. Calvin threw him a tight-lipped smile and a nod.

"That'll be f-f-fine," John confirmed. "We'll head back in the m-morning. Unless you want us to stay for the viewing and the service. We typically help with that as well."

"Oh, that's not necessary. We've been in contact with the reverend. We're having the viewing starting tomorrow and then the service later. I believe everything is set for both."

John furrowed his brow. If Hall and Wright Funeral Services would only be performing half of the work, perhaps they ought not to charge. Charging for the embalming alone would make sense, but . . . God, these circumstances were horrible. And Theodore had been his father's friend. Providing the embalming for free . . . well, it was the least John could do.

"Well, if that's the case, I'd like to offer the embalming free of charge."

Theodore's eyes widened. "Free?!"

John nodded once.

"Thank you," Theodore said. "Really, that means so much to me."

"Just let me know if there's anything else we could help with. I-I'm not sure where the . . . the boy is, but maybe he could m-m-meet Agathe or—"

"Little Lewis is with my brother for now."

"Ah." John chewed on his lip. "W-w-will he live here? After?"

"He will," Theodore said, his voice shaking a little.

John winced, wondering if he might have overstepped. He typically tried not to pry about things like that. But it had been hard to remember himself when he'd known Theodore for over ten years. He had only wanted to help.

Before John could fumble through either a platitude or an expression of his regret, Calvin spoke up.

"I'm so sorry for your loss, Theodore," Calvin said, his voice so light and kind that John found himself a little taken aback by it.

"Thank you," Theodore choked out before turning to leave.

John's heart clenched. Goodness, he had made Theodore cry with his inquiry. How horrible of him to have pressed the bereaved man like that. He let out a breath and rested some of his weight on the worktable.

"Sorry," John said, running his free hand over his face. "I'm sorry, Calvin. God, I . . . I shouldn't have upset him like that."

"What? Why are you sorry?" Calvin said, coming closer and leaning on the surface next to him. "I'm sure he knows that you meant well. For heaven's sake, John, you're performing the embalming for free. You traveled all the way here from Philadelphia, too. Most people wouldn't have done that."

With a sigh, John rotated to rest his back against the heavy wooden table and folded his arms over his chest, holding himself tightly as though he could somehow contain his burgeoning embarrassment too.

"Wh-wh-when I went to Eckels, we were taught that it was an invasion of p-privacy to venture into those sorts of topics. I believe they even said something like 'it is f-frowned upon to provide excessive expressions of sympathy.'"

Calvin scoffed. "Alright, well, first, that seems unnecessarily cold, and I think whoever came up with it is probably missing part of their soul. Second, Theodore is a family friend of yours. I'm sure those etiquette rules can be tossed out the window for people you know personally."

Calvin reached over and squeezed John's bicep, and despite their current situation and the serious discussion they'd been having, John's stomach fluttered excitedly from the contact. God, it was hard to think of Calvin *only* as a friend. Every time they touched . . . it felt like magic. If such a thing existed. John had never been one to believe in that sort of thing. But Calvin was . . . spellbinding.

John recalled the way Calvin had held his hand while they'd worked together on the casket lid in the basement, and his stomach fluttered once more.

"Yes, maybe . . . maybe you're right," John said before his eyes flitted over to his tools, his stomach still topsy-turvy. "I should start."

"Alright." Calvin removed his hand and took a step back. "Go ahead."

John waited for Calvin to leave. When Calvin stayed fixed to the same spot, John raised an inquisitive eyebrow.

"Are you really staying?"

"I'm not sure if I should," he said. "Do you want me to?"

John's body began to hum with nervous excitement. Of course he wanted Calvin to stay. He wanted the two of them to spend as much time together as possible.

"I'd love that," John said softly before he caught sight of the bodies and remembered himself. He couldn't ask Calvin to stay for this. "Or . . ."

Calvin's eyes wandered over to the cooling boards, too, and a look of uncertainty seemed to flash in them.

"Sorry, Calvin, I-I shouldn't have said that," John said quickly. "I mean, I'd like it if you stayed, but only because I want us to spend t-t-time together. I like it when we're together and—"

"Yeah, I'll stay," Calvin said.

"Only if you're sure."

Calvin smiled. "I'm sure. I like it when we're together, too."

Fondness and happiness erupted in John's chest with such force it left him feeling lightheaded. He took a breath to try to temper it.

"Alright," he said, clasping his hands together. "P-p-perfect."

Over the next few hours, the two sat side by side, with John working while Calvin watched. Aside from Calvin's handful of interesting facial expressions—scrunching up his nose or wincing a couple of times—he seemed to be handling everything rather well. By the time John was finished with Rose, he thought that perhaps he had overestimated how much Calvin would be impacted by witnessing the embalming itself.

But, once John then began to work on Lewis, Calvin's behavior started to change. Rather than sitting calmly beside John while he worked, Calvin pushed his chair backward, putting more space between him and the body. John pretended not to notice, but once Calvin then began bouncing his leg, he knew he had to say something.

"Calvin, if it's too much . . ."

"It's not," Calvin said.

John searched Calvin's face for insincerity, but he couldn't find any. Still, Calvin continued to bounce his leg. He was upset. John *knew* he was. But if Calvin wouldn't be honest, John couldn't press him. Not like he had pressed Theodore earlier. He couldn't hurt Calvin like that.

Returning his focus to the embalming, John pushed his worries aside. Cotton squares ready on the end of the table, John stood and picked up his scalpel. He prepared to make the incision in Lewis's throat, one that would be long enough to insert the cotton—a necessary, but unpleasant step when embalming someone who had perished from a lung disease—when Calvin spoke up behind him.

"Little Lewis," Calvin said. "It's sweet that they call him that, isn't it?" John looked over his shoulder to see Calvin staring at the floor tiles. "Guess he'll have to be Big Lewis now. Or . . . The Only Lewis."

Chest tightening, John lowered his scalpel and set it back on the table. God, he felt so horrible for Calvin. He obviously felt sorry for Lewis as well, but it was terrible to see Calvin like this. It wasn't only terrible, but it *pained* him. It was physically painful to witness Calvin's upset. John wasn't accustomed to feeling this way—to feeling a painful sort of compassion—and he wasn't accustomed to having to comfort someone, either. He wanted to, though.

God, how he wanted to. John opened his mouth to respond—to try to say something to rid Calvin of his pain—but then Calvin looked up, and John froze. His breath caught, the sight of sorrow shimmering in Calvin's eyes ripping his heart in two. He couldn't even begin to know what to say now.

Calvin buried his head in his hands.

"I have no idea how you can stomach this. Fuck, it's sad."

Sorrow continued to twist in John's chest, its sharp edge shredding him from the inside. Seeing Calvin like this—eyes teary, crumpling in on himself—John could easily imagine his business partner as a small, frightened boy, one who had lost too much too soon. It made John's chest swell and his heart ache, and it made it even more impossible to speak.

Squeezing his eyes shut, John tried to will the words to come.

"I'm so sorry for what you've been through, Calvin," he wanted to say. *"What a strong man you are for having survived so much loss."*

But the words stayed trapped in his throat.

Calvin looked up at him with pleading eyes. "How?" he asked. "How can you stand this kind of thing over and over?"

John wasn't sure himself.

He swallowed hard and said, "It's . . . easy for me. Always has been."

Bottom lip trembling, Calvin shook his head and said, "John, you're a nice man, but sometimes . . . sometimes I think there's something wrong with you."

Calvin's words struck John in the chest, paralyzing him on the spot.

Those words—the very same ones Michael had said so many times when they were children—continued to play over and over in his head, each repetition causing shame to coil tighter in his stomach, making him want to retch.

There's something wrong with you.

There's something wrong with you.
There's something wrong with you.
Calvin stood to leave.

"I think I'll find out where the bedroom is," he said, walking away, his voice wrought with unmistakable heartbreak. "I want to rest for a while."

John stayed frozen in shame and uncertainty, unspoken words of sympathy still trapped inside him, blocked by the tightness in his throat.

Hours later, once John was finished with the embalming, he and Theodore relocated both bodies to the front room. Afterward, the kitchen needed to be cleaned. Melted ice needed to be mopped up, wet towels had to be moved, surfaces needed to be cleaned. Rather than possibly be in the way, John left to see Agathe while Theodore and his wife, Beatrice, scrubbed the room. Stroking Agathe's mane, John confessed to everything that had happened between him and Calvin lately, telling his horse about their intermittent and confusing closeness and about his own inability to help Calvin whenever he seemed to need consoling. All the while, John hoped that Calvin would come outside to meet him. But Calvin never did.

Later, John had supper with Theodore and Beatrice. Concerningly, Calvin never came out of the spare bedroom. While John lazily moved his baked chicken back and forth with his fork, he kept looking out into the hallway, praying for Calvin to show up. But he didn't. Guilt and shame sat heavy in John's stomach, robbing him of most of his appetite. He barely had ten bites of food.

After supper, John excused himself to feed Agathe, and then he went upstairs to wash up. Theodore and Beatrice had explained which one was the spare bedroom where he and Calvin would be sleeping for the night. When John reached it, he paused outside the closed door, his hand hovering just in front of the wood. Would Calvin even want to see him now?

After knocking twice, John called out Calvin's name.

"Come in," Calvin called back.

Carefully, John poked his head inside. He found Calvin sitting up in bed, reading while wearing his night-shirt—brown-and-white-striped linen, long enough that it probably reached past his knees when standing, though right now, it was bunched up slightly, the fabric only coming halfway down his thigh.

"I have to, to w-w-wash up," John said, his cheeks heating up from the sight of Calvin's bare thighs.

Even from feet away, John could see the brown hairs, the way they looked so coarse and yet somehow also soft. He had the sudden intense urge to touch them, to nuzzle his face into the flesh of Calvin's thighs and feel the hair tickle his cheeks. Oh, what was the matter with him?! Calvin was his friend!

John blurted out, "Did you wash up yet?"

Asinine. He knew Calvin had. Because Calvin was in his bed clothes.

"Earlier," Calvin confirmed. He cocked his head to the side. "Can you not tell that this is my nightshirt?"

"Oh, no, I-I-I can tell," John spluttered before scrambling to find his own nightshirt in his luggage. "Definitely, yes, I can tell."

John's cheeks burned hotter. Why was this happening? He was supposed to be busy feeling bad for continuing to be such a horrible friend, not standing here fixating on Calvin's thighs. Not to mention what lay beneath his nightshirt, only a mere six inches or so from the hem. Goodness, hopefully he could leave for the bathroom before Calvin noticed the bulge forming in his pants.

Quickly, John snatched his black leather toilet bag from his luggage, then hurried to the bathroom, where he breathed a long sigh of relief, happy to have a moment to rein in his sordid thoughts in private.

First, John changed into his own blue nightshirt, and then he washed his face and brushed his teeth. All the while, his heart kept on pitter-pattering, the memory of Calvin's thighs practically seared into his brain, its vibrancy blocking out every other thought. And, of course, John still had the pesky bulge to contend with, too. Dammit. He liked Calvin a lot. Romantically. Sexually. Did Calvin reciprocate these feelings? Likely not. But . . . possibly. Once again, the thought of their basement hand-holding session burst into John's mind, sending his heart aflutter. It wasn't as though John could ask Calvin what his feelings were, not unless he wanted to risk losing his business partner and, more importantly, his friend. Or even his entire *business*.

But, *God*, the sight of Calvin like that was stirring up some very intense feelings, ones that John couldn't ignore. Still, he needed to lock these feelings—these *urges*—away if he wanted to make it through the night with Calvin in the same room. Or, oh Lord, the same *bed*.

Pressing a palm to his erection, John tried to force it away with a silent scolding. But unsurprisingly, that failed to work. It seemed that there was only one solution to his problem. Letting out a frustrated sigh, John took his cock into his hand and prayed that when he returned to the room, Calvin wouldn't somehow sense what he would have just done.

Slowly, John began to pump his fist, his now-uninhibited thoughts of Calvin's pale, hairy thighs exciting him even further, making his cock throb for release. Closing his eyes, John tried to imagine what it would feel like to place one of his hands on one of those lovely thighs. Would Calvin's leg hair tickle his skin as he massaged it? Moving his fist faster, John then tried to imagine himself inching his hand up higher, eventually slipping it beneath Calvin's nightshirt and—oh, *God*—finding Calvin's cock. And Calvin's cock would be hard. Not only hard, but hard for *him*. Next, John would pepper soft kisses on Calvin's neck. And then, he would take Calvin's member in his hand and—

With a low moan, John started to come, shooting the evidence of his very inappropriate lusting onto the floor. Slowing his strokes, John continued to rub himself a few more times, coaxing out every last shameful drop with the hope that it might make it easier for him to get through the night with Calvin in their shared bed. Afterward, John stayed put for a little while, his heart still hammering wildly from having touched himself to the thought of his new friend, and then, once he felt like he had composed himself enough, he cleaned up his mess and washed his hands.

By the time he returned to the room, Calvin had moved to the floor, and as soon as John saw him, his stomach sank. Wouldn't he be uncomfortable? Probably this meant that Calvin did *not* feel the same way. Or . . .

Or maybe Calvin was not only *not* harboring romantic feelings for him but was truly so upset over John's inability to comfort him—to be a true friend to him—that he'd rather freeze on the hardwood floor than be near him.

Remorse pulled at John's heart as self-loathing burned in his belly. What was the matter with him? Why was he so . . . so strange? No wonder he had never . . .

John's eyes fell. No wonder he'd never had a friend before.

After John set his clothing in the corner and returned his toilet bag to his luggage, he stepped over Calvin and climbed onto the mattress. Calvin only had a thin blanket, probably something he'd found in the closet. John tried to ignore the niggling feeling in his chest telling him that Calvin's plight was John's own fault and that Calvin might have been more inclined to share the bed had John not been such a socially stunted person. But still, his heart continued to ache.

"Ready for me to lower the light?" Calvin asked, hopping up and heading over to the oil lamp hanging on the far wall.

Adjusting his position on the mattress—tucking one hand under his pillow and curling his knees closer to his chest—John stuttered a pathetic "y-yes."

After fiddling with the lamp, Calvin settled back onto his spot on the floor. Under the blanket of night, John's shame intensified, coiling tighter in his stomach with each tick of the clock, like the winding of a spring. He had to fix things somehow. John couldn't let Calvin ruin his back on the stiff wooden floor because of his own miserable inability to say what he needed to say *when* he needed to say it. All John's life, he had struggled to connect with people. While it had been a problem as far back as he could remember, back when he'd been a little boy, Lucy had made up for it. Gregarious and sweet and talkative, Lucy had been personable enough for both of them. John had let her be his voice. But then, when he'd lost her, he had lost part of himself, too. And now John *still* hadn't figured out how to talk to people. He hadn't figured out how to connect with them.

Until Calvin. With Calvin . . . there was something there. John was certain of it. Even if that something was only friendship, it was still something. It was still *important*. God, between running the business together and having fun together, that something was becoming the *most* important something. John couldn't let himself lose it. He needed to be a better friend to Calvin. Starting now.

"Calvin . . . I . . ." John could feel his throat closing, fear of saying the wrong thing beginning to wrap itself around his vocal cords, but he forced himself to push through it. "I'm sorry. For everything."

"I'm fine, John," Calvin said, his voice weary.

Clearly he wasn't fine.

"Cal . . ." John tried again, wincing when he realized that he had inadvertently shortened Calvin's name. "Come up here."

There was a pause.

"Are you sure?" Calvin asked.

"*Yes*," John answered emphatically, trying his best to sound very, very sure. "I'm sure it's uncomfortable on the f-floor there."

After a moment, Calvin climbed up into bed, and John nearly heaved a sigh of relief. One fewer thing to feel horrible for. At least Calvin could be comfortable now.

Calvin rolled over to face him.

"I thought you were probably mad at me," he said. "Because of what I said earlier."

How could he be mad at Calvin for speaking the truth?

"Not in the least."

"I'm sorry if I was mean," he said. "Or childish."

"You weren't," John said.

"When I started to think of Little Lewis, I . . . I mean, I know his pain too well. I lost my parents when I was young and—"

Sympathy clutched at John's heart.

"I know," John said.

But it wasn't enough. John *knew* it wasn't enough. And yet . . . he still couldn't make himself say what needed to be said. Because he was terrified. He had never had a friend before, not a friend that was his and his alone. He had never comforted someone before. God, he had barely even talked to people outside his family for most of his life. John clenched his teeth, wishing so badly for the words to come. But they wouldn't.

Struck with the sudden urge to coil in on himself, John tried to tuck his legs closer to his chest, but ended up knocking knees with Calvin. Heat flooded his cheeks. *Why* was he continuing to fumble like this? Verbally *and* physically?

"Sorry," John managed.

He was sorry for bumping Calvin's knees. He was sorry for never having the right words. He was sorry that he couldn't seem to show Calvin how much his heart hurt for him—for current Calvin and for little Calvin, too. He was sorry for so many things.

Calvin rolled over without saying a word.

John had hurt him. Again. Regret and self-reproach hardened in John's stomach, pushing bile up his throat.

There's something wrong with you.

There's something wrong with you.

No.

John swallowed once, trying to shove his self-loathing back where it couldn't continue to hurt either him or his friend. He had to fix this. He *would* fix it. But how?

Closing his eyes, John tried to think back on the times he *could* recall receiving comfort, few that there were. One specific memory floated into his mind, hazy and half-formed like a faded photograph.

Missing his sister, John had crawled into bed with his mom. And then . . . then she had held him close. Other times—instances prior to that one—she had pushed him away, but that time, for whatever reason, she had hugged him. And it had made him feel safe. Safe and warm and loved. It had helped John internalize the fact that, even though she often struggled to show it, she still cared for him.

And John wanted Calvin to know that he cared for him.

Perhaps Calvin would like to be held for a moment, too.

Determined to provide Calvin with comfort, even if that comfort couldn't come from words like it probably should, John scooted closer, close enough that his chest was nearly flush with Calvin's back, and then, tentatively, John lifted his hand to Calvin's shoulder. Calvin flinched.

"Calvin . . ." John's voice shook.

He wanted permission to hold his friend, but he was too nervous to speak. And so, he waited for Calvin to say something. Or to move away.

But Calvin stayed both still and silent.

It wasn't explicit permission, but maybe it was something.

Slowly, John hooked his arm around Calvin's midsection. When his hand came in contact with Calvin's stomach, he paused and braced himself for Calvin to push him away or to chastise him for touching him like this. But Calvin shuffled backward instead, melting into John's embrace with a soft sigh.

John's heart fluttered, his chest warming, and tears sprang to his eyes. Had he finally managed to help the man he had come to care for so very much?

"Thank you," Calvin whispered, his voice cracking.

After a moment, John squeezed Calvin one more time before starting to pull away, but then Calvin's hand came to rest on top of his.

"Stay. Please."

Stay? Calvin wanted him to stay? John's heart fluttered once more. Did this mean what he hoped it meant? Because friends . . . friends didn't *normally* hold each other like this, did they? Probably not. Not for this long.

John's face caught fire, his heart slamming into his chest from a mixture of fear and excitement and more emotions he couldn't even name. Was there . . . something else here, then? Something romantic? God, he really hoped so.

Heart now pounding wildly, John squeezed Calvin a little more.

Oh, he never wanted to let go.

Calvin laughed softly and said, "Not *too* tight, John."

"Sorry," John said, laughing a little, too.

John's whole body burned with excitement and elation and fondness.

Goodness, how would he *ever* be able to sleep now?

But they had to sleep. Because they had to travel back early in the morning, before the viewing started, which meant that they would have to leave before ten. At the very least, they both needed to *try* to sleep.

In a hushed voice, John said, "Goodnight, Calvin."

Entire body still engulfed in the flames of yearning, John closed his eyes.

Minutes or seconds passed. John wasn't sure which.

Then, Calvin tapped one of his hands and said, "John?"

"Hmm?"

"I liked it when you called me 'Cal.'"

Huffing a soft laugh, John tapped Calvin's hand in return.

"I liked it, too," he said, smiling. "Goodnight, Cal."

Calvin squeezed one of John's fingers. "Goodnight, John."

Chapter Ten
Calvin

Sunlight was starting to stream through the window, the beams of soft yellow peeking through the space between the curtains and the window frame, when Calvin's eyes fluttered open. Immediately, heat bloomed in his chest, the warm happiness making his skin tingle.

Because John was still holding him.

In the middle of the night, Calvin had woken to the feeling of John shifting on the bed, letting out what had sounded like a pain-filled sigh as he shuffled in place, moving like maybe he was trying to rotate his shoulder without letting Calvin out of his embrace. Calvin had realized that John had probably been enduring some sort of stiffness for a while so that the two of them could stay cuddled close. Knowing that John wouldn't complain, Calvin had simply unhooked John's arm from around his own waist, crawled to the other side of the bed, lay back down facing the other way, and then said, *"Come here, John."* And then John had rolled over and hugged Calvin close. *"Is this better?"* Calvin had asked, to which John had replied, *"Yes, it is. Thank you, Cal."* Almost immediately, Calvin had fallen back asleep. He assumed that John had as well.

And now, with morning upon them, John was still holding him. And Calvin had no idea what such a wonderful thing might mean.

Despite the fact that John had cuddled him for the entire evening, Calvin still couldn't be sure whether it meant that John liked him in a romantic sense. Because John wasn't like most people. Ergo, it seemed possible John might think that two men snuggling like this could be a normal occurrence between business partners, especially ones who happened to be friends.

Calvin frowned. Perhaps not, though. Because that . . . that would be too silly. Wouldn't it?

Oh, God. Calvin couldn't be sure *what* John was thinking.

Anxiety began to buzz beneath Calvin's skin, the hum of energy making his skin itch and rendering it impossible for him to stay still. If he couldn't stop wiggling, he'd wake up John. Regardless of whether or not the cuddling was supposed to have been romantic, the closeness had helped Calvin feel better when he'd been lying there feeling as though his heart was cracking in two. Waking John up earlier than necessary wouldn't be a very nice way to repay him, would it?

After taking a few more moments to enjoy John's comforting touch, Calvin slipped away and rolled out of bed. And then, as silently as he could, he rummaged through his luggage for his robe. Once he tied it on, he left to relieve himself, praying that it was early enough for him not to bother either of their hosts. After he was finished, he headed for the kitchen. Perhaps he could make both himself and John some breakfast.

Luckily, no one else was in the kitchen yet. Even better, there was a skillet resting on the stove, one that had probably been left out to dry the evening prior, so Calvin wouldn't need to make noise looking for one. After opening a couple of cabinets, Calvin found some eggs that had been stored in pickling lime. Perfect.

He spent some time starting the cast-iron stove by reigniting the fire in the firebox, which involved first cleaning it out and then putting in new wood, and then, Calvin was ready to cook. Using a splash of olive oil and a pinch of salt, Calvin cooked a large helping of scrambled eggs. While they sizzled in the skillet, he brewed some coffee too, first pulverizing some beans he'd found with a mortar and pestle. Hopefully they weren't too old.

It took a little while to clean up once he was finished making everything. He had to close the vents for every burner and hope no one would mind that he had started the fire for the cast-iron stove this early.

And all the while, Calvin's heart continued to thump with excitement. After having a couple of bites of eggs himself, he saved the rest for John. Since he'd only made enough coffee for one mug, he opted not to have a mug himself.

When Calvin reached the bedroom with the coffee and a plate of cooked eggs, John was still snoozing.

Sitting on the edge of the mattress, Calvin whispered a soft "Good morning," feeling a little sad that he had to wake John now. But the two of them couldn't overstay their welcome here.

At first, John only stirred a little and then settled again. Calvin's heart began hammering with even more intensity as he watched John's chest rise and fall slowly with sleep. God, he had no clue how John would react to either the breakfast or the night of snuggling.

His hands began to tremble as thoughts swirled around in his head. Holy hell, why was he putting himself through this? He had promised that he wouldn't let himself become too close to John. Wouldn't let their lives become too entangled. And now, he had spent the entire night in the man's embrace. Dammit, what if those cuddles were meant to have been platonic? Could Calvin stomach that? Could he even stand to continue working for John if that was the case? Calvin knew himself. He'd be pining for more of those embraces every Goddamned moment that they were alone.

Calvin moved to stand, thinking he'd sneak back into the kitchen, try to endure his moment of panic in peace, but his sudden movement was rough enough to rouse John from his slumber.

Before even fully opening his eyes, John started to smile, the corners of his lips twisting up ever so slightly, and the sight made Calvin's breath catch. Goodness, he was handsome.

"I, uhm, I cooked you some breakfast," Calvin said, sitting back down on the mattress. "Just some scrambled eggs."

John's mouth stretched into a proper smile as his eyes fluttered open the rest of the way.

"Mmm . . . that was very kind of you," he said.

"I wanted to thank you for . . . everything. I was horrible to you yesterday."

"No, Calvin, you weren't." John's voice was slow and sweet like honey. "You were hurting."

Calvin's cheeks warmed. How could John be so forgiving?

When John moved to sit up, Calvin scooted back a bit. John propped himself up with a pillow, resting it against the headboard, and then Calvin handed him the plate, praying John wouldn't notice that his hands were still slightly shaky. He held on to the coffee so that John could focus on the food.

"I normally only have coffee for breakfast," John said. "But I c-c-c- . . ." John paused, flinching from his error. Affection bloomed in Calvin's chest. "But I c-can't say no to this."

Calvin's face flushed from the implied compliment.

Thank God John seemed to be unbothered by the fact that they had spent the night together in bed. Calvin couldn't help but feel more hopeful that maybe the nighttime closeness *had* meant something.

Questions began flitting into Calvin's mind, each of them bringing forth more and more fluttery feelings. Would John like the eggs? Would he ever want to cuddle in the future? Tonight, maybe? Or . . . or every night? Soon, Calvin's entire body was humming from the flurry of them.

Overcome with the need to busy himself with something else, Calvin took a sip of coffee. As soon as the liquid sloshed over his tongue, however, he remembered that the coffee was supposed to be for John. Upon realizing his error, Calvin opened his mouth, letting the coffee fall back into the cup. His eyes went wide. Oh, God, what the hell was that? Why hadn't he swallowed it?

John's eyes snapped up to meet his. Calvin froze, his mouth still hanging open.

"Sorry, I, uhm, I . . ." Calvin stammered. "See, I brewed it for you."

As though *that* somehow explained his ridiculous faux pas.

Crooking an eyebrow, John said, "Really?"

Smiling sheepishly, Calvin nodded.

"But you spit in it."

"Yeah . . ." Calvin scrunched up his nose. "Not on purpose."

Slowly, John said, "Right."

John and Calvin continued to stare at one another as Calvin's face began to heat, embarrassment creeping up his neck. And then John started to laugh, and Calvin's embarrassed blush turned into something else: longing. John's melodious hum of a laugh tickled Calvin's ears. Jesus Christ, how Calvin wanted him!

After John composed himself, he heaved a long sigh and closed his eyes, tilting his head back to rest it against the pillow.

"Oh, Calvin, you're too f-f-f-funny," John said. "May I still have the coffee?"

"Yeah? I'm surprised you still want it."

Lulling his head to the side, John opened one eye and said, "Yes, I want it. Well, unless there's m-more?"

Calvin frowned. "No, there's not."

"Well, then . . ." After balancing the plate of eggs on his lap, John took the mug from Calvin. He wet his lips, lifted the mug with a little "cheers" motion, and then chugged some of the tepid, spit-contaminated liquid down.

Upon swallowing, he recoiled slightly and scowled.

"Tastes fffunny," John said before smacking his lips a few times. "I wonder why."

Now this was interesting. Was John teasing him? *Without* the help of hard liquor? Calvin narrowed his eyes, scrutinizing John's expression. He honestly couldn't tell. God, why was the man so hard to read sometimes?

"Are you trying to be silly?" Calvin asked.

"No," John said, tilting his head. "Should I be?"

Calvin continued to study him. He *still* couldn't tell if John was teasing. Perhaps he could figure it out by being playful himself and then trying to interpret John's response.

Smiling wryly, Calvin flicked John's leg as hard as he could, though he wasn't sure how much John would feel it from beneath the blanket.

John's response was to stick his foot out and try to nudge Calvin with it, curling his knee and swinging his foot over toward him. When the ball of John's foot made contact with Calvin's lower back, a few pieces of egg fell off of John's plate and rolled onto the covers.

"Now look wh-wh-what happened," John said, his voice this strange mixture of seriousness and playfulness that Calvin hadn't heard from him before. "Really, Cal, you're supposed to be my business partner, not a thorn in my rear end."

Once again, John prodded Calvin with his foot, poking him with his big toe this time, but now, he was smiling, and the sweet little way he then said "hmm?," like maybe he was waiting for Calvin to play along, was enough to convince Calvin that, even though John had seemed a smidge serious before, he really *was* trying to have fun now.

"Are you serious?" Calvin spluttered through a very fake scoff. "I can't believe you'd blame me for a couple of rogue egg pieces!"

Calvin thought that John might push back, banter with him some more, but he only chewed on his lip for a moment, looking like he was maybe trying to contain a second bout of laughter, and then turned his attention to the mess on the bed. So, now John was finished being playful? What was happening? Calvin was starting to consider saying he was sorry for the food mishap when John plucked the small clump of eggs off of the mattress.

And threw it in Calvin's face.

The instant the cool mush hit Calvin's cheek, he let out a yelp, but then cupped a palm over his mouth, embarrassment rushing to his cheeks and making his face burn. God, Beatrice and Theodore had probably heard him!

John set his mug on the nightstand. And then, while Calvin was busy feeling stupid for his reaction to the egg pelting, John scooped up a few fingerfuls of eggs from his plate and flung them over. One of the bits hit Calvin on the nose.

Alright, so, John was very clearly being playful now.

"John!" Calvin scolded, chuckling. "Stop!"

John moved to scoop up even more. Calvin's hand shot out to clutch John's wrist, preventing him.

"Stop! *Please*," Calvin begged, still laughing a bit.

"Alright, fine," John said, now smiling madly.

Wow, that boyish smile of his. It was such a strange thing to see. Strange and wonderful. Surely there had to be *something* more than friendship between them. Right?

Heart thudding from the possibility, Calvin released John's wrist. He let his hand linger on the mattress, however, wishing he had the courage to take John's hand in his. While Calvin was busy trying to muster up the courage to chance his entire livelihood by brazenly holding his business partner's hand, the most marvelous thing happened: John covered Calvin's hand with his own.

John's hand curled around Calvin's, and for a few precious seconds—seconds that seemed to last forever in the best possible way—they held hands. John squeezed Calvin's hand—once, lightly, and then one more time, but with more *oomph*—before letting go. Calvin's heart pinched, the loss of John's touch making his chest ache, but then John set his plate on the nightstand and said, "I can't imagine you're c-comfortable like that," before scooting over.

And Calvin couldn't believe what was happening.

After lying his pillow flat, John lay back on the bed, and then raised up one of his arms, silently inviting Calvin to join him. Calvin's stomach flip-flopped from excitement. Swinging his legs onto the mattress, Calvin's could barely contain his elation as he rested his head on the pillow and settled next to John. Immediately, John snuggled close.

With a soft sigh, Calvin said, "I'm sorry I spat in your coffee."

"I know." John nuzzled his nose into Calvin's hair. Calvin squirmed a bit, though he loved the way it was tickling him. "When I told you that I thought the coffee tasted funny, I was being serious, though. Wh-wh-where'd you find the beans?"

"In a little sack."

"Hmm . . ." John's nose rubbed the side of Calvin's head a few more times. "I think m-m-maybe they were old."

"Damn," Calvin said. "I'm sorry." He took care to keep his voice level, even though every one of John's movements was threatening to make him unravel, causing his heart to soar and his breath to shake. "I hadn't noticed. If the coffee really *did* taste too bitter, though, it's probably for the best that I ruined it. Otherwise, you'd have felt obligated to pretend to like it, right?"

"Probably." Pulling him closer, John said, "We'll make some more at home."

Home. Calvin's heart stuttered, a little lightning bolt of happiness shocking his system. He had a *home.* He hadn't had a home since . . .

Quick as the wind, a rush of worry slammed into him, making Calvin's breath catch. He hadn't had a home since New York. And even then, that home had been a lie. What if *this* home was nothing more than a lie, too? No, John wasn't David. John was John.

Before Calvin could spiral further, John hummed sweetly, and that beautiful, melodious sound brought him back to the present moment. God, it was probably the loveliest sound in the world.

"Such f-funny ears," John whispered. "I hope you aren't upset with me for saying that."

Calvin huffed a soft laugh. "Don't you remember how much you yammered on about them when you'd had those cocktails?"

"Shhh . . ." John hushed him, and the sound sent a shiver up Calvin's spine.

Calvin couldn't help but be surprised that John was being so talkative and so silly. Maybe John was a little sleepy. People could be silly when they hadn't had enough sleep. Not that Calvin was complaining. It was nice to see John like this—playful and carefree. Calvin was fond of John's typical shyness, though, too. Calvin found it endearing.

While Calvin was lost in his thoughts, John nudged his nose against Calvin's ear, and the puff of warmth from his breath made Calvin shudder.

"Sorry," John said, his voice still quiet.

"No one has ever liked my ears before. Or, well, no one has ever *told me* that they liked them."

"Who says I like them?" John asked, and once again, Calvin was surprised that John could take such a serious tone when he was obviously trying to be silly.

"So, you're fixating on them because they're so hideous?"

"Mm-hmm." John's mouth moved right next to Calvin's ear again. "Grotesque, even."

Calvin chuckled. "Sure."

And then John's lips brushed the tip of Calvin's ear. It wasn't a kiss, exactly, but it wasn't *not* a kiss, either. Calvin's stomach tumbled. He wondered whether John might kiss him for real. Especially if Calvin rolled over to face him. Because they were definitely becoming something more than just business partners and friends. It was clear to him now.

Calvin let out a breath. "John . . ."

"Was that alright?" John asked, and Calvin managed a nod. John kissed Calvin's ear again, and though it was soft—his lips barely brushing Calvin's skin—it was more of a real kiss this time. "And—and that?"

Before Calvin could respond, there was a knock, and the sound caused both of them to startle, their bodies spasming in tandem. Calvin's heart began pounding even harder.

"Good morning," Beatrice said from the other side of the door. "If either of you made coffee with those beans that were on the table, I'm so very sorry for how it must have tasted. I went to throw them away last night, but I must have walked away before finishing the task."

Calvin sighed while John chuckled a little.

"Don't worry about it!" John said loudly, forgetting to move his mouth away from Calvin's ear. Calvin let out an "ack!" and reached up to cover his ear. "Sorry," John whispered.

"Did you two eat breakfast earlier, then?" Beatrice asked.

"Yes, we're fine," Calvin called back. "Thank you."

John sat up on his elbow some more, propping himself up higher, and called out, "W-w-w-we'll be leaving for home in a bit. Unless you need more help?"

"No, no, you've already helped us so much. We'll see you off soon, then."

"Great, thanks," John said back.

They listened to Beatrice's footsteps retreat toward the staircase. And then they both let out a breath. When John subsequently unhooked his arm from Calvin's waist, Calvin immediately felt a small pang of sadness from the loss of contact.

"We should probably pack up and put on some clothes." John sat up the rest of the way. "I told Michael we'd be back for lunch. Katherine might prepare something."

"Yeah," Calvin said, sitting up and clearing his throat. "Alright."

Over the next half hour, they took turns in the bathroom to wash up and ready themselves for their trip home. Once they were packed, they said a fast farewell to Theodore and Beatrice, promising to visit the next time they were in town, and then loaded everything into the hearse.

They sat in silence for the first stretch of the trip. Calvin let his mind wander as they rode through town, passing trolleys and other carriages on the way, and once they exited the Borough of Media, nearing Swarthmore, Calvin began to fret, uncertainty over the nature of his and John's relationship making his skin prickle with unease.

"Thank you for c-c-coming with me," John said, shifting closer to Calvin, close enough that their thighs were now pressed together.

Calvin let out a long breath, hoping, wishing, *praying*, for this to be romantic, but still too scared to broach the topic.

John said, "I really love working with you, Cal. And, well, the trip was m-m-mostly only for the embalming so there really was no need for you to have come."

"I enjoyed myself," Calvin said, putting as much reassurance and warmth into his voice as he could. "Not the embalming, but, uhm, everything else."

"I'm so happy to hear that."

John balanced the reins in his right hand and let his left fall to rest on Calvin's thigh. Calvin's breath hitched, want and fear mingling together and shooting through his veins. Thank *God* they were on a relatively vacant road now. What if someone saw them? Calvin's heart began hammering, terror still surging through his veins. He and David had *never* been so brazen. Sure, there were men who liked to show their friends they cared for them by being publicly affectionate in some way, but not Calvin. David had impressed upon him how important it was for people never to know that the two of them were together in a romantic sense. It would have been foolish, David had said, to be physically close with each other while people had been watching.

Calvin's cheeks burned. "John, maybe this isn't . . ."

Quickly, John removed his hand, recoiling as though he'd been burned by a hot pan.

"Sorry. I-I'm sorry," John stammered. "I shouldn't have . . . and, oh, back in Media . . . if—if I made you uncomfortable wh-wh-when we were in the bedroom—"

"No!" Calvin exclaimed. "You haven't made me uncomfortable. Not even for a second. I'm only trying to remind you that we're in public."

John crooked an eyebrow and looked around.

"We are?"

"Yes!" Calvin nearly shouted, but then John smiled this very sweet, sly-looking smile, and Calvin sighed. "You're trying to be funny. I'm having trouble knowing whether or not you're being serious lately. Which is new for me, by the way. I pride myself on being able to read people."

"Yes, Calvin, I'm being silly. I . . . well . . . there's no one nearby, so I thought . . ." John shook his head, his cheeks turning pink. "Doesn't m-m-matter what I thought. I'll keep my hands to myself while we're out. All of this is new to me."

"All of what?" Calvin asked, his tone slightly cheeky, though there was an unmistakable tinge of seriousness in it, too.

Calvin needed to hear John name what the two of them were.

"All of everything that's happened since last night," John said. "I hope I haven't . . . well, I hope you're . . . interested? In me, I mean? In a—a romantic sort of way?"

Calvin's chest pinched. *God*, how he wanted to pull John close and kiss him right then and there. What a sweet man he was.

"I'm interested," Calvin said. "I'm very interested."

John's lips curled into an uncertain smile. "Really?"

"Yes," Calvin confirmed. "Would you, uhm, like to read together when we're finished with lunch later? Spend some time in one of our rooms without Michael and Katherine?"

John's small smile blossomed, and so too did the blush on his cheeks, his entire face turning a lovely shade of crimson.

"Yes, Cal," John said. "Absolutely, yes."

"Good," Calvin said, intentionally knocking his knee with John's a few times in a playful manner. "I can't wait."

Chapter Eleven
Calvin

Hours later, John and Calvin reached home. After unloading the embalming supplies from their carriage, John left to take Agathe back to her stable while Calvin went inside. When Calvin stepped through the threshold, the scents of stewed vegetables and simmering broth filled his nostrils and caused his stomach to rumble. Well, John had been right about Katherine making lunch. Hopefully it would be ready soon. Obsessing over the state of his relationship with John had really worked up his appetite.

Luggage in hand, Calvin started toward his bedroom. Michael passed him on the staircase, clipping Calvin with his shoulder. Michael mumbled a curt "sorry" and continued to hurry toward the kitchen. Calvin rolled his eyes. When he reached his bedroom, his shoulder was still tingling from the unexpected physical contact. Michael's very essence seemed to be lingering, and Calvin's blood ran hot with irritation. But then . . .

Calvin's eyes fell upon the mahogany chest of drawers located in the corner of the room, and his stomach suddenly churned with a nauseating flare of self-reproach. Guilt rippled over Calvin's skin, making him feel warm and itchy, the image of those beautiful cuff links floating into his brain like a specter. Calvin released his hand, letting his luggage fall to the floor with a thud, and reached up to massage his temples, the knowledge that he had proven

Michael right—that he was a thief and a criminal—making him want to vomit on the spot. Dear God, what had he done? John liked him. John had made him his business partner. John wanted to be *romantic* with him. And Calvin had stolen from his brother. By trying to ensure that he would have a nest egg if and when he ever needed to stop working for Hall Funeral Services, Calvin had only increased his likelihood of losing what he now had with John.

Fuck!

What if Michael found out? What if Katherine found out? Oh, *God*, what if John ever stumbled upon those cuff links himself? He'd know they were Michael's. Even if Calvin managed to keep them hidden until Michael and Katherine moved out, John could still find them someday. Dammit, those cuff links, they'd be haunting him forever, their very existence threatening to unravel Calvin's life. He had created his very own version of the *Tell-Tale Heart* right here in his bedroom.

He had to return them. He had to return them and make it look as though he hadn't fucking stolen them. Calvin let out a long, slow breath to try to calm himself. He'd have to be clearheaded to make this work.

Desperation clawed at Calvin's insides, its sharpness making Calvin clench his teeth as he headed toward his sock drawer. Flustered, Calvin searched for the pair of off-white cotton socks where he'd stashed the cuff links.

Immediately upon finding them, Calvin stuffed them into his front pants pocket. He ran a palm over his face, telling himself that he needed to wipe away every trace of upset if he ever wanted this to work. Then, holding his head high, wearing what he hoped was a casual and neutral expression, he went out into the hall.

Minutes later, he was standing in the threshold of Michael's study, his heart threatening to burst right out of his chest. Michael was flipping through a stack of something. Receipts, perhaps. Calvin cleared his throat.

Michael looked up. "Can I help you with something?"

"Not exactly . . ." Calvin took a step forward and reached into his pocket for the cuff links. Extending his hand, Calvin unfurled his palm, and the two emeralds sparkled in the light that was pouring in through the window. "I found these in the hallway upstairs. Thought they might be yours."

Michael's eyebrows shot up. He looked down at the cuff links and then back up at Calvin.

"You . . . found them," he said slowly.

"I found them."

"In the hallway."

"In the hallway."

Pursing his lips, Michael narrowed his eyes, studying Calvin's face.

"Right," he said, his voice tinged with incredulity that made Calvin's insides turn into a soupy porridge of nervousness.

Michael took them and pushed them into the pocket of his pants. When Calvin turned to leave, Katherine called out from the kitchen.

"Lunch is ready!"

Calvin continued forward. Michael brushed past him, shoving Calvin with his shoulder even more forcefully than he had before.

At the table, Michael and Katherine sat on either end, while Calvin and John took the chairs in the middle, on opposite sides. When minutes passed and Michael had yet to make a spectacle, some of Calvin's lingering worry fell away. Michael seemed to relish making Calvin uncomfortable. If by now, halfway through the meal, Michael still hadn't brought up their conversation in the study, it seemed that Calvin had successfully fooled him. Thank God.

While Katherine was chattering about the recent engagement of a woman she knew from church, John's foot nudged Calvin's underneath the table. Even though Calvin thought it must have been a mistake, his heart fluttered all the same. But then he looked up to see John's lips firmly pressed together, almost like he was attempting to conceal a smile. So, Calvin tapped his foot back.

And then John tapped his.

And then Calvin retaliated.

And then, the second John's foot made contact with Calvin's shin, Michael cleared his throat very loudly, and both John and Calvin froze, their eyes widening in tandem.

"So, Calvin," Michael began, "Katherine and I were thinking that perhaps you could come to church with us sometime."

Katherine knitted her brows together. "We were?"

"Yes, we were. Don't you remember us talking about it a few weeks ago?" Michael asked, but before Katherine could reply, he waved a hand in the air and continued. "Anyway, we thought it might give you a chance to meet someone. I mean, now that you're no longer barely scraping by, it should be easier for you to find a wife. I *assume* you want to be married someday, yes?"

"Uhm . . ." Calvin's stomach was suddenly in his throat. "No. I mean, yes, maybe. I mean . . ." Calvin tried to catch John's eye, but John's gaze had fallen to his soup. "I'm not interested in church. We oversee so *many* church services for our business and every-thing."

What the hell was happening? Was this related to the cuff links? Or had it been the playful kicking? Or, hell, maybe both? Fear continued to percolate in Calvin's veins. Why was Michael suddenly so interested in his life?

"Well, that's true," Michael said. "But one shouldn't stay single forever."

Calvin opened his mouth to speak, but it made this horrible clicking sound. He shut it, looking to John for help. While John was no longer just staring at the little cooked vegetables floating around in his bowl, Calvin knew by the way he was sitting—his shoulders pulled forward like he was crumpling in on himself—that he was probably as flabbergasted as Calvin.

Calvin tried to calm himself. He had to think of something. Michael had hired him because of his charm. Or, well, not exactly. Calvin had convinced Katherine to feel sorry for him because of his charm, though, which had *led* to him being hired. Good enough.

Finally, Calvin said, "Agreed. In fact, I'm hoping to return to New York eventually. Temporarily. I met someone there a couple of years back. Someone through church. Lovely woman."

"And she's been waiting for you all this time?" Michael asked, a bemused smile pulling at his lips.

Calvin had to bury the urge to punch him in the nose. "I can't say. But I hadn't been in a position to try to court her before. So, well, I think I ought to try now that I have some more stability." He took a pause, folding his hands in his lap. "Don't worry about me, Michael. I have my prospects."

"Glad to hear it," Michael said, some harshness in his tone. Quickly, Michael wiped his mouth with a napkin and then flung it onto the table. "Alright, I'm heading back to the factory. I'll be home later."

While Michael and Katherine exchanged a kiss, Calvin tried to catch John's eye, but John was too busy shriveling up like a fallen leaf to notice. So, Calvin kicked John's shin with his foot. When John looked up, there was unmistakable hurt in his eyes. Worse, his face was pale. Ashen, even. Oh, how Calvin wished he could tell him right then and there that there was no woman in New York! Only a horrible man named David and his pretty new lover whose spindly mustache made him look like a buffoon.

Once Calvin heard Michael slam the front door, he offered Katherine what he hoped was a convincingly pleasant smile.

"Soup was excellent, Katherine, thank you." He pushed himself to stand. "Even though I'd love to stay and chat, I need some time to relax. It was a long trip."

"Alright, well, let me know if you ever change your mind about church. I still have a few friends who haven't married yet. I'm sure they'd—"

"Yes, I will," Calvin said curtly, interrupting her. "Thanks."

All the way to his bedroom, Calvin continued to feel slightly lightheaded from the intensity of everything that had transpired since he and John had come home from the embalming. God, he hoped John would come upstairs soon so they could read together. John would still want to, wouldn't he?

Thirty minutes passed. Calvin left briefly to relieve himself, but otherwise, he stayed in his room trying to read, though his book couldn't hold his attention. Once, Calvin crept out into the hall to see if he could hear John and Katherine talking from up here, but he couldn't.

Then, while Calvin was sitting cross-legged on the floor in front of some playing cards, setting up solitaire, the sound of heavy footsteps floated in from the hall. Calvin held his breath, *praying* that John would knock. Several seconds of silence followed.

Unable to stand even one more minute of waiting to see if John would come in, Calvin hopped to his feet. He yanked open the door and found John on the other side.

Calvin let out the breath. "Where were you?"

"Sorry, I wasn't sure if . . . if you'd still want to read with me," John said, his voice small.

"Of course I want to read with you." Calvin motioned for John to come inside, but then stopped him once he remembered that Katherine was still home. Katherine and Michael's bedroom shared a wall with Calvin's. He hated to think that Katherine might come up and hear what they were talking about. "Actually, mind if we read in your room instead?"

John shook his head. "Not at all."

Calvin snatched a book from his bookshelf at random, not even bothering to see if it was the one he'd been trying to read earlier (hopefully he wouldn't really be reading it much anyway), and followed John across the hall. Once they were both inside, Calvin caught John's hand and urged him closer.

"I hope you know that there's no woman in New York," Calvin said, kicking the door shut with his foot. "I only wanted Michael to stop trying to provoke me."

"I thought there m-m-might not be."

"Why were you worried that I wouldn't want to read with you anymore, then?"

"Don't you f-f-feel . . . ashamed?" John asked, eyes falling to the hardwood floor. "Of this? Of us?"

"Why—" Calvin started to say, but cut himself off. Oh. He'd never told John that he'd been with a man before. John probably thought that Michael's . . . whatever-the-hell-that-was had made him feel uneasy. It *had* made Calvin feel uneasy, but not because he was experiencing shame over liking a man. With every bit of tenderness he could muster, Calvin said, "No. I'm not ashamed. Not even a little. I . . ." He trailed off, biting his lip. Calvin wanted to tell John that he'd been with a man, but he couldn't bring himself to tell him about *David*, specifically, not with how things had ended. He couldn't bring himself to tell John that his old business partner had ripped out his heart, betrayed him in their shared home, and then had thrown Calvin out onto the streets. "I've liked men before," Calvin said instead. "Haven't you?"

"Yes, but only from afar," John answered. "I've k-k-kept to myself for most of my life."

"But you're not ashamed of us," Calvin said, needing to confirm. "Are you?"

"Heavens, no, Calvin. I-I like you. I wanted to continue . . . the . . . the . . ."

"Cuddling?" Calvin finished for him. John nodded, smiling. Tentatively, Calvin took a step closer and placed his hands on John's waist, letting his book fall to the floor with a thud. "Do we *have* to read, then? Or can we relax in the bed together instead?"

"Yes, I would prefer the . . . relaxing," John said.

Grinning, Calvin tugged John toward the bed. "Good. Because I'm a little cold. I'm hoping you can help me warm up," he said, a playful hitch in his voice.

All of Calvin's worries over Michael melted away the moment they reached the mattress. Simultaneously, both men removed their suit jackets and waistcoats. As Calvin tossed his over John's chair, John's hand found the small of his back.

"I thought you said you were c-cold," John teased.

"Don't make me spit in your coffee tomorrow."

"Oh, *that's* why I have a headache," John lamented, closing his eyes and throwing his head back. "We forgot to make more coffee. I normally have two or three cups every m-m-morning."

"I'll help you feel better."

Both men swiftly removed their neckties and unfastened their stiff linen collars before Calvin then took John by the hand. Calvin sat on the bed, tugging John's fingers as he lay back and coaxing him to follow. John settled next to him, and the two faced one another. With a gentle smile, Calvin reached up to push his fingers through John's hair. Luckily, John hadn't coated it with pomade that morning. Probably because there hadn't been a service for them to run. "How's this?"

John smiled. "Heavenly."

"Does it help?"

"Not really," John said, chuckling at Calvin's subsequent scoff. "Sorry. I still like it, though."

"Well, that's something," Calvin said. "Would coffee help? I'd be happy to make some for you."

"Oh, no, I wouldn't want to be awake all night," John said. "Or maybe we'll be awake n-now anyway."

Excitement shot through Calvin's veins. God, *now* he'd be awake all night—now that John had implied that they *both* might be awake for . . . potentially sexual reasons.

Calvin's cock started to swell. How *wonderful* it was to imagine that he might spend the next ten or twelve hours wrapped up in John's embrace, threading his fingers through John's hair. Or, oh *God*, kissing him. Or *more*.

Heart thumping wildly, Calvin studied John's lips. They were perfect. Plump and pink. With the tiniest bit of wetness from when John's tongue had skirted out of his mouth earlier. Calvin *really* wanted to kiss them. But . . .

Oh, hell, he wanted their first kiss to be perfect. Because John was perfect. And it couldn't be perfect now, could it? Not while John's head was pounding from not having had his favorite morning beverage. What a sad memory that would be. Especially if it was John's first kiss ever, which seemed likely.

"I will happily stay awake with you the entire night," Calvin said. "But I won't kiss you. I need you to know that."

After a loud snort, John said, "What? Wh-wh-why not?"

"Because you have a headache," Calvin said, letting his hand fall so that his thumb could trace John's jaw. "And I want our first kiss to be perfect."

"Oh. I see." Averting his eyes, John licked his lips again, making them look even *more* kissable. It had Calvin regretting everything he'd said less than three seconds ago. "Well, what if . . . what if I k-kiss you instead?"

"Nope. No. I won't let you."

"N-not a real kiss. Not . . ." John paused and let out a huff. Calvin knew it meant that he was becoming tongue-tied, probably because he was nervous. It was magnificently sweet. "Let me show you."

When John leaned forward, Calvin placed a finger to his lips.

"I'm not sure if I should trust you," Calvin said.

And then, John pursed his lips and kissed the tip of Calvin's finger.

"I meant like that," he said.

Elation bubbled up inside Calvin's chest, starting as a little tingly warmth near his heart and rippling outward to the top of his head and the tips of his toes. He almost felt like he was weightless enough to fly.

"Ah, well, that's . . ." Calvin's voice faltered, so overwhelmed by that itty-bitty kiss that he'd momentarily forgotten how to speak. After letting out a breath, Calvin said, "I think that's the sweetest not-real kiss I've ever received."

He and John smiled at each other, and then John leaned forward and kissed the tip of Calvin's nose. And then he planted one soft kiss on Calvin's cheek. And then one more slightly lower. Calvin's breath shook.

"I think this might be cheating," he said as John pressed a kiss to his jaw. "God, I thought I was the one with the criminal mind."

John hummed in response, the sound almost a laugh, and then he scooted forward on the mattress, still propping himself up with his elbow, and nuzzled Calvin's nose with his own.

John whispered, "It isn't cheating. Because you're not k-kissing me back."

"But you're making me *want* to kiss you back."

"I know." John's lips traveled back toward Calvin's ear again, planting tiny kisses on the way, and then he pressed them to the tip of Calvin's earlobe, sending shivers up Calvin's spine.

When Calvin felt John pause and let out a long breath of his own, he knew that John was working up the courage to say something. John couldn't have been more endearing if he tried.

"Are you mine, Calvin?" John finally whispered.

"Only if you're mine too."

"I've been yours, I think. Only I couldn't t-t-tell you before."

He kissed Calvin's ear again, and Calvin sighed and then let out a whine, one that sounded so needy it had him blushing with embarrassment.

"Cal, I want to keep kissing you," John whispered.

Calvin swallowed thickly and replied, "I want that too."

Slowly, John began peppering kisses down Calvin's neck, and then Calvin let out that embarrassing whine again.

"If you continue kissing me like *that*, I'll continue making that silly noise," Calvin said, his breathing slow and shallow and rough.

"I like that noise." John placed a palm flat to Calvin's chest and urged him backward. Calvin didn't resist. He fell back onto the mattress, and John followed, pressing his lips to Calvin's neck again. "Keep m-m-making it."

Calvin was practically overcome with the need to have John kiss every inch of him. Except maybe his lips. Because, somehow, it was really, really exciting to throw logical progression out the window like this. Calvin unfastened the top buttons of his shirt, and the moment some of his chest was showing, John began kissing him lower, first pressing his lips to Calvin's collarbone and then to the top of his chest. John moved Calvin's shirt out of the way and then started venturing toward Calvin's nipple, but paused when he was only an inch or two away.

Looking up to meet Calvin's eyes, he said, "Is this . . ." He trailed off, and his face reddened. "Do you like this? I-I can stop. I know you said no k-k-kissing. I swear I had only intended to kiss your cheek and maybe your f-f-funny little ears. But n-now I want to keep going."

"I love it," Calvin said, touching his fingers to John's cheek. For a moment, he wondered what could be causing John's face to burn with such intensity, but then he realized that John had been stuttering a bit more ever since they'd climbed into bed. Perhaps that was it. "If you're feeling embarrassed right now, like maybe you feel as though you're not finding the right words, I need you to know that I'm never bothered by it. Not when we're having meals together or running a funeral together. Not in bed, either."

Huffing a laugh, John said, "I will never understand how you're able to read my m-mind like that. So, may I . . ."

"Keep kissing me," Calvin confirmed. "Please."

Lowering his head, John resumed kissing Calvin's chest. When his lips lightly brushed Calvin's nipple, Calvin sucked in a breath, and then John flicked his tongue over the tip. Blood rushed to Calvin's crotch, making his pants feel tight.

"Oh, *God*." Calvin's eyes rolled backward as he pressed his head more firmly into the pillow. John teased his nipple again, running his tongue over it. Jesus Christ, it felt so incredible. David had never played with his nipples. Not ever. Hell, David had barely seemed concerned with Calvin's pleasure at all. "More of that."

John continued to tickle Calvin's nipple with his tongue, his hand moving to unfasten the next button on Calvin's shirt. In mere seconds, John finished unbuttoning the rest, but paused when he reached Calvin's pants. Sitting up, Calvin swiftly shrugged off his suspenders, and then scrambled to unbutton his pants himself, stopping only when he realized that John's face was now as red as a ripe tomato.

"Sorry," Calvin said. "Am I moving too fast?"

"No." John's eyes flickered to Calvin's pants. "But I've never . . ."

"Wherever you want to kiss is fine. I'm not expecting . . . *everything* right now. But I'm excited, and my excitement is becoming uncomfortable. Because of these pants, I mean."

"I-I want to kiss you. Everywhere. Everywhere you'll let me."

Affection tugged on Calvin's heart. "Alright, well, I'll take these off, then."

While Calvin worked to remove his pants, his stomach started fluttering madly, nervousness percolating inside of him. Naked, Calvin lay back on the mattress, and John settled beside him, kissing Calvin's cheek. He buried his face in the crook of Calvin's neck.

"I haven't looked yet," John said. "May I?"

Calvin's heart was now thudding so wildly that blood was whooshing past his eardrums. All of this was so strange. Not only because John was lying here fully clothed while he himself was completely naked. Not only because the two of them hadn't even kissed yet. But because Calvin knew that John was the sort of man who would take care of him better than David ever had. And that realization, while wonderful, was a little terrifying, too. Calvin had never been with someone so sweet. Calvin's eyes flickered to his very hard, very exposed cock, standing straight up, the tip of his foreskin wet from leaking so much precum, and he had to inhale a couple of breaths to try to rein in his nervousness.

"Yeah," he said. "Yeah, of course."

Calvin felt John's head shift against him.

"*Mmmf.*" John let out a little sound before burying his face in Calvin's neck again. "I think I need a m-m-moment." His lips brushed Calvin's collarbone. "May I touch you?"

"I'd love it if you touched me."

Slowly, John's hand moved down Calvin's torso, over the smattering of light-brown chest hair, over the taut muscles of his stomach, and then John's fingertips brushed the base of his cock. Calvin inhaled a shaky breath. When John then wrapped his hand around Calvin's length, Calvin responded instinctively by bucking his hips. Before Calvin could speak, John let out a long, low moan.

"*Oh, God, Cal*," John breathed, shuddering and trembling against Calvin's side. "Sorry. I'm sorry. I . . . I . . ."

It took Calvin a few seconds to realize what it was that John was trying to say, and the moment he knew what it was, a warm fondness filled his chest.

"Did you come?" Calvin asked, cupping John's chin and forcing him to meet his eyes.

John nodded, his cheeks crimson.

Calvin's heart swelled, the fondness he felt toward John now too much to contain. He *had* to kiss him. Right now.

"I love that," Calvin said. "Really. It's . . . oh, God, that's so sweet and so flattering." Calvin's thumb brushed John's bottom lip. "Does your head still hurt? Please say no."

With a small shake of his head, John said, "No."

"Good."

And then they both lunged forward, slamming their lips together, and a needy moan escaped Calvin's mouth. Again and again their lips met, each time sending little bolts of electrical current shooting through Calvin's veins. His body buzzed with elation and desire. While they kissed, John started to pump his hand, the sensation causing heat to pool low in Calvin's belly. He lifted his hips once more, fucking up into John's hand.

"I want to come too," Calvin said, breaking their kiss.

"Should I . . ." John ran his tongue over his lips. "I still want to k-kiss you. Everywhere."

"Then kiss me. Everywhere."

Calvin turned onto his back. John resumed kissing him, first on his neck and then on his chest and then on his stomach. All the while, his hand lazily traveled up and down the length of Calvin's shaft. Calvin's entire body continued to thrum, excitement making his skin tingle. John pressed his lips to Calvin's cock, first to his foreskin and then, once he'd pulled the foreskin back, to its naked head. Calvin let out a low moan, his head swimming with anticipation.

Parting his lips, John took the tip into his mouth and sucked. One of Calvin's hands found John's head, and he threaded his fingers through John's hair. Gingerly, John swirled his tongue, encircling the head of Calvin's cock, and then took more of him into his mouth.

"Incredible, John. You're incredible," Calvin said, a hint of wonderment in his voice. It wasn't as though he hadn't been pleasured like this before, but nothing he'd ever experienced with David could compare. Gentle and caring and tender, John was unlike David in every way. And the way John was touching him, like John was completely besotted with him, it was making every second of their intimacy immensely special. Pleasure building, Calvin fucked upward into John's mouth and said, "I'm so close."

In response, John increased the speed of his movements, taking more of Calvin's cock into his mouth with each bob of his head, his hand continuing to work the base. Calvin's muscles started to tighten, his balls lifting, toes curling. The hair on the back of his neck seemed to stand on end.

"I'm coming," he moaned softly only seconds before his cock started to pulse.

Calvin's eyes widened, his mouth hanging open, as he watched John swallow every drop of his ejaculate. And when Calvin's cock stopped pulsing, John lingered and sucked once more, as though he really wanted to consume every bit of Calvin's orgasm.

"Dear God," Calvin blurted as John climbed up to join him. "I hope I can return the favor soon."

John nuzzled the side of Calvin's face and kissed his cheek.

"Cal, I'm sorry for before," he said, his nose still pressed to Calvin's skin.

"Don't be. Please. Everything was perfect," Calvin said, turning to capture John's mouth in a kiss. And, *oh*, how he loved that he could taste himself on John's lips. "Completely perfect."

"I became too excited."

"I know. And I loved that. Truly."

"W-w-was I . . ." John trailed off and cleared his throat. "Did you like the rest?"

"*Way* too much. Where'd you even learn?"

John fell backward onto the mattress and stared up at the ceiling.

"I saw two men once. Back in M-Media. I'd been working, and one of the poles had broken off a casket I'd finished. Only one hour or so before the start of the f-f-funeral. I had to fix it, but there was no time for me to run home and find my t-t-tools, so the lady of the house—a woman named Florence—said I could borrow some from her husband. I went to the shed, and . . . there her husband was with a c-c-cock in his mouth."

Calvin burst out laughing, and then John laughed too.

"I think the other man was one of Florence's cousins." John lulled his head to the side, locking eyes with Calvin. "I know it's strange to say this, but I've been w-w-*wishing* I could try that ever since. God, that . . . that was probably four years ago now."

Chuckling still, Calvin scooted closer, and they shared a kiss.

"Well, you must have seen enough," Calvin said. "It certainly seemed like you knew what you were doing down there."

John replied, "Twenty seconds or so."

"Did you ever tell Florence?"

"Heavens, no." John seemed to shudder from the thought. "I haven't ever managed to look her husband in the eye since it happened. Especially . . . especially because I've thought of that moment so many times in private. God, he's not even that handsome, but . . . there you have it."

Laughing warmly, Calvin pressed a kiss to John's shoulder, kissing the fabric of his shirt. God, John was so fucking perfect. Hopefully John wouldn't try to ask Calvin about his previous sexual experiences. Calvin still had no interest in talking about David, especially since the mere thought of his former lover still sometimes made him feel as though his heart was being crushed. Best to change the subject, probably.

"I feel so strange that you're still fully clothed while I'm not," Calvin said. "I think we ought to fix that."

"Yes, it is rather uncomfortable with my clothes . . . wet like this," John remarked, making a sour face. "But I-I'm a little worried about the fact that the first time you'll see me, I won't be . . . erect. N-not like you were."

"Are you worried I won't like what I see?"

"Somewhat."

"I am *positive* that I will," Calvin said, tugging on the top buttons of John's shirt. "Hm, you'll need to clean yourself up too, won't you? Mind if I fetch a wet rag from the bathroom?"

"Ugh, how embarrassing," John groaned, covering his face with his hands for a moment before removing them again. "Alright. Go ahead."

"I'll borrow a robe," Calvin said, scrambling off the mattress. "Be right back."

After Calvin found a robe, he rushed to the bathroom, snatching a towel from the linen closet on the way, and then wet it with water from the sink. Thank God Katherine still hadn't come upstairs. When he returned to the bedroom, John was standing next to the bed, completely nude, his hands covering his privates.

Stopping a few feet away, Calvin took a moment to admire him. John was perfect, with a broad, beautiful chest and a stomach that had the sweetest bit of pudge. Both his chest and his stomach were covered in a smattering of beautiful brown hair. Taking in the sight, Calvin was finding it hard to breathe. Slowly, Calvin came closer. John's tentative half smile was immensely cute.

"Beautiful," Calvin said, his breathing still a little shallow. "John, you're so beautiful."

John's mouth twisted into an uncertain smile. "Really?"

"Every inch. Or, every inch I can see. But . . ." Calvin's eyes flitted to John's hands. "Maybe I can see the rest of you too?"

After a moment of hesitation, John removed his hands, revealing his flaccid cock—thick but short—and the mass of pubic hair with some white still clinging to it. Calvin fell to his knees. When he looked up, he saw that John's smile had faded and had been replaced by a grimace.

"I p-promise it's a little more impressive when I'm excited," he said.

Calvin snorted. "It's plenty impressive now too." He touched the towel to John's skin, causing him to startle. "I love how intimate this is," Calvin remarked. "Thank you for letting me see you. And clean you up."

"It's . . . strange," John said. After a pause, he added, "But I like it."

After one more rub of the towel, Calvin stood and wrapped his arms around John's neck, pulling him in for a kiss. John's hands slipped inside the robe.

"Will you sleep here t-tonight?" John asked, his voice back to a whisper.

Calvin's heart thudded, that swell of nervousness returning. It was so scary to think that he might have his heart broken. Or lose his home. But how could he say no? He liked John. More than he thought he ever would. And they'd had such a wonderful afternoon together already.

"Every evening from now on," Calvin said, ignoring the pinprick of worry that was still making his stomach churn slightly. "We'll have to be secretive, but that shouldn't be a problem, right?"

"No, I wouldn't think so," John said, before kissing him once more.

They rested their foreheads together, and then John exhaled a shaky breath that made Calvin want to pull him even closer. Calvin's hands traveled to John's hips, and then he took a small step forward, pressing his pelvis to John's.

Calvin swallowed thickly and said, "I'm not sure I can believe this is real."

"It is real, Cal," John said. "I p-promise."

Calvin's lips curled into a small smile. It was real. God, how lucky he was.

"I won't ever break your heart, John," Calvin remarked, saying the words that he himself wanted to hear. Perhaps John would like hearing them as well. Calvin pressed a kiss to John's nose. He waited for John to say the same thing back, but John only nuzzled his cheek.

It was enough. At least, it was enough for now.

Calvin took John's hand and pulled him toward the bed. Then Calvin shimmied out of his robe, and the two lay together, cuddling close.

And then they kissed and kissed and kissed. Until their lips were sore.

Chapter Twelve
John

By the time John woke in the morning, Calvin was no longer in bed. Curling into a smaller ball, John winced as his stomach began roiling unpleasantly from worry. Perhaps Calvin was regretting everything. Wouldn't he have stayed in bed otherwise?

After spending the next couple of minutes too lost in his worries to move, John sat up, surrendering to the need to relieve himself, and as soon as his blanket slid off of his bare torso, he was struck with an intense feeling of unease. Being naked was making him feel vulnerable, even more vulnerable than he'd felt when Calvin had been on his knees in front of him, cleaning the ejaculate off of his pelvic area. Calvin must regret their intimacy, if not because they were both men, then because maybe Calvin had come to the conclusion that John wasn't right for him. Because why on earth would a personable man like Calvin ever want someone like him?

Uncertain of how Calvin might react when they saw each other again, John thought that he'd better put on a proper suit, rather than only a nightshirt and a bathrobe. After throwing on a robe—the very same one Calvin had borrowed the previous evening—John chose a suit from his closet. It was one of his favorites—tweed and the color of chocolate and a perfect fit. Never once had he not felt handsome in it. Hopefully Calvin would think he was handsome in it too.

John's stomach continued to churn as he made his way to the bathroom. After washing up, John changed into his suit and headed to the kitchen for some coffee, his heart hammering nervously while he mentally prepared himself to see his . . . his what? Lover, maybe? Or, ex-lover, perhaps, if Calvin no longer wanted their closeness to continue.

When John rounded the corner to the kitchen, he found Calvin by the cast-iron stove and oven, baking something.

"Cal . . ." John's throat tightened, and he cursed inwardly. Apparently, he was back to being strangled by his godforsaken shyness.

Calvin turned to face him, a huge smile stretching across his face the moment their eyes locked. Relieved, John tried to smile back, but he was so overwhelmed that he seemed to be having trouble connecting with his body. It felt like he was floating, Calvin's beautiful smile making him weightless. *Thank God* Calvin seemed to be happy to see him.

"Good morning," Calvin said, coming toward him. John's stomach tumbled. He hoped that Calvin would hug him, but Calvin held up his hands instead, revealing his flour-coated palms. "I'm baking."

"I thought I smelled something sweet. Wh-what are you baking, exactly?"

"Funeral cookies!" Calvin exclaimed excitedly. "I've been wanting to make some ever since we had that whole terrible mishap with the scarf. I thought that maybe we could start offering them for an extra charge. Let me show you."

Calvin motioned for John to come closer. On the worktable was a batch of overly browned cookies, each of them with a little cross on top. John moved to take one, but Calvin smacked his hand.

"Don't eat those, you silly man! Look how burned they are!"

Heat rushed to John's cheeks. Well, Calvin wasn't *exactly* behaving like he regretted the previous evening, but that smack hadn't been the nicest, either.

While John kept his gaze fixed on the little crosses atop the cookies, Calvin said, "John, what's wrong?" in a soft voice that was so much sweeter.

"N-nothing," John lied, though he suspected he wasn't sounding particularly convincing, which was then confirmed when Calvin let out a forceful breath and repeated his name. He'd better tell Calvin the truth. "Wh-why'd you leave without waking me?"

Calvin tilted his head slightly. "What do you mean? I woke you before I came down here."

Both of John's eyebrows shot up, and he swiveled to face Calvin.

"Oh. Really?"

Calvin snorted. "*Yes!* And you fell right back asleep. Don't you remember?"

John shook his head. Michael had told him that he was a heavy sleeper, someone who could fall back asleep in the middle of a conversation if he hadn't yet woken fully when he was having it.

"No," John said sheepishly.

"I wouldn't have left without making sure you knew everything was fine between us," Calvin said tenderly before taking John's hand. "More than fine. Fantastic." He pressed a kiss to John's knuckles. "I'm sorry I smacked you. I was only trying to be silly."

Lowering his voice to a whisper, John asked, "Are you . . . still mine, then?"

"Of course." Calvin looked over John's shoulder, probably checking the entrance to the kitchen to make sure there was no one nearby. Then, he pressed a kiss to John's lips. "I'm yours, John."

John was too touched, too relieved, to even manage a reply. He'd have chastised himself for it, but Calvin continued to look at him with such remarkable fondness that John hoped Calvin wasn't too upset that he couldn't say something sickly sweet right back to him. Instead, John ran his tongue over his lips, relishing the way they were still tingling from Calvin's touch, and wished that they could kiss some more.

"Do you want to help me with the next batch?" Calvin asked. "Hopefully I won't burn those too."

With a shy nod, John said, "Yes, I'd like that."

Calvin picked up a tin measuring cup and handed it to John.

"I made up the recipe myself since I have no clue what *real* funeral cookies are supposed to taste like. I thought caraway seeds might be interesting? I feel like I've seen them in baked goods. Biscuits, maybe? Or muffins? Either way, I wanted to try them so I roasted a few in a pan. What are your thoughts on them?"

"I have no problem with them."

"Alright, well, then we'll try them." Calvin rubbed his hands together. "Would you mind scooping two and a half cups of flour into the bowl?"

"Simple enough," John said.

Well, he hoped it would be. He had never baked anything before. Tin cup in hand, John reached into the flour sack, collecting enough that the white powder extended well beyond the rim, making a little mound on top. When he then moved to dump it into the bowl, Calvin's hand caught his forearm, and John inadvertently released the cup, sending flour wafting into the air as soon as the tin made contact with the worktable. After the little white cloud cleared, John noticed that both of their suits were now speckled with white. And, funnily enough, so was Calvin's face.

"So, thank you for that," Calvin said.

"Sorry, I—"

"One second," Calvin interrupted, holding up a finger, and then, before John could react, Calvin took a bit of flour off of the tabletop and blew it in John's face.

John recoiled, but sputtered a laugh. "Calvin!" he scolded.

And then Calvin blew a second bit over at him. John sneezed.

"Why are you punishing me?" John asked, still laughing. "Everything was going well before you knocked my hand!"

"I was stopping you from putting too much flour in the bowl."

"But that was only one c-cup!"

"That's not how you measure cups!" Calvin said through a cackle.

"Why not?"

With a shake of his head, Calvin took the tin from the work-table and plunged it back into the bag of flour. When he lifted it out, it looked exactly the same as John's had.

"I know you think I'm saying that this is correct, but I'm only trying to show you why it's not." Calvin lifted the cup until the top was level with John's eyes. "See the markings? One cup means filling it to the top. *Only* to the top. Not *over*filling it."

"Ah." John lowered his head. "Now I feel f-f-foolish."

"Don't," Calvin said before taking a pinch of flour and flicking it onto John's suit. "Alright, *now* you can feel foolish."

"Oh, for heaven's sake, Cal!" John said with a chuckle.

In retaliation, John plunged his hand into the bag and took out a whole fistful of flour. By the time he had enough, Calvin was already backing away, saying things like "let's not be hasty" and "we're partners, remember?," but John ignored Calvin's pretend pleas. Lunging forward, John clutched the lapel of Calvin's suit with his free hand and then proceeded to smash the clump of flour into Calvin's hair with the other.

"John!" Calvin cried.

And then they both erupted with laughter as their hands found each other's waists.

"We keep fighting with food," Calvin said, beaming at him.

"Sorry," John said, though he wasn't really.

"I think this must be how you show someone you like them, hmm?" Calvin towed their hips together, and they both swayed a little. "By being silly."

John's cheeks began to tingle with the most wonderful warmth. He loved when Calvin was playful with him. It was wonderful. He had been having fun being playful right back. It was as though he'd refound a part of himself that he'd long forgotten.

"Well, I'm not silly with anyone else, so, yes, I think that's a f-f-fair statement." John pulled Calvin closer. "Back in Media yesterday morning, I was confused for a m-m-moment when you flicked my leg and made me drop those bits of eggs. At first, I thought maybe you were mad that I'd pointed out the funny taste in the coffee. But, then, once I realized you were trying to have fun with me . . ." He shrugged. "It made me want to try to be silly too. Because I wanted to . . . to make you laugh."

Calvin's smile broadened, and he sighed. "God, what a sweet man you are, John."

Staring into Calvin's lovely brown eyes, John felt a sudden pressure in his chest, as though his heart were swelling from the rush of *like*. Goodness, he liked Calvin so much. More than he would have thought possible.

Their lovesick stares were interrupted by a loud clearing of the throat.

Both John and Calvin immediately pushed off of one another, turning toward the sound in tandem.

It was Michael.

"John, I need to speak with you," he said, his tone harsh. "Privately."

In an instant, every ounce of blood left John's face. Lightheaded, John took a step back, and one of his hands found the edge of the worktable.

"Go ahead. I'll finish the cookies," John heard Calvin remark, his voice seemingly miles and miles away.

It took John a few extra seconds before he could move, and even then, even once he finally forced himself to follow Michael, his legs shook with every step.

When they were both through the entryway to Michael's office, Michael turned to him, rolled his eyes, and sighed.

"Jesus Christ, John, you look as though you might faint," he said, taking John by the forearm and leading him over to the little love seat. John sat without hesitation. "Breathe."

"Don't hurt him," John pleaded, his voice so soft he could barely even hear himself.

"Did I hurt him for stealing Katherine's necklace? No. So, why would I hurt him for . . . for *that*? Especially when you were clearly a . . . a willing participant." Michael closed his eyes and pinched the bridge of his nose. "Look, John, you being with a man, it isn't . . . I mean, most people wouldn't like it, but that's not what bothers me. I've known for forever that you . . . that you like men. I've had some time to sit with the information."

"But, then, what—"

"I'm not upset that he's a *man*. I'm upset that he's *Calvin*." Michael opened his eyes and let out an irritated huff. "Calvin isn't some random man. He's a man in your employ. Worse, he's a thief. He *stole* from me. Seeing you two together . . . it's obvious to me now that I shouldn't have let Katherine talk me into letting him work for you. Dammit, Katherine *begged* me to take a chance on him, especially because of that ridiculous sob story he tried to feed us, most of which was probably a lie, and so, I caved. I convinced myself that since he was only to be your subordinate, it would be fine for a while. And then, when you *immediately* offered him the spare room, I nearly threw him out of the house, but . . . but then I let *you* convince me that nothing unsavory would happen. And now . . . hell, now something *has* happened. John, he's trying to con you!"

John reeled back, those two words ripping a hole in his heart.

"Are you a . . . a . . . wh-wh-what's the term? Con man?"

"Yes."

He choked out, "What are you t-t-trying to say?"

Michael sighed. "Calvin's probably trying to cheat you out of money. He's trying to make you think that he likes you so you'll become complacent. Perhaps he's hoping you'll eventually be less cautious with your earnings, or he thinks he can trick you into paying him more or—"

"I am paying him m-m-more."

Michael's eyes bulged. "I'm sorry—what?"

"I-I made him my partner. Weeks ago."

Covering his face with his hands, Michael threw his head back and let out a frustrated groan.

"You're not serious," Michael said. "John, tell me that *you're* still the one handling the money. Tell me you haven't been letting him manage *that*."

Why shouldn't he have let Calvin start collecting the payments? John had never enjoyed talking of financial matters himself.

"Well, I—"

"For heaven's sake, John!" Michael roared. "I thought you were smarter than this! I mean, I know you have trouble with people, but . . ." He turned and thumped his fist once on the desk. "Fuck!"

Michael's shouted cuss word struck John in the chest with such strength that it knocked the wind out of him. Squeezing his eyes shut, he forced in a breath. Calvin wasn't trying to trick him. He had made a promise to John that he'd never steal from him. John still kept his own money in his own safe.

John managed to eke out, "Why'd you hire him if you . . . if you thought you couldn't t-t-trust him?"

"Because of my wife! Katherine was very convincing, looking up at me with those big, puppy eyes of hers!" Michael hollered as he started to pace. "And you know how she is, John. She's so innocent and caring and—"

He cut himself off to let out a small, frustrated scream, and the sound made John want to collapse in on himself. Curling his shoulders forward, John tried to hide from the rush of shame and fear and embarrassment. Meanwhile, Michael continued to walk back and forth across the round rug, seemingly unaware of John's plight.

"And *you* needed help!" Michael spat. "God, ever since you enrolled in that mortuary school, I've been worried that you'd never meet someone who would like working with you, not while you're still so . . . so painfully shy. So, when we stumbled upon Calvin, I let myself think that maybe Katherine was right. Calvin seemed like a *wonderfully* convenient find. I mean, the man was practically a beggar! Desperate and pitiful! He was living in one tiny room with a fucking urinal next to his bookcase, for Christ's sake! Him working for you, it was only ever supposed to be temporary! God, John, even though there was a part of me that was nervous to invite a petty thief to work with you, the other part of me was *relieved* that I managed to find someone hopeless enough to—" Michael looked over at John midsentence, and the moment the two of them locked eyes, Michael's face fell. "Oh, John, I'm sorry. What I mean to say is that I was only ever trying to look out for you. I only wanted to help you find someone who could help with some of the more . . . social parts of the business. You're my little brother. I'm supposed to take care of you."

But Michael's softened tone couldn't erase the hurt he'd already inflicted. Michael's harsh words echoed in John's head, mixing with every venomous insult that Michael had ever thrown John's way when they were children.

"Why can't you be normal?"

"No one wants to listen to you talk about Lucy anymore!"

"God, John, why are you so strange?"

John's face burned with shame.

Michael continued on. "And now you've made the criminal your business partner." He heaved a long sigh. "And Calvin has clearly figured out that you like men. And so, he's pretending that he likes men, too. Or, hell, maybe he's *not* pretending when it comes to that, but, John, he's pretending to like you. It pains me to say it, but you're . . . well, you're still a little strange for most people. I have to think that . . . that he's trying to lull you into a false sense of security. Probably so that he can cheat you out of money. Goodness, I bet he's hoarding some of the cash from your business. Or, heaven forbid, stealing from clients." He knelt in front of John, catching John's eye. "Look, I wasn't sure if I should tell you this, but I think I have no choice." He clicked his tongue once. "Calvin stole a pair of my cuff links."

John's eyes went wide with horror. "No. He—he wouldn't. He—"

"He would. He *did*. Trust me. Yesterday, Calvin came by and handed me my emerald cuff links. He said he'd found them in the hall."

"Wait. I thought you said that he stole them."

"John, they vanished the *moment* he moved in and then magically resurfaced even though I *know* that Katherine and I had looked everywhere for them over the last couple of weeks. I'd convinced myself that I'd simply lost them, probably at work or something."

"But Calvin handed them back to you. How . . . how is that stealing?"

Even if it was stealing, it sounded like Calvin had come to his senses. He had returned them. No matter what had happened, John knew, in his heart, that Calvin was a good man. Just one who'd been struggling.

John wouldn't fault him for that.

"I can't have this conversation," Michael said as he pushed himself to stand, his voice weary. "Just . . . John, be careful. If you want to keep Calvin as your partner, well, so be it. But I hope that, if you *really* think about it, you'll see that you need to be more careful. I hope you'll see that, whether you like it or not, there's a possibility, or, hell, *probability*, that Calvin is trying to trick you."

John's stomach tightened. Michael wasn't right. He couldn't be.

"He's n-n-not," John said. "I trust him."

"Fine," Michael said. "If you want to throw away your business, fine. Uncle Frances and I are opening up a second factory, and I have plenty of money for my own place now, too. I basically bought you this one, and, well, if you want to burn it to the ground, then burn it to the ground. I can't take care of you anymore. I wouldn't have thought you'd be naïve enough to make a criminal your business partner, but, well I suppose that means I'm a fool." He turned on his heel to leave. "I hope your relationship with the criminal works out, John. I really do."

Michael left, slamming the door behind him.

John buried his head in his hands and prayed that Michael was wrong.

For the next several hours, John stayed in Michael's office, too confused and upset to leave. What if he bumped into Calvin? He probably *would* bump into him the moment he stepped out into the hall. And then Calvin might want to kiss him. And of course John would want to kiss him back. But now . . .

Now John couldn't banish the worry that Calvin might be trying to fool him. Even though John couldn't see why Calvin would want to. John had made Calvin his business partner. Ergo, Calvin made exactly as much money as he did. Since they were equals, they were to split the money from each funeral exactly in half. Unless . . . Calvin was keeping some of the money for himself? No. He wouldn't. John nibbled on his bottom lip as this possibility wormed its way inside his head. But . . . if Calvin was merely tricking him, why the kissing? Surely a man who preferred the company of women wouldn't let a man suck his—

Abruptly, John forced the thought out of his head. No, Calvin *liked* him. Calvin wasn't a cheat. Sure, Calvin had cheated plenty of people out of money in the past, but that had only been because he hadn't had a home. Now, he had one. Why would he steal money? Michael was wrong. He *had* to be wrong.

Once the sun started to set, John expected someone—either Michael or Katherine—to call him for supper. But no one came. Given the fight he'd had with Michael, this made some sense. Michael may have taken Katherine out for the evening instead. Dinner. Theatre. Anywhere, really. What about Calvin, though?

Had Calvin cooked for the two of them? John sniffed the air. He couldn't *smell* anything cooking. Even the faint smell of the funeral cookies had long since faded. John's stomach gurgled. God, he was so hungry.

Tentatively, John crept out into the hall and made his way to the kitchen. On the worktable, there was a plate of cookies with a note.

John,

Thank you for helping me with these.

Calvin

Even though John knew it wouldn't have been sensible for Calvin to have even *hinted* that there was something romantic between the two of them on paper, the platonic tone of Calvin's note hurt John's heart. He wished it would have been more poetic, maybe, or more loving. It would have been nice to have stumbled upon some kind of proof that Calvin hadn't been toying with him.

Stomach still rumbling, John took two of the cookies off of the plate and forced himself to eat them, though their sweetness couldn't compete with the bitter insecurity he now felt, one that was souring the memory of his and Calvin's fun in the kitchen earlier and souring the taste of the cookies, too. Even though the two tiny treats were barely enough to curb his hunger, John couldn't fathom trying to eat more of them. He left the rest in the kitchen and went upstairs to his room, the lingering worry that he might see Calvin making his heart race as he ascended the stairs. Thankfully, Calvin must have been keeping away from him as well, because he was nowhere to be found.

While John sat on his wooden chair, Michael's words—old and new—continued to play on loop in his head. He opened up the top drawer of his desk to see everything he had saved from Lucy, things he still couldn't part with—some marbles, a well-loved rag doll, and a silver locket, the bail of which was broken. Michael had been right, hadn't he? John should have let himself forget his sister. Once Lucy had been buried, John should have left her in the past, but instead, John had carried her with him throughout his life. He had let himself become obsessed with her passing, and that obsession had been like . . . well, perhaps like embalming fluid, one that had preserved his childhood eccentricities—his shyness, his inability to connect with most other people, even his stammer—and had transformed them into something permanent. Now, these flaws had become part of him. Interwoven with the fabric of who he was. But who would he have become had he not struggled to move on from the past? He supposed he'd never know.

Goodness, even when his parents had been lost in their grief, John hadn't managed to let Lucy rest. Instead, he had brought her up every chance he'd had. He would be served a meal only to tell everyone whether he thought Lucy would have liked it. He would meet someone and tell them he had a twin sister, speaking of her like she was still there. He would talk to her and pretend that she could hear him. He hadn't had the sense to move on.

No wonder his parents had retreated into themselves.

And then, once his parents had pulled away, John had stopped speaking for a while, becoming sullen and shy and confused in his state of near-constant bereavement. Soon, nearly everyone in the Borough of Media had begun commenting on how odd of a child he was. Oh, the names that some of the other children in town had started calling him then. It was still so painful to remember them now.

Because they'd been true.

Because they still *were* true.

John heaved a sigh. He wanted so badly to believe that Calvin liked him. Closing his eyes, John replayed the last forty-eight hours in his head.

He remembered how Calvin had melted into their first embrace.

He remembered how Calvin had been the one to tell him to stay.

He remembered how Calvin had cooked him breakfast.

He remembered how Calvin had said, *"I'm yours, John."*

Clutching tight to these memories, John chose to believe that Michael was wrong. He chose to believe that Calvin liked him. Despite every horrible thing that John had ever been called, Calvin still liked him.

Praying that he was right, John left for Calvin's bedroom.

Chapter Thirteen
Calvin

Hours earlier...

Calvin's hands shook as he plopped the cookies onto the baking sheet, his mind continuing to conjure up horrible possibilities about what kinds of things Michael must have been saying to John right then. Calvin's heart clenched. Even though he himself had never felt one ounce of shame over the fact that he liked men, he knew it might not be the same for John. What unkind words might Michael have been saying to John over their obvious romantic bond? Or, *God*, what if Michael was trying to convince John that Calvin needed to be reprimanded for stealing those cuff links? But Calvin hadn't stolen them, really. Had he? It had taken him some time, but he had eventually returned them. That had to count for something.

Please let it count for something.

While Calvin was putting the tray in the oven, someone came into the kitchen, their footsteps causing him to startle. But it was only Katherine.

"Smells wonderful," she said warmly.

"Thank you," Calvin said, his voice trembling and shy and barely like his normal voice at all.

Katherine frowned. "What's wrong?"

"Um . . ." He shook his head. How could he even begin to explain this to her? Probably he shouldn't. But, oh, how he wanted someone to talk to! And Katherine seemed so kind. "Michael . . . he saw . . . John and I were . . ."

Goodness, was this how John felt all the time when he was stumbling over his words?

Katherine's eyebrows shot up. "Oh!" She came a few steps closer and lowered her voice. "Last night, Michael said he thought that you were . . . staying in John's room?"

Calvin's cheeks began to burn, and when he opened his mouth to confirm, he found he couldn't bring himself to speak. Katherine seemed to take this as confirmation.

She said, "Did Michael say something to you?"

"Not to me, yet, but probably to John."

Katherine shook her head. "Oh, I'm sorry, Calvin. Michael only wants to protect him. Not from *you*, specifically. Or *maybe* from you, but that's only because he needs some more time to . . . to move past the . . . ehm . . . the necklace incident."

Calvin winced. "I'm sorry I sold it. Really, I am."

"I know." Katherine sighed. "It's not only *you* who Michael is worried about. Michael has *always* been protective of his little brother. When I first met John, I remember asking Michael why his brother wasn't married yet. I wanted to know whether I should try to see if I could find someone for him." She huffed a soft laugh and shook her head. "Michael reacted poorly to that. At first, he seemed . . . irritated with me. He said that I shouldn't be sticking my nose in other people's business. But, well, me being me, I came right back and said that I was to be his wife. I was to be part of his family. Part of *John's* family. And, so, that was when he told me that John wouldn't ever be marrying. Michael had only tried to keep that from me because he'd been worried that I might say something cruel with regards to . . . the sort of company John prefers. But that isn't me."

Calvin's cheeks warmed. No, that wasn't Katherine. God, Calvin had picked the nicest woman in all of Philadelphia to steal from, hadn't he?

"Anyway," she continued, "what I'm trying to say is that Michael is very protective of his brother. John has *always* struggled with people. I'm sure Michael is only worried that you'll hurt him."

"I won't," Calvin promised, wishing he could reassure Michael of that instead. "I swear I won't."

"I believe you." Katherine began playing with her skirt. "And, Calvin, I want you to know that I won't tell anyone. About you and John, I mean. I simply wish you the best." She pursed her lips, as though thinking. "Or, well, I'll say one thing, perhaps: Be careful with John's heart. He's a sweet man, one who is more sensitive than he lets on."

"I will be," Calvin confirmed.

Moments later, Michael came into the kitchen.

"Calvin, I need to speak with you," he said.

Calvin's stomach leapt up into his throat as Katherine excused herself. Michael waited a few extra seconds, probably to make sure that she was out of earshot.

"Look," Michael started, clasping his hands together, "I know what I saw earlier, and I have to say—"

"Michael, listen—"

"*Don't* interrupt me," Michael said, his nostrils flaring. "I came here to warn you."

"Warn me?"

"Leave John be. Keep your relationship professional. Otherwise . . ." Calvin steeled himself, preparing for some sort of threat. "Otherwise, someone will end up hurt. Probably John."

Calvin clenched his teeth. *Never.* He'd *never* hurt John.

Michael narrowed his eyes. "Don't think you have me fooled so easily, Calvin Wright." He made a show of fiddling with the sleeves of his suit, his movements causing the emerald cuff links to peek into view. "I have my eye on you. If you hurt my brother, that'll be it for you. One day, John will know the truth. And you, my friend, will find yourself back out on the streets."

Without waiting for Calvin's response, Michael turned to leave.

Anxious, Calvin was sitting on the edge of the bed, bouncing his leg while his mind ran through every possible thing that might have happened in Michael's office. What had Michael said to John? Whatever it was, it must have been horrible. Dammit, the sun was starting to set, wasn't it? Would John even sleep in Michael's office tonight?

When someone then rapped their knuckles on the door, Calvin startled. After taking a moment to calm himself, he stood to go see who it was, whispering a prayer that it wasn't Michael. He was still reeling from what Michael had said to him earlier. He couldn't stomach a *second* conversation like that one.

He took a deep breath before opening the bedroom door, and relief washed over him as he saw John waiting, his head low.

"Oh, I'm so happy to see you," Calvin said.

"I'm sorry that I stayed away for so long," John said, casting his eyes to the floor. "Michael said some things that . . ."

Calvin took John by the hand and pulled him into the bedroom, only breaking contact for the briefest moment to shut the door before finding both of John's hands once again.

"Whatever Michael said, I'm here now," Calvin reassured him with a squeeze.

Immediately, John captured his mouth in a kiss, one so intensely passionate, it nearly knocked Calvin off of his feet. Once he regained his footing, he began kissing John back with that same intensity, lifting one hand to run his fingers through John's hair as his other hand hooked around John's waist. But while they kissed, the image of Michael's emerald cuff links flashed in Calvin's mind, and his stomach twisted with shame. Quickly, he forced the image away. He hadn't hurt John by temporarily borrowing those cuff links, had he? He had only ever meant to hurt Michael by taking them. And, even then, he had returned them.

When they broke their kiss, John said, "I'm sorry for taking so long to come see you, Calvin. Michael tried to m-make me think that . . . that you . . . oh, I c-c-can't even say it."

Grimacing, Calvin looked away. He knew what Michael must have said. Michael must have mentioned the cuff links. He *had* to have mentioned them.

And Calvin knew, too, that he ought to confess.

"One day, John will know the truth."

Calvin's heart sank as Michael's words came back to him. Other memories began to flood Calvin's mind, too, every one of them slamming into him like the waves of a violent storm.

Being rejected by his family members and sent to the orphanage.

Being overlooked by prospective caretakers over and over and over.

David taking him in, only to later toss him out like trash.

Heartache filled Calvin's chest, forcing the oxygen from his lungs.

"And you, my friend, will find yourself back out on the streets."

He couldn't tell John the truth. He couldn't lose his home.

John's hand cupped his chin. Slowly, Calvin peeked open his eyes.

"Cal," John said. "What is it?"

Calvin merely shook his head. John's expression turned pained.

"John, I . . ." Calvin's truth stuck in his throat. "I . . ."

"Are you worried about what M-M-Michael said to me?" John asked, and Calvin managed a nod, his eyes filling with tears. John pressed a kiss to Calvin's lips. "Don't be. I trust you, Calvin. I w-w-won't ever let Michael ruin what we have. I promise."

Calvin swallowed thickly and nodded once more.

Wordlessly, John pulled Calvin in for an embrace, and the warmth of John's body curled around him, comforting him and reassuring him that he still had a home.

But Calvin's heart stayed heavy.

And he wondered whether he was worthy of a home at all.

Chapter Fourteen
Calvin

On a Friday, Calvin and John were taking a trolley to Walnut Street to see a play together. All week long, Calvin had been contending with occasional bouts of nausea, something that he had initially convinced himself was merely a bit of tummy trouble, perhaps a sickness that had been making its way through the city. But the more time passed, the more Calvin recognized the upset for what it was. Guilt.

It wasn't that he felt sorry for taking Michael's cuff links, exactly, since Michael had barely even managed to be cordial to him since he had moved in, but that he knew it was wrong for him not to have confessed everything to John. He had been presented with the perfect opportunity, but he'd been too cowardly to take it. John hadn't brought it up since. He hadn't once pressed Calvin to admit to taking those stupid cuff links. It seemed that John really *did* trust him.

But Calvin felt unworthy of that trust.

Worse than that, perhaps, was the fact that Calvin couldn't rid himself of the worry that John only liked him, both romantically *and* as a friend, because he was unaware of the extent of Calvin's past crimes. Calvin had stolen from *a lot* of people. He had cheated other struggling criminals out of money in cards. He'd tricked people into overpaying for minor handiwork. He had even sold bottles of what had essentially been snake oil on the streets of New York. But John only knew, in the vaguest sense, that Calvin had cheated his way through life. At least, he had been cheating his way through it ever since he had met David, which had been . . . God, over ten years ago now.

Even though Calvin should have been pleased that John was happy to look past his misdeeds, even so far as to not ever ask what they even were, Calvin wasn't. Not really. Because he *wanted* John to know him. Insecurities over how David hadn't ever really loved him were still lingering, their shackles preventing Calvin from ever feeling truly comfortable, truly *safe*, with John. Part of him still worried that John would leave him someday.

And so, Calvin needed to prove to himself that, if John really knew him—if John knew *all* of him—he would still want him. Because Calvin had fallen in love with his business partner. He had fallen for his shy-but-sweet mortician friend. And, *God*, how he wanted John to fall in love with him too.

But John had never asked about Calvin's past. Not even once. And Calvin had been left to wonder, then, whether John might not have wanted to know him. Perhaps John was only with Calvin because . . . well, because he hadn't ever been with anyone else before. John had said himself that Calvin had been his first real friend. He was his first lover now, as well.

Perhaps John was only falling for the *idea* of Calvin Wright.

And that possibility broke Calvin's heart.

While the trolley moved through the streets of Philadelphia, rocking lazily back and forth, Calvin clutched tight to the little bar above his head and tried to work out how and whether he should broach the topic.

First, the *whether*. Normally, Calvin would have been reluctant to even consider confessing to stealing those cuff links, no matter how nauseated he was. *But*, thanks to a recent funeral they'd organized for a city official, Calvin had finally saved up enough money to pay Michael back for that necklace. Which meant that, if John threw him out, Calvin could simply make use of that money for himself instead. He could start over. Either in Philadelphia or elsewhere. And so, it seemed that now was the perfect time to confess to having stolen those cuff links. And to confess to having conned people out of money for over ten years, too.

Good Lord.

Second, the *how*. It wasn't only important to Calvin that John listened to his silly confessions, but that John *wanted* to know who Calvin was. David had never wanted to know. David had only ever seen Calvin as a . . . a *thing*. Something to help him run schemes and con people out of money. Something to use for pleasure. Every time Calvin had tried to be emotionally close with the man, David had pushed him away. Calvin wanted—no, *needed*—to know that John wanted to know him. Hell, he needed to know that John *wanted* him in the first place. Not only needed him as David had needed him.

Soon, John and Calvin reached their stop on the corner of Walnut and Second and hopped off the trolley. They then started walking west toward the theatre together. Neither of them talked much. Calvin knew that John not talking didn't mean the man wasn't enjoying himself. In fact, John seemed to like it best when the two of them were simply cuddling or kissing or reading together. And Calvin liked those things plenty himself.

But right now, listening to the sounds of the city—the clip-clop, clip-clop of horse hooves hitting the cobblestone, and the occasional birds chirping overhead—the near-silence felt suffocating. Calvin wanted the two of them to talk—to *really* talk. About nothing. Or everything. About nothing and everything. He wanted to know that John was interested in him. All of him.

Not only in what he brought to the business. Or the pleasure he brought to the bedroom.

Walking past Lawyer's Row, Calvin's eyes wandered over to Washington Square Park, located on the other side of the street. It was empty, save for a handful of people, most of whom were only passing through. Several benches were free. When a cool breeze blew past, Calvin had the thought that it might be nice to spend a while there before the show, provided there was still time, and then, while they were there, maybe the two of them could talk. He pulled out his father's pocket watch to check.

"I like your w-w-watch," John said as Calvin clicked it open. "I can't remember ever seeing that before."

Calvin's stomach fluttered.

"I only wear it on certain occasions," Calvin said, closing the watch and returning it to his pocket. "It was my father's."

"Ah," John said.

Calvin waited for John to say something more.

Seconds passed.

Nothing.

"I wouldn't mind if you asked about him," Calvin offered.

After a pause, John said, "Alright." He cleared his throat. "If I remember correctly, you said he was a . . . a c-c-carpenter?"

"Yes," Calvin confirmed. "Well, really, he owned his own shop. I believe I mentioned it before. It was small, but popular. I think you'd have liked him."

John smiled a little. "I'm sure I would have."

Calvin's chest warmed. He waited for John to say more, but still . . .

Nothing.

Calvin sighed. He'd have to pay Michael back tomorrow. Tonight was the last chance he'd have to tell John about the cuff links for weeks. Or, God, probably even for longer. It had taken quite a bit of luck to save up enough to pay Michael back in such a short time. Had that city official not sought out their services, Calvin wouldn't have even considered confessing yet. He'd have had to contend with the weight of his secret for *weeks* longer. Not to mention the constant niggling worry that John wasn't even falling in love with the real him.

After a few more paces, Calvin nodded toward the park.

"Would you mind sitting with me for a bit?" he asked. "We have a whole half hour before the play's scheduled to start."

"Not at all," John said with a warm smile. "It would be nice to spend some t-t-time out here with you."

Calvin's chest fluttered with hope, even as his stomach nearly fell out of his rear end. It was now or never.

After the two men secured their tickets, they returned to the park and immediately sat next to each other on one of the benches.

Another breeze blew past. Calvin closed his eyes and inhaled, relishing the way the unusual midsummer chill felt so refreshing. Cleansing, even.

He was ready.

"John?" Calvin said.

"Hmm?"

"What Michael said the other day—"

"Cal—"

"I want you to know that I only took the—"

"Cal, *please*." John shook his head. "Let's not t-t-talk about that. I-I told you that I would never let Michael ruin what we have. I want us to f-forget about it."

Calvin's eyebrows pinched together. "Are you *sure*?"

"Yes. I'm sure."

Minutes ticked by. Cool breezes continued to blow past, rustling through Calvin's hair. He knew he ought to keep trying.

He knew he ought to confess. Whether or not John wanted to *hear* it, Calvin needed to say it.

But . . .

Calvin curled his hands into fists. He couldn't.

"Let's find our seats," Calvin said, fighting to keep his voice steady. "I'm not much in the mood for talking right now."

"Oh." John furrowed his brow in confusion but then nodded. "Alright."

Together, they stood, and with trembling hands, Calvin pulled out his father's watch, pretending to check the time but really only wanting to hold it for a little while.

It was his most prized possession.

He wished that John had asked him more about his watch. Or his father. Or him.

"Are we late?" John asked.

"No," Calvin said as they cut through the grass. "Just being cautious."

Sorrow continued to build, bringing tears to Calvin's eyes. After running his thumb over the watch's face one more time, he clicked it closed. And he prayed that he could muster the courage to try confessing to John again later that evening.

Calvin was still feeling unsteady when they took their seats, but the thrill of being in a theatre was thankfully pulling him out of the well of self-pity he'd created for himself. Walnut Street Theatre was even nicer than Calvin had imagined it would be. From the beautiful white brick exterior, to the expansive theatre itself with the semicircular balcony where John and Calvin were seated, to the luxurious-feeling red velvet seats, everything seemed so grand. Despite being in his twenties, Calvin had only been to the theatre once before, back in New York. And it hadn't even been one of the larger, more well-known theatres, but a little playhouse. He and David had won their tickets playing faro.

Calvin frowned at the realization. He ought to try not to ruin this experience for himself. Or for John.

Shortly before the show began, John leaned over and whispered, "Oh, Cal, it's m-magical here, isn't it?"

Swallowing his upset, Calvin forced a playful wink and said, "It is."

Before the lights were lowered, Calvin had the pleasure of seeing John's beautifully pink cheeks. How he loved making John blush like that.

Calvin's sorrow waned throughout the course of the show, enough so that he was able to truly enjoy the play. Calvin especially liked it when his and John's fingers briefly brushed each other's once in a while, though it made him wish that he could have held John's hand for the entirety of the production.

Later, when they reached their home in the Frankford neighborhood of Philadelphia, they found Michael and Katherine spending time together in the front sitting room, Katherine knitting and Michael flipping through a book. Michael looked up from the page as soon as John and Calvin entered the room.

"So," Michael began, locking eyes with Calvin. "John said earlier that you might have something for me?"

Nausea came back in full force, its vile coils settling in Calvin's stomach, and he suddenly wanted nothing more than to curl into a ball and disappear.

He had missed his chance.

"Yes, I . . ." He paused and swallowed past the bile rising in his throat. "I have the money for the necklace."

Michael smiled. "Excellent."

And Calvin had to fight the urge to retch.

Chapter Fifteen
John

In the morning, John awoke to an empty bed. Groaning, he rolled over and pressed his face into Calvin's pillow, inhaling his scent. He missed Calvin already. Despite the fact that they had cuddled close for the entire evening, John hated when they had to separate, even if it was only for a little while, like for Calvin to make breakfast or when either of them went outside to feed Agathe. While John lay with his face smushed into the fabric, he felt a sudden pang in his chest.

Calvin had seemed upset last night. Distracted. Morose, even. Still struggling to know when to press his lover to tell him *why* he was upset, John had opted to simply hold Calvin close, hoping that his touch would offer some comfort. Perhaps Calvin hadn't liked Michael's smugness when he had paid Michael back for the necklace. John himself wouldn't have liked that. He could see Calvin being irked by it. But John couldn't really be certain if that was what had Calvin behaving so strangely. He hadn't been interested in physical intimacy before bed, which had been so unlike him. John had to hope that he would find Calvin in better spirits this morning. Later, they were supposed to run a funeral together. John had performed the embalming earlier that week. Before the funeral, though, John had promised to teach Calvin some more carpentry.

Remembering that they'd have limited time for the lesson prior to the funeral later, John sat up and stretched. He'd probably find Calvin waiting for him in the kitchen, baking cookies for the service or cooking breakfast for the two of them. Eager to see his partner, John hurried to pick out an outfit and then left for the bathroom. Once he was finished, he made his way to the kitchen, but Calvin wasn't there. Only Katherine.

"Good morning, John," she said from the table.

John nodded. "Morning, K-Katherine." He looked around the room. "Is there—"

"Coffee?" she said. John nodded again. "Calvin brewed some for you." She stood and retrieved a mug from the worktable. "It's still warm."

"Thank you," John said, taking the mug from her. "Do you know where he went?"

Katherine pursed her lips. "I believe he went for a walk."

"Mmm." John took a sip of the coffee. God, it tasted incredible. Everything Calvin made for him tasted incredible. It was as though he could taste the care that Calvin put into meals and cookies and even tea. What a strange and wondrous thing that was. "Well, I hope he'll be back soon. We're supposed to work on a p-p-project together."

"Carpentry?" she said.

"Right."

Katherine furrowed her brow. "I'm not sure if he'll be interested in that this morning."

"Oh." John tilted his head. "Why not?"

Katherine began chewing on her bottom lip.

After a few seconds of pause, she said, "He seemed upset."

"Ah, yes, I n-n-noticed that last night."

John frowned at his coffee. He hated that Calvin was still sad. Even more than that, though, he hated that he had no idea *why*.

"John?"

John looked up. "Hmm?"

"I know that I shouldn't concern myself with your . . . relationship, but . . ." Sighing, Katherine sat back at the table and motioned for John to join her. "Look, Michael told me something that surprised me. He said that Calvin had stolen his emerald cuff links."

Bristling from the comment, John sat with her. "I know."

"Did Calvin tell you?"

"No," John said with a shake of his head. "I heard from M-M-Michael."

"I wonder why he'd have taken them. I mean, you two make plenty of money from the funerals, if I'm not mistaken."

"We do."

"What stuck with me most, though, was that he returned them. He hadn't sold them straightaway. Not like he had my necklace."

John took another sip of coffee. He hadn't thought about that.

Katherine leaned forward to rest her cheek on her hand, propping her head up with her elbow. "It's interesting, is it not?" She tapped her face with her index finger several times. "He seemed so upset when he paid Michael back last night, too. Truthfully, I thought he might make himself sick right there on the floor."

John let out a breath through his nose. "I thought the same."

"Did you try to talk to him about either of these things?"

Shutting his eyes, John shook his head. "No, I-I-I couldn't. I'm not upset with Calvin for the cuff links. If he even really stole them. I suspect he did. But . . ." John winced from the painful rush of compassion that suddenly seized his heart. "But I'm not mad at him. I couldn't be. N-n-not with what he's been through."

John peeked his eyes open to see Katherine smiling warmly.

"I feel the same way."

"And," John said, "I'm not sure wh-wh-why he seemed upset to pay Michael back, but I'm worried that I'm not . . . that I'm not the right person to c-c-comfort him. I'm worried that I might make things worse."

"I see." Katherine hummed thoughtfully. "But, John, I think that, whether you like it or not, you *are* the right person to comfort him. I mean, you're his . . ." She laughed softly. "I'm sorry, I'm not sure what to call the two of you, but I hope you know what I'm trying to say. John, you're his *person*."

John's cheeks warmed. Goodness, Calvin had told him that Katherine had been so surprisingly sweet to him when she'd found out that the two of them were together, but John hadn't imagined how lovely it would be to really converse with her about his and Calvin's relationship himself. It was . . . well, it was nothing short of wonderful.

Katherine continued, "I know you sometimes have trouble connecting with people. I know it's hard for you to be comfortable talking to others. But I think that you might need to try to talk to Calvin. He needs to feel as though he can come to you when he's upset."

Furrowing his brow, John fixed his eyes on his coffee and watched the black liquid swirl in his cup. Katherine was probably right. Perhaps Calvin needed more than cuddles sometimes. And, so, John would have to figure out how to talk to him. About everything. Because he so badly wanted Calvin to know how much he cared for him.

Calvin only came back home forty minutes before he and John needed to prepare for the funeral. It had to have been purposeful. Before their trip to the theatre, Calvin had been excited to learn some more carpentry techniques. He wouldn't have missed the lesson had he been in a better mood.

A half hour before they were scheduled to arrive in Rittenhouse Square for the funeral, John and Calvin left. While they drove the hearse carriage through the streets, John considered broaching the topic of Calvin's upset then and there, but ultimately realized that he and Calvin may not have enough time to thoroughly explore the reasons behind Calvin's upset before the service. So, he thought he might hold his tongue until the funeral was behind them.

When John and Calvin reached the home of Alice Odell, a woman who had lost her husband, Richard Odell, to cancer, Calvin's lack of tact was reminiscent of the way he had behaved back when John had first hired him. Rather than feel exasperated by it, as John had back then, John instead felt completely crushed. God, Calvin must have really been hurting to be behaving this way.

Fifteen minutes into their visit, Calvin led Mrs. Alice Odell, who had insisted that John and Calvin call by her first name, into the kitchen, the basket of funeral cookies hanging on his wrist, while John stayed back in the front room with the casket. Raking a hand through his hair, John spun on his heel, at a loss for what he should do. He wished he could tell Calvin to rest. But, oh, how would he ever manage to run a funeral on his own?

Standing in the middle of Alice's sitting room, surrounded by the sea of folding funeral chairs that he himself had set up the morning before, John couldn't help but feel purposeless. He and Calvin were meant to be partners. He ought to have the skills and confidence to step in and help when Calvin was struggling, but instead, he could only stand here stiffly while Calvin tried his best to be personable enough for the both of them, even when he likely wasn't feeling well emotionally. John sighed. Without Calvin, he was simply an embalmer, not a mortician, and once he was finished performing his tasks, he was left unmoored.

Someone knocked, and John's stomach jumped at the sharp sound of knuckles rapping on wood. Pleadingly, John looked toward the kitchen, praying that Calvin would come back to welcome the first mourners.

The knocking resumed.

Squeezing his eyes shut, John winced from the sound. He hadn't even had to *attempt* this part since before Calvin had first started working with him. Oh, Lord, there was no way it wouldn't be a complete catastrophe. But he had to try. Perhaps it would lighten the burden on Calvin. Probably not by much, but it was the best he could offer right now, wasn't it?

Steeling himself, John walked over to the door and opened it, forcing a smile as he turned the knob.

"Hello. W-w-welcome to—"

"Where is he?" The woman on the other side of the door looked past John as she asked the question.

"I'm sorry?"

"Richard," she said, her eyes puffy and pink. John's stomach roiled from the sight. He had barely even mentally prepared himself to try to verbally comfort Calvin. He was *not* equipped to console some random woman off the street. "Where's my Richard?"

Her Richard?

John opened his mouth to speak, but shut it again. Her Richard? Wasn't Richard *Alice's* Richard?

Over the next several minutes, the crying woman, whose name John discovered was Elizabeth, proceeded to first push her way into the house and then reveal a lot of surprising information, such as the fact that she had been Richard's mistress and that Alice not

only knew her but had been aware of the sordid relationship between her and her husband as well. Complicating matters, Alice's
family had heard about the affair from her. *Before* Alice had made
peace with it. And so, even though Alice was completely fine with
this Elizabeth woman coming to the funeral, her family would very
likely *not* be fine with it.

It was a *lot* to take in.

John's mind was still reeling from trying to make sense of it all
when Elizabeth reached out to touch John's forearm and said, "So,
where should I sit?"

John froze, thunderstruck.

"I . . . I . . ."

He looked over at the rows of chairs. Good God, where should
he sit her? Calvin would know. Dammit, John ought to know,
too. But this was so far beyond his scope of knowledge. Sure,
John knew simple etiquette rules. He knew them even better than
Calvin. But "where to sit someone's mistress for a funeral service"
had *not* been taught at Eckels.

"Let me think on that," John said. Desperate to buy himself
some time, he then blurted out, "In the m-m-meantime, I bet you
would like to try my partner's c-c-*cookies*."

He then forced what had to be the most awkward smile in human existence. Elizabeth's eyes bulged, and her mouth fell agape. It
took John a moment before he registered the faint pink hue on her
cheeks and realized that perhaps she thought he had been trying to
tease her.

Panic rose in John's chest.

"Uhm . . . no, thank you," she said, cautiously.

John looked over his shoulder and spotted Calvin coming out
of the kitchen.

"Just one m-moment," he said to Elizabeth before rushing over
to Calvin. "Cal . . ." He took Calvin by the sleeve and pulled him

into a corner, only feet from the casket. Calvin scrunched up his nose a little. "I need to talk to you."

Right then, there was a knock, and, dear God, *Elizabeth* moved to answer the front door. John's eyes went wide with horror. Either he or Calvin should have been welcoming the mourners!

Thankfully, it was only the reverend. John breathed a sigh of relief.

"Small problem," he whispered to Calvin. "That woman whom I was talking with, she's Richard's mistress. Or, *had been* Richard's mistress, rather."

"Oh. Uhm. Interesting."

"Trust me, it's stranger than you think," John said.

He proceeded to tell Calvin everything. How Elizabeth and Alice knew each other. How Alice's family members knew who Elizabeth was and hated her. How Alice and Elizabeth had somehow become friends. All the while, Calvin's eyebrows slowly ticked up higher on his forehead, his eyes blowing wide as though this was, indeed, one of the strangest things he'd ever heard.

Last, but certainly not least, John prepared to confess about his verbal blunder regarding the cookies.

"I *think*, though of course I can't be certain, that she thought that I was trying to insinuate something *sexual*." John shuddered, and Calvin snorted. "It must have been because of how I had said it. Perhaps it was my . . . my stammer? Oh, God, the look on her face! Calvin, she seemed m-*mortified*! It was like . . . it was like she thought that I was trying to insult her for having b-been his mistress!"

"Hmmm . . ." Calvin tapped his chin, obviously only pretending to think. "Well, I have to say, I like the thought of *you* trying my cookies."

Calvin chuckled while John rolled his eyes, though the comment *was* a little funny. Just not right now.

"Calvin, *please* help me here," John implored.

"Alright, well, find her some of our real cookies while I think about where to put her for the service."

"But she said she wasn't interested in the cookies," John said.

"Jesus, John, then find her a piece of fruit!" Calvin said with a sigh before a small, sly smile stretched across his face. "Maybe not a banana, though."

John pursed his lips to fight back a laugh.

"Calvin," John scolded, leveling a look. "Not helping."

"Hmm." Calvin chewed on his lip. "Well, Elizabeth is one of the first people here. Other than the reverend. So, maybe we find her a veil. And . . . we'll sit her in the back? Or, no, maybe in the front corner. For the viewing and short prayer service here *and* the full service in the church. It'll keep people from seeing her face very well. I hope."

"Brilliant," John said, his shoulders relaxing a little. "Now we have to hope we can f-find an extra veil."

Calvin shrugged. "I have one in the hearse. Several, actually."

"Really?" John asked.

"Yeah. I learned my lesson from that whole scarf fiasco. Now we have a whole sack of scarves and veils and handkerchiefs and even one of those collapsible opera hats. In the little fabric bag."

"Genius," John said, his muscles finally relaxing as he managed a smile. "Thank you, Cal."

"Of course," Calvin said, beaming.

Calvin rushed outside to find a veil. John stayed near the casket, and slowly, the lingering relief he felt transformed into shame. Even though he had tried to help Calvin, he had ended up needing Calvin's help all the same. Why was he still so inept when it came to interacting with other people?

There's something wrong with you.

Shame intensified, creeping up the back of John's neck and making his face burn. He covered his face with his hand. He had to try harder for Calvin.

Mercifully, the entire viewing passed without issue. Either no one noticed who the mistress was or no one really cared as much as John had feared. Toward the end, Alice even had a pleasant exchange with Elizabeth without her family noticing and commenting on it.

After the viewing, everyone traveled to the church, which meant that John and Calvin had to travel there too, casket in tow. Once everyone reached Christ Church, Calvin collected hats from the six men who would carry the casket and then put them in the back of the hearse, which would enable the pallbearers to focus on carrying the casket into the nave and then back out without having to worry about their hats. John hung back, wishing that he could help but still too shaken by his earlier error to try.

When the service was over, everyone made the last trip for the funeral—the one to the cemetery. John and Calvin led the procession in the hearse while others followed in carriages—some of the carriages rented, some not—and once everything was then set for the short service by the burial plot, John breathed a long sigh of relief. Since they weren't staying for that, they could head home.

Finally, he could try to talk to Calvin.

But then, halfway back to the hearse, John realized that Calvin had forgotten to return the hats. Calvin seemed to realize it at the same time.

Throwing back his head, Calvin let out an overly exaggerated groan.

"I forgot the hats," Calvin lamented. "Now I'll have to run the rest of the way to the hearse to fetch them and then run all the way back to the burial site, too."

John could see how tired Calvin was. Whatever had been bothering him had clearly wiped out his reserves. Now was his chance to help.

"I'll return them," he said.

Calvin's expression softened. "Oh, John, that's sweet of you, but it was my responsibility to return them in the first place. I know you're probably tired. More tired than I am, I'm sure, since you were the one who performed the embalming. All I'd been responsible for was bringing your tools back into the house when you were finished. And then, earlier today, you helped me with welcoming that Elizabeth woman into Alice's house, which couldn't have been easy. I know that you normally prefer to sit off to the side rather than chat with strangers. It was well beyond your scope of responsibilities to help with that. I mean, you hired me to take care of these things—talking to clients and handling finances and welcoming the mourners and carrying people's hats."

"Ah, but you were the one who came up with the c-c-clever veil solution. And you even had the veil in the hearse for us. Really, Calvin, you were m-my savior back there. Let me help you with this."

"Alright," Calvin relented, smiling up at John fondly. "If you're sure."

"I'm sure."

John increased his pace to a brisk walk and headed over to the hearse so that he could collect the hats, cradling them in his arms. Once he had them all, he started toward the burial plot, where the service was underway. John's chest swelled with a mixture of relief and pride. Returning the hats to their owners was turning out to be the perfect way for him to help Calvin.

Until a strong breeze blew past.

Wind whipped through the air, lifting up one of the bowlers and sending it sailing a few feet ahead. It began to tumble through the grass, moving farther and farther away. John tried to rush after it, but he was having trouble not losing one of the other hats in the process.

Chasing the runaway bowler through the cemetery, John's face began to burn. God, he couldn't even do *this* right!

"John?" Calvin asked, hurrying to meet him. "What—"

"I lost one!" John cried out, tilting his chin toward the rogue hat. "Look!"

"Oh," Calvin said through a chuckle. "Do you want me to catch it for you?"

John's cheeks burned hotter. "Please!"

Calvin ran off, maneuvering between headstones while keeping his eye on the bowler. After only a few seconds of chasing, Calvin scooped it up effortlessly. John slowed his pace, sighing with relief, even while his stomach twisted unpleasantly over the nagging notion that he couldn't seem to run even one small part of the service himself without Calvin's help.

"Easy enough," Calvin said, coming back over to John. "Especially since I was empty-handed otherwise."

"Thank you, Cal," John replied. "I'm so lucky to have you."

Calvin's warm, loving smile caused John's chest to flutter. He really had fallen in love with Calvin. What a wonderful man Calvin was. Resourceful. Confident. Smart. Kind. Funny. Goodness, he was . . . well, he was perfect. If only there was some way for John to show him how much he cared.

John tried to smile back, hoping that might give Calvin a little hint, at least until John could speak with him, but just as he did, Calvin tripped on a little hole in the field and stumbled forward, bashing his knee onto the corner of a headstone. He cried out in pain as John's eyes flew wide with horror.

"Fuck," Calvin cursed under his breath.

"Oh my God, Calvin!" John took a few fast steps over to him. "Are you . . . Oh, heavens, I hope nothing's broken!"

Clenching his teeth, Calvin blinked a few times in rapid succession, as though trying to force away the tears that had pooled in his eyes. Despite his efforts, a single tear escaped. John longed to wipe it away, but they were in too public an area. It was too risky. Calvin squeezed his eyes shut. After a moment, Calvin tried to move his leg, stretching it out straight and then curling it.

"No, I think I'll only have a bruise," Calvin choked out, and then he sucked in a short breath through his teeth. "But, *fuck*, it hurts like hell." He took another couple of breaths, more measured ones, and John's whole body burned with the yearning to wrap him up in an embrace. "Sorry for the profanity."

Sympathy swirled in John's chest, as furious as a summer storm.

"Oh, Cal, it's fine," John murmured, making his voice as soft and sweet as he could manage as his mind worked to figure out how to make Calvin smile, if only to perhaps ease the pain. "Don't fffucking worry about it."

Calvin burst out laughing, and John smiled proudly in response.

"Thank you for that," Calvin said, standing up straighter. He reached over to take some of the hats from John. "Let's work *together* to return them."

"Good idea." John handed Calvin half of the hats. "Are you sure you can w-w-walk, though?"

"Yes, I'm sure," Calvin said.

Halfway to the mourners, John looked over to see Calvin making a sour face. Calvin nodded to his pant leg, which appeared to be quite wet from the knee down. John grimaced as he realized that the apparent wetness had to be blood, and it only just appeared wet because of the black fabric.

Thankfully, no one mentioned Calvin's leg while they were returning the hats. Even with Calvin occasionally wincing from pain, the men were seemingly too preoccupied with the service to notice.

Once Calvin and John were within a few paces of their hearse, Calvin's breathing became labored, and each shaky inhale sent a wave of worry rushing through John's veins.

"God, John, this is terrible," Calvin said, tears springing to his eyes again. "I haven't felt this much pain in years. And I've probably ruined these pants."

Approaching the hearse cabin, John said, "Come sit back here with me."

John climbed in first, and Calvin followed, his body noticeably trembling. Calvin's visible upset made John's hands shake too, tremors of painful sympathy rippling through him. After hoisting himself up, Calvin settled onto the floor, clenching his teeth to keep himself from crying out in pain as he sat, and the sight pulled at John's heart. Quickly, John shut the cabin door and then crawled around the cabin on his hands and knees, closing each of the curtains. He left one of them open a smidge to let in a small stream of sunlight.

Afterward, John took a seat behind Calvin, stretching out his legs to rest one on either side of Calvin's body, and wrapped Calvin up in a backward embrace. Wordlessly, he urged Calvin to recline back.

"Let's relax for a minute," John whispered into Calvin's ear. "We'll take a look soon, but I n-n-need you to catch your breath first."

"Fuck, it hurts," Calvin hissed. He sniffled once. "Everything hurts."

John wasn't sure whether Calvin was only talking about his knee.

"I know, Cal. I know," he said softly. "I'm here."

After a moment, John pressed a cautious kiss to the tip of Calvin's ear. Slowly, he began peppering kisses on the side of Calvin's face, first up toward his temple and then on his cheek, hoping that every one of them would not only provide a bit of physical comfort but would also reassure Calvin of his love for him. Because even though John hadn't managed to say the words out loud yet, he so badly wanted Calvin to feel his love. He wanted Calvin to know it and for his love to feel as true and real and everlasting as time itself.

Calvin began to cry.

"I'm sorry, John," he said. "I'm so sorry."

Now John *knew* that Calvin wasn't talking about his knee anymore. He continued to kiss Calvin's face.

"I only stole those cuff links because I was scared. God, I was terrified that I'd end up back on the streets, especially because Michael really seemed to hate me so much. I thought for sure that working with you would be temporary." Calvin exhaled a long, trembling breath. "I told myself that once you eventually became more comfortable running the funerals, you would try to find someone else. I *still* . . . Christ, John, I *still* worry about that. I'm fucking terrified."

John shook his head in confusion. "What? Wh-wh-why?"

"I'm scared that there will come a time when you no longer need me and—"

"Oh, Cal, I'll always n-need you," John said.

But Calvin only began to cry more, his sniffles transforming into sobs. John's stomach churned with self-reproach. He knew he'd say the wrong thing. He never seemed to find the right words, no matter the situation. John began kissing Calvin's neck over his stiff shirt collar, his own eyes filling with tears.

"I'm sorry, Cal," he murmured. "I'm sorry."

"I want you to *want* me, John."

John's tears began to fall, wetting Calvin's clothing.

"I want you. Of course I want you. Did I . . . Oh, God, have I m-m-m-made you feel otherwise? I never meant to—"

"But *how* can you want me?" Calvin asked. "You barely even know me."

John shook his head, words of protest catching in his throat. Why was Calvin saying that? It wasn't true. It wasn't true at all.

"All the time we've been partners and friends, you've barely ever asked me about my life. At first, I thought that maybe . . . maybe it was only because it was too hard for you to hear about my childhood. Because it's so Goddamn sad. But every time I've brought up New York, you've changed the subject, too." Calvin's sharp words made John wince, and more tears fell from his eyes. John tried to kiss Calvin's cheek, to wordlessly apologize for making Calvin feel as though he didn't care, but Calvin turned away. "Even when I tried to tell you that I had stolen the cuff links, you cut me off and told me you wouldn't hear it. I wanted to explain myself. I wanted to tell you how sorry I was. I *needed* to. But . . ."

But John hadn't let him. John's heart splintered from the realization. Shame and regret coiled tighter inside him, making John want to collapse in on himself. He hadn't known that he'd been hurting Calvin like this. He had only ever wanted to protect Calvin from what he'd assumed would have been his own continued failures to provide the right kind of comfort, whether about Calvin's personal losses or everything else. But, God, how he wished he could turn back all the world's clocks now. He'd have happily spent the last weeks fumbling with words of sympathy and kindness if could have prevented Calvin from feeling like this.

"I'm sorry," John eked out, his voice shaking. "I know I've n-n-never asked for specifics, but I never meant to hurt you." He nuzzled the side of Calvin's head with his nose. "I m-m-may not know everything about you that I should, but I know your heart, Cal. Still, if that's not enough—"

"No, John, it's fine if you're not interested in—"

"I-I-I *am* interested," John insisted. "I want to know you, Calvin. All of you. Everything there is to know. P-P-*Please* believe me."

Calvin stayed silent for a few long, excruciating seconds while John continued to chastise himself for making such an egregious mistake, and then Calvin turned slightly to face him.

"Do you really want to know . . . everything?"

"Yes, Calvin."

"Even the terrible parts?" he choked out. "John, I was a con man."

"I know you were," John said, reaching up to touch Calvin's cheek. He wiped a tear away with his thumb. "But I know, too, Cal, that there's nothing you could ever say, n-n-nothing you could ever do, to make me not want us to be . . . *us* anymore."

"Are you mad at me for stealing Michael's cuff links?"

"No."

"Do you promise?"

"I promise."

"Would you have been if you had found them yourself?" Calvin asked, lowering his eyes. "If I had never returned them, I mean?"

John furrowed his brow, thinking.

"I can't say. But I'd have w-w-wanted to hear your reasons for taking them. Because I know you, Cal, and I know you'd have had a reason."

Calvin smiled half-heartedly. "Thank you."

John leaned forward and caught Calvin's mouth in a brief kiss.

"Does your knee still hurt?" he asked. Calvin nodded. "C-can I look at it?"

Calvin scooted away and turned, stretching out his leg toward John.

"Do you have vinegar in here?" he asked.

John nodded. "I keep some in my embalming kit."

"It's not that hopeless, is it?" Calvin said with a wry smile.

John had to fight back a laugh.

"I certainly hope not," he said, a smile tugging at the corner of his lips.

Calvin leaned back and rested his weight on his palms, and the moment that John started lifting his pant leg, he let out a whimper. John paused.

Calvin asked, "Does it look bad so far?"

"I can't see your cut yet," John said. "But there *is* a lot of blood."

"Oh, God," Calvin complained. "What if I need stitches?"

Warm sympathy swirled in John's chest again.

"Then I will come with you and hold your hand," he said. "Even if people think it looks f-f-funny."

"I've never had stitches."

"I have. Once." John moved closer to Calvin's face. He lifted his hair to reveal a small scar. "Here."

"Was it horrible?" Calvin asked.

John sat back. "Only because I was little."

"Do you think we'll be able to tell if I need stitches?"

"I'm not sure. I think my parents only thought that I needed them because it was my head that had been injured. I might n-not know if you need them on your knee. I'm not a physician."

John rolled up more of Calvin's pant leg to reveal a large laceration on Calvin's knee. He studied the cut for a few moments, wondering if it would need stitches, but eventually came to the conclusion that it would heal fine on its own. He nodded to himself and then began searching through his bag for the vinegar.

"Why would you keep vinegar in there?" Calvin asked.

"I've cut myself with my scalpel a few times. It hasn't happened in a while, but I like to be prepared."

John then soaked a rag in vinegar before pressing it to Calvin's wound. Calvin startled, hissing in pain. Frowning, John set the bottle of vinegar by Calvin's feet and then reached his free hand up to stroke Calvin's thigh as he continued to clean the cut.

"I'm so sorry, Cal," John said after a while. "I'm sorry I hurt you."

"I'm sorry, too," Calvin said. "I knew I needed to tell you about the cuff links. I've been making myself nauseated over it. I should have confessed anyway. Even when you basically urged me not to. You couldn't have known how important it was for me to tell you the truth." He sighed. "And I should have been more honest about everything else, too. But I had convinced myself that . . . well, that you weren't interested in knowing more about me."

"But that was my fault, wasn't it?" John said. "Because I n-n-never knew how to . . . how to respond to the things you t-tried to tell me."

"It wasn't only that," Calvin said. "Back in New York, I . . . I had a lover. David. We met when we were kids and . . ." Calvin shrugged. "David never liked it when I talked about my parents or the orphanage. I think it made him uncomfortable. Not because he struggled to know what to say, necessarily, but probably because he wasn't interested in becoming close with me. Emotionally. Funny that we lived together for ten years and I never felt close to him."

"I want to be close with you, Calvin," John said, trying his very best to sound sincere. "I want it m-m-more than anything."

"Do you mind if I tell you about him, then? About David? Or if I talk about my parents? Or even if I tell you about how I made money?"

John pulled a long white bandage out of his bag with some scissors. After he cut it to size, he began bandaging Calvin's knee.

"Tell me everything," he said. He paused his wrapping to look in Calvin's eyes. "Everything there is to know about Calvin Wright."

Calvin smiled, and John's words briefly hung in the air around them before Calvin finally spoke.

"Alright, well, David and I met when we were kids. I was thirteen, and he was fifteen. He was struggling, too. Orphaned, like me. I had recently left the orphanage to try to make it on my own, and then the two of us met when we were both helping unload cargo at one of the ports. Just, you know, to make money. I think David felt sorry for me when I told him that I'd been sleeping in a park, and so, he let me come live with him in an old warehouse."

John finished tying the bandage and scooted closer to Calvin. He wrapped Calvin up in a hug. Calvin hummed happily, and they shared a kiss.

Calvin continued, "After that, we stuck together, taking whatever work we could. Sometime later, we started stealing. Just pickpocketing, initially, but that eventually turned into other things. Once we were much older, when I was nineteen or so, our friendship changed into something more."

"What happened? With your relationship?"

"Wasn't meant to be," Calvin said, sadly. "David never loved me."

"I'm sorry to hear that." John furrowed his brow as he considered what he should say next. But he couldn't think of anything helpful. So, instead, he pressed a kiss to Calvin's temple and said, "Keep going."

Over the next fifteen minutes or so, Calvin talked without stopping, sometimes without seeming to take a breath, either. He told John about his childhood. About how his parents had been killed in a train crash. About how lonely and hopeless he'd felt in the orphanage.

OURSELVES AND IMMORTALITY

All the while, John pressed soft kisses to Calvin's head and cheeks, trying to imprint some of the love he felt with every single one. Despite the fact that John couldn't even *begin* to know what to say to most of what Calvin told him, he needed Calvin to know he cared. Not one thing that Calvin said was making John love him any less. Actually, learning more about Calvin's childhood and realizing how *much* pain and uncertainty and struggle Calvin had been forced to face was only making John love him more.

When Calvin finally went silent, John captured his mouth in a kiss. Pulling Calvin close, John poured every bit of love he had into it, trying hard to impress upon Calvin how very enamored he was, even though he hadn't yet tried to say the words. But, oh, he *wanted* to say them.

When they parted, John tipped their foreheads together.

"Cal, I have something I want to say, and—and I hope it's not too f-fast."

Calvin smiled sweetly, pulling back to look in John's eyes. "What is it?"

John swallowed past the nervous lump in his throat.

"I love you." Calvin's bottom lip trembled, and John touched it with his thumb. "And I-I think I've fallen more in love with you now, knowing everything that you've been through."

Calvin's lips curled into a tentative smile. "Really?"

John nodded, smiling back. "Really."

"Oh, John, I love you too," Calvin said, letting out a shaky breath.

Before John could even react, Calvin pulled him in for another kiss. Now John knew for certain that he loved every part of Calvin Wright.

Every single part.

Chapter Sixteen
Calvin

For hours, Calvin and John stayed cuddled together in the cabin of their hearse carriage, only emerging once the sun had set. Both of their stomachs rumbled from hunger. Calvin wasn't bothered by it. It seemed like John wasn't either. It was so wonderful to spend time together like this—away from the world. Hopefully no one from the funeral noticed that their hearse was still parked nearby, but, in truth, Calvin couldn't bring himself to care very much, not when he felt so safe snuggled with John. He wished that they had brought some blankets with them. Or pillows. Instead, they settled for taking off their waistcoats and suit jackets, and bunching them up beneath their heads as they lay cuddled together.

Once the stars came out, John and Calvin climbed out of the cabin. Together, they looked up at the sky. Surrounded only by the cloak of night and the barely visible cemetery headstones, Calvin reached for John's hand.

"Thank you for listening earlier," he said softly.

"Anytime, Cal."

Calvin turned to John. "It's beautiful out here, isn't it?"

"It is. I love the stars," John said, releasing Calvin's hand. He cupped Calvin's chin. "But, you, Calvin Wright, shine b-b-brighter than every single one."

Letting out a soft sigh, Calvin closed his eyes and basked in the light of John's love.

"See, John, you are plenty skilled with words," Calvin said, opening his eyes.

"I've had that line in my head since we saw the play together," John said. "I w-w-wanted to say it on the ride home, but you seemed . . . sad."

Calvin hung his head. "I was. But it was silly of me. I know that now."

"Never," John said. "Sadness is never s-silly."

"Mine was," Calvin said. "I can't believe I thought you wouldn't want me once I confessed to stealing the cuff links. I thought for sure you'd leave me. Either right when I told you or once I eventually managed to tell you how many people I'd tricked over the years." He frowned as Michael's hateful words floated into the forefront of his mind. He wondered how long they would haunt him. "I let Michael poison my mind, it seems."

"I know how that is," John said, his voice suddenly sullen.

Calvin still wasn't sure what Michael had told John then.

"Don't buy whatever falsehoods he tried to sell you," Calvin said. "Because we're perfect together."

John nuzzled Calvin's nose. "You're right, Cal. We are. God, sometimes I wish that I could t-t-tell the whole world about us. I want everyone to know how much I love you."

"Sometimes I want that, too," Calvin said, a small pang in his chest. "But what we have is wonderful. Even if we have to keep it to ourselves. It's real, and it's beautiful. Too beautiful, maybe, for the rest of the world."

John's mouth found his, and when their tongues swirled together, Calvin's head began to spin, leaving him in a state of light-headed bliss. John clutched tight to his shirt, pulling Calvin's body flush with his own, and Calvin felt John's hard length pressing against him. Letting out a soft moan into John's mouth, Calvin scrambled to find one of John's hands. Burning with the need to bring John pleasure, to make the man he loved writhe and moan and climax in the cemetery, Calvin broke their kiss and started back toward the hearse.

"Come here, John. Let me take care of you."

Both of them climbed inside, and as soon as they had privacy, John lay back, resting his head on his rumpled suit jacket. Calvin crawled over and began unfastening John's pants as John slipped off his suspenders. Without light from either an oil lamp or the sun, Calvin could only barely make out his lover in the black blanket of nightfall. He tugged John's pants to his knees and took John's beautiful cock into his hand. Settling beside John in the hearse, Calvin started to pump his fist.

"I love you," he whispered. "I love every part of you."

"Oh . . ." John moaned. "Oh, God, Cal." He turned to bury his face in the crook of Calvin's neck. "I'm so close. Already, I'm . . . oh, Lord, I'm . . ." His cock started to pulse in Calvin's hand, warmth spilling over Calvin's fist. Groaning, John pressed a kiss to Calvin's neck. "I'm sorry. I'm sorry."

"Why are you sorry?" Calvin said through a light chuckle.

"It was so f-fast," John said. "But being here with you . . . hearing you say those words . . . I couldn't help myself."

Calvin's cheeks warmed, fondness blooming in his chest.

"Oh, John, I love how passionate you are about us. I love how excited I seem to make you."

"Everything about you excites me," John said. "Cal, you're m-m-magical to me. Truly."

Calvin's stomach fluttered as John pressed lightly on his shoulder, wordlessly instructing Calvin to recline back. Then John climbed on top of him and began kissing over the top of Calvin's clothes, working his way down toward the hem of Calvin's pants.

Calvin shrugged off his suspenders. In only seconds, his cock was free.

John took the tip into his mouth, and Calvin's eyes rolled back as John began to lower his head, the warm slick of his tongue massaging Calvin's shaft with every motion. Faster and faster, John bobbed his head, seeming to easily find a rhythm, and Calvin's eyes became unfocused, his vision blurring slightly as he lost himself to pleasure. Soon, John took Calvin's whole cock into his mouth, his nose bumping Calvin's pubic bone, and the sensation of having the entirety of his length enveloped in the wet warmth of John's mouth threatened to send Calvin over the edge.

And Calvin might have been able to last, had John not held himself there.

"Oh, hell . . ." Calvin's cock started to pulse.

Intoxicated by the rush of bliss, Calvin's hands found the back of John's head, and, without thinking it through, he held John still, his need to keep his cock surrounded by comforting, pleasurable warmth overtaking every other thought in his head. With a long moan, he emptied himself inside John's mouth, shooting ejaculate to the back of his partner's throat.

Once his cock stopped pulsing, he came to his senses.

Removing his hands, he said, "Oh, John, I'm sorry! I forgot myself."

Laughing, John came up beside him. "I loved it. I loved seeing you lose control like that."

"Did I hurt you?"

"Not even a little."

John captured Calvin's mouth in a surprise kiss, and Calvin's heart fluttered excitedly when he realized he could still taste himself on John's lips.

"God, I love you," he said to John.

"I love you too, Calvin."

Over the next few minutes, the two continued to kiss, murmuring occasional sweet nothings into each other's ears, and then, when they both started to feel sleepy, they finally pulled up their pants and left for home.

On the way, Calvin began ruminating on the past few days. Oh, how wrong he had been about John and the love they shared! Calvin's cheeks prickled with shame. Even though he had already sensed that John seemed to struggle with providing comfort over emotionally heavy situations, especially *words* of comfort, Calvin had still let his past hurt cloud the way he had viewed John's silence. He had still let it nearly ruin his relationship. God, he had been mentally preparing himself to run off with the money he had saved to pay Michael back for the necklace. Somehow, Calvin had let both Michael's harsh words and David's constant coldness scare him into thinking that John could never really love him. How shameful it was that he'd let his own mind manipulate him.

More shameful, though, was the fact that, even now, Calvin could feel a lingering fear still lurking inside him, hiding in the shadows of his brain.

If only Calvin could reason with it.

Despite everything, Calvin still hadn't managed to tell John about David's betrayal. John had requested honesty. And Calvin *had* been honest. He had revealed the truth about the cuff links. Had told John about his past crimes. He'd even told John about David. And yet . . .

David's willingness to break what they'd had, it had been too painful to share. Calvin's chest tightened, his heart feeling as though it was cracking in two. God, David had thrown him away. And Calvin had lost *everything*.

How could Calvin ever stand to tell John how callous David had been? Or, especially, how worthless he had felt ever since?

Calvin swallowed thickly, hurt bubbling up inside him.

"John?" he said. "Do you think you'll always need me?"

"I thought you w-w-wanted me to *want* you," John said.

"Yes, of course I want that. But . . ." He looked at his shoes. "I was just wondering if you thought you'd need me, too."

"Always," John confirmed. "I will *always* need you, Calvin."

Calvin closed his eyes and repeated the words to himself, hoping that their power might banish his lingering worries and praying that they were true.

Chapter Seventeen
Calvin

One week went by. Calvin was in the middle of fixing his cravat in the hallway mirror when John came out of the bathroom and wrapped him up in a backward embrace, pressing their cheeks together as they both eyed their reflections.

"Ready?" he asked.

"Almost," Calvin said.

John tugged on one of the ends of the cravat. "May I help?"

"Of course." Calvin turned to face him, and John took hold of the silky fabric. John's uncle had died earlier that week. And it was *John* who had embalmed him. Calvin couldn't help but be curious as to whether or not it had been strange for him, though he suspected that John hadn't been very fazed by it. "How are you feeling? Was it, uhm, strange to work on your uncle yourself?"

"Somewhat," John answered.

"I'm really sorry for ever calling *you* strange for the work you do. Really, I'm so impressed by you, John. I mean, you and Michael could have found someone else for the embalming, but—"

"He asked for me," John said. "Before he passed. Uncle Frances and I, we had never c-connected much, so I think . . . I think him telling Michael that he wanted me to be the one to help lay him to rest, it was his way of maybe saying that he loved me. He, like everyone else, had thought that I was an eccentric boy, but it seems he never forgot that I was his n-n-nephew."

Calvin tried for a comforting smile. "I hope the funeral isn't too hard for you."

"It won't be," John said with a shake of his head. "Death is a part of life. I'll be fine."

"Right."

Despite having helped organize a significant number of funerals thus far, Calvin still had trouble keeping his mind from circling back to everything he had lost. Ever since he'd first talked with Katherine, he'd been struggling to keep his past hurt from resurfacing. Talking with John the previous week had helped, though. What had been a near-constant pain, one that pulsed with every beat of his still-broken heart, had been reduced to a mild throb, something he only really noticed when they were in the middle of a funeral.

After John was finished tying the cravat, Calvin leaned forward and pressed their lips together.

"Come on," he said. "It's time for us to impress Michael."

"Oh, yes, I'm sure he'll be impressed," John replied, voice thick with sarcasm. "Uhm, in case you thought I was being serious—"

"No, I *know* you were being sarcastic," Calvin said fondly before taking John's hand. "But I really meant what I said." He started for the stairs, tugging John along with him. "You've blossomed over these last few months. I mean it."

"Don't lie, Cal," John said wearily. "Goodness, you saw how f-f-flustered I became while talking to Richard's mistress last week. I couldn't even . . . God, the c-cookie comment . . ."

When they reached the bottom of the stairs, Calvin stopped and turned to face him.

"Even *I* would have been flustered in that situation."

"Doubtful."

"No, really, I would have been." Calvin pursed his lips, thinking. "Did you have exams when you went to Eckels?"

"Only one. After I was finished with the program."

"Alright, well, I think that if that . . . *encounter* with Elizabeth had been the exam, nearly every student would have had to repeat the course. John, no one could have prepared you for that sort of strangeness. All things considered, you were very welcoming." Calvin couldn't fight the smile. "Almost *too* welcoming."

John flicked Calvin's shoulder with his free hand.

"Not nice," he said.

"I'm still intrigued by the prospect of playing with each other's cookies. Perhaps the next time we're in the bedroom, instead of sucking my cock, you could—"

"Cal!" John scolded, his cheeks reddening

He released Calvin's hand and shoved him forward.

Calvin tried to stay in his spot. "I was only—"

But John shoved him again. "Don't want to be late." Another shove. "Out." One more toward the back door. "Keep moving."

Laughing, Calvin finally relented, and the two left for the funeral together.

Together, they traveled to John's uncle's home in Kensington. After the funeral, Michael would be putting it up for sale. Or perhaps he would want to live here himself. Calvin wasn't sure. God, was it nice to fantasize about Michael moving out, though.

When they reached the right home, they parked the hearse in front of the house, and then John and Calvin walked Agathe over to the nearest hitching post, which was half a block over. After securing her, the two men walked back to the house.

Katherine came out to meet them before either of them had a chance to knock, welcoming both of them with a hug. When they then went up the four cement steps to John's uncle's home, Michael was waiting by the foot of the inside staircase, leaning against the post. He threw Calvin a thin-lipped smile, one that was very obviously fake, and a curt nod. God, the tension was so uncomfortable. It was practically thick enough to cut with a knife. Or perhaps one of John's scalpels.

Calvin merely nodded back, though part of him wanted to say something biting instead. He and John followed Katherine through the front room toward the kitchen.

Coming up behind them, Michael said, "Are you two *always* this friendly to your clients?"

Calvin clenched his teeth. Michael wasn't a real client. Real clients never sneered at him in lieu of welcoming him into their homes.

Luckily, John tried to shift the topic of conversation.

"Have you thought about wh-wh-wh-wh- . . ." He paused to restart. "Have you thought about wh-whether or not you were interested in having me create some kind of pin or—"

"Not interested, thanks," Michael said with a wave of his wrist.

Katherine huffed a sarcastic laugh, barely even loud enough for Calvin to hear. What was *that* about? Hopefully he could find out later.

In the kitchen, Katherine explained how she wanted the refreshments served—Calvin's funeral cookies in the sitting room with the tea and coffee, not in the front room where the viewing and small service would take place—while Calvin tried not to react to the feeling of Michael's eyes boring into him from behind. Ugh, that man. He was so infuriating.

After the rest of the preparations were made—scarf hung on the front door, cookies and beverages set out, funeral chairs unfolded and arranged neatly into rows in the front room, casket open and ready—Calvin caught Katherine heading back into the kitchen. He blurted out that he needed some water and followed.

"So, I hope you'll tell me why you were laughing before," he said with a little teasing smile. After playfully tsk-ing a few times, he continued, chiding, "Mocking waning funeral customs. It's frowned upon, for sure."

"I wasn't *laughing*!" she protested, one hand coming to her chest as though she was physically wounded by the accusation. Calvin raised an incredulous eyebrow in response. "Oh, fine. I *was* laughing. Or scoffing a bit. See, *of course* Michael wouldn't be interested in some sort of mourning trinket. Goodness, he refused to even let my father hire a photographer."

"Well, that's because Uncle Frances hadn't been much to look at *before* he passed, so—"

Katherine smacked Calvin on the bicep, barely suppressing a smile with her pursed lips.

"Sorry. I'm trying to be funny," Calvin said.

"I know." She leaned in close, and her previously repressed smile bloomed to life on her face. "But the thing is, you're right."

Shielding his mouth with his hand, Calvin huffed a soft laugh. Thank God Katherine enjoyed his type of humor, crass as it could be. He scooped up one of the extra funeral cookies from the tin on the table and took a bite, friendly fondness swirling in his chest. He really liked Katherine.

After taking a bite, he said, "So, has Michael always been uncomfortable with funeral stuff, then?"

"I'm not sure, really," she said, taking a cookie too. "I think . . ." She paused to take a bite. "I think he struggles with knowing how to grieve."

"Well, keeping everything inside only makes it worse. I think. I'm starting to learn that myself. I kept so much inside over the years. David—my, uhm, previous . . . friend—wasn't very caring. Every time I tried to talk to him about my parents, he'd become sort of irate, which . . . well, made me not want to bring them up anymore. But that was fine. I mean, even when he and I were kids, I was vaguely aware that David was probably only mad because hearing me blather on about *my* parents forced him to think about *his* and . . ." Calvin heaved a sigh. "Anyway, now that I have John, I've found myself talking about my parents more often. It helps ease the pain, surprisingly. It's like . . . like when I talk about them, they're still here with me. In my heart or . . . something. Sorry. Maybe that's too sentimental."

Katherine smiled warmly. "You're wise for a con man, Calvin Wright."

Though he wasn't entirely sure whether or not she meant it to be a real compliment, blood still rushed to Calvin's cheeks. "Thank you. I think."

"I mean it, though. Not only wise, but sweet. I bet you help your clients feel relaxed with that lovely personality of yours. I bet you make them laugh, too."

"I try."

Katherine took another bite of her cookie before her eyes flew wide.

"Oh! Look!" She fished a necklace out from beneath her neckline. It was beautiful—silver with what looked to be a sapphire and a pearl in the center of the heart pendant. "Michael bought it for me with the necklace money. Thank you for paying us back so quickly."

Shame swirled in Calvin's stomach, and his face reddened.

"You're welcome," he said uneasily.

"What's wrong?"

"Nothing," he said. "Or, something. It's . . . I had kind of considered *not* paying you back. Not because I wanted to steal from you. Again. But I wanted to make sure I had some money saved. In case John no longer . . . wanted me."

Katherine sighed sweetly and touched Calvin's shoulder.

"John *adores* you."

"I know. I mean, I *think* I know." Calvin met her eyes, and an uncertain smile tugged on his lips. "Does he really?"

"Yes, Calvin. He's smitten," Katherine said with a laugh.

"Well, then, I'm happy I paid you back for the necklace." Katherine removed her hand, and Calvin looked at the necklace, its chain draped over Katherine's high neckline. "It's a beautiful piece. Actually, I think this one is even nicer than your old one." He playfully scrunched up his nose. "Sorry. Maybe I shouldn't have said that."

"It's fine, Calvin. We're friends. We can be honest with each other."

"Really? Friends?"

"I think so."

Calvin's body buzzed with happiness. God, he had a real friend now. Not one he was trying to bed, either.

"Speaking of our friendship," Katherine said before taking a bite of her cookie. She took a moment to chew and swallow. Then she continued. "I keep thinking about something you said to me a while ago."

"Hopefully nothing bad."

"No, nothing bad. I've been considering what you said about married women working, and, well, that made me wonder about working myself." Calvin's eyebrows shot up. He'd nearly forgotten his mortician suggestion. "I think I might like it. I keep picturing myself having my own shop or something." Katherine blushed and shook her head. "It's silly."

Calvin smiled. "It's not."

"Do you think I'm personable enough?" she asked.

"Without a doubt."

"Smart enough?"

"Yes."

"Organized enough?"

"Katherine, I think you are *everything* enough that you need to be to run a business. And if you should ever choose to open a shop, I'm confident that it will be one of the most beloved in the entirety of Philadelphia."

Katherine's entire face reddened even more, her smile practically stretching from ear to ear. One of her curls spilled out from her mess of hairpins, springing in front of her face, and she blew it away. Calvin chuckled.

She said, "See, Calvin, you are so easy to talk to. I've never even shared that with anyone else. Not even with Michael. Goodness, he can be so tight-lipped when it comes to personal things. Especially certain matters. If only one of us could convince him to talk about—"

Michael burst into the room, pushing the swinging kitchen door so forcefully that the wood smacked the edge of the closest work space, causing both Katherine and Calvin to flinch.

"Sorry." He cleared his throat. "Guests should be here soon."

"Be right there," Calvin said, shoving the second half of his funeral cookie into his mouth, and then Katherine copied, eating the rest of hers in one bite too.

Michael sighed, his eyes flickering up to the ceiling as he shook his head. Ducking their chins, Calvin and Katherine moved past him, both of them still smiling mischievous little smiles, like children who had been caught sneaking treats.

Out in the front room, John was sitting on one of the folding chairs, wringing his hands nervously. Calvin sat beside him.

"What is it?" he asked.

John shook his head, his hands continuing to move. "Nothing."

"Liar," Calvin scolded, knocking John's shoe with his own.

"Michael thought I should try to help you welcome people," he said softly. "But I k-k-keep thinking about that Elizabeth woman and—"

Calvin placed a hand on top of John's. "Do you *want* to help?"

"Not exactly, but I probably should. I mean, Michael's right. There will be old f-f-family friends coming. Extended family members too. But . . . Cal, I'll n-n-need your help."

Calvin squeezed John's hands. "Of course, John. We'll work together."

Nodding, John met Calvin's eyes and smiled. "Thank you."

Over the hour, John and Calvin worked together to welcome people into Uncle Frances's home. And, *God*, John was magnificent. Even though John sometimes struggled to know what to say or otherwise struggled with saying what he *wanted* to say, he kept on trying. He never once crumpled in on himself. Never once went off to sit on his own. And when John looked like he needed a bit of reassurance, all it had taken was a smile or a touch from Calvin to boost his resolve. All in all, John was wonderful. And Calvin was so proud of him.

Thankfully, the first part of the service then passed without issue.

Later, while the pastor read from scripture, Calvin, who was seated in the front row closest to their makeshift aisle, fiddled with his pocket watch, repeatedly clicking it open and then clicking it closed, while trying to keep his mind in the present, though it kept returning to his parents' funeral instead.

Letting his eyes fall to the beige-and-brown carpet, Calvin's focus shifted, reality itself blurring while images of the past flashed in his mind.

Seeing his parents in their caskets.

Disingenuous looks of mild sympathy from relatives, their smiles thin-lipped and eyes uncaring.

Little Calvin clutching tight to the pocket watch while he sobbed in his bedroom, legs curled close to his chest, blanket pulled up over his head.

Weighty sorrow fell upon Calvin's shoulders. He sat with his head low for the rest of the service, startling from John's soft voice when it ended.

"Cal, the service is over," he said.

"Sorry," Calvin said with a single shake of his head. "Just thinking."

"Not paying you to think," Michael said, coming up the aisle. Calvin barely fought back the urge to say that Michael was barely even paying them at all, only reimbursing John for the money that he had spent on the embalming fluid. Tapping his foot, Michael said, "Don't you want to see everyone to their carriages so that we can head to the cemetery?"

Placing his hands on his knees, Calvin pushed himself to stand. "Yes, of course. Sorry."

"I can try to see them out by m-m-myself instead," John offered, squeezing Calvin's shoulder.

Calvin's stomach fell. While it was sweet that John wanted to take care of him, Calvin had promised they'd work together. He couldn't break his promise to John.

Swallowing his upset, Calvin reached up to squeeze John's hand and said, "No, I'll come too. Really. I was lost in thought for a little while, but I'm fine."

Together, Calvin and John started toward the back of the room, and for the next fifteen minutes, they exchanged a mixture of pleasantries, platitudes, and expressions of regret with everyone who had come to pay their respects (save for the three other men who would help them carry the casket to the hearse) and then showed the mourners to their carriages while instructing them on how to find the cemetery later.

After the casket was taken from the house and lifted into the hearse, Michael and Katherine left to freshen up while John started packing up the chairs, which they would pile off to the side for now and come back for later or the following morning, as was typical. Calvin began to help collapse them.

"What were you thinking about earlier?" John asked, leaning one of the folded chairs against the wall.

"Just my parents. How painful their funeral was."

John froze, his brows knitting together. "I'm sorry. I-I can't even imagine . . ."

He trailed off as affection unfurled in Calvin's chest. He knew how hard John was trying to comfort him.

"Thank you," Calvin said, warmth in his voice.

John raked a hand through his hair, mussing it up.

"Tell me, how was their service? Did mmmany people come?"

"Yes," Calvin said, sorrow twisting in his chest, even as he still felt full with gratitude. "They were both very loved in our little community, especially my father. I still can't believe that no one"—Calvin paused to swallow, a lump forming in his throat—"wanted me."

"Oh, Cal . . ." John set the chair he had folded up against the wall before coming over to wrap Calvin in a hug. "I w-w-would have wanted you."

Calvin chuckled softly, his eyes brimming with tears. "John, you're only four years older than I am."

"Still." John squeezed tighter. "I would have wanted you then, and I want you now."

"Thank you," Calvin said. "Even though that sentiment is a *tiny* bit silly."

"Sorry."

Calvin pulled back to fix John's hair. "Don't be. It was silly, but it was perfect, too. It was a perfectly silly thing for you to say." His hand trailed lower to brush John's cheek. "I love you."

"And I love you, Calvin."

"It really helped to talk to you," Calvin said. "Thank you for listening."

"Anytime."

"If you ever need me to listen, I've been told that I'm easy to talk to." John only hummed a little in response. Calvin continued, boasting, "Actually, Katherine said that to me earlier. Isn't that incredible? It's hard to believe that she still wants to be my friend even though I was such a bastard to her when we met."

"I'm sure you weren't *that* horrible."

"I *stole* from her."

"And I'm sure you were very n-nice while doing it."

Calvin huffed a laugh. "Yeah, I wasn't too bad, maybe." He nodded toward the remaining chairs. "We better finish up or Michael will have our heads on a platter."

"Yes, let's."

For the entirety of the burial, Calvin felt lighter than he had for some time, the support from John and Katherine making the heaviness of his past loss easier to bear.

Once Calvin and John were finally home, they slipped away into John's bedroom together before Michael and Katherine came back. As soon as the door closed behind them, Calvin snaked his hands inside John's suit jacket, pulling him in for a passionate kiss. John's fingers threaded through Calvin's locks, and the two men pressed themselves closer together. Their knees knocked together, and Calvin pulled back, hissing in pain.

"What is it? Your knee?" John said, slightly breathless.

"Yeah," Calvin replied with a wince. "Damn. It still hurts."

"May I clean it for you?"

"It's probably fine," Calvin said.

"Cal . . ." John took a step back and fell to his knees. He began pulling up the fabric of Calvin's pants. "I won't have you ending up on my c-c-cooling table."

Calvin merely pursed his lips. He waited for John to finish rolling his pant leg past his knee and then unravel the bandage.

"Yes, we ought to clean it," John said right away. "It's healing, but I can't help but be worried."

For the first time, Calvin looked down to inspect his injury. It wasn't as bad as John seemed to fear. Calvin had suffered worse throughout the years. Even the cut on his finger had been far worse than this one.

"Alright, you can clean it," he said. "I think it looks fine, though."

"Let me take care of you." John pushed himself to his feet. "Isn't that wh-wh-what you said to me back in the cemetery?"

"Uh, well, I was referring to making you come, so . . ."

Chuckling, John kissed Calvin briefly on the lips.

"Mmm . . . that'll come later."

"That'll *come* later, hmm?"

John rolled his eyes playfully and started toward the door. "I'll be back in a few. I n-n-need my supplies."

As John left, Calvin made his way over to the bed and sat. John returned not two minutes later with honey, vinegar, one of his square cloths from his black bag, and a long linen bandage.

Wordlessly, John crossed the room, stopping in front of Calvin, his brow creased slightly with worry. Calvin's chest fluttered from the sight. How foreign and yet how splendid it felt to be cared for like this.

Over the next few minutes, John cleaned the cut with vinegar and then spread a thin layer of honey on top, explaining that honey was thought to prevent infection. Calvin already knew this from his mother, but he let John explain it anyway.

When John was finished with the honey, Calvin curled his knee to inspect his injury again. Upon seeing the shimmering honey—evidence of John's care—Calvin's body tingled with unexpected warmth.

Reverently, Calvin said, "No one else has ever made me feel like this. Like I'm *home*. You make me so happy, John. We're like a lock and key, you and I. Made for each other."

With a happy hum, John said, "I think so too."

Calvin's eyes began to tear as he watched John tie the bandage. It had been so Goddamned long since he had felt this loved. He suddenly wished he could have something to remind him of this moment and John's care forever.

"I hope it leaves a scar," he said.

John's eyes went wide with horror. "Wh-wh-what a horrible thing to hope for!"

"It isn't horrible," Calvin laughed. "It'll remind me of how well you took care of me. I'll be upset if it heals too well. Actually, maybe we ought to remove the bandage. Thwart the healing process a little."

"Bite your tongue," John said, a smile cracking through his fake sternness. "It better heal well. I wouldn't ffforgive myself if it became infected."

"It won't. Not with how well you've cleaned it."

"If you take this off before I tell you to—"

"I won't, I won't," Calvin said through another laugh. "I still hope it scars, though."

"I heard that," John mock-scolded in return, settling beside Calvin on the bed. Calvin rolled onto his side, nuzzling John's nose. Sighing, John said, "Alright. I'll hope for it too."

And then Calvin took hold of John's lapels and pulled him in for a kiss.

Some weeks later, Calvin took John to a baseball game. Calvin wasn't exactly a fan of the Philadelphia Phillies, but he wasn't *not* a fan, either. In truth, Calvin loved baseball so much that he would have been happy to root for whichever team he was supposed to in whichever city he was in. All that mattered to him was that, for the first time in a *long* time, he would soon be watching it.

Waiting in front of the grand stand entrance, Calvin could barely contain himself. Energy flowed through his veins with such intensity that it was taking every ounce of strength he had not to bounce on the balls of his feet as they waited to purchase their tickets.

When they reached the front of the line, Calvin let out a tiny squeal. Catching Calvin's eye, John chuckled, the fondness in his laughter only ratcheting up Calvin's elation.

By the time Calvin and John found seats in the bleachers, Calvin was completely beaming, smiling from ear to ear like a fool, and now, he was completely unable to scale it back. He looked over to his companion. John's eyes were slowly moving across the field, and he was nodding in a way that suggested he was still taking everything in.

"When's the last time you came here?" Calvin asked.

"Oh, I've never been here before," John said, now seemingly inspecting the stands beside them instead of the field. "I've never even seen a b-b-baseball game."

"What?!" Calvin spluttered

Turning to him, John tilted his head. "What?"

"I can't believe you've never watched baseball!"

"Because it's our country's so-called n-n-national pastime?" John asked with a chuckle, to which Calvin simply widened his eyes and blinked very slowly, trying to communicate how incredibly shocked he was feeling. John shrugged and said, "Well, I-I've never had so much as one friend. Who would have come with me to see it played? Michael isn't the type to care for sports. He prefers the theatre."

Of course Michael preferred the theatre. Ugh. Calvin pretended to scoff while trying not to think about how much he himself loved the theatre as well. Then he said, "Oh, you poor, sweet man."

John laughed heartily. "Don't pity me for never having spent hours sitting on w-wooden bleachers in the blazing sun watching men toss a ball to each other."

"Baseball is more complicated than *that*," Calvin said.

John wiggled his eyebrows playfully.

"Oh, is it? Teach me, then, Calvin Wright," John said with a sparkle in his eye. "While we w-watch, you can explain everything that's happening. Make me love baseball."

Calvin sucked on his lip. God, he loved playful John.

"Alright, I will."

Simultaneously, both men intentionally bumped their knees together, leaving them touching even though they had plenty of room. Within seconds, their brazenness had turned John's cheeks bright pink and made Calvin's burn in the most exciting way.

When the first pitch was thrown, Calvin let out a very happy sigh.

He was home.

Over the next hour, Calvin took care to explain everything that was happening on the field, and, when there was a lull, he tried to teach John a little of the sport's history as well. While Calvin couldn't be *one hundred percent certain* that *everything* he was saying was correct, he *was* confident that he was relaying what his father had told him when he was a boy. So, the information was true enough. It was true for him, anyway.

Regardless, by sharing these facts, whether they were completely true or not, Calvin felt a connection to his past, to his *childhood*, similar to that he'd felt when John had tried to teach him carpentry. Watching baseball with John, explaining the sport to him, being in the stadium, it was *perfect*.

All the while, John seemed to eat up every word Calvin said, whether it was commentary on what was happening on the field or an explanation of the various types of throws that the pitchers liked to use (fastballs, curveballs, slow balls), and even though Calvin was sure John wasn't really *that* interested in baseball itself, he could tell John was very obviously interested in *him*.

And that was truly wonderful.

Halfway through the sixth inning, someone tapped Calvin on the shoulder from behind.

"Excuse me, sir," the man said. "Do you have the time?"

Calvin's breath caught, the memory of the final baseball game he'd seen with his father bursting into his mind like a concentrated beam of sunlight and then replaying with radiant clarity. Some seconds must have passed while Calvin remained transfixed by the flash of the cherished childhood memory because John's hand found his knee and squeezed, pulling Calvin back into the present.

"Time?" Calvin blurted out with a shake of his head as John removed his hand. "Apologies. Yes, let me . . ." He reached into his inner breast pocket and took out his father's pocket watch. With a shaky breath, he pressed the little button on top to reveal the watch's face. After a clearing of his throat, Calvin replied, "Seven past four."

"Thank you, young man."

Calvin continued to stare at the timepiece, watching the seconds tick by. After a moment, John's hand came to rest on the bleachers in between them. Ever so slowly, he inched it toward Calvin.

Stealthily rubbing Calvin's thigh with his fingers, John said, "It's a fine watch, Calvin."

"It is," Calvin said with a small, wistful smile.

In a whispered voice, John added, "And you're a f-f-fine man."

Calvin tilted his head, his small smile broadening a little.

"Do you really think so?"

"I *know* so."

What a fine man John was too. No one else had ever made Calvin feel like this. Like he was worthy of care. Of respect. Of a proper life, not one on the streets. No one other than his parents had ever made him feel like he mattered. Somehow, John had seen Calvin's worth from the start, back when they were strangers, back when Calvin had been, in truth, less than worthy of either respect or care. He had been a criminal. Worth*less* in the eyes of some (even in Calvin's own eyes when he was feeling particularly low). Certainly not worthy of becoming John's business partner and roommate. Not worthy of second chances or friendship. Or love.

Without John, Calvin would still have been languishing in his one-room rental, stealing to make ends meet. He'd have had nothing.

And now, Calvin had *everything*.

Calvin's eyes fell back to the watch.

Ever since losing his parents, Calvin had considered the pocket watch to be his most treasured possession, not only because it had belonged to his father but also because the watch had come to symbolize the home he'd once had. Whenever Calvin held it, he sensed his father's presence. The feel of the cool metal beneath his fingertips had rarely ever failed to comfort him, to remind him that he had once been loved. Hearing the *tick-tick-tick* of the timepiece always transported Calvin back into the past, and he knew that as long as he had the watch, he wouldn't forget his parents or their love for him.

But ever since Calvin had shared his memories of his parents with John, he had come to realize that his parents weren't ever far from his mind, nor was their love ever not in his heart. He would never forget them. Or their love for him.

Once, the watch had been Calvin's everything.

But now . . .

Calvin said, "Did I tell you that my father gave this to me when we were watching a baseball game together?" He stroked the watch's face. "In New York."

"No, you hadn't told me that," John replied before slowly lifting his hand to touch the timepiece too.

"Yes, he, uhm, he passed not two months later."

After a brief pause, John said, "I'm sorry."

"I know. I'm sorry too."

Their fingers touched.

All of a sudden, the crack of a wooden bat reverberated through the stadium, causing everyone to stand and cheer. Everyone except for John and Calvin. Even though they were surrounded by the roar of the crowd, sitting in the middle of a sea of Philadelphians, it seemed as though the entire outside world had fallen away.

All that remained was the fierce love that he and John felt for one another. Even though Calvin still sometimes worried that John would cease to need him—cease to *want* him—he wanted

John to know how very much he treasured their relationship. He wanted to prove to John—and to himself—that he believed in it.

Calvin leaned in close and clicked the watch closed.

Unhooking the watch's chain, he said, "I want you to have this."

John's eyes flew wide as he retracted his hand.

"Cal, I-I couldn't possibly—"

Calvin smiled warmly. "Take it." He snatched John's hand and pressed the timepiece into his palm. "All this time, it's been a symbol of home for me. I only needed it because, well, because I had lost my home. But I have one now. With you."

Everyone was starting to sit, making further conversation somewhat risky. Still, Calvin had one more thing to say.

Carefully, Calvin closed John's fingers over the watch, and then he whispered in John's ear, "I want you to have it. Really. Because you gave me everything, John. And I want to give *you* everything in return."

When Calvin sat up straighter, he noticed that tears had formed in John's beautiful brown eyes. Oh, how he wanted to embrace his sweet, perfect mortician and prevent those tears from falling. Instead, Calvin offered what he hoped was a warm smile. And a nod.

After a moment of stunned hesitation, John smiled back.

And Calvin's entire chest warmed as John clipped the timepiece to his suit.

Chapter Eighteen
John

John awoke to the sound of heavy footsteps in the hall. Covering his head with the pillow, he tried to hide from them. He knew what they meant, and that knowledge weighed on both his mind and heart.

It was the morning of Michael and Katherine's move to Uncle Frances's home in Kensington. Michael had hired a couple of men from his factory to help him relocate his belongings. He wasn't taking too much with him, other than his and Katherine's clothes and books and other personal items. He would likely take their mattress and bed frame as well as some of their favorite smaller pieces of furniture as well.

Unsurprisingly, Calvin had climbed out of bed sometime earlier. He tended to wake when the sun came up, and he was probably trying to stay out of Michael's way, either out walking somewhere or down in the basement, tinkering by himself.

Groaning, John pressed the pillow to his ears. He hated that Michael was leaving. He and Michael had never lived apart. Well, except for the brief period of time when John had stayed in Ardmore so he could practice what he had learned from Eckels. But even then, it had only been for a month, and Michael had visited constantly. John had barely made it through his stay there without Michael's presence. He had hardly even spoken to the mortician with whom he had been training. At least now John had Calvin to live with. And John had become a bit more used to speaking with people. Still, he'd miss his big brother.

Over the next hour, John stayed in his bedroom, covers pulled up over his head as though he was hiding from a monster when he was really only hiding from the fact that his brother no longer wanted to live with him. Truthfully, Michael probably wanted to move so soon because he still seemed to loathe Calvin. God, what horrible circumstances these were. John wished that he and Michael could be parting on happier terms.

Eventually, the constant pitter-patters and thuds slowed and then stopped completely. Perhaps the movers had finished. Reluctantly, John came out from his nook. He found a bathrobe in the closet and threw it on.

After relieving himself and washing up, he headed to the kitchen for coffee, but when passing Michael's office, he halted in his tracks. Michael was still there, packing.

"Good morning," John said.

Michael looked up briefly. "Morning. Just finishing up here."

He placed a few things—notebooks and pens and other materials—into a brown leather suitcase and clipped it closed.

John asked, "Are you leaving the desk behind?"

"I'll use Uncle Frances's old one. It's bigger."

"Could C-Calvin and I use this one, then?"

"Calvin." Michael's eyes flickered up toward the ceiling. "Are you really going to continue this . . . *partnership* of yours?"

John wasn't sure if Michael was referring to their romantic partnership or their business one. He supposed it was both. Nervousness twisted in his stomach as he mentally prepared to reply.

"Yes, I intend to," he said with as much confidence as he could muster.

"Well, I'd rather that *he* not keep *his* things in here," Michael said, running his hand over the cherry-colored wood. "I'm leaving it for you. Not for him."

John's face flushed from a burst of indignation. Calvin was the love of his life, and as such, he ought to be able to use Michael's old desk.

But rather than push back, John held his tongue. Unsure how to respond to what Michael had said with even the tiniest bit of civility (what he wanted to say to Michael wouldn't have been very nice), John turned on his heel and left. Michael followed with a huff.

"John," he said, "don't be like this."

Upset simmering in his blood, John hurried up the stairs, wishing he had the courage to throw propriety out the window and yell at Michael for continuing to harbor such contempt for Calvin. Perhaps Calvin had made a mistake by taking the cuff links, but John knew for certain that he had a kind heart. If only Michael would show Calvin some kindness, he would see that for himself.

Michael caught John's arm. "Look, I'll only say this one more time: Calvin is *not* someone whom you should trust with half of your business. He was only ever meant to be a temporary employee while he paid me back for the necklace and while you had some practice having someone in your employ. Nothing more."

John twisted out of Michael's grasp.

Michael sighed and said, "God, I've never seen you like this. Really, John, it seems to me that you've let yourself become fooled by his serpentine tongue."

John's irritation burned hotter. "Calvin is not t-t-trying to—"

Michael cut him off, holding up his hand. "Let's not keep talking in circles, little brother. Just . . . be careful."

Talking in circles. It was only Michael who was talking. He had yet to let John explain why and how he had fallen in love with a so-called criminal.

John turned away as his stomach started to roil. He wasn't used to this sort of rage, never having been the sort of person to experience the emotion either often or easily. Shame and sorrow, he was plenty familiar with those. But Michael's contempt for Calvin truly enraged him.

John continued toward his bedroom with Michael following close behind, and the fury that had been burning through him slowly cooled. Dammit, this was *not* how he had wanted the two of them to part.

When John reached his desk, he turned toward his brother, forcing himself to meet Michael's eyes, only to be hit with a rush of familial love, which then pulled at his heart. His big brother was only trying to watch out for him.

"Thank you for your c-concern, Michael," John forced himself to say. "I'll respect your w-w-wishes regarding your old desk." He tapped the surface of what would soon be *his* old desk with his index finger. "Calvin can have this one instead."

Michael smiled weakly.

"Thank you," he said back before looking at his watch. "I ought to take that last suitcase over to our new home now. Katherine is probably overwhelmed with trying to unpack by herself."

John waited for Michael to hug him, but Michael started toward the door. Sorrow welled up in John's chest.

Once John heard Michael's footsteps on the stairs, he sank to his knees, sadness pulling him to the floor. How horrible it was that he'd finally fallen in love, only to have somehow fractured his relationship with his brother.

John's eyes found the top drawer of his soon-to-be former desk. Straightening, he opened the drawer to view the collection of Lucy's things. It seemed that his love for people tended to break things. Huffing a quiet, bitter laugh, John scooped up Lucy's belongings.

Michael's scornful words rang in his ears.

There's something wrong with you.

And they rang true.

He still loved his sister. Even though that love had broken his family.

Shame coiled itself around him, its hold painful and yet familiar. Pushing himself to his feet, John cradled Lucy's things in his arms and took them downstairs to his new desk, all the while feeling so intensely silly—so completely *wrong*—for how much he still treasured them. And for how much he still treasured her.

John carefully placed Lucy's things into the new desk, and then, just as John shut the desk drawer, Calvin came in.

"We officially have the house to ourselves!" Calvin declared.

Looking up, John tried to smile. He hummed in acknowledgement.

Calvin's face fell.

"What's wrong?" he asked, coming over to John.

Before John could try to respond, Calvin pulled him in for a hug, and though shame still lingered, Calvin's love made the tightness of its terrible, strangling tendrils easier to bear. John buried his face in Calvin's neck. After a minute passed, John found he finally had the strength to speak.

"Am I strange?" he murmured into the fabric of Calvin's shirt collar.

"Uhm . . . is this a trick or something?" Calvin teased. He moved his fingers through John's hair. "You *are* strange. And I love it. I love *you*."

John's cheeks burned, and a pathetic whimper of self-reproach escaped his lips. He tried to keep his face hidden, but Calvin pulled back and lifted his chin.

"Every person in the world is strange in their own way," he said.

John shook his head. "Not like me."

"No, not like you," Calvin confirmed, his voice soft and kind. "I've never met one single person who was even a *little* like you. I've never met someone so sweet, so soft, so kind. I've never met someone who can focus like you or who feels as intensely as you. John, you are utterly unique in the best possible way."

John swallowed thickly, tears pooling in his eyes.

Calvin said, "I'm enamored with you, John. With every part of you. Even the parts that are strange."

"Really?" John choked out, a tear rolling down his cheek.

Calvin wiped it away. "Really."

Closing his eyes, John let out a shuddering breath.

And tried to make himself believe it.

In early fall, John and Calvin were traveling back to Media, setting off as soon as John was finished with an embalming in their Frankford neighborhood. On the way, Calvin expressed his intrigue over the "party" they had been invited to. It would be a strange event, for sure, because the woman who had insisted on having it was no longer living. Apparently, Betty Roberts had been telling her children for half of forever that when she passed, she wanted them to host a party celebrating the life she had lived, rather than having a traditional funeral. She had asked not to be embalmed. She had asked not to have a service. Instead, she'd wanted her large, lovely yard to be transformed into a wonderful party locale.

Her children, now in their forties, were happy to honor her wish. Practically everyone in the Borough of Media had been invited (or so John had heard). Since John and Michael had both known Betty, they had been invited as well. John had fond memories of Betty. In fact, looking back, John thought that the Hall children had probably been Betty's favorite neighbors. Every time she'd baked a new treat, she'd brought some over to their house, and one summer, she had tried to teach Lucy and John how to play cards (though they had been too young to really play properly). Revisiting the memory, John let out a wistful sigh. He could still remember how fun it had been to spend time with Betty. He was happy to have been invited to her postmortem "party."

Despite the fact that, thanks to having helped Calvin run a few funerals, John was feeling more confident about talking to folks that evening, John's stomach was still roiling unpleasantly during their carriage ride. Because of Michael. Ever since Michael had moved out, it was as though a chasm had formed between them, and that had never happened before, not even when they'd lost their sister. It was incredible (in the negative sense of the word) that Michael could loathe Calvin *that* much. Michael had come to visit John a few times, but he seemed to have made an effort to stay away from Calvin. Katherine, on the other hand, had visited Calvin specifically on several occasions. Those two had truly become friends. Still, the four of them hadn't been in the same room since their final, awkward supper on the eve of Michael's move.

God, John was nervous for them all to spend time together.

As John and Calvin's hearse carriage neared the party, John's worry spiked, and the swirl of energy prevented him from continuing to sit still. Instinctually, he wanted to wring his hands—something that often calmed him—but he couldn't because he needed to keep holding the reins. So John began tapping his foot instead.

Calvin's hand settled atop John's closest thigh.

"We'll have fun," he said. "I promise."

John managed a nod but continued *tap-tap-tapping* his foot.

"I-I'm worried that Michael will say something . . . bad," he said.

"About . . . ?"

"Me. You. Us." John closed his eyes. "I hate c-c-conflict."

"I know." Calvin squeezed John's thigh. "We'll try not to spend too much time chatting with him, then. We'll talk with everyone else. And if you're ever uncomfortable, either with Michael or with others, we'll sneak off to the hearse."

John opened his eyes and said, "You wouldn't mind that?"

"Never. All I want is to enjoy some beer or wine while spending time with the most interesting man I've ever met. Which is you, by the way. In case you thought I meant someone else."

John couldn't help but smile. "I knew you m-m-meant me."

"Good." Calvin knocked John with his elbow. "What time is it, by the way?"

Balancing the reins in his left hand, John retrieved the pocket watch from his suit breast pocket and clicked it open, his cheeks flushing.

"Nearly six."

"Gorgeous watch," Calvin said. "Was it a present?"

"Yes, Calvin," John said, feigning exasperation.

"Wow," Calvin said before trying to whistle but failing miserably. "The handsome and funny man who gave it to you must really love you."

"Yes, I think so," John said, his entire face now on fire, though it wasn't burning nearly as hot as the love he felt in his heart. "And I love him, too."

"Well, he's a *very* lucky man," Calvin said with a wink.

Shaking his head, John let out a laugh.

For the next few minutes, John continued to clutch the watch in his palm, and as they traveled past the shops in the town center, he reminded himself that Calvin loved him and that Michael's inevitable comments weren't to be taken to heart and that soon enough, he and Calvin would be by themselves in the hearse for the *entire* evening and no one would be the wiser.

Now *that* he was excited for. Instead of bothering to rent a room, John and Calvin had simply packed the hearse with a whole bunch of blankets and pillows so they could sleep there together. If someone happened to wonder where they were staying, they would lie (well, Calvin would lie) and say that they had rented a room at one of the inns. God, it would be fun.

By the time John and Calvin reached Betty's home, the party was in full swing.

"Do you want me to talk to someone from the family first? Confirm that there's space for Agathe in the stables?" Calvin asked as they stopped their hearse carriage.

"No, I ought to be the one to bring up Agathe, I think," John said, climbing out of the hearse. "I'm not so n-nervous about talking to everyone else tonight. Only Michael."

"Ah, well, maybe we won't see him much," Calvin suggested, hopping out too. "It looks like there are plenty of people."

"Yes, that's true."

Over the next ten minutes or so, John and Calvin talked with some of Betty's relatives—her children and second cousins—and it was a pleasure to see that everyone was excited to meet John's business partner. Everyone seemed happy for John, too. Happy to hear that he had founded a successful business and that he enjoyed his work. Thankfully, no one had a problem with Agathe taking up some room in the stables. In return, John offered to feed the other horses in the morning and said he wouldn't mind brushing them, either. It wouldn't be a problem. He loved horses.

After parking their hearse carriage and then securing their horse, John and Calvin started back toward the party. When they were getting closer to the cluster of people, Calvin stopped suddenly.

John stopped beside him. "What is it?"

Calvin took off John's hat and fiddled with the brim.

"Just wanted to take one last opportunity to be close to you," Calvin said, putting John's hat back on his head and then subtly touching John's cheek with the back of his hand. "I thought I'd make it look like there was something wrong with your homburg."

"Oh, Cal." John's heart fluttered wildly as the two of them smiled at each other. "Perhaps . . . I w-w-wonder if my tie might need—"

"Ah, you're right, it *is* kind of crooked," Calvin said before straightening it out. Both of them then needed to purse their lips a little to keep their smiles to a relatively normal size. "There. Much better."

"I could foresee it becoming lopsided later. In an hour's time or so."

"Well, if that should happen, I will be happy to fix it."

Footsteps on the path sounded in John's ear, and he turned to see Michael and Katherine come to see them. Almost immediately,

John began to sweat, despite the fact that the sun was moving close to the horizon and the trees shook with a cool, intermittent breeze.

"I hope you two aren't planning on being this obvious the *entire* evening," Michael said.

"It's nice to see you too, Michael," Calvin said flatly before looking at Katherine with a welcoming smile. "And it's very nice to see you, Katherine. I hope you've been well."

"I have, though I've been missing one of my friends. We haven't had lunch in over a week."

With a cheeky smile, Calvin asked, "Is it me?"

Katherine shrugged. "Perhaps."

Michael let out a sigh, his eye twitching from either irritation or impatience or both. Calvin snorted. Michael then leveled him a look.

"Sorry," Calvin remarked before sniffling. It was . . . surprisingly realistic. "Milkweed. It bothers my nose."

"Milkweed? At this time of year?" Michael said.

"Either that or I'm coming down with something."

"What a shame *that* would be," Michael said, not even trying to make his fake concern sound the least bit convincing. "Well, we wanted to say hello before we started mingling." He looked past John's shoulder and narrowed his eyes, scrutinizing. "Is that the hearse?"

"It is," Calvin answered. "We're leaving it here for the night."

Michael hummed and said, "Where are you staying?"

"Oh, the little inn in the center of town. I forget the name," Calvin said.

John silently marveled at how easily Calvin could lie through his teeth.

"The Chestnut Inn?" Katherine offered.

"Yes, that's the one," Calvin replied effortlessly. "We left our bags there earlier."

Worry curdled in John's stomach as he watched Michael suck on his teeth, thinking this over. He wondered if they'd be found out. Within the first few minutes of the party, too.

"Very well," Michael said finally, and John felt a rush of relief. "Katherine, let's find some wine, shall we?"

"Perfect," she said, beaming up at her husband.

As Michael and Katherine turned to head toward the party, Michael leaned in to whisper in Katherine's ear, telling her how beautiful she looked that evening. John smiled to himself. For his flaws, Michael certainly treated Katherine well. He really loved her. John was certain of that.

John and Calvin followed, lingering a few feet back. And then, in order to keep their space from Michael and Katherine, they found some beer to enjoy, rather than wine. Soon, Calvin became engrossed in a conversation with one of the neighbors. While the two men chatted about the challenges of funeral planning, John stood by silently, thankful that Calvin was happy to talk enough for the both of them.

Over the next few hours, John and Calvin moved through the party, with Calvin excitedly talking to whomever they happened to bump into. He handed out a few business cards as well. Unsurprisingly, Calvin was perfectly charming, though sometimes a little too brash or brazen or both, especially once he'd had a couple of beers. No one seemed to mind, though. Probably because everyone else had been enjoying the refreshments as well. John even tried his hand at conversation a few times. He couldn't help but be a touch proud of himself. It seemed that Calvin had been right: He had really blossomed.

Once, John intentionally unfixed his tie a little and then Calvin took the time to straighten it, letting his hands linger a *little* too long, which was so incredibly thrilling. Another time, Calvin pretended that he was having some trouble with a *particularly* stubborn peanut and so John helped him crack it. And he, too, let his fingers linger on top of Calvin's a *little* too long.

After they had both enjoyed a significant amount of alcohol (or, well, it was significant to John, who had only ever had those two whiskey fizz cocktails before, so three beers in four hours' time felt like a lot), Calvin leaned in close to whisper in John's ear.

"Follow me."

John startled, letting out a little yelp, which then made Calvin chuckle. John wasn't sure whether Calvin had been too loud or whether his own ears had become oversensitive. Did beer work like that?

"Sorry," Calvin chuckled.

He turned and began walking toward the hearse. John followed. Were they really heading back so soon?

Calvin started walking faster and faster, and John soon struggled to keep up. Eventually, the two of them were practically running, but instead of continuing to the hearse, Calvin took a sharp turn and slipped into a vacant-looking barn.

Once John was inside, Calvin shut the barn door.

"Isn't this perfect?" Calvin said with a wolfish smile, one that John could *barely* make out from the light streaming in through the spaces between the wooden beams—moonlight above and light from the bonfire through one of the walls. "Earlier, while you were picking out some sweet bread, I was chatting with Betty's niece, Mildred, and she mentioned that they'd be selling the horses. And *then*, she mentioned this barn. Said it was empty." Gently, Calvin took John by the lapels and urged him backward, only stopping once John hit the wall. "I couldn't wait any longer. I needed to be alone with you."

Before John could reply, Calvin's lips crashed into his. Calvin moaned while they kissed, and John smiled in response before breaking away.

Humming happily, John said, "Why not sneak off to the hearse instead? Why c-c-come in here?"

Calvin's eyes widened, and he raised his eyebrows in a playful manner.

"I thought it would be exciting."

John bellowed a laugh. "Ah."

John took Calvin by the lapels and pulled him in for another kiss. While their lips moved together, their tongues twirling intermittently, both of them shrugged off their coats, which they then tossed aside onto some hay. Next, they removed their hats, flinging them in the same direction. Calvin then moved closer, pushing his body flush with John's, and John could feel Calvin's hard cock pressing against his thigh. Desire flooded John's veins as he began stroking Calvin through the fabric of his pants. Momentarily lost in his bliss, John let out a whimper. Dammit, how he wanted Calvin to pleasure him, too.

"Cal," he murmured, slightly breathless.

Placing his hands on Calvin's shoulders, John coaxed Calvin to his knees. Before Calvin could even settle, John began shrugging off his suspenders, and then Calvin started fiddling with the buttons on John's pants. In seconds, they fell to John's knees, and John's cock sprang free. Looking up at John through his lashes, Calvin took John's thick cock in the palm of his hand and pumped twice.

"Oh, God," John moaned.

Calvin brought his lips close, hovering them inches from John's cock, and the puff of warmth from Calvin's next exhale sent shivers up John's spine.

"May I?" Calvin asked.

"Yes." John's voice cracked. He cleared his throat and tried again. "Yes. Please."

When Calvin then pressed a soft kiss to the tip, John's heart stuttered as he sucked in a breath, a fiery rush of heat pooling low in his belly, both from the wonderful, beautiful sight and from the softness of Calvin's lips.

Fuck. Calvin was so exciting. And John was already so close to coming.

Quickly, John took his own cock in his hand, pushing Calvin's hand back in the process, and then squeezed the base, hoping to buy himself some more time.

"*God*, Cal, I need a m-m-moment," John said. "You look so handsome like this. And your breath, it's so warm."

"Am I that talented?" Calvin teased.

Without hesitation, John answered with an emphatic "Yes."

John took one more relaxing breath before removing his hand, confident that the sudden rush of excitement had been successfully contained. With a nod, he gave Calvin permission to continue.

Slowly, Calvin took John's length into his hand again, and John sucked on his bottom lip as Calvin stroked him a few times. Small trickles of warmth spread throughout John's body, each one making him burn for more. Calvin's tongue barely brushed John's naked head, and John sucked in a breath through his teeth, a low moan escaping the moment Calvin's lips closed over the tip.

"Good Lord," John whispered. "I can't believe how incredible this feels."

Calvin hummed in response as he took more of John into his mouth. Enraptured, John fisted some of Calvin's hair. And then Calvin's hum turned into more of a low, closed-mouth laugh. The sensation sent a rumble of pleasure rolling through John's body, making him moan. Calvin began to bob his head, taking more and more of John's cock into his mouth each time, and it wasn't long before the warmth that had pooled low in John's belly began to make his cock swell with the urge to come.

"I'm close," John rasped, holding tight to Calvin's hair. "So, so close."

One of Calvin's hands cupped John's balls, sending him closer to the edge. Without John needing to request it, Calvin started increasing the speed of his movements, tightening his fist while massaging John's balls with his other hand. Goodness, the warmth of Calvin's mouth, the slickness of his tongue, the wet, filthy sounds . . .

It was too much.

With a soft cry of pleasure, John started to come, his cock pulsing as waves of pleasure rippled through him. He watched Calvin swallow every bit of his ejaculate, and the sight had John's heart fluttering. The moment Calvin was on his feet, John pulled him in for a kiss, relishing the way he could still taste his own orgasm lingering there on Calvin's lips.

"I love you," John sighed before clutching tight to Calvin's shirt and kissing him hard on the mouth one more time. "God, I ffffucking *love you*, Calvin."

Calvin burst out laughing. "I love you too, John. So very much."

Calvin's beautiful words swirled in John's chest. Calvin loved him. All of him. Even the parts that were strange.

They nuzzled each other's noses, and then, once Calvin's cock was free, John started to stroke him, coaxing Calvin close to the precipice. All the while, he whispered sweet nothings, occasionally nibbling on Calvin's ear.

"John, I'm . . . fuck, I'm coming."

In an instant, John was on his knees. He took Calvin's swollen member into his mouth and swallowed every ounce of warm pleasure that spilled forth.

Resting his head on Calvin's thigh, John said, "Perfect, Cal. You're so perfect."

"So are you," Calvin replied, wistful.

After John pushed himself to stand, the two of them stayed in the vacant barn for a while, kissing and hugging and swaying, the faint music—cello and violin—from the party floating in through the cracks in the structure. Minutes passed before they finally managed to fix their clothing and hair so that they might make one or two more rounds to socialize before eventually sneaking off to their hearse.

After sharing one more brief kiss, they rushed back toward the main house to the party, where they found most of the remaining townsfolk completely intoxicated, laughing and dancing and none the wiser to John and Calvin's trip to the newly empty barn.

Breathing a sigh of relief, John removed his hat and ran a hand through his hair. Calvin then reached up to smooth his locks.

"Sweet, silly man," Calvin whispered. Calvin's tender care brought tears to John's eyes. He was still struggling with his emotions when Calvin said, ever so sweetly, "If you insist on continuing to move your fingers through your hair seemingly every time you become the least bit nervous, might I suggest a little less pomade?"

Face tingling from embarrassment, John shut his eyes briefly and managed a soft, "Yes, that w-would be sensible, wouldn't it?"

When John opened his eyes, he realized, to his horror, that their intimate moment hadn't gone completely unnoticed.

From just a few feet away, Michael stood, staring at them. He caught John's eye, and John's face burned hotter. Michael raised one curious—or maybe incredulous—eyebrow, pursing his lips as though to try to communicate how very *not* pleased he was. Heart pounding, John struggled to swallow, the lump in his throat ballooning to the size of a billiard ball. He braced himself for Michael to come over and chastise him for being so reckless with Calvin, but Michael merely turned and headed over to the wine table for a refill.

"Think he saw us?" Calvin asked.

With a subtle nod, John hummed in response, not even caring to try to make the words come.

"Are you mad?" Calvin whispered. "At me?"

John shook his head.

"Alright," Calvin said, but John could tell it wasn't.

Even though John could barely focus past the fierce beating of his heart, he knew he had to try to speak.

"N-n-not mad," he managed. "Only m-momentarily stunned."

"One more round of socializing," Calvin suggested. "And then we'll head to the hearse. I want to hold you. Make you feel better."

John let out a long breath. "Yes, that sounds sensible."

Calvin smiled a cheeky smile and said, "I'm not sure what we should say if someone notices us heading over there. Perhaps"—he snickered—"perhaps we could say that we have to inventory our tools?"

As John turned Calvin's silly sentiment over in his head, the shock over his encounter with Michael faded away, and then he started to laugh.

God, Calvin was so funny. Oh, to hell with Michael!

With a boisterous laugh, John said, "Only if you're the one to say it."

Over the next half hour, the two men managed to chat with a few people—friends of John's parents—and then, as soon as more people began trickling out, Calvin suggested that they leave too.

Moving through the field to the hearse, John's heart began to race, a mixture of excitement and elation and nervousness starting to swirl inside of him, making his palms sweat. Now far from the bonfire, John and Calvin needed to navigate through the blackness of night, and when Calvin took John by the hand to help steady them both, fear and happiness shot through John's veins, and the thrill of being outside with his fingers intertwined with his lover's caused him to laugh some more. And then Calvin was laughing, too.

"Shhhh . . ." Calvin scolded. "Someone will hear us."

"Oh, they can't p-possibly see us out here, can they?" John asked, though he tried to reel in his laughter. "Still, it's thrilling to be touching so intimately so close to the party."

"I won't be falling to my knees in the open field, if that's what you're insinuating," Calvin teased. "Not so close to where people would recognize us."

"God, Cal, I was *not* suggesting *that*!"

Calvin squeezed his hand. "Are you sure? I could change my mind."

"Don't tempt me," John scolded.

When they reached the hearse, they climbed inside and settled next to each other. Neither of them could see much with the curtains blocking out even the last bits of light from both the roaring bonfire and the moon above. Still, they managed to find each other's lips. Despite John having orgasmed less than one hour prior, his cock started to stiffen. Being with Calvin thrilled him in a way he would have never thought possible.

Later, when they were both spent, half-lost in the bliss of post-orgasm tranquility, they snuggled together for a long while before eventually fumbling to fix their clothing.

And then John pulled Calvin close.

And they slept peacefully.

In the morning, John woke with a smile, the crisp fall air chilling his face in a pleasant way, even as his body remained snug beneath the blankets. What a spectacular night it had been. Stretching out his legs, John let out a yawn and then rolled over to face Calvin, only to see him shivering, curled into a little ball.

"Oh, Cal, I'm sorry if it's too c-c-cold. I was w-worried that we hadn't packed enough blankets," John said, wrapping Calvin up in a hug.

Calvin shifted to face him.

"It's not that, I don't think," he said, his voice slightly raspy. "Seems like I must have caught something."

Frowning, John placed a hand on Calvin's forehead. While he wasn't burning up, John could have sworn that his skin felt too warm. His brow creased with concern as he pressed a kiss to Calvin's temple.

"Let's get you home," he said.

"Mind if I stay back here?" Calvin asked, tucking his knees close to his chest.

He closed his eyes before John could answer.

"Not at all," John said. "I n-n-need to feed the horses and fetch Agathe from the stable, but we'll leave as soon as I'm f-finished. You stay here and rest."

Calvin's breathing had already slowed. Poor sweet Cal. God, normally Calvin was the first to rouse. He had never not woken refreshed and energized. Whatever sickness this was must have hit him hard.

After pressing one more soft kiss to Calvin's forehead, John left to fulfill his promise to Betty's children. He first fed the horses and then brushed each of them, though more hastily than he would have liked. All the while, he told them how concerned he was for Calvin and apologized for not taking his time tending to them. He hoped that Betty's children would come out soon to spend more time with them instead.

Concern sat heavy in John's stomach the entire way back to Frankford. By the time they reached their home, John's skin had started to itch with the urge to check on Calvin.

After leading Agathe to her stable, he returned to the hearse. Calvin, though, was still fast asleep, no longer shivering, likely thanks to the warmth of the morning sun spilling in through the hearse's windows. Breathing a sigh of relief, John retreated toward the house. He would let Calvin sleep for a while longer.

On his way to make Calvin some tea, John passed by the study, and a flash of powder blue caught his eye. He turned to see Katherine sitting at Michael's old desk, the top drawer of which was open.

John's stomach leapt up into his throat. Katherine had found his secret keepsakes. Lord.

"Morning K-Katherine," he spluttered. "What . . . ehm . . . wh-wh-why are you here?"

"Michael thought that he might have left one of his checkbooks here in the office," she said. "I thought I could come look for it myself."

John rocked back on his heels, hooking his hands behind him. "Ah."

Katherine looked back in the open drawer. "Were these Lucy's?"

John's heart stuttered, his breath catching. *Lucy.* He hadn't heard her name spoken out loud in years. He managed a nod.

Katherine sighed. "I wish Michael would tell me more about her."

John's eyes widened, but he still couldn't manage to speak. Katherine had never mentioned Lucy to him before.

After a moment, she picked up Lucy's rag doll. With a small smile, she smoothed its yellow hair.

"It's a shame that Michael has closed off that part of his life to me. I mean, he told me that Lucy was your twin and that she passed from some sort of illness, but that was it, really. Whenever I've brought her up—the few times that I've tried to, anyway—Michael became so ornery. He was so . . . so unlike himself. Normally, Michael is so sweet to me. Gentle. Supportive. Yes, Michael can be stubborn, but he's never *mean*. Not to me. But whenever I try to bring up Lucy, something changes. One time, when he'd had a little too much wine, he said something like 'I can't talk about her, Katherine. She stole everything from me.'" Katherine frowned. "I thought that was so . . . uncharacteristically cruel. Goodness, I still can't believe he would say something like that. About his little sister, too."

Spots began to form in front of John's eyes. It was only then, once he started feeling lightheaded, that he realized he hadn't been breathing. He took a breath, but it didn't stop him from feeling woozy, a heaviness in the room pressing on him and constricting his chest. How could Michael have said such a horrible thing?

"Michael said that?" John rasped, his voice barely above a whisper as he struggled to fill his lungs with enough oxygen.

"I'm sorry. That must be hard to hear."

John closed his eyes. "Yes, it is."

It was as though John's entire reality had suddenly shifted, like the world itself had changed, tilting the opposite way on its axis, and now John's brain was working to recontextualize every childhood memory to try to make sense of what Katherine had said. When John and Michael had been little, Michael had berated John so many times for continuing to bring up Lucy. John had been made to feel broken for wanting to remember her. Or even for loving her. Desperate to make sense of Michael's harsh chastisements, John had come to the conclusion that "normal" people moved on when someone passed. After a brief period of mourning, they forgot their sorrow, mended the holes in their hearts, and carried on with life. And, of course, since John had never managed that, he had internalized the notion that he was simply broken. He had thought that Michael had—*childhood* Michael—had hated him for it. But Michael had hated *Lucy*?

Katherine's hand came to rest atop John's shoulder. He startled and fluttered open his eyes.

"Why?" John asked. Even though he knew that Katherine wouldn't have an answer. "Why would he . . . hate her?"

"I wouldn't say that he *hates* her. I have the sense, though, that he blames her for her own passing." She squeezed his shoulder. "Perhaps that's not much better, is it?"

John shook his head.

"And . . ." She trailed off and John looked over to see her cheeks turning pink as her hand fell away. "Never mind."

"What?"

"I shouldn't say."

"Katherine, p-please, I-I need to know."

Katherine's eyes fell to the floor and she began fiddling with the rag doll's hair, twirling it between her fingers.

Softly, she said, "Sometimes I think he wishes that she had never existed."

Katherine's words cut through John's heart. He clenched his teeth to try to block out the stinging pain.

Katherine said, "I know that's horrible, but I think Michael must have really been heartbroken when she died. I'm happy that you don't seem to feel the same way. It's very sweet of you, John, to keep some of your sister's things."

"It's not . . . shameful?"

Katherine smiled warmly and shook her head.

"No," she said, her voice soft and kind. "Have you talked to Calvin?"

"About Lucy?" John asked, and Katherine nodded. "No, I-I haven't managed to tell him yet. I can't seem to make the words c-come."

Shame bubbled its way to the surface, turning John's face hot. He still couldn't think of his lost sister without Michael's old insults and chastisements resurfacing, their power making John want to curl in on himself, to shield himself from the world so that no one else could see how strange and broken he was.

Even now, even though John had learned of Michael's lingering pain, there was still a voice in his head telling him that he was wrong for missing his sister. And for loving her.

"I think he'd want to know about her, John," Katherine said. "I'm sure he'd love to know what she was like and what it was like having a twin. And even what it was like for you when she passed. Don't forget that Calvin lost people who were important to him, too. He knows how that feels."

John's heart clenched. Katherine was right.

"I'll tell him," John said, his throat tightening as he spoke. "Once he's feeling better, I'll show him these k-k-keepsakes."

Katherine knitted her brows together. "Oh, is Calvin sick?"

"I think so, yes."

"I'm sorry to hear that. He seemed fine last night."

"It came on suddenly. He's sleeping right now. In the c-carriage."

Katherine hummed and said, "Maybe you should try to find him some medicine. Oh, what's the name of it? It has cinnamon and . . . hmm . . . something else. Qua-something?"

"Quinine?"

"Yes, that sounds right."

"Does it work?"

"It's meant to. I mean, it's not something that Calvin is simply peddling on the street."

Chuckling, John said. "I'll pick some up later, then. Do you w-w-want some help searching for the checkbook? Perhaps I'll let C-Calvin sleep for a bit longer."

"Yes, that would be wonderful. Thank you."

Afterward, Katherine and John continued to chat a bit while they searched for Michael's checkbook. Although they couldn't manage to find it, John did manage to tell Katherine how *much* he cared for Calvin. It felt so good to talk with her so openly. Little by little, John could feel himself breaking free of the chains of self-reproach that had kept him prisoner all this time.

It had been Michael's words, really, that had wrought those chains, with the rejection of his parents having contributed, too.

But it was Calvin's love that had broken them.

All except for one.

Chapter Nineteen
Calvin

Thirty minutes earlier . . .

When Calvin's eyes fluttered open, he let out a pained moan, rolling onto his back. His head was pounding, his nose stuffy, his clothes wet from excessive perspiration. Slowly, Calvin pushed himself up. Looking around, he realized that they were no longer in the Borough of Media, but back in the city. It seemed that John, the sweet man that he was, had let Calvin keep sleeping for the whole trip.

Calvin shivered. Despite the sun's warmth, he was starting to feel chilled. Just as he had earlier that morning. He'd better head inside.

Groggy from illness, Calvin climbed out of the hearse and started for the house. On the way, he tried to smooth out his clothing, but it was hopeless. He heaved a sigh, struggling to even stay upright as he made his way up the steps. Why had John parked out front? God, hopefully no one had seen him sleeping in the hearse. After opening the door, Calvin's ears tickled from the familiar sound of John's voice. He paused, hovering in the entryway. Who was John speaking with? He listened some more. It sounded like Katherine.

Slowly, Calvin crept forward, continuing to listen. He never could break the habit of eavesdropping. Not that he'd had a lot of motivation to thus far.

"Have you talked to Calvin?"

"About Lucy? No, I-I haven't managed to tell him yet. I can't seem to make the words c-come."

Calvin's heart clenched and stuttered, making him feel faint in an instant. He began backing away, now only hearing the sound of blood whooshing past his eardrums.

John was keeping something from him.

No, John was keeping some*one* from him. But why?

Calvin hurried back to the hearse. Inside, he shut each of the curtains, one by one, worry curdling in his stomach, making him nauseated. Or was that the sickness? Grimacing, Calvin lay on the cold carriage floor and covered himself with the blankets. Who was Lucy? Why wouldn't John tell him about her?

Perhaps . . .

No, John wouldn't replace him.

Temporary.

Calvin was John's partner. He helped run the business. He wasn't only some random person in John's employ. Not anymore.

Even though Calvin knew, logically, that this half-formed worry of his made little sense, even though he *knew* that he was overreacting to whatever John was keeping from him, he couldn't manage to make himself see it that way.

Calvin squeezed his eyes shut and told himself that he was being silly.

For the next half hour or so, Calvin tossed and turned. He tried to make himself sleep, but couldn't, even though he knew it would make him feel better.

Eventually, Calvin heard a light knock on the door of the hearse, and then the door opened, letting in bright sunlight.

"Cal," he whispered, climbing inside. "I think you ought to try sleeping in our bed. It's warmer in the house. M-m-more comfortable, too."

Calvin swallowed thickly, mentally preparing himself to tell John what he had heard. But then . . .

Memories of David flashed into his mind, each of them so clear and bright and painful that they made him wince. David had replaced him. He had found someone better to work with, someone better to love. Why wouldn't John?

Calvin flinched from the feeling of John's lips pressing to his forehead.

"Come inside," John said, his voice sweet and soft and not even a little like David's. "I'll make tea."

Calvin inhaled a shaky breath. John loved him. John loved him and respected him and cared for him. And whatever it was that John was keeping from him, he would reveal in his own time. John wasn't like other people. He often struggled to find the right words. It would be wrong for Calvin to rush him.

"Thank you," Calvin said, sitting up and sniffling. "I'd love some."

Calvin followed John into the house.

While Calvin waited in bed, trying to warm up and to calm his worried mind, John brewed tea. It was only a few minutes before he came back with a cup for Calvin (and a mug of coffee for himself). Cup in hand, Calvin scooched over to make room for John, who then sat beside him. For the next several minutes, they sipped their hot beverages in silence.

Eventually, John said, "I n-n-need to cancel the funeral today, don't I?"

"What?" Calvin said. "Why?"

"Because you're sick. I can't expect you to come with me. Not only will you infect everyone, but you m-might make yourself feel worse."

Calvin chewed on his lip. John shouldn't cancel. The James family was counting on Hall and Wright Funeral Services to ensure that the funeral would run smoothly. Even though the entire service was scheduled to take place in the client's home, they would still need someone to help welcome everyone inside. Calvin had baked funeral cookies too. What would the family serve for refreshments without Hall and Wright? Who would hang the silly scarf outside? Who would make sure that mistresses weren't served suggestive fruit before the service? God, how would they even transport the casket to the cemetery?

"Don't cancel," Calvin said. He thought for a moment longer. Dammit, John would have to run the whole thing by himself, wouldn't he? But he could. Calvin was sure of it. "John, I think . . . I think you'll have to run it on your own."

John's eyes went wide with fear. "Cal, I can't."

"You can," Calvin said earnestly. "I *know* you can."

"But wh-wh-what if I make a mistake?"

"You won't."

"What if I forget something?"

"Then you forget something," Calvin said. "I've made mistakes. Everyone *makes* mistakes. But the family *needs* you, John."

John tilted his head back to rest it against the headboard. He heaved a sigh.

"God, I'm n-n-nervous."

Calvin smiled with as much warmth as he could muster. Turning slightly, he reached his free hand inside John's suit and pulled out the pocket watch.

"I'll still be with you," he said. "I'll be with you the whole time."

John put his hand on top of Calvin's. "Thank you, Cal."

He brought Calvin's hand to his lips and kissed it while Calvin still clutched tight to the watch. Calvin closed his eyes and tried to memorize the feel of John's kiss. Tried to hold tight to the tingling warmth that lingered.

John's brow wrinkled with concern. "Should I . . ."

"Get ready, John," Calvin said. "Wash up. Change. Run the funeral. Don't worry about me. I'll be in here, napping."

"Alright."

John moved to leave, but then stopped and kissed Calvin on the lips.

"Well, you may have had a chance of avoiding this illness before but *now*—"

"I know," John said before kissing him once more. "Doesn't matter."

John leaned in to kiss Calvin once more, but Calvin held up his hand, blocking him.

"*Go!*" he instructed through a chuckle.

"Fine, fine," John said, climbing off the bed.

He left, taking both of their mugs with him.

And Calvin shimmied lower, pulling the covers up to his neck. Once he was comfortable, he closed his eyes and tried to sleep. But, as he teetered on the edge of slumber, he kept on asking himself the same thing: *Who was Lucy?*

Even wrapped up in three blankets, Calvin couldn't stop shivering. He was beginning to feel fatigued from his muscles shaking so violently for what seemed like hours. His teeth were starting to chatter, too. Every time he closed his eyes to try to sleep, he'd fall into some sort of half-conscious slumber that wasn't even restful. Hopefully John would come back from the funeral soon.

While Calvin's fever burned and his muscles trembled, his thoughts lazily floated back into the past, to the life he and David had shared together. David had thrown everything away so easily. He had started seeing Ed *right* under Calvin's nose. And while David had been wooing Ed, he had been treating Calvin the same. Sleeping next to him. Running schemes with him. Fucking him. But still, David had been seeing Ed on the side, the two men stealing little moments together here and there as David had figured out how best to break Calvin's heart.

When Calvin then heard the click of the lock—the metallic clang echoing through the otherwise silent house—his heart soared with excitement, practically pelting him in the ribcage. John was home. He was finally home.

"Cal!" John called out. "I'm home." His voice was coming closer, footsteps tap-tap-tapping on the stairs. "Sorry if I'm waking you, but I'm so excited to tell you how everything went. After we c-c-cuddle, I thought I'd make some soup. I'm not particularly t-t-talented in the kitchen, as you've noticed, but still—"

John's voice cut the moment he reached the bedroom.

Through bleary eyes, Calvin looked up at John and said, "John."

God, his voice sounded so weak.

Without hesitation, John rushed over. "Cal, you're shaking."

"I know. I'm sicker than I thought I would be."

After kicking off his shoes, John climbed into bed. Calvin moved over to make room. When John pulled him close, Calvin's eyes teared even more, now from relief rather than only the sickness. John kissed his head. Over and over.

"I'm here," he said.

"Thank you," Calvin whispered. "How was the funeral?"

"It went well, I think. I forgot to collect the p-payment, but otherwise I managed fine on my own."

Worry seized Calvin by the throat, drowning the swell of pride that should have had him happy and joyful. John had managed fine without him. Calvin hadn't been needed. At all.

"I know I said I would make you some soup, but I think I ought to try to buy some m-medicine instead. It'll mean that I have to leave again, though." John stroked Calvin's hair. "But only for a little while."

Calvin nodded weakly. "Medicine sounds good."

"Alright, I'll hurry." John hopped back out of bed and immediately began putting on his shoes. "I p-promise I'll be back soon."

Calvin pulled the covers over his head and listened to John's retreating footsteps. When he heard John leave, his eyes welled up with tears. John had run the whole funeral without him. He had completed the embalming, too. Before they had left for the party. Calvin couldn't embalm people. He couldn't make mourning trinkets. Calvin's entire purpose was to organize the services.

But John hadn't needed him.

One tear fell from Calvin's eye. And then another. And then more. Over the next few minutes, he continued to cry, worry twisting inside him. Soon, in his hazy, feverish state, thoughts of David and Ed began flickering in his mind, each of them ratcheting his worry even higher, and somehow, Calvin couldn't seem to reason them away.

David and Ed having lunch together.

David and Ed shaking hands, their fingers lingering a touch too long.

David and Ed laughing while they loitered in the hall of their building.

David and Ed falling in love. Or in lust. Whichever or both.

All the while, David had continued to spend the nights with Calvin. Probably *wishing* that he was Ed. Perhaps even imagining that he had been.

And who was Lucy? Did John no longer need him? Did John no longer want him? Why was John keeping things from him? Did John not trust him?

Slowly, Calvin's past hurt began intertwining itself with the fear that John no longer needed him, and before he could even *try* to talk some sense into himself, their fabrics were woven so tightly together that Calvin couldn't separate them. Especially not with his sickness-riddled mind.

Calvin let out a small scream of frustration. He sat up and began rubbing his forehead. God, something was wrong with him. Something was wrong with his brain. He couldn't think straight.

Calvin then walked to the bathroom to splash water on his face, hoping that the shock of coldness would provide him with some clarity.

Hovering his face over the sink, Calvin turned on the water and cupped his hands beneath the faucet. Over and over, he splashed himself, telling himself that there was something he wasn't seeing. John had run the funeral. By himself. He had run the funeral by himself and everything had gone smoothly. He had only forgotten to collect the payment.

Calvin froze.

John had forgotten the payment. John had made a mistake.

And Calvin could correct the mistake. He could prove to himself and to John that he was still needed. Calvin wrung his hands together, his mind racing, eyes wide and wild. Yes, he could collect the payment himself. And John would be thankful and proud. He would realize that he still needed Calvin as a partner.

It made perfect sense.

Didn't it?

Calvin hurried to change. After wiping his face with a towel, he blew his nose on a handkerchief and then put on one of his suits. Despite the fact that the weather seemed pleasant, warm for the early fall, Calvin threw on a coat too, in case he might suffer through a second—third?—bout of chills while he was out. Then he found the notebook they'd been using to write up their receipts.

Mind still hazy from illness, Calvin walked to the home of Elliott James, only a few blocks away. By the time Calvin reached the beautiful brick building, he was sweating profusely, enough that the front of his hair had become wet. And yet, he was still shivering. Dammit, he should have stayed in bed.

No.

He needed to prove that he was still needed.

After wiping his forehead with the sleeve of his coat, Calvin knocked. Moments later, Mr. James opened the door, an inquisitive look on his face.

"Mr. Wright?"

"Hello!"

"I thought Mr. Hall said you weren't feeling well."

"Oh. That. I had some . . . stomach troubles, but I'm fine now." Calvin was hit with a wave of something. Something that was making him feel lightheaded. He could feel his false smile faltering, and so, he made sure to smile even harder. "Apparently, my partner forgot to collect the payment earlier. I thought I'd—"

"Ah, you're right. I'm sorry. I must have forgotten as well."

"Not a problem."

"So, how much will it be for the embalming and the viewing?"

Calvin rubbed his chin, trying to remember what he and John had settled on for this one. Hall and Wright's pricing was flexible. Depending on the complexity of the services requested (how much help was required for the viewing, whether they would need to help the family coordinate with the church, how far Calvin and John would have to travel to the cemetery, how *many* services there were [one in the home and one in the church or only either], whether the funeral was for a small child [they tended not to charge for those], whether John needed to build a casket [rare nowadays], whether they wanted mourning trinkets or funeral biscuits or other such things), the pricings could vary a lot.

Something *else* that Calvin had been wanting them to consider was the wealth of the clients themselves. In Calvin's mind, there was no reason not to charge more money to someone who controlled half of one of the city's neighborhoods, for example, either because they were a politician or because they owned and operated several businesses, but John had always refused.

Well, John wasn't here now, was he? What harm was there in trying it out this one time? Mr. James was wealthy. He owned not one, not two, but *three* markets in Frankford. God, Calvin would not only prove to John that his presence was essential for things like organizing the funeral and collecting money, but for his financial sense as well.

"One twenty," Calvin said confidently, even though that was *way* too much. Normally, they'd charge eighty for the services they had provided (or, well, that John had provided). But not today. "I know it's steep, but—"

"Ah, no, I completely understand," Mr. James said with a wave of his wrist. "Accounting for the embalming and the viewing and the cemetery transport, I'd say that it's a fair price."

Calvin's chest swelled with pride. Hah!

"Great," Calvin said, trying to keep his voice level so as to not show how elated and shocked he was by the man's response. "I'll write up a receipt, then."

Heart still pitter-pattering from the rush of having charged this man *forty more dollars* than their typical price, Calvin hastily scrawled two copies—one for Mr. James and one for Hall and Wright. After the man then paid—in *cash* no less—Calvin stuffed the bills into his front pocket. Forty extra! Twenty extra *each*!

Calvin then left for home. For the first half of his walk, he was busy feeling ecstatic over the extra money, but, when the rush of excitement began to wane, Calvin's thoughts found their way back to *Lucy*.

Even though Calvin was ninety-nine percent certain that it was impossible for John to have found someone else, either to work with or to bed, he couldn't seem to stop worrying over that last little one percent. Because there was a chance, a *tiny* chance, that Calvin could lose his home. Again.

God, how horrible it would be. And Calvin had so much more to lose now, too. He could lose his home and his business and his only friend. Not to mention the most painful loss—the loss of the love of his life.

Oh, Calvin was so fucking tired of conning people. He was tired of working in factories and barely scraping by. He was tired of being lonely. He was tired of feeling unloved. Finally, *finally*, he had built a beautiful life for himself. He could hardly believe that there was a chance, however small, that he could ever lose it.

Desperation seized Calvin's heart and a heaviness pressed on his chest. He couldn't seem to pull enough oxygen into his lungs to keep up with his racing pulse. Within seconds, Calvin's chest hurt so much that he had to stop walking to try to recover. He wiped the sweat from his brow once more.

Damn, he was exhausted.

Slowly, the heaviness on Calvin's chest lifted as his heart rate returned to normal. Still, there was one weight that remained—the extra money in his pocket.

Calvin ran a hand over his still-sweaty face. What if . . . what if he kept it? And what if he kept some next time, too? What if he *kept* keeping it?

Calvin could have himself a little private stash of emergency money. Just . . . in case John thought he wasn't needed anymore.

When Calvin returned home, he found John waiting for him in the kitchen. Calvin's stomach churned unpleasantly.

"Cal, wh-wh-where were you? I came back with the medicine but—"

"Sorry," Calvin said. "I, uhm, I went to collect the payment myself."

Letting out a long breath, John came closer.

"Why would you exert yourself like that?" he said, putting his hands on Calvin's hips. "You're sick." John reached up and touched Calvin's forehead with the back of his hand. "Goodness, Cal, you still have a f-f-fever. You shouldn't have been out exerting yourself like that."

"I'm sorry," Calvin said, hanging his head low.

"We n-n-need to take you back to bed," John said, finding Calvin's hand. He started toward the stairs. "How much did you charge Mr. James? Eighty? Ninety?"

"Uhm . . ."

Calvin paused. He thought of David and Ed. He thought of those horrible words of warning Michael had thrown at him months back. He thought of how terrible it had felt to lose his home and be left with *nothing*.

And, so, he spluttered a lie.

"One hundred."

His heart thudded. He had lied. He had lied to John.

Abruptly, John stopped walking. "*One hundred*?!"

Calvin's stomach soured, and the taste migrated up his throat. He tried to swallow, to banish the bitter taste, but couldn't. John sighed.

"I'm not mad, Calvin," he said. "Really."

Calvin licked his lips, wincing from the wretched taste still sitting on his tongue.

He said, "I know that I should have charged eighty, but I thought . . . well, I thought that we could try charging him a bit more since he's so wealthy."

"Cal, I thought we talked about this," John said, his voice a mixture of weary and stern. He resumed walking, tugging Calvin along. "I want us to be f-f-fair. I can only imagine how hard it is for our clients to pay us to bury someone they love. We shouldn't exploit the families who hire us."

Calvin's face burned. "You're right, John. I'm sorry."

"Well, m-m-maybe we can put the extra into the business. I've been considering purchasing a telephone. I remember reading that the cost per month shouldn't be too much, not for people like us. We're very lucky with the money we make. I'm not sure how much the w-w-wiring might be, but what are your thoughts? Should we put the extra into a telephone fund?"

Calvin swallowed hard. "Sure."

"Alright."

Once they were in the bedroom, John turned to face Calvin, pulling him close. He kissed Calvin's cheek, and Calvin's entire face warmed, not from the fever, but from shame. He could still feel the extra twenty, the secret bit of cash, sitting heavy in his pocket, and every second that ticked by, it became heavier.

Calvin opened his mouth to tell John everything—to say that he had overheard part of John's conversation with Katherine and that he had overcharged the client even more than he had said and that he had been planning to *steal* the extra money, but then . . .

But then he started to imagine what it would be like to be rejected by the man he loved, either because John would confirm that he had found someone else or, more likely, because John would be upset with him, both because he had lied and because his first instinct had been to *steal*.

God, was he even worthy of John's love?

"I think I'll try to sleep for a while more," Calvin said, head swimming and heart beating fast as sickness and worry and shame still raged inside of him.

He felt as though he might faint.

"Do you want the m-m-medicine I purchased?"

"No," Calvin said with a shake of his head. "Just need to rest."

"Of course," John said, his voice filled with tenderness. "I'll start on the soup."

After one kiss on the forehead, John nuzzled Calvin's nose, and then he turned to leave. Calvin stayed frozen as he listened to John's retreating footsteps. When Calvin was sure that John was no longer nearby, he hastily shoved the wad of cash into one of his socks and then climbed back into bed.

All the while cursing himself for being a liar and a coward.

The wall clock began to chime, the bells seeming sluggish, as though their notes were traveling through honey before they reached Calvin's ears. Slowly, Calvin poked his head out from beneath the covers. He sat up, expecting to feel the same way he had yesterday—sore and fuzzy-headed—but was surprised to find that he felt a tad more like himself, other than a somewhat stuffy nose and mild headache. And except, of course, for the knot of regret balled in his stomach.

Bong. Bong. Bong.

Bleary-eyed, Calvin turned toward the clock, wondering how long it had been since either he or John had wound it. While Calvin was thinking about this, John came into the bedroom. He was still wearing his big, billowy night shirt. Probably John hadn't wanted to change earlier so that he wouldn't wake Calvin.

How unworthy Calvin was of such consideration.

"Goodness, Cal, the clock sounds sicker than you," John remarked, holding a T-shaped metal key in hand. Instead of heading over to the clock, John walked to the bed and sat on the edge. He ran his free hand through Calvin's hair, caressing him sweetly. "Are you fffeeling better than yesterday?"

Calvin nodded. He wanted to speak, but the truth was on the tip of his tongue, and he worried that if he opened his mouth, it would fly out of its own volition like a bird that had been trapped in a cage.

It was only a matter of time before he let it escape. But he couldn't bring himself to confess to stealing the money yet. Last night, once his fever had finally broken, he'd been able to think more clearly, his rational mind teasing apart the interwoven tapestry of new worries and past traumas, and he'd realized what a fool he had been. Whoever Lucy was, the chance that she was either John's lover or prospective new business partner was infinitesimally small. He and John were together constantly (except for an embalming here and there). And even though John had run *one* funeral by himself, that by itself didn't mean that he would no longer need Calvin. Or that he would no longer want him.

If only Calvin hadn't collected that payment by himself. Or if he hadn't overcharged. Or, hell, if he hadn't *lied*, then maybe his partnership with John—both business and romantic—would have still been salvageable. But, of course, Calvin *had* collected the overly inflated payment, he *had* kept the extra money, and, worst of all, he had lied. Once Calvin confessed the truth to John, there was no way John would still want him. Calvin had broken John's trust.

He had broken his own heart.

John pressed a hard kiss to Calvin's forehead.

"It seems like your f-fever hasn't returned," he said. "Are you hungry yet?" Calvin shook his head, and John hummed, frowning. "Do you want some tea, then? I think you ought to have something, even if it's only tea with honey."

Guilt coiled tighter in Calvin's stomach. Dammit, it hurt that John was trying to take care of him. Before Calvin could decline John's offer, John kissed Calvin's head once more and stood.

"I'm m-m-making it anyway," he said, walking over to the clock.

Calvin twiddled his thumbs as John wound the three mechanisms on the clock's face, and every second that passed, Calvin's self-loathing and regret twisted tighter, too.

After John left, Calvin climbed out of bed and fetched a robe from the closet, his movements shaky and slow. Even though John had made him soup the previous night, Calvin hadn't managed to eat more than two bites, and even then, he had been too lost in some mixture of worry and regret and delirium to taste them. John, on the other hand, had eaten more than he normally would have, trying not to waste the food. In the end, he had brought the rest over to the neighbors. And Calvin had climbed back into bed to hide from himself and from his future and from John.

Calvin walked to the kitchen where John was steeping the tea. After John poured him a cup, John nuzzled the side of Calvin's face and left to change. Calvin stood fixed to the spot, the cup of tea cradled in his hands. Heat permeated the porcelain and warmed his skin, reminding him of John's love.

And how unworthy he was of it.

Seconds later, Calvin heard the metallic click of the front door being unlocked. It was probably Michael. Ugh. Why had he and John let Michael keep his set of keys?

Calvin was still staring at his tea when Michael and Katherine came into the kitchen.

"Good morning, Calvin," Michael said. "Where's John?"

"Bedroom," Calvin said, his voice hoarse. "Changing."

Michael responded with a hum. He hooked his hands behind his back and walked off. Katherine and Calvin smiled at each other.

Gesturing to the tea kettle, Calvin asked, "Want some tea?"

"Why not?" she said before turning to retrieve a mug from one of the cupboards. "How are you feeling?"

"Better," he said. "And . . . not better."

Katherine furrowed her brow. "Why?"

Calvin shook his head. "I can't tell you. I need to talk to John first."

"Well, Michael and I shouldn't be long. He's looking for one of his checkbooks. I came by yesterday looking for it, but I couldn't find it. He wanted to take one more look in the study before we check the factories. He seems to think that I couldn't have searched hard enough in the study myself."

She rolled her eyes, and Calvin chuckled. While Katherine poured herself a cup of tea, Calvin shifted his weight from one foot to the other. Hopefully Katherine would still want to remain his friend once John threw him out.

But probably not.

Heart heavy, Calvin sat with a sigh, and Katherine sat next to him. Stomach churning, Calvin forced a smile.

And told himself to try to enjoy this one last cup of tea with his friend.

Chapter Twenty
John

In the bedroom, while John was putting on his suit, button-ing his long-sleeved shirt in front of the standing mirror, unease settled heavy in his stomach. Calvin had been behaving strangely. Yes, Calvin was sick, but that wasn't it. Or, that wasn't *all* of it, rather. Last night, Calvin had barely even spoken while nibbling on the soup and crackers that John had prepared for him, and then, later, in bed, Calvin hadn't wanted to cuddle. But Calvin loved cuddling.

Something was wrong.

When John was finished buttoning his shirt, he tucked the ends into his pants and then looped his suspenders over his shoulders. Next, he put on his blue waistcoat, his mind still stuck on the possibility that something was wrong with Calvin. He then took a step toward the closet, but the feel of the cool hardwood on the ball of his foot made him pause, pulling him out of his thoughts. Drat. He lifted his foot to find a hole in his sock. He was really running through them lately. He probably ought to be more careful when washing them. Poor Calvin. John had really kept him busy over the last few months mending his things.

After checking his own sock drawer (empty), John moved over to Calvin's (nearly empty except for two pairs). At random, John chose one, only to realize that there was something stashed inside one of the feet. He crooked an eyebrow.

Tentatively, John stuck his hand inside. At the bottom, by the toe, the tips of his fingers touched what seemed to be a ball of paper. Money, perhaps? Gripping it tightly, he pulled it out. It *was* money—twenty dollars to be exact—with a piece of paper as well. Confused, John unfolded the paper. His eyes scanned the page. It was a receipt from their most recent funeral service yesterday, only it indicated that Calvin had charged Mr. James one hundred twenty for their services, not one hundred like he had said. Why on earth would Calvin lie?

Michael's words rang in his ears.

"He's trying to lull you into a false sense of security. Probably so that he can cheat you out of money. Goodness, I bet he's hoarding some of the cash from your business. Or, heaven forbid, stealing from clients."

Each portion of Michael's statement was like a swift, hard punch to the stomach, and the blows were so fierce, so painful, that John nearly fell to his knees from the force of them. He could barely comprehend what he was seeing. Calvin was *purposefully* overcharging their clients? And secretly keeping the extra money? It was unfathomable.

Faintly, he heard the sound of footsteps in the hall.

Michael called out, "John?"

But John couldn't seem to make himself respond.

Michael strolled into the room.

"Ah, there you are," his brother said, coming closer while John remained frozen, his feet stuck to the floor and eyes unfocused. With a light laugh, Michael said, "Are you keeping money in your stockings now? I think the safe is probably safer. Hence the name."

Heart hammering, John merely shook his head, hurt and confusion tangled in his throat.

"What is it?" Michael asked.

"Calvin . . . he . . ."

Oh God, it couldn't be true, could it?

"Christ, John, what now?" Michael said, the familiar irritation in his voice sparking a fierce protectiveness in John's heart. He couldn't tell Michael what he had found, especially without first knowing for sure whether Calvin—

"John?"

It wasn't Michael's voice this time, but Calvin's. John turned to see Calvin standing in the threshold of their bedroom, with Katherine behind him.

And then, John watched Calvin's eyes blow wide with horror the moment he spotted what John was holding in his hand.

And John knew, then, that his suspicions were true.

"I can explain," Calvin spluttered. "*Please* let me explain."

Michael crooked an eyebrow. "Explain what?" He seemed to follow Calvin's line of sight to the cash and the receipt, and then his mouth fell open for the briefest instant before he snatched both from John's hand. "Oh my God, John, he was stealing from you, wasn't he?"

"No!" Calvin protested. "Not . . . not exactly. I—"

"I *knew* he shouldn't have trusted you," Michael said to Calvin. "My brother takes you into his home, makes you his business partner, trusts you with his heart and *this*"—he paused and held up the money—"is how you repay him?!"

Calvin took a step forward, his eyes pleading. "Of course not. Listen, I—"

"Get out," Michael snarled. "Now."

Locking eyes with John, Calvin tried once more. "John, please listen to me, it was *one time*, and, trust me, I know it was wrong, but—"

Michael scoffed. "*Trust you?!* Why the hell should John *trust* you?"

John flinched from Michael's words, that fierce protectiveness flaring to life inside of him once more, but he fought to keep it contained.

Calvin continued, "I know, I know, but if you'll let me explain—"

"No, I *won't* let you explain. I want you to leave," Michael said, his shoulders visibly tensing. "*Now.*"

Katherine piped up, saying, "Michael! Stop!"

Calvin tried one more time. "Listen, I only—"

"Get the hell out of my house!" Michael exploded.

And with that, John's fury exploded forth too.

"Oh, for God's sake, M-Michael, will you let him talk?!" John bellowed. "And it's not *your* house anymore. It's mine. I can fetch the—the—the fffucking *deed* to prove it to you if you've somehow forgotten. And Calvin isn't leaving. I w-w-want to hear what he has to say."

With a shaky hand, John took back the money roll and receipt, and then he started toward Calvin—his best friend, his business partner, his lover—with his head held high. He would *not* let Michael make this choice for him.

When John came close, he noticed the faintest hint of what looked to be a proud smile on Calvin's face, and it ignited a tiny spark of self-love within him, too, one that burned so brightly he nearly melted on the spot. John could *feel* how much he had changed over the past several months, thanks to Calvin's love, and it was nothing short of miraculous. *His and Calvin's love* was miraculous. No matter what had happened, no matter what supposed crime Calvin had committed, John still loved his partner. He'd never *stop* loving him.

John would forgive Calvin. Even before finding out the truth, John knew that he would forgive him. Still, John had to know what had happened and why.

"Cal," he began, keeping his voice soft, "wh-what is this?"

Calvin's small smile fell. Lowering his eyes, he whispered his response.

"It's the extra money from yesterday's service. I'm sure you saw the receipt. Initially, I wanted to keep it for myself, but I . . . fuck, I realized I shouldn't have taken it. I shouldn't have lied to you."

"Why did you?"

"I overheard you talking to Katherine yesterday morning." Calvin paused. A light-pink hue crept across his cheeks. John's heart twinged with sorrow. How he loathed to see Calvin this way—so timid and unsure. Calvin lifted his eyes to meet John's and then he said, "About Lucy."

John's breath caught, and a wave of emotions—worry and sorrow and shame—coalesced inside him.

"Lucy," John repeated, barely able to say her name himself.

"I'm not mad," Calvin said, his voice wrought with urgency, and the words helped calm some of John's emotions, the wave of relief and fear and shame receding like the tide. "I'm not sure who she is to you, but I shouldn't have . . . I mean, I thought that maybe you were leaving me like . . . like David left me."

"Oh, Cal, never. Why would you think that?"

"I, uhm, I never told you this, but David . . . see, we were business partners, right? Obviously what we had wasn't a real business, not like Hall and Wright, but our schemes *were* our business. And David . . . eventually, he found someone else. He replaced me. I think the reason why the two of us were never close in the, uhm, in the way that you and I are close is because David never really loved me. With David, I was only ever meant to be . . . temporary."

Calvin's bottom lip started trembling. John could see the tears pooling in his lover's eyes, and he could sense the strength that it took for Calvin to keep them from falling. It hurt. God, it hurt so much to see Calvin's pain.

Without so much as a word, John pulled Calvin in for an embrace. After a brief moment of hesitation, Calvin hugged him back, burying his face in John's neck. Michael and Katherine stood nearby silently, though John could have sworn that he heard Michael let out an irritated huff.

"I would n-n-never replace you," John whispered into Calvin's ear. "You're not t-temporary. Don't ever think that you are."

"I'm sorry," Calvin whispered back. "I panicked."

John ran his fingers through Calvin's soft brown hair and wished that he had never kept such a large piece of himself from the man he loved. Just as Calvin had kept the specifics of David's betrayal a secret, probably because the hurt and shame surrounding it had been too much to face, John had kept Lucy a secret as well, and for the same reasons.

But John wouldn't keep Lucy from Calvin anymore.

Pulling back to look in Calvin's eyes, John said, "Lucy was my sister. Actually, she was my t-t-twin. But she passed. When Michael and I were little." Calvin reached up to touch John's cheek, his eyes still shimmering with unshed tears, and John melted into his touch, welcoming the wordless comfort. "I'm sorry I never told you that I had a sister. It wasn't because Lucy wasn't important. But because she was . . . because she was *so* important. Lucy was the reason why I became a m-m-mortician. Losing her . . ." John heaved a sorrowful sigh. "It changed me somehow. I was never able to move on. I still can't seem to. It's hard for me to t-t-talk about her. Goodness, Cal, I'm sorry my silence caused all of this."

John and Calvin's conversation was interrupted by a scoff. John looked over to see Michael rolling his eyes.

"Why are *you* asking for forgiveness, John? No matter his ex-cuse—which, by the way, barely even sounds like a reasonable one—Calvin *stole* from you." He rubbed his forehead. "And, *of course* his excuse involves Lucy somehow. Why am I not sur-prised?"

"Michael, please," John said. "I know how you f-f-feel about Lucy. I know how hard it must be for you that I . . . that I still m-miss her."

"Still miss her," Michael repeated with another scoff. "After she passed, you practically became obsessed with her. It seems you still are. God, even our parents wanted you to stop with the constant Lucy-related commentary."

Shame started to creep up the back of John's neck, the familiar burn turning his ears hot and making him want to curl in on himself, to coil into a ball so small that he somehow wouldn't be seen. But then Calvin caught his hand, and when John saw the hurt and shame and regret on Calvin's face, he realized that it was his own shame—the shame he felt for missing Lucy, the shame that *Michael* had helped to cultivate over the course of his life—that had started this horrible course of events and put that pain there. He needed this to end.

After clearing his throat, John straightened his posture and said, very pointedly, "Lucy was our sister, Michael. I refuse to keep feeling bad for missing her. Wh-wh-when we were little, the three of us were inseparable. And you *loved* her. I know you loved her. Heavens, I remember how you seemed to *cherish her*, even. But now you're behaving like she m-m-meant nothing to you. Like she had n-*never* meant anything to you. Why?"

Michael stood frozen for a few seconds, his expression hard-ened, but then, slowly, his eyes fell to the floor. John wanted to press him further, but his heart was still beating wildly, his nervous system reeling from the confrontation. Uncomfortable silence followed.

And then, to John's wonder, Michael seemed to curl in on himself.

Head low, Michael shook his head and said, "That's not true."

John felt a pinprick of pity for his older brother. He released Calvin's hand and started toward Michael.

"I still can't understand why everyone seemed to stop missing her. Everyone except for me." He took a pause to compose his thoughts. "Everyone else stopped w-w-wanting to talk about her, stopped wanting to remember her. Even though I was little, I could tell that our p-p-parents weren't happy with me whenever I'd bring her up. But you were the only one who—who seemed to really *hate* it. Or—or hate *her*, maybe." Catching Michael's eye, he said, "*Do you hate her?*"

After a long pause, Michael said, "How could I not?" John's heart splintered, and even though he wanted to cover his ears—to protect himself from Michael's truth—he waited for Michael to say more. "When Lucy left, she took everything from me," Michael choked out, tears pooling in his eyes. Hugging himself, he looked away and then shuffled his shoe back and forth across the floor in front of him. It looked like . . . like maybe he was struggling not to cry. "And, yes, I hated her for it. I really hated her for it. I still hate her for it. God, is that . . . is that what you wanted to hear, John?"

Tears began to fall from Michael's eyes. John's heart clenched, a rush of painful sympathy rippling through him, and he had to tense his muscles in order to try to endure it. Michael sniffled, and John felt one more painful tug on his heart. He could barely stand the pain.

Michael said, "I'm not sure how much you remember, but our parents *changed* when she died. Mother started sleeping all the time. Father . . . he . . . he practically stopped talking. He barely ever . . . I mean, he never hugged me *once* after that. Or you. And then you . . . you *never* stopped talking about her. Not for those first few months. And it hurt so much. Here you were, practically *bursting* with love for her, while I was . . . not." He swallowed hard and sniffled once more. "I was angry. I was so, so angry. And I *hated* my anger. So . . . so, I tried to make you stop. But you *wouldn't*. Not until I managed to make you feel horrible for missing her. But then you . . . God, you became like our father, I think. Quiet. Sullen. Awkward. And I never knew how to *fix* it. I *wanted* to fix it. I wanted to fix *you*. Because I thought that maybe everything could somehow return to normal. Before Lucy passed, you had your stammer, but otherwise, you were fine. Shy, maybe, because some kids hadn't been the nicest whenever you tripped over your words, but a lovely, if not somewhat eccentric, person otherwise. You had some interesting mannerisms, too, if I recall correctly, but . . . oh, everything is so fuzzy now. Still, I remember that time fondly." Michael squeezed his eyes shut. "And then . . . oh, God, I think I *broke* you." He sniffled. "Didn't I? All this time, I thought that maybe you were the way that you were because of Lucy. Because of her leaving us. But . . . but it was because of me, wasn't it? It was because I made you think there was something wrong with you."

John's brows creased together as he considered Michael's words. Carefully, John unraveled them, tugging on each thread so that he could examine them separately. Michael was right in some respects. He was right that John had always had his stammer. John had always wrung his hands whenever he was upset. He had always been shy. God, he had always struggled to connect with people, too. It had never come easy for him. Not even when Lucy had been by his side. Despite those things, Michael seemed to have viewed the whole of their early childhood favorably. Michael seemed to have viewed *John* more favorably. But John had always been himself, even back then. John had never been "normal." And

Calvin *liked* that he wasn't normal. Truthfully, John was starting to like it himself. Perhaps things like Lucy's passing and Michael's constant reprimanding and his parent's lack of care had played a part in John becoming the man that he was. But, at his core, John Hall had always been John Hall. Yes, Michael had hurt him. But he hadn't broken him.

Because John wasn't broken. He never had been.

"Michael," John finally said, "I won't p-p-pretend that the way you treated me hadn't hurt me back then. Or even now, sometimes. But . . ." When John paused, Michael sniffed, and John knew that he couldn't wait to comfort his brother even one second longer. He pulled Michael in for a fierce hug. "But you didn't break me. I'm still me."

"I'm sorry," Michael said, his voice muffled by John's shoulder.

"I never stopped to c-c-consider that you were hurting back then, as I was," John said. "And so, I'm sorry, too."

"John, you were six. I was nine. I never expected you to coddle me."

John huffed a soft laugh. He squeezed Michael tighter, his heart twisting as Michael inhaled a trembling breath.

"I'm not upset with you for hating her," John said into Michael's ear. "And Lucy w-w-wouldn't be either."

"Don't lie to me," Michael said, a hint of levity, of *teasing*, in his voice. "Remember when I broke her porcelain horse? God, it wasn't even on purpose, and she still punished me for it. If I close my eyes, I swear I can feel her little five-year-old fists pummeling me in the chest."

With a chuckle, John said, "You're right, she w-w-would be mad. But she would forgive you." He paused, wondering something. "Do you really still hate her?"

Michael waited for a second before replying, "Sometimes."

"Do you hate me?"

Another pause. "Sometimes."

For some reason, even though John knew he probably should have been hurt by this, he found it extraordinarily funny instead. So, he started to laugh. And then Michael laughed right along with him. And John thought about the fury he'd felt toward Michael lately when it came to Calvin.

"I hate you sometimes, too," John confessed. Both of them laughed a little more before John then released Michael from the embrace. Placing one hand on each of Michael's shoulders, John harnessed every ounce of courage he had and said, "Look, Michael, I know you still hate Calvin."

"No." Michael heaved a sigh. "It's not that I *hate* Calvin. Not in a playful, brotherly way, and not in a real way, either. It's that I want to protect you. I was worried that he . . . that he was only *pretending* to like you."

"You w-w-wanted to protect me even though you hate me?" John teased.

"Well, I'm your big brother. I'm obligated to protect you. It's in the contract."

With a smile and a chuckle, John shook his head. He let himself enjoy the moment for a little while—to bask in the warmth of familial love—before remembering that he needed to confront Michael about how he had been treating the man he loved.

John's smile faded, and then, with as much sternness as he could muster, he said, "Calvin and I love each other. I n-n-need you to respect that."

"Do you really not care that he stole from you?"

"No," John said with conviction. "I trust that it was a mistake."

One that Calvin had made before and could potentially make again, but that was something that he and Calvin would work through themselves.

"Alright, I'll *try* to respect your . . . relationship," Michael said, though the words seemed hard for him. "Because I respect you."

Katherine came over and placed a hand on Michael's back.

"Give Calvin a chance—a *real* chance."

"Give him a chance," Michael repeated in a playfully sarcastic manner. "Didn't he steal from you, too?" Chuckling, Katherine nudged him, and Michael nudged her back. "*Fine.*" He pointed at Calvin. "But if you *ever* steal from John even one more time—"

"Never." Calvin reached for John's hand and squeezed. "I promise."

Warmth unfurled in John's chest. Whether or not Calvin kept his promise, John wouldn't stop loving him. He knew Calvin had a kind heart.

Smiling fondly, John squeezed Calvin's hand back.

Michael cleared his throat. "Well, Katherine and I will let you two have some privacy. But *please* let me know if you need me, John. Come straight over if—"

With a curt nod, John turned to his brother and said, "I will."

Still, Michael lingered a moment. John could tell that, no matter what Michael had *said*, he was struggling to not be John's protector right now. And John could hardly blame him. *He* knew that Calvin was a lovely person, one who was still struggling to break free of his past. But to Michael, Calvin was first and foremost a criminal—someone not to be trusted.

"Michael," John began, "I will be f-fine. Calvin and I care for each other. Truly."

"Alright," Michael said again before taking a breath and then letting it out slowly. "I wish there was an easier way to reach you later. I ought to . . . to purchase you a telephone."

John and Calvin turned to each other, their eyes widening in tandem.

Calvin said, "I bet we're thinking the same thing."

"Yes, probably," John said, breaking their linked hands so that he could hand the wad of stolen money to Michael. "Cal and I would love a t-telephone. Neither of us knows how to even *begin* the process of acquiring one, but—"

"I can take care of it," Michael said, taking the money. "I'll put some of my own money toward it as well. Of course, you two will have to pay the monthly fee, but I can reach out to the fellow who helped install one for me in Kensington." He shoved the cash into his pocket. "Smart choice. It's the right thing for your business. And hopefully this means that I can check up on you sometimes?"

"Anytime," John said, now smiling so broadly his cheeks were starting to hurt.

"How exciting!" Katherine said, practically beaming, too.

With a wry look, Michael wagged his index finger at her and said, "Don't think you can call your new friend all the time once they have a telephone."

"Ah, well, Michael, if you prefer, I'd be happy to come over several times a week instead," Calvin suggested in a teasing tone.

Michael's eyes flickering up to the ceiling as he shook his head.

With a sigh, he took Katherine's hand and said, "Why I let you become friends with him is beyond me."

But there was a levity to his voice, a small smirk threatening to break through his obviously fake expression of exasperation. Katherine laughed softly.

"Come on, let's not overstay our welcome," she said.

"Right." Michael offered a curt nod. "Take care, little brother."

John replied, "I will."

After Katherine and Michael left, Calvin collapsed into John's waiting embrace.

"I'm so sorry. I never meant to hurt you. I swear. When I found out that you were keeping something from me, I lost my head. I kept thinking of David and Ed and Ed's fucking horrible mustache and—"

"I know." John hushed Calvin, rubbing his back with long strokes.

John continued to comfort him, to shush him and caress him and hold him close as he cried. What a beautiful heart Calvin had. Oh, the poor man must have been so worried, so hurt. Nothing short of heartbreak—and the sorrow and fear that came with it—could have caused Calvin to resort to reverting to the man he'd once been but no longer wished to be.

Softly, John kissed the top of Calvin's ear and whispered, "Such a beautiful person." One more kiss. "With a wonderful heart." And another. "And such f-f-funny little ears."

Calvin chuckled, his sweet little laugh mixed with a sniffle. John loosened his hold and pulled back so that he could wipe Calvin's wet cheeks with his thumbs. Even though words of comfort were still hard for him, he knew he had to try his best to put both Calvin's mind and heart at ease.

He said, "I'm not mad. I'm not hurt. Right now, my only c-c-concern is you."

"I'm sorry," Calvin repeated.

John's chest clenched. Calvin would probably be saying those words a lot.

Sighing, John said, "All these months, Cal, you've been taking care of me. C-c-comforting me with lovely, lovely words while too often, I struggled to know what to say when you n-n-needed the same sort of care in return."

"Oh, John, there's no need to—"

"Wait, there's more." Still holding Calvin's face in his hands, John looked intently into Calvin's beautiful brown eyes and said, very earnestly, "I kept things from you. Important things. For that, I am sorry. I p-p-*promise* I won't let it happen again. I will make the words come. If not out loud, then on paper. No more secrets. No matter how hard something is for me to say."

Calvin leaned forward, kissing their foreheads together.

"Thank you," he said, his voice barely even a whisper and his breathing still shaky. Sweetly, he pulled back to nuzzle John's nose. "I want to know more," he said, "about Lucy."

"Then I will tell you more," John said, a magnificent rush of warmth spreading through his chest, his love for Calvin somehow burning brighter and hotter by the moment. "I'll t-t-tell you everything."

John and Calvin climbed into bed. And then, for the first time since he was six years old, John spoke freely of his sister Lucy, letting himself love her and miss her and mourn her and even celebrate her.

All without even the tiniest bit of shame.

Chapter Twenty-One
Calvin

That evening, Calvin was curled up on the sofa with a blanket over his shoulders, waiting for John to finish making soup. Despite having taken the medicine that John had purchased for him, Calvin wasn't feeling much better than he had been that morning. Physically, that was. Emotionally, Calvin felt as though he had been reborn. He still felt terrible for having stolen from John and silly for having worked himself into such a frenzy, but the weight of shame had been lifted. Somehow, even though Calvin had confessed to having overcharged their client, even though Calvin had confessed that he'd been planning on keeping the extra money, John still loved him. John's capacity for love was unlike anything Calvin had ever known.

God, was he ever lucky to have found him.

Musing on this, Calvin couldn't help but think that he ought to thank Katherine for bringing them together. If Katherine hadn't been *Katherine*, Calvin wouldn't have managed to steal her necklace, nor would Michael have ever let him work with John. Calvin owed her more than he could ever repay. He had to hope that, for now, his friendship could be enough, though he wouldn't stop trying to figure out some other way to make it up to her. Hopefully it would come to him. In time.

"Soup is ready," John said, coming into the sitting room with a piping hot bowl of bean and vegetable stew. He sat on the couch beside Calvin. When Calvin reached for the bowl, John pulled it back. "Let me feed you."

Calvin pretended to roll his eyes. "I'm not *that* sick. Anymore."

"Humor me," John said, scooping up a spoonful of broth with a piece of carrot floating in it. "I like taking c-care of you."

"*I* should be the one taking care of *you*. Everything we went through today, God, it was a lot. I can only imagine how tiring it was to confront Michael like that. And when you first found the money . . ." Groaning, Calvin closed his eyes, a flicker of self-reproach striking him in the chest. "Dammit, John, I'm—"

"Cal," John said, a hint of sternness in his voice. "I *know* you're sorry."

"I feel—"

Gently, John interrupted, saying, "Terrible. I know."

"Worse than terrible. Worse than . . . worse than I've ever felt in my whole fucking life."

Huffing a light laugh, John shook his head. "Good thing we have soup, then."

"Soup cures emotional wounds now, too?" Calvin jested.

"We will soon find out." John brought the spoon closer to Calvin's lips. "Open."

Rolling his eyes, Calvin took the spoonful into his mouth. He hummed as the liquid moved over his tongue.

"I thought you said you couldn't cook," he said. "Why have I been the one cooking for months when you can make food like that?"

John chuckled. "It's only soup."

"Amazing soup."

Calvin made a big show of opening his mouth for more soup, and John's cheeks reddened from the wordless compliment.

"I will make the soup w-weekly if you will stop this c-c-commentary."

"Deal."

Over the next fifteen minutes or so, John fed Calvin the soup. Unlike the last batch, Calvin now tasted John's love in every single morsel. And it was *everything*.

When Calvin was finished eating, John served himself a bowl, and Calvin rested his head on John's shoulder while John ate beside him on the couch. Every once in a while, John stopped to kiss Calvin's head. And Calvin couldn't believe he had ever thought, even for a second, that John would replace him.

"We're perfect together," Calvin said with a sigh. "Aren't we?"

John set his empty bowl on the floor and wrapped Calvin up in a hug, and then Calvin curled up on John's chest, soaking up every bit of John's care. While they cuddled, Calvin found the pocket watch in John's suit. He took it out and held it, the chain still clipped to the black fabric of John's waistcoat.

"Do you w-w-want it back?" John asked.

Calvin shifted his head to look up at him. "No. Why would I?"

"It's special to you."

"It is. But so are you." Calvin crooked an eyebrow. "Do you not like it?"

"I love it. B-but it belonged to your parents."

Calvin narrowed his eyes. "Do I have to explain it again? I thought I was pretty thorough the first time."

John smiled. "You were. But . . . there are things I have of Lucy's that . . . well, I'm not sure I could ever p-p-part with."

"Really? Like what?"

John held up a finger. Gingerly, he urged Calvin to sit up, and then he left the room. He came back a minute later holding a few things. One by one, John set them on the couch cushion next to Calvin. Calvin picked up the rag doll first.

"Lucy loved her," John said.

"What's her name?"

"Jennie."

Calvin smoothed its hair and set it back on the cushion. Next, he picked up the locket—only the clamshell, no chain. Upon closer inspection, Calvin realized that it was missing its bail.

"I broke it when I was ten," John said. "By m-m-mistake."

"I'm sorry."

"I shouldn't have been w-wearing it in the first place."

"Why not?"

John shrugged. Calvin's expression softened as he felt a pinching in his chest.

"It's not wrong to miss her," he said. "It never was."

John's lips curled into a tiny smile. "I know. Or, I should say, I know that n-now," he said. "Perhaps it had been strange of me to w-w-wear her necklace, though."

"Maybe," Calvin said, pushing himself to stand, the blanket falling to his feet. "But it was sweet, too."

Calvin stepped over the blanket, nearly tripping over the folds, and placed his hands on John's waist, one still clutching tight to the locket.

He pressed a light kiss to John's lips. Then he lifted the locket to inspect it some more, running his finger over the silver, over the swirl pattern that vaguely resembled curling vines, and wondered if he could somehow fix it.

"Would you wear it now? If you could?" Calvin asked.

After a pause, John replied, "Maybe."

John touched the locket, too, his fingers bumping into Calvin's.

"It would be like one of those pieces of mourning jewelry," Calvin said.

"Minus the hair."

"Thankfully," Calvin said with a teasing edge in his voice.

John laughed and shoved Calvin back a half step.

"What?" Calvin chuckled. "Come on, the hair is the most unsettling part."

But John only shook his head, continuing to laugh, a beautiful blush coloring his cheeks. Calvin's heart fluttered as he let out a happy sigh.

"God, I love you," he said. "I love every part of you."

"And I love every part of you, Calvin Wright. Every single part."

John took hold of Calvin's shirt and pulled him in for a kiss.

That night, even though Calvin was still recovering from his illness, he couldn't resist the pull to be close to John. He wanted sexual intimacy, especially because of everything that had happened between them recently. He needed it, *craved* it, and, luckily, John was happy to oblige. And so, Calvin and John snuggled together in bed, enjoying slow and sensual kisses.

After some minutes of becoming lost in their lovely little touches, Calvin finally worked to remove John's night shirt, and then John began unbuttoning his. Calvin's heart thudded hard in his chest, the intensity of the sudden surge of lust making his breath catch and shudder. Once both of them were fully undressed, John climbed on top of him, kissing him passionately once more, and the moment their bare chests pressed flush with each other's, Calvin let out a moan against John's lips. Running his hands up John's back, Calvin let out a sigh, and then John rocked his hips. Calvin couldn't help but wonder whether John might be interested in fucking him. It was what David had enjoyed most, after all.

"John . . ." he said between kisses. "Would you . . ."

But then, Calvin was struck with an intense feeling of unease as memories of his and David's intimate times together flooded his mind. Calvin's stomach roiled as he recalled how easily he and David had fallen into their bedroom routine. Calvin hadn't ever felt empowered to consider whether he liked being taken by David. Probably there were better phrases for it—for having a man thrust his cock into you—but that one seemed most fitting for what he had experienced with his former lover. Taken. Used.

David had taken many things over the years. Because he'd been bigger and stronger and more forceful and surer of himself. And Calvin, having never known a more equal love, hadn't ever thought to wonder what it was that he himself had wanted.

But now he was free to wonder.

And he found himself wondering how to finish the thought.

"Mmm?" John started to kiss his neck. "Would I what?"

"Nothing."

After one more kiss, John stopped and looked up, his brow furrowed with concern.

"It's something."

"No," Calvin replied, feigning nonchalance. "It's nothing."

"Cal."

"John."

With a sigh, John sat up on his elbow and leveled a serious look. Calvin relented.

"Are you interested in . . . other ways of pleasuring each other?"

Confused wrinkles creased John's brow. "There are more?"

Calvin nearly laughed, but then he realized from the look in John's eyes that he was serious. God, how fucking endearing John was.

Calvin moved his fingers through John's hair.

"Silly man," he said sweetly. "Of course there are more."

"Really?" John asked, and Calvin nodded. "Well, t-tell me what they are."

Affection bloomed in Calvin's chest, its tender warmth making Calvin smile.

"Alright, well, I'm not sure if I really want to try it, but . . . I feel strange not . . . offering. I *thought* I might want to try it with you, but . . ." Calvin pursed his lips, hoping he could figure out how to put everything into words. "It's something that David and I . . . well . . . it's what David liked best. But now that I've had some time to be with you, I'm not so sure that I'm interested in it. Not that we wouldn't have fun. I mean, if you really *wanted* to try it—"

"Uhm, Cal, c-c-could you be more specific? I think you've lost me."

"Sorry. It's strange for me to name it. When I was little, I went to church with my parents, and the word I learned for it . . . it makes me uncomfortable. I'm sure there are other names, but I haven't heard them."

"Ah."

"I take it that you know what it is now?"

"Yes, I . . . I think so."

Calvin's cheeks began to warm. "So, is that something you want?"

"You w-want to know if I would like to fuck you?"

Calvin snorted. He liked it when John was charmingly blunt.

"Yes. Or me you."

John seemed completely lost for words. Calvin's entire face felt like it was on fire.

Calvin said, "I'm not sure if I would like the former. Just bad, uh, memories, maybe. I'm not sure if I ever really even enjoyed it much. But, uhm, we could try the latter if—"

"No, no, I have no interest in that," John said, his face starting to redden too. "I-I have no interest in either, really. I n-n-never have."

"Really?"

"It's not something I think of when I touch myself. I-I picture us rubbing each other or pressing our c-cocks together or pleasuring each other with our mouths, but not . . . *that*. I tried my . . . my fingers once on myself, and it wasn't for me. I'm not sure I want *you* back there."

Calvin felt some tension leave his shoulders.

"God, so, you wouldn't mind it if we're never together like that?"

"Not in the least. I love the other ways we find pleasure together."

"Oh, thank the Lord," Calvin said, letting out a long breath as relief hit him like a bucket of water. "Goodness, John, you're a saint."

John laughed. "Sorry, what church was it that you said you went to when you were a k-k-kid? It's thrilling to learn that I have been canonized so easily. I'd like to find m-m-my statue. Assuming that I have one."

Calvin cackled. "I've erected one for you, yes, but I'm afraid it isn't to be shown to the public."

Wearing a playful smirk, Calvin took John's hand and moved it to his still-hard cock.

"I thought it was supposed to be in my likeness," John quipped, wrapping his hand around Calvin's length.

"Oh, sorry, I thought it was only supposed to be something that you *liked*."

"Wrong." John began to move his fist. "Because this? This I *love*."

Calvin's mouth fell agape as he rolled onto his back.

"Show me," Calvin said before bucking his hips into John's moving hand. "Show me that you love it."

"Gladly."

Slowly, John kissed a trail from Calvin's chest to his cock. When John took the tip into his mouth, Calvin's eyes screwed shut as he let out a needy moan. John began to pleasure him—taking more of Calvin's length into his mouth with each of the first few bobs of his head—and at the same time, John rocked his hips, massaging his own cock on the sheets. Calvin felt a fresh surge of intense need pulse through him, making his cock swell. It was wonderful. Too wonderful. He was so close. But he wanted to make it last.

"Wait, wait," Calvin blurted out, cupping John's chin and stopping him. "Come up here. I need to see you better."

After John placed one more sloppy kiss to Calvin's cock's head, he climbed up higher, and then their mouths met. Calvin moaned hungrily.

"I love that I can taste myself on you," he said.

"I love that too," John panted, slightly out of breath.

"I want to finish both of us," Calvin said, pushing himself up to sit and therefore, coaxing John to sit up with him. John straddled him, one knee on either side of Calvin's thighs, and then Calvin took both of their cocks in his hand. "*Please* tell me you're as close as I am."

Slowly, carefully, Calvin pumped his hand once. Twice. Three times. Fuck, it was heaven.

After the fourth time, John muttered a curse and said, "*God*, Cal, of course I'm close. Even when I try to . . . to fight it, I can barely c-c-contain myself when we're together."

Arousal pulsed hot in Calvin's veins. He moved his hand faster and watched John close his eyes. Oh, but he wanted them both to watch. He wouldn't last much longer now.

"Open your eyes," Calvin said, his breaths becoming more ragged as he lost himself to pleasure. "I want you to watch us come."

After a brief moment of hesitation, John opened his eyes. He then let out the most tantalizing, most thrilling moan, seemingly overwhelmed by the sight of Calvin pleasuring them in tandem.

John's cock began to pulse, hot and hard in Calvin's hand, and seeing that first spurt of white pleasure was enough to send Calvin over the edge too.

"Look how beautiful that is," Calvin whispered through his pleasure. "We're so beautiful together, John."

With a low, husky moan John said, "C-Cal . . . my God . . ."

Once Calvin was finished, his clean hand found John's chin.

"Beautiful," he said, urging John to meet his eyes.

He proceeded to leave a series of small kisses on John's nose and cheeks and chin. John was so beautiful.

Huffing a laugh, John said, "Really? Me? B-b-beautiful?"

"Yes," Calvin said with a sigh, kissing him some more. "Irrefutably yes."

After a moment more, John hummed sweetly.

"Cal," he said, his voice filled with such warmth. "You're beautiful, too."

Calvin's stomach fluttered and roiled, the conflicting sensations triggering simultaneously. His face reddened. How could he be?

"I'm not," he said in a whispered voice, his eyes lowering.

"You are," John said. "Look at me, Calvin." Slowly, Calvin raised his chin. His bottom lip trembled, tears suddenly pooling in his eyes as self-reproach twisted inside him. God, how he wanted to protest. "Don't *ever* think that you are *less* because of the m-m-mistakes you've made. If I can be b-beautiful, then *you* can be, too. N-n-no matter your mistakes."

Calvin exhaled a trembling breath as a tear slid down his cheek. John caught it with his thumb, and said, "Beautiful."

Calvin sniffled. "Do you really think so?"

"I *know* so."

Calvin buried his face in John's neck to cry.

And tried to believe that he, too, was beautiful.

It was the first frost of the season in mid-November when Calvin finally saved up enough money to fix Lucy's locket. He would have managed to procure enough sooner had he planned on fixing it in some boring, typical manner like simply replacing the bail, but he had something *much* more interesting (and, therefore, more expensive) in mind. Because John Hall was *far* from typical. And Calvin wanted the locket that John might wear to be as extraordinary and unique as him.

So, Calvin was taking the trolley to one of Michael's factories with the hope that Michael might know of a skilled metalworker in the city who would be willing to take on the project. He had been friendlier to Calvin lately. Both Michael and Katherine had come over to John and Calvin's home for supper several times, and they had invited John and Calvin to their place for lunch on a few occasions as well. Michael really had been true to his word with regards to giving Calvin a chance. He'd been much more cordial, even once suggesting that Calvin borrow (in the real sense of the word) some of his books to take home and read. Calvin couldn't help but be hopeful that Michael would be happy to assist him with this idea of his. And, hell, Michael owed John for the lifetime's worth of shame. Surely that would make him feel even *more* compelled to help.

Still, Calvin's heart pitter-pattered from nervousness, icy worry shooting through his veins while he walked up the front steps to the factory. Attempting to calm himself, he took several long breaths before making his way into the building. Immediately upon entering, Calvin's ears were pelted with the furious clanging and whirring of machinery. There, on the first floor, was the factory itself, with rows and rows of machines and tens, if not hundreds, of workers. Seeing the men and women in their well-worn work clothes, sweat upon their brows, brought forth a flurry of unpleasant memories, most of which were from childhood, and Calvin's stomach churned as they replayed with painful clarity in his mind. Panic rising, he touched the scar on his finger, running his hand over the raised bit of skin. Even though, to Calvin's knowledge, Michael was not one to employ children, he still found himself too lost in his upset to move.

"Calvin!" someone called from nearby. "Calvin!"

With a shake of his head—one sad attempt to break free from the chains of the past that had seemingly trapped him in his particular spot on the factory floor—Calvin tried to find the source of the sound. Across the expansive room, near the flight of stairs to the office space above, was Katherine. Goodness, the machinery was so loud and Calvin's mind was so shaken that he hadn't even recognized the voice as hers.

He held up a hand before starting to hurry over.

"Katherine! Good morning!"

When Calvin reached her, the two exchanged chaste kisses on each other's cheeks, and then Calvin followed her up the stairs to a room that was probably Michael's office. Even though it wasn't exactly peaceful up on the second floor, being inside the office with the door shut was a vast improvement, both for Calvin's ears and for his sanity.

"I'm surprised you're here," he said. "Do you come to the factory often?"

"Not often, no, but Michael wanted to meet with my father this morning. I think they're coordinating for some sort of business venture. Probably Michael wants to source some wool from him or something. I thought I'd come with Michael to say hello to him."

"Ah, were they not working together before?"

"No, surprisingly, they weren't. I met Michael through church. It was merely a coincidence that they both work in textiles. Actually . . ." Katherine leaned in close. "My father is a bit envious of Michael. Michael is very successful, you know, with his two carpet factories. And now he's considering purchasing and expanding one for upholstery. I think every businessman in the city must know Michael by now. It was no wonder my father was so happy when he noticed that Michael was smitten with me. I bet he's been hoping for this collaboration for a while."

Calvin tried to suppress a scoff, but failed, and it came out like some sort of scoff-cough-snort mixture, one that sounded silly, but probably communicated how much her statement bothered him. Even though Calvin knew it was churlish of him to react like that, he hadn't been successful in stopping himself. It irked him to know that Mr. McGough might have thought of Katherine as some sort of chess piece. Luckily, Katherine wasn't bothered by Calvin's reaction. Instead, she chuckled a bit, shielding her mouth with one of her hands.

"Sorry," she said, composing herself. "What about you, Calvin? Why are you here?"

"I think I've come up with a present that I want to have made for John. And I'll need Michael's help with it. He seems to have connections."

"What is it?"

"Well . . ." Calvin took the pocket watch and the locket out of his inner coat pocket. "I *think* I want to—"

Calvin was interrupted when the office door was flung open, the movement forceful enough that the doorknob knocked into the wall. Michael and Mr. McGough came through the threshold, both of them laughing. But when Mr. McGough and Calvin locked eyes, Mr. McGough's smile fell. Calvin's cheeks burned with embarrassment. Katherine's father must have recognized him from the mill.

"Michael, why is that . . . that *criminal* in your office?" he asked, his lip curling into a snarl. "Is he *still* working for John?"

Oh, God, Michael had been insulting Calvin behind his back, hadn't he? Not that Calvin hadn't been a criminal when he and Michael had met, but, still, Calvin wouldn't have thought Michael would ever tell Mr. McGough that the necklace thief was now employed by his brother.

"I know what I called him before, but . . ." Michael took a pause and clasped his hands together. "Calvin is John's partner now."

It was curious that Michael had said partner, rather than business partner. Even though Calvin and John hadn't exactly figured out how to refer to each other, relationship-wise, Calvin had been thinking of John as his partner in *life*, not only in business, and it was an interesting thing to learn that Michael might have been thinking the same. What was even *more* curious, though, was that Michael's formerly friendly smile now seemed so strained. Calvin couldn't miss the way Michael's shoulders were tensing, either.

"I thought you were putting a stop to that," Mr. McGough said. "When you came to me to see if I recalled employing a man fitting his description, I had been shocked to learn that I'd had a literal thief working for me for so long. And then to later learn that he had started working for your brother . . ." He tsked and shook his head. "I remember meeting John prior to the wedding, though. I suppose I shouldn't have been surprised. Not when I remember how strange—"

"Patrick," Michael said sternly, leveling a look. "I won't have you speak of John that way." His eyes flitted over to Calvin. "Or Calvin, for that matter. Calvin is . . . he's a fine man."

"Fine man?!" Mr. McGough scoffed. "Bastard stole my kitten's necklace."

"Daddy, stop. Calvin has more than paid us back for that. Besides, he's my friend," Katherine said, looking to Calvin with a warm smile, one that pulled on Calvin's heart.

Mr. McGough let out a huff. "Puh! Friend! Michael, she can't be serious. Are you really letting my little girl be friends with a . . . a *thief*?"

"Yes," Michael said, standing up straighter. "I am. And she's not your little girl anymore. She's a grown woman. She can make her own choices when it comes to her friends. And in this case, I have to say that I think she . . . well, she couldn't have made a better choice. Calvin is practically family." After a moment, he cleared his throat and straightened his lapels with a fierce tug. "He *is* family."

"Well, not to me he's not."

Michael pursed his lips for a moment. "You know, maybe we ought to rethink our collaboration for my next business venture."

"What?!" Mr. McGough spluttered, his face pinching and twisting as though he was barely maintaining the last vestiges of decorum.

OURSELVES AND IMMORTALITY

Calvin's eyes flew wide, his brows shooting up, and he looked over at Katherine to see her mirroring his shocked expression. Both of them kept their lips clamped shut as they waited to see how things would unfurl.

Michael continued, "Yes, I think that might be best. I can find the recycled wool elsewhere."

"Fine," Mr. McGough spat. "Don't bother sitting with me in the pew on Sunday."

Katherine's father turned on his heel to leave. Calvin's muscles tensed as he braced himself for the inevitable slamming of the office door.

Thud.

Despite being ready for it, Calvin still flinched from the sound, self-reproach punching him in the stomach. Michael hadn't needed to tarnish his relationship with his father-in-law because of him. And, oh, poor Katherine. Would she even want to be his friend anymore?

Everyone stood in frozen, stunned silence for a few moments.

And then Katherine clapped her hands once and said, "Michael, you're a treasure!"

Calvin's eyes snapped up to see her throwing her arms around her husband's neck.

"I couldn't be more in love with you if I tried!" she said, beaming.

"Thank you, love," Michael said, nuzzling her nose. "I wasn't too happy with his terms for our business venture, anyway. It would have benefited him more than it would me."

"Neither of you are upset with me?" Calvin asked.

Katherine tilted her head. "Why would we be upset with you?"

"It seems like Michael broke both of your relationships with your father by sticking up for me."

Katherine waved her hand back and forth. "Daddy will be fine."

"Yes, he's prone to histrionic outbursts," Michael said with a roll of his eyes. He looked at Katherine and narrowed his eyes. "What was it last month?"

"Ah, he was upset that we only had twenty minutes for lunch. Not that he refused to share a pew with us over that later, but still, he can be very theatrical. I'm sure he'll be fine. Eventually. One month from now, maybe two."

"Two very peaceful months from now," Michael mused and Katherine smacked his chest. Michael stopped laughing, and he turned to Calvin and said, "Calvin, I meant what I said to him. You're family."

"Am I really?"

"Of course," Michael responded with a nod, and Katherine hugged him tighter. Raising one curious eyebrow, Michael then said, "So . . . why are you here? Were you and Katherine supposed to have lunch or . . . ?"

"Oh!" Calvin thrust the pocket watch and locket forward, practically shoving them into Michael's chest. "I came to see if you could help with these."

Michael took both of them into his hands and then slowly raised the locket to eye level.

"Oh . . . is this . . . ?"

"Lucy's locket," Calvin confirmed. "And that watch there was my father's. It's the one I gave to John. I sort of . . . lied to him so that I could bring it here. Told him I wanted to have it professionally cleaned."

With a wry smile, Michael said, "Didn't I say you were a trickster?"

Calvin shrugged his shoulders, feigning nonchalance, though he was smiling a little now, too. "Only when necessary."

"Well, if you're not having them cleaned, then what is it you need help with?"

"First, I need to know if you have a relationship with a metalworker. Jeweler. Someone like that. Someone talented." Calvin tried what he hoped would be an innocent-looking smile, one that might make him look charming and maybe a *smidge* pathetic, too. "Someone . . . cheap? Or perhaps someone who owes you a favor?"

Michael smirked. "Yes, I know someone."

"Someone cheap?"

"Someone who owes me a favor."

"Whose prices are . . . reasonable?"

Michael huffed a half-laugh. "How much can you spend?"

Calvin held up his finger and then retrieved his wallet. He took out a wad of cash and fanned it out. "This much?"

Michael stared at it for a few seconds, counting it.

"That'll be plenty. Probably." Calvin frowned, and Michael chuckled a bit. "I'll make sure it's enough. Even if I have to pay for the remainder myself."

"Really?"

"Really."

"Thank you," Calvin said, sincerely.

Michael asked, "So, what is it that you want to have done?"

Calvin rubbed his hands together a few times, excitement buzzing beneath his skin, the electricity making him feel like he needed to move or else he might burst. "Now, this *might* not be possible, but hear me out . . ."

And then, Calvin revealed his plan. While he talked, he could feel a shift in the room, the hum of enthusiasm he felt infecting both Michael and Katherine as well. Calvin began bouncing on the balls of his feet, unable to contain the excess energy flowing through his veins.

More surges of exhilaration moved through him when Katherine squealed and said, "What a sweet idea, Calvin!"

And then it happened once more when Michael then said, "Yes, very creative. I like it. And I'd be honored to help."

How perfect this surprise would be! Sure, neither Katherine nor Michael seemed to be as ridiculously thrilled as Calvin was, but . . .

But they seemed content to help him. It felt as though both Michael and Katherine were happy that Calvin wanted to make John happy. Or maybe . . . maybe they were happy that *he* was happy, too.

Because he was family now, wasn't he?

Chapter Twenty-Two
John

In the kitchen, while waiting for Calvin to return from having tea with Katherine, John stood by the worktable munching on some extra funeral cookies, ones that Calvin thought he had baked for a smidge too long, though John still thought they tasted fine. Minutes passed. Even though John was starting to feel full, he couldn't seem to stop eating. Because eating was keeping him busy, helping him pass the time until Calvin eventually returned.

Calvin had been behaving strangely for the past week. Not that Calvin had been less lovey or was behaving in a way that made John worry that Calvin's feelings had changed. Quite the opposite, really. Calvin had been so happy. Probably, John should have been thankful for the extra energetic kisses and enthusiastic cuddles, but because John wasn't sure what was making Calvin so chipper, he couldn't help but feel a little unsettled by everything. It seemed like Calvin was hiding something. Nothing bad, most likely, because why would he be cheerful over something bad? Still, now that John had seen how secrets could harm their relationship, he hoped that neither of them would ever keep secrets from each other in the future, even happy ones.

Frowning, John shoved one more cookie in his mouth and then raked his hand through his hair while he chewed.

Before he could reach for another cookie, he heard someone come into the house. Hopefully Calvin, though it could have been Michael instead. Ever since that fight, Michael had been visiting more often, which John liked. It was nice that they were becoming close again. Closer than ever, really.

"John!" Calvin called out. John's heart fluttered excitedly upon hearing Calvin's voice. "I have a surprise for you!"

Hurrying into the hall, the nervous feeling in John's stomach eased a little. At least whatever secret Calvin had been keeping wouldn't be a secret for much longer.

When John came to the end of the hall, he was surprised to see that it wasn't only Calvin in the front room, but Michael and Katherine as well.

"Ah, well, this *is* a surprise," John said, coming over to see them.

"Disappointed?" Michael asked, pulling him in for a hug.

"Only that you're here," John teased, mimicking the same silly sentiment that Michael voiced sometimes. "I'm happy to see Katherine, though."

When John pulled away, Michael playfully pushed him back a step. John and Katherine embraced each other next.

"I'm surprised that you're happy to see me. I could have sworn that Michael told me you thought I was too loud," she said, hugging him.

"Oh . . ." John's face warmed. "I . . . well, I—"

Katherine laughed next to his ear. Goodness, it really *was* loud.

"Don't worry, I'm not upset," she said. "I know I'm very . . ."

"Lively?" Calvin offered.

"Dramatic?" Michael suggested.

"Oh, yours sounds worse," Calvin said to him.

"Does not," Michael scoffed right back.

"N-neither are very nice," John said, releasing Katherine from her hug.

And then, without a moment's more hesitation, John wrapped Calvin up in a fierce embrace, holding him so tightly it probably seemed like they hadn't seen each other in much longer than a measly couple of hours.

"Wow, I missed you too, John," Calvin said through a laugh.

After squeezing Calvin for a few more seconds, John finally loosened his hold. Calvin leaned back and reached up to fix John's hair.

"Why are there cookie crumbs in it?" Calvin asked.

He put one in his mouth, but immediately spit it onto the floor.

"Calvin!" Michael scolded while Katherine erupted with laughter.

"Tastes like pomade," he said before spitting some more. "Ugh. *God*." Wiping his mouth with the back of his hand, he said, "Why were you keeping food in your hair?"

"I was feeling n-n-nervous. Eating helped," John said, shrinking into his shoulders a bit. "Sorry, Cal."

"Don't *you* say sorry, little brother. Calvin is the one putting things in his mouth."

With a cheeky smile, Calvin said, "I'm not sure that John has a problem with the things I put in my mouth."

"Cal!" John spluttered, embarrassment scorching his cheeks.

"I thought you'd like that! It was funny!" Calvin said, reaching up to finally finish smoothing out John's hair.

"He's my b-brother!" John protested, now feeling like he might burst into flames.

"I know, but I still thought you'd have found that funny."

Even though John's embarrassment was still lingering, burning beneath his skin, it slowly cooled from Calvin's soothing touch as Calvin finished fixing his locks.

Calvin touched the tip of John's nose with his index finger and said, "Besides, *you're* the brazen one. I'm not the one making bold moves in public."

Michael sighed. "Don't tell me you two are *this* unprofessional on the streets of Philadelphia."

John had to fight to contain a smile as a comment popped into his head. Well, there was *something* that he could use to tease Calvin with in retaliation for what Calvin had said before.

"Only if cemeteries are p-public," John remarked.

"Oh, for heaven's sake," Michael said. "You aren't actually risking your reputation, your *business*, by having *relations* in the city's churchyards?!"

"No, no," Calvin said. "Just in the larger cemeteries *past* the city." God, Calvin hadn't been fazed by John's comment in the least! "Don't worry, Michael, I'm sure no one would open some random hearse in the middle of a cemetery. Could be a couple of *stiffs* in there."

By the time Calvin managed to say the last two words, he began to lose himself to a fit of laughter. Katherine started roaring with laughter right along with him. And John, of course, couldn't keep it together either. He loved Calvin's sense of humor. Meanwhile, Michael looked like he was caught between passing out from having to witness Calvin's unabashed lack of propriety and feeling shame that he very likely found that inappropriate comment funny himself.

After a few more seconds, Calvin reined in his laughter.

"Alright, enough silliness." Calvin moved to pull something from his pocket but paused and looked at John. "Are you ready for your present?"

"I suppose I have to be," John said.

Calvin thrust his hand into his pocket.

"All three of us worked together on this," he said.

Michael replied, "It was Calvin's idea, though."

Calvin's cheeks reddened, and he smiled. It warmed John's heart to see the two of them interacting like this.

"Thanks, Michael," Calvin said.

With a flourish, Calvin held out his hand. There was something that looked like his father's pocket watch in his closed fist. Maybe Calvin hadn't only cleaned it but had it embellished somehow?

"I really hope you like it," Calvin said before biting his lip. "If you hate it, though, I take full responsibility."

Slowly, Calvin uncurled his hand. In his palm was the pocket watch, only, the clamshell face had been changed. Somehow, it had been swapped with the face of Lucy's locket, the outer rim seemingly reworked to incorporate some of the watch's original brass, possibly because the shell from the locket wouldn't have been a perfect fit otherwise.

John's entire body began to warm, tears springing to his eyes as his heart stuttered in his chest. He was so completely touched by the beautiful present that he thought he might faint. With a slightly shaky hand, John took the timepiece from Calvin, still too overwhelmed to find even one word that could express how much this meant to him. Heavens, the metalwork was beautiful. He hadn't ever seen something like this before. None of the mourning trinkets that he had ever created or that he had commissioned over the years could hold a candle to this watch's loveliness. It was, in a word, exquisite.

If only John could move his leaden tongue and say that word out loud.

"Do you like it?" Calvin asked, his voice soft and tentative and oh-so-hopeful.

Wordlessly, John nodded once. And then his tears began to fall. John's cheeks reddened, embarrassment twisting inside him. Calvin reached up to catch some of the tears with his thumb.

"I can't tell whether you hate it so much that it's making you cry or whether you're touched," he said, swiping his thumb over John's cheek. "Either way, I *can* tell that you're embarrassed. But there's no need for that. I've cried in front of you, haven't I?" John nodded, his bottom lip trembling. "Don't be scared to tell me if you hate it. I know it's a strange present. And probably I should have sought your permission before ruining the locket."

Inhaling a shuddering breath, John tried to find the right words. Because it wasn't a strange present. It was a perfect present. And he needed Calvin to know that.

"Cal, it's . . . it's lovely. I can't even begin to express how m-m-m-*much* I like it," he said, his voice trembling while he spoke. "Thank you."

"I'm so happy to hear that," Calvin said, warmth in his voice. He took the watch back and moved to clip it to the inside of John's coat. "I love you."

Without a second's more hesitation, John leaned forward to touch their lips together. He wasn't so bothered that Michael and Katherine were watching. Because John needed Calvin to feel all of his love for him.

After breaking their kiss, John whispered, "I love you, too."

And then they nuzzled each other's noses.

Some seconds passed with John and Calvin still lost in each other's eyes, and then Michael shuffled toward them, the sound of his shoes swishing on the hardwood breaking their lovesick trance.

Michael said, "I'm happy that Calvin included me in this. I've been trying to figure out how I could even begin to atone for the years I spent hurting you. John, I'm sorry I made you feel so horrible for missing our sister. And I'm sorry for the times I made you feel like you were strange for your interests or your profession or, hell, for your *person*, too. In truth, I'm very proud of you. I'm proud of the man you've become. And of the business you've built

OURSELVES AND IMMORTALITY

with your partner." He paused to swallow, emotion welling in his eyes. "I hope you can forgive me."

John's body began to tingle with the most wonderful warmth, the words he'd been hoping to hear for so long setting his heart ablaze with familial love.

Michael was proud of him. His big brother was proud of him.

"Thank you, Michael," John said. "I f-f-forgive you. *Of course* I forgive you."

Over the next few minutes, Calvin, Michael, and Katherine told John a little about the timepiece—where they'd commissioned the work, how Katherine had come up with the idea to rework some of the watch's original brass into the locket's face, how Michael and Calvin had "split" the cost. All the while, John simply stood by in somewhat of a stunned silence, still struggling to internalize how very loved he seemed to be. Accepted *and* loved.

What a miraculous thing it was.

Afterward, Calvin and Katherine left for the kitchen so that they could prepare some lunch for everyone. Since John and Michael were both fairly useless when it came to cooking (except for John's supposedly incredible soup), they left for the library. Both of them took a seat on either of the two chairs that were fanned out in front of the unlit fireplace.

Once John was settled, he took the watch out once more to admire it.

Running his fingers over the clamshell face, he said to Michael, "Are you f-f-feeling better lately? About Lucy?"

"Somewhat," Michael said, crossing his legs. "I'm still working on not hating her. Seeing how happy you've been lately has been helping. Because now I know that *I* was the cause of most of your misery."

"Oh, Michael, I blamed m-myself for my own misery before. I even blamed Lucy a little. But no one was really to blame. I told you, you never broke me. Because I'm not b-broken. I'll never not be hurting over the fact that we lost our sister, but it's n-nice to have my brother back. I feel so much better now, like a . . . a weight has been lifted." He paused to put away the pocket watch. "Shame is a heavy thing to c-carry."

"I can imagine," Michael said, his voice low and sad. "Grief, too, probably. Which is why I haven't managed to not hate her fully yet. I know that when I stop hating her, I'll have to be sad instead. I mean, you saw a bit of that when we had that fight. But that was a mere crack in the dam. I can feel it."

"I'll be here," John said. "I'll be here wh-wh-when it breaks."

"I know you will," Michael said.

Goodness, the fact that Michael knew that John would be there for him . . .

It was wonderful.

Michael began strumming his fingers on the cushion.

After a moment, he said, "I hope you know that I'm not bothered by the fact that you and Calvin are together romantically. Everything that happened between us, or between me and Calvin, none of it was because of your sexual and romantic proclivities. I mean, when Calvin was being silly back there in the other room . . . none of that *really* bothers me." Michael turned to meet John's eyes. "I need you to know that, John."

John smiled. "Thank you."

Michael shifted in his seat, making the leather cushion squeak. "Remember that party in Media?"

"When you saw me and Calvin coming out of the barn."

"Do you want to know why I was upset?"

"Wasn't it because you knew that Calvin and I were . . ."

John's stomach flip-flopped, the rush of memories turning his ears hot.

"It wasn't *that*, though of course I hadn't been too fond of Calvin back then. But no, I hadn't been bothered by the fact that you two were engaging in those kinds of things. I *was* upset, however, that *because* you two were being so brazen, I had been forced to spend the entirety of the time that you and Calvin were in there *having fun* trying to keep other people from realizing what you were doing."

John's eyes widened. "What? Really?"

"Really," Michael said, huffing a laugh. "It seemed like every two minutes, someone was coming up to me to ask where my little brother had run off to. I can't even remember the excuses I was forced to come up with. Sometimes I said you were inside, sometimes I said you went to the inn, sometimes I tried to steer the conversation elsewhere. One time, I caught those newlyweds wandering toward the barn—Marie and William Peterson—and I had to scramble to tell them that there was a rotting raccoon in there so that they'd rethink their evening plans." He started to laugh in earnest, and John couldn't help but laugh too. "Probably they'd been hoping to have the same kind of fun *you* were having!"

John looked at Michael with wonder. "I c-c-can't believe you protected us."

"I protected *you*," Michael corrected. "I hadn't liked your partner back then, remember? Even so, I knew I needed to keep you safe."

"Thank you. You're a good brother."

"I wasn't," Michael said. "Not most of the time. But I hope I can be one from now on."

They smiled warmly at each other.

Before John could express his love in return, Calvin and Katherine came into the room.

"We made some cream of wheat," Katherine said cheerily. Michael only scrunched up his nose, which made Katherine frown. "What? Calvin and John's cupboards are practically bare! Did you expect me to somehow create a proper meal with two potatoes and some coffee beans?"

Michael's eyebrows shot up. "Is that *really* all you have?"

"We were planning on heading to the market today," Calvin said defensively. "Besides, coffee beans are the most important pantry staple."

Michael snorted. "John, is that *still* your breakfast? Multiple cups of coffee?"

"Maybe."

"It is," Calvin said. "Though he'll eat slightly burned funeral cookies sometimes too."

"I need you to start having proper meals more often," Michael chastised, wagging a finger. He looked over at Calvin. "Can you make sure he eats a real breakfast sometimes? Lunch when we're not together?"

"We have lunch," Calvin reassured him. "Our kitchen is only empty because I was too preoccupied to remember to shop for more food recently." Hooking his hands behind his head, Calvin turned to John and said, "Speaking of things that were preventing me from remembering to take care of our home, what time is it?"

Affection swirled to life in John's chest. He took out the watch and pressed the little button on top to open it.

"Quarter past one," he said before clicking it closed. "And I love you too, Calvin."

Calvin grinned.

"Alright, let's eat some porridge," Michael said, pushing himself to stand.

Everyone started for the kitchen, but then John caught Calvin's sleeve, holding him back.

"We'll be there in a m-minute," he called out and then placed his hands on Calvin's hips. When Michael and Katherine were out of earshot, he said, "I-I need you to know, this w-w-watch is the most spectacular present that I've ever received. I cannot ever thank you enough for it."

"You're very welcome."

"*But . . .*" John tethered their hips together, and the two of them swayed back and forth a little. "I can only imagine how hard it was for you to part with your f-father's watch. And not only that, but to break it so that you could have this m-m-made for me. I—"

Calvin put a finger to John's lips.

"It wasn't hard for me, John."

John kissed Calvin's finger and then wrapped his hand around it to pull it away from his face.

"At least before this, though, you knew you could t-t-t-t- . . . you knew you could t-take it back someday. If you ever needed to. Or wanted to."

"I never thought that," Calvin said, his voice soft and sweet. "All these months, it's been yours. I only needed to borrow it for a little while."

"Thank you, Calvin," John said, tilting forward to touch their foreheads together. "I love it so much. Whenever I see it, I'll think of everyone I love."

Calvin reached up to stroke John's cheek. "Good. Because I never want you to forget how loved you are." He let out a sigh. "I love you, John Hall. You are *everything* to me."

John's heart fluttered from the swell of fondness, the torrent of love he felt for Calvin so powerful it nearly knocked him to his knees. Overwhelmed with emotion, John couldn't even begin to find the words to respond. Instead, he captured Calvin's mouth in a kiss.

And he hoped it told Calvin everything.

Epilogue
Calvin

Five months later...

The moment Calvin flung out the red-and-white checkered picnic blanket to spread it on the ground, a strong breeze blew past, causing the fabric to flutter and twist in the wind.

"Let me help you with that," Michael said, taking hold of the other end.

Together, the two men laid the blanket flat. Katherine then set their picnic basket on top and turned to fetch the container of lemonade that she'd placed nearby while John brought the cups and plates from the hearse. Over the next minute or so, everyone finished setting up for the picnic, and then, they sat together on the blanket. Calvin and John settled close to each other, both of them relaxing back on Lucy's headstone. Calvin took two halves of one of the lettuce and mayonnaise sandwiches that he'd made earlier and handed one to John. Meanwhile, Michael and Katherine inspected theirs with interest.

"Is this really your favorite sandwich?" Michael asked, turning up his nose.

"Lettuce and cottage cheese is better, but the market was out," Calvin said. "Why? What's wrong with lettuce and mayonnaise?"

"It's so . . . overly simple," Michael said.

"Picky, picky," Calvin chastised.

"I'm sure you'll like it, Michael," Katherine said. "I mean, you like both of these separately."

"Can't I put some of our salted meat in the middle?" Michael asked.

"Nope. *No,*" John said emphatically. "We each brought one of our favorite meals to celebrate mine and Lucy's birthday." He stretched out his leg and poked Michael in the thigh with the toe of his black leather shoe. "Lucy would have liked that we're sharing our f-f-favorite foods. Don't you remember how much she liked to share? Or, well, she liked wh-wh-when people shared with *her.*"

"Alright, *fine,*" Michael said, his eyes flickering to the sky, though Calvin knew Michael well enough now that he could tell Michael was only pretending to be irritated.

When Michael took a tiny bite of the sandwich only to *immediately* follow it up with a bite that was substantially larger, Calvin threw him a wink, not even bothering to be subtle in his teasing. Michael rolled his eyes in a *much* more exaggerated manner in response.

And that was how Calvin knew that Michael really *did* like the sandwich. Probably a lot.

Calvin took a bite of his own. While he was chewing, John leaned over to nuzzle his cheek, and Calvin squirmed a little from the feel of John's nose rubbing on his skin.

"Stop," Calvin said through a laugh, barely managing to swallow his half-chewed food.

"Why?" John whispered. "We're in the largest cemetery in M-M-Media. Far from the main road and p-prying eyes."

Calvin chuckled some more. "Sometimes I find myself missing the times when you were too embarrassed to be lovey in front of your brother."

Before Calvin could take a second bite, John wrapped him up in a backward hug, silently coaxing Calvin to cuddle up on him, rather than continue to rest against the marble. Calvin obliged but regretted it as soon as John started kissing his ear.

"Alright, now you *really* have to stop," Calvin said, though, *hell*, he really loved it when John played with his ears. Way, way too much.

How John had become so bold over the last few months, Calvin couldn't be sure.

"Funny little ears," John whispered before softly biting the top of Calvin's ear.

Calvin pursed his lips to contain his smile. At least Michael and Katherine were kind enough to pretend to be preoccupied with their food.

"Eat your sandwich," Calvin scolded playfully. "I'm afraid you'll smear mayonnaise on my coat."

"I won't. I p-promise." John hugged Calvin tighter, wiping some of the condiment on the back of one of Calvin's hands instead. Groaning, John whispered a soft, "Sorry."

Calvin heaved a teasing sigh.

"I'll fix it." John lifted Calvin's hand and licked it off. "Better?"

Calvin sputtered a laugh and mentally prepared to chastise his brazen companion but was hit in the face with sandwich remnants before he could contain his laughter. He yelped when more bread hit him in the chest. John's reaction to the sandwich-pelting was to laugh, and the sound of John's low chuckle next to Calvin's ear sent a small shiver up Calvin's spine, causing him to shudder.

"Michael!" Katherine scolded. "Leave them be!"

"Don't pretend the two of them weren't being obscene."

Calvin scoffed and said, "It wasn't *that* bad."

John proceeded to press one hard kiss to Calvin's cheek before then starting on his sandwich. Calvin's cheek was still tingling pleasantly as he went back to eating his own food.

After everyone finished their sandwiches, Michael unwrapped the salted pork he had chosen to bring, and Katherine took out a box of crackers. John scooted to the side to fetch what had come to be his favorite food (or, really, his favorite meal probably, too)—Calvin's funeral cookies. Even though Calvin had seen John choose the cookies earlier (he had seen John put them in a tin while they were packing for the birthday picnic), watching John pry off the tin's lid to serve them was so much more emotional than he would have ever imagined.

His chest warmed and his heart fluttered as he sucked in a trembling breath. Knowing that John wanted to serve Calvin's funeral cookies on this special occasion, one that was meant to not only celebrate John's birthday but also honor his sister's memory, too, was the sweetest, most wonderful feeling in the entire Goddamn world.

Calvin closed his eyes and tried to keep the rush of emotions from spilling forth as he settled back against John's chest. God, the last thing he wanted was to cry right now.

When Calvin's eyes fluttered open, he craned his head to see John watching, smiling at Calvin like he was the most important, most exquisite thing.

Calvin swallowed past the lump in his throat, barely holding back tears. "Thank you." In response, John tilted his head, and his forehead wrinkled in confusion. Elaborating, Calvin said, "Thank you for choosing my cookies."

As soon as the words left Calvin's mouth, the lump in his throat vanished, and he began cackling instead. Immediately, John threw his head back, howling with laughter, too.

Once John composed himself, he tried a wink, one that was probably meant to be subtle, but was slow and unpracticed and not subtle in the least.

"I will *always* choose your c-cookies," John said, a teasing lilt in his voice.

He shoved one of the cookies into his mouth.

Calvin shook his head. When he looked over at Katherine, he saw that she was shielding her mouth with one of her hands. But she couldn't hide her smile. Because when Katherine smiled, her eyes smiled too.

Prim and proper Michael had clearly caught on to the innuendo as well. Michael was sitting there with his lips pinched shut, so obviously trying to suppress a smile like his wife. Calvin's own smile broadened, his heart fluttering with happiness.

Everyone began munching on some of the cookies, each of them still very clearly trying not to laugh. After a few minutes, the silliness passed.

Michael tried to restart the conversation.

"Oh, Calvin, John tells me that you're having some people come to change things in the house?"

Calvin looked over at John. "Did you not tell him?"

"I thought you would want us to tell him t-together."

Calvin smiled warmly. "Thank you." He turned back to Michael. "Yes, we're, uhm, we're transforming our house into a funeral parlor. Funeral home? I'm not sure what to call it, but we won't have to travel for the embalmings anymore. Or the viewings."

Michael's eyes went wide. "Really?"

"Yes, well, times are changing, and it seems like more and more people are hoping to move the funeral events out of their homes entirely."

"Oh, that's wonderful news!" Michael said, slapping his thigh. "God, that'll be so much simpler for you both. And I'm sure *you're* especially excited for the change, John."

"Yes," John said. "I can't wait." He kissed Calvin's cheek. "It was C-Calvin's idea."

Calvin's face reddened. "Well, one that I stole from one of the other morticians in the city," he said. "But I suppose I was the one who proposed it to you so it was *a little bit* my idea."

"Now this kind of stealing, I can support," Michael laughed.

Calvin rolled his eyes.

"So, Michael, how're the factories?" he asked. "Anything new to share?"

"Both of them are fine," Michael said. "Business as usual." He and Katherine then exchanged a knowing look. Michael raised both his eyebrows, as though he was perhaps requesting permission for something, and Katherine nodded in response. Michael clapped his hands together. He swept them back and forth, wiping off some crumbs, and then took Katherine's hand.

"Katherine and I have some news," Michael said, excitement in his voice. Calvin braced himself. "Katherine will be opening her very own yarn shop."

Calvin sucked in a fast breath, his eyes widening in surprise.

"Congratulations!" he exclaimed with an enthusiastic smile, his heart swelling with the warm rush of excitement and pride for his friend.

"Thank you," Katherine replied, beaming.

Michael continued, "If you remember, back in the fall, I had been thinking of partnering with Katherine's father for recycled wool. I had intended to use his shoddy to manufacture clothing, mostly to make soldier's uniforms or cheap blankets, but since that fell through . . . for *some* reason . . ." He paused to throw Calvin a look of playful annoyance. "I partnered with someone else in

the city instead, someone who procures very fine wool from some
of Pennsylvania's farms, and we'll be taking some of that wool to
make balls of yarn. Katherine's shop will sell them. She'll sell other
types of yarn, too, of course."

Calvin could hardly contain his excitement.

"God, Katherine, that's incredible," he said.

"We've thought of a nice name for the store as well," Michael
said.

"Little Lucy's Yarn Shop!" Katherine practically shouted.

Calvin's hand flew to cover his mouth. How sweet of a name it
was!

"Michael came up with it," Katherine said.

"Oh, well . . ." He trailed off and began pulling on a loose
thread in the picnic blanket. "I wanted to honor my sister somehow. Especially now that I'm not . . . upset with her anymore."

Against him, Calvin felt John let out a shuddering breath,
and Calvin's chest twinged with sympathy. Probably John was
momentarily too touched, too overwhelmed, to find his words.
Calvin waited a few seconds in case John might push through it,
but John only sat there silently. Calvin looked back to see John's
beautiful brown eyes shimmering with evidence of his overwhelm.
Sympathy still swirling in his chest, Calvin found John's free hand
and squeezed.

"That's very kind of you, Michael," Calvin said on John's be-
half. "What a beautiful way to honor your sister's memory."

Michael's cheeks turned red.

"I know," he said, still twirling the blanket thread. "But thank
you for saying that."

Behind Calvin, John cleared his throat.

"I-I'm very p-proud of you, Michael," John said. "I know how
hard these last few m-m-months have been."

Michael shrugged. "Well, I had you so . . ." He took a pause, perhaps to keep himself composed. "It wasn't too bad."

John smiled fondly in response. And Calvin's heart beat with pride.

Ever since John and Michael had reopened those wounds from their childhoods, Michael had often struggled with facing what had to have been extremely painful memories, not to mention uncomfortable truths of the past. And John had been the most wonderful support, offering comfort however he could, sometimes with words, but often in other ways, like with phone calls and visits and shared pots of tea.

What a sweet man John was. Calvin couldn't have loved him more if he tried. He stroked John's hand with his thumb. And he hoped that John knew how very loved he was.

Katherine chimed in, "Calvin?"

Crooking an eyebrow, Calvin looked over at her.

"I have to thank you, especially. Without you, none of this would have been possible. I never would have had the courage to open my own shop. I wouldn't have even considered it. It was you who planted the idea in my head. And then, later, it was you who helped it take root. Thank you for believing in me."

Calvin smiled.

"Of course," he said warmly. "And I'm sure it will be a wonderful little shop." Calvin smiled a playful smile. "*Although*, the offer to become a mortician still stands."

Katherine chuckled and shook her head. "No, thank you."

"Are you sure? We would see each other more often," Calvin said in a singsong voice. He looked over at Michael and smirked. "And I would *love* to have more opportunities to bother your husband."

"Nope, there are plenty of those right now, thank you," Michael said.

Cackling, Calvin picked up one of the half-eaten cookies and chucked it at him. It hit Michael in the chest.

Michael leveled a look, and Calvin threw him a simpering smile. He was still struggling to contain his happiness for Katherine. God, it had been nice of her to thank him, but he felt so unworthy of it. He had hurt her so badly when they'd met. Even though Calvin had *financially* made up for stealing Katherine's necklace, he couldn't help but feel like it wasn't enough. He still needed to *truly* make it up to her. Somehow.

Chewing on his lip, Calvin racked his mind for ideas.

His eyes flew wide when he thought of one.

"Katherine?" he said.

"Hmm?"

"Do you have a sign for your shop yet?"

"Not yet, no. Michael thought we could purchase one in—"

Calvin cut her off. "Could I maybe try to make one for you?"

Katherine covered her heart with her hands. "Oh, Calvin, that would be wonderful! Can you really make one?"

"Well, not by myself," he said before craning his head to look at his partner. "But hopefully with John's help?"

"I-I-I'd love to help," John said, sounding overwhelmed, but in a happy sort of way.

"Goodness, that's so nice of you," Katherine said. "Of both of you."

Calvin's cheeks warmed. "It's nothing."

John planted a firm kiss on Calvin's temple.

Next, everyone shared what had been Lucy's favorite food—molasses spice cake. While everyone enjoyed a slice, Michael and John took turns telling stories from their childhood, mostly ones featuring Lucy, showing how kind she could be, but how stubborn and feisty and opinionated, too. Listening to the two Hall brothers reminisce so freely, both men sharing memories of their sister without shame or resentment or even sorrow, was truly wonderful.

And Calvin was so happy for them. Oh, how he loved his new family.

Later, back in Philadelphia, John and Calvin were cuddled together in bed, both of them feeling tired from the cemetery picnic. Eager to relax in what they both thought was the best way possible, they began to remove each other's clothes, pausing intermittently while they sometimes became lost in long, sensual kisses. Once they were naked, Calvin took John's cock and stroked him to completion, only pumping his hand for a couple of minutes before John came with a heady moan, burying his face in the crook of Calvin's neck.

Afterward, while Calvin reached for one of their stockings to wipe the ejaculate from his hand, John began leaving a trail of kisses on Calvin's torso, starting up by his shoulder and then moving to his chest. Letting out a small, contented sigh, Calvin threaded his fingers through John's hair and smiled to himself when he saw the result. John's hair was so beautifully messy, so perfectly John. Calvin continued to play with it while John's lips moved lower, first brushing Calvin's stomach and then finding his legs. John kissed the small scar on Calvin's knee, the one that had formed from the injury he'd sustained in the cemetery.

"You were right, Cal," John said. "I love this scar. I love wh-what it represents." He pressed one more kiss to the raised bit of skin. "I love every part of you, Calvin Wright. Even the scars."

Calvin's eyes filled with tears. Over the past several months, John had never once made him feel bad for having stolen that money. And whenever Calvin had begun feeling worried that he might someday lose his home, Calvin had come to John for comfort and reassurance. And John had never hesitated to provide it.

"Thank you," Calvin choked out. "I love you, too, John."

Sweetly, John kissed the scar once more. He then moved to kiss the head of Calvin's cock. Calvin let out a shuddering breath the moment John's lips brushed his skin. When John then took the pink head of Calvin's cock into his mouth and sucked, Calvin's eyes rolled back as his hips lifted off the mattress.

Under his breath, Calvin whispered, "I love you, I love you, I love you."

One of John's hands softly squeezed Calvin's thigh in return.

John began to pleasure him, to take care of him, and when Calvin climaxed, he cried out, moaning and trembling, John's name on his lips.

Afterward, the two men lay on their backs, contented, their minds hazy with bliss.

Still lost in the feeling of tranquility, Calvin rolled over to face John, and then John rolled over to face him, too.

"Cal," John murmured, reaching over to stroke Calvin's cheek. "Are you really mine?"

Slowly, John's hand moved toward Calvin's ear. John began massaging the earlobe between his fingers, and Calvin closed his eyes, letting out a happy hum.

"I am," he cooed. "I'm yours, John. I'm yours forever."

Minutes passed like this, with John sweetly playing with Calvin's ear. Calvin relaxed into it, letting himself be taken care of by the man who had become his everything. Listening to the faint ticking of a faraway clock, Calvin's thoughts wandered, first to the concept of time itself, and then to his parents and how much he missed them, and then to the cruelty of mortality and how much he or John would someday have to miss each other, too.

I'm yours forever.

God, how he wished that could be true. He had experienced so much loss in his life. It pained him to think that there would be more.

Calvin's eyes fluttered open.

"I know this will probably seem silly considering the nature of our work," he began, his voice barely a whisper, "but I'm a little terrified of the future, of the time when one of us leaves for whatever there might be waiting for us when we pass on, and the other is left behind." He took a pause, trying to keep himself composed. "Somehow, that's the happiest ending there we could ever hope for, and yet, it's still so incredibly sad."

"Is it?" John asked.

Calvin had to smile a little now. "Of course it's sad. We have no clue what *really* waits for us on the other side. Hell, what if there is no other side? What if there's nothing? If there's nothing, that means that we'll never be reunited. And our love will perish with us."

"It won't," John said simply. "I mean, the love I feel for my sister n-n-never left."

"Because you're still here, you mean?"

"Even when I'm no longer here, m-m-my love for her will still be here. Loving her, it influenced my life. And therefore, I think it influenced other people's lives, too. Michael's and Katherine's. Yours. And everyone's whom we've ever helped with our b-business. And—and more people I can't even think of right now.

W-w-we touch other people's lives, Cal. It's how . . . it's how we live forever. It's how our love lives f-forever."

Calvin blinked back tears. "I like that, John. Thank you for sharing it."

"Our love will stay forever," John said, nuzzling Calvin's nose. "Remember that."

Calvin smiled, nuzzling him right back. "I will."

He pressed his lips to John's.

And basked in the beauty of their immortal love.

About the Author

Logan Sage writes queer historical romance with plenty of sweetness, a little heartache, occasional humor, and hard-earned happily ever afters. Their work explores themes like healing from loss, finding the courage to fall in love, learning to love oneself, and overcoming trauma.

Logan Sage harnesses her love of learning in order to paint rich, immersive worlds for her readers to fall into. She especially enjoys writing love stories between everyday people, and typically sets her stories in the 20th century, mostly in the United States.

When she's not writing or reading, Logan Sage can be found working, cooking, and spending time with her supportive family.

Follow their Instagram:

@logan.sage.adams

Join their Facebook Group:

Logan Sage Adams – MM Romance Readers

Subscribe to their newsletter for book news and cool historical facts: www.logansageadams.com

Printed in Great Britain
by Amazon

60833089R00204